SPRINGFIELD 1880

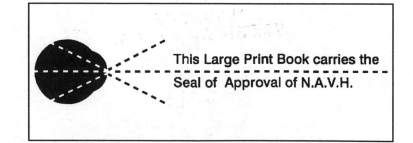

This Large Print Book carries the
Seal of Approval of N.A.V.H.

SPRINGFIELD 1880

Copyright © 2018 by J. A. Johnstone.
Wheeler Publishing, a part of Gale, a Cengage Company.

ALL RIGHTS RESERVED
Wheeler Publishing Large Print Western.
The text of this Large Print edition is unabridged.
Other aspects of the book may vary from the original edition.
Set in 16 pt. Plantin.

LIBRARY OF CONGRESS CIP DATA ON FILE.
CATALOGUING IN PUBLICATION FOR THIS BOOK
IS AVAILABLE FROM THE LIBRARY OF CONGRESS

ISBN-13: 978-1-4328-6768-3 (softcover alk. paper)

Published in 2019 by arrangement with Pinnacle Books, an imprint of
Kensington Publishing Corp.

Printed in the United States of America
1 2 3 4 5 6 7 23 22 21 20 19

SPRINGFIELD 1880

WILLIAM W. JOHNSTONE
WITH
J. A. JOHNSTONE

WHEELER PUBLISHING
A part of Gale, a Cengage Company

GALE
A Cengage Company

Farmington Hills, Mich • San Francisco • New York • Waterville, Maine
Meriden, Conn • Mason, Ohio • Chicago

PROLOGUE

In 1880, the Springfield Armory of Springfield, Massachusetts, sent roughly one thousand new Model 1880 trapdoor .45-70-caliber rifles to Army troops stationed on the American frontier for testing in the field. The factory and the US Army hoped the new rifles would be an improvement over Springfield's Model 1873 rifle.

This is the story of two hundred and fifty of those Springfield 1880s.

CHAPTER 1

The last thing Second Lieutenant Grat
Holden wanted to see was the dust he just
spotted. It drifted in the cloudless sky
beyond the "Two Heads," the outcropping
of rocks that topped the Dos Cabezas,
which was how the mountains got their
name. He had seen dust earlier, too, on the
other side of the trail and had shrugged that
off as a dust devil. Now, he unfastened the
flap that protected the Schofield .45-caliber
revolver on his left hip.

Hooves beat toward him. Sergeant Byron
Lusk reined in his dun gelding and turned
his head to water a rock with tobacco juice.
"Beggin' yer pardon, suh, but —"

"I see it, Sergeant," Holden said.

"Figured you would, sir. Almost didn't
even ride up to tell you."

"Be glad you did, Sergeant. I don't see
everything."

"Like that, suh?"

Holden followed the gray-haired sergeant's crooked finger, which pointed southeast, toward the pass they found themselves bound to pass in a few minutes. The lieutenant, however, saw only Arizona rocks, Arizona sky, and felt the Arizona heat. He was soaked with sweat beneath his dark tunic, but it wasn't just the heat that caused him to sweat.

"What was it, Sergeant?" Holden asked.

"Looked like the sun reflectin' off somethin'. Rifle. Knife. Pretty brass concha." He chuckled. "Maybe gold. Wouldn't that be somethin'?"

Pulling the reins up on his bay gelding, Holden raised his right hand and heard the command called out from the first wagon behind him down to the fourth. As soon as the horse stopped, he turned to his saddlebags and found the pair of binoculars, which he brought to his face after pushing up the brim of his battered slouch hat and studied the trail, the hills above the trail, and the split between the "Two Heads."

"More dust, suh," Lusk said.

Without lowering the binoculars, Holden asked, "Where?"

"On the trail. Somewhere between the hills."

The lieutenant swept another look through

his glasses, but, seeing nothing, lowered them in his left hand and studied the road before him. "On the trail?"

"Yes, suh. But if it's a rider, he ain't come out yet."

"Unless he's riding toward Dos Cabezas, Apache Pass, or Fort Bowie," Holden said. Dos Cabezas wasn't much of a town to be riding to at a pace fast enough to raise dust seen by the naked eye from that distance.

"He ain't, suh." Lusk pointed to the road. "Rained yesterday. Good soaker."

Holden nodded. "I know, Sergeant. No tracks. Maybe he sees our dust, though."

More tobacco juice splattered the road. Sergeant Lusk wiped his mustache, beard, and lips with the brown-stained end of one of his gauntlets. "We are close to Bowie, suh."

"Close to Apache country, too, Sergeant."

The noncommissioned officer chuckled. "Hell, suh, we're surrounded by Apache country."

Holden looked back at his command. He was twenty-seven years old. The men behind him made him feel ancient. Five years out of West Point, five years in Arizona Territory, and he was a battle-hardened veteran of the frontier. The men he commanded, with the exception of his sergeant, were as

11

new as what they were hauling in four government freight wagons.

Brand-spanking new Springfield trapdoor rifles, fresh from the armory in Springfield, Massachusetts. Crates of them, not to mention the new triangular bayonets that could be affixed underneath the barrel and enough .45-70-caliber cartridges to start a war. The Army didn't need to start another war. They had a good one going on with the Apaches. Sometimes, Holden thought the Apaches might win.

Back at Fort Bowie, Colonel Carlton Smythe didn't think much of sending experimental Springfield rifles to be tested by troops, most still wet behind the ears, against veteran Apache guerrillas. Nor did Colonel Smythe like rifles. The cavalry used shorter carbines, easier to maneuver on horseback. And he despised bayonets. Shoot, Holden hadn't even seen one saber carried by an officer in that desert country except during parades.

So Colonel Smythe had sent Lieutenant Holden to Fort Lowell in Tucson to fetch the weapons, the ammunition, and some new green troops, and bring them back to Fort Bowie.

Rubbing the beard stubble on his cheeks and jaw, Holden tried to figure out his best course. Make it through the little pass, and they would be a few miles from the village of Dos Cabezas. Another twenty-five miles, through Apache Pass, and they would be home safe at Fort Bowie.

It was just getting there . . . alive . . . that troubled him.

"You know what the colonel says." Sergeant Lusk shifted his chaw to another cheek.

"Yeah." Holden leaned back in the saddle. "But he hasn't fired a Springfield or any rifle in the five years I've been here. He leaves that to his junior officers and their men. He hasn't led anything but Fourth of July parades and courts-martial."

"That's one reason I like you, suh. You speak your mind. You tell the truth. And you fight, suh. You fight alongside the rest of us. I figure you ain't no officer at all."

That led Holden to grin . . . till the sergeant said, "Just gettin' kilt over weapons that might not be worth spit . . . I dunno, suh."

"Want to leave the wagons behind?"

"No. Don't reckon we should do that, suh."

Again, Holden looked back. He had eight troopers on four wagons. Ten men.

"Maybe the Apaches heard the same

Colonel Smythe heard, suh. That these weapons ain't worth spit."

Holden shook his head. "I've seen Apaches armed with a blunderbuss that likely hadn't been fired since the Revolution. I've seen them throw rocks. And, begging the colonel's pardon, I don't think the Springfield Armory would send us a rifle that will blow up in our faces. Might not be better than what we have now, but an Apache or some Mexican bandit would likely sell his soul to have one. Especially as many as we're carrying."

"Lieutenant!" Sergeant Lusk pointed to the opening of the passage.

A rider came loping out. He was raising a lot of dust.

CHAPTER 2

Holden let out a curse, wheeled his horse around, and loped back to the first wagon where he barked orders at the two blond-headed troopers, one pudgy, the other weighing about as much as a cholla cactus.

The troopers — he couldn't remember their names — stared at him blankly.

"Ich verstehe nicht."

The other said, *"Ich Rann Sie nicht verstehen."*

Then both said, shrugging, *"Nein."*

Holden cursed the two Germans probably just off the boat. He cursed the recruiters who sent those two pilgrims to Arizona. He cursed his father for sending him to the United States Military Academy, and he cursed his commanding officer. Then he yelled at the two men, both Americans, in the next wagon.

"Set the brakes to the wagon and crawl into the back. Cock your weapons and wait for me. But if somebody shoots me off my horse, do your best to stay alive. And pass the word down!"

It was a silly order. He'd shouted so loud the men in the last wagon understood, and maybe even the two Germans got an idea about what he wanted because both took their Springfield carbines.

Those were 1873 trapdoor models with twenty-two-inch barrels, and they fired the same caliber as the ones in the crates they had been hauling for close to a hundred miles. He doubted if the recruits with him had fired a weapon since Jefferson Barracks, and if shooting started . . . *God help the mules pulling our freight.*

The bay gelding carried Holden back to Sergeant Lusk, who had brought up his Springfield, also a carbine, and rested the butt against his right thigh while keeping the reins in his left hand.

Holden reined up and studied the dust and the rider. "Still just one?"

"Yes, suh. Ain't slowed down."

"Watch the hills, Sergeant, especially where you saw dust earlier."

"You are somethin' cautious, Lieutenant."

Holden grinned. "I'm alive, Byron. I'm alive."

He found the binoculars again, and

brought them to his face. It took him just moments to find the rider and bring him and the horse into focus. What he first saw, at least clearly, were the spurs. Brass. Army-issue. On black boots, also provided by Uncle Sam. He saw blue pants.

The horse was steel dust. He saw the beaded gauntlets gripping the rein, the posture that told him the rider had likely been born in the saddle. The saddle seemed to be a McClellan. By then Holden's heart-beat had steadied and his lungs had stopped heaving. He still sweated. He figured he would always sweat. But he was about to think that he had worked his men up, his horse up, and himself up for nothing.

The binoculars raised, and he saw the rider's face. The damned prankster seemed to be smiling, and his eyes, though squint-ing from the pounding in the saddle and the wind and the dust, might have been staring all the way across the remaining three hundred yards at Lieutenant Grat Holden. Laughing.

"Sergeant Lusk." Holden lowered the binoculars and shook his head.

Lusk turned toward him.

"Have the men stand down," Holden said. "It's the captain."

The noncommissioned officer stood in his

stirrups and trained his bare eyes on the approaching galloper.

"You sure, Lieutenant?"

"I'm sure."

"What's Captain Foster doin', suh, ridin'
a horse like that?"

"Other than acting like one son of a bitch,
Sergeant, I don't have a clue. But I'm sure
he'll tell us directly."

Captain Jed Foster's cackles could be heard
over the pounding of the steel dust's hooves.
An expert rider, Foster pulled on the reins
and the gelding slid to a stop in front of
Holden and Lusk. By the time the dust
cloud had settled, Foster was removing his
buckskin gauntlets and shoving them into
the deep pockets of his golden buckskin
jacket with fringes longer than eight inches
on the sleeves.

"Hello, Mr. Holden." Jed Foster was forty
years old, and after close to twenty years in
the service — the first four with the Seventh
Michigan Cavalry during the War of the
Rebellion, and the last decade and a half in
the regular Army — he looked no older than
Holden. Foster had a golden mustache with
the ends twisted, a pointed goatee, and hair
that fell to his shoulders.

"Captain," Holden said, offering a salute

18

that was not returned, "you're looking a lot like Custer today, sir."

"I sure hope not." Foster pulled at the stampede string securing his white hat dangling on his back and set the hat on his curly blond hair. "He is dead, you know, Mr. Holden. I'm very much alive."

"Yes, sir." Holden had to smile. *Very much alive* described Jed Foster to a T. Tall, muscular, athletic, Foster was the envy of practically every junior officer at Fort Bowie . . . and quite a few of the married officers looked upon the dashing figure with a good amount of jealousy. He could waltz. He could do everything from the French contra dance to the mazurka or the galop or the quadrille.

Holden noticed the bedroll and grip strapped behind Foster's saddle.

"Are you going somewhere, Captain?"

"Taking a leave, Mr. Foster. The Army owes me six months. They're giving me one."

"Where to, sir . . . if I may ask?"

"I think Mexico, Mr. Holden. There's nothing like celebrating Independence Day on the Fourth of July in Mexico."

"I don't believe Mexico celebrates our independence, Captain."

Mexico. Jed Foster belonged in a place

19

like San Francisco or New Orleans. Maybe the new mining metropolis just south of there called Tombstone. Chicago, New York, Boston, Charleston, or even Washington City.

"Then I'll celebrate her. By myself if I have to."

"Why Mexico, sir?"

Foster grinned. He had perfect teeth, too, and dark blue eyes. "Mr. Holden, have you ever heard of tequila and señoritas?"

"I have met tequila on two occasions and have conceded that he is the better man."

Foster laughed his thick laugh, shook his head, and beat the dust off his clothes. "And what about señoritas?"

"I don't get out of Bowie much, sir."

"You were just in Tucson."

"Only saw Fort Lowell, sir."

Foster's tongue clucked. "One day, Grat, you and I will need to take us a trip. I can show you some fine places. Let you grow up some."

"Thank you, sir."

Foster looked at the wagons, the men, and then turned around in his saddle to stare at the road to Fort Bowie.

"You nervous, Lieutenant?"

"Cautious, sir."

"Want some company?"

"You have Mexico, sir."

"Well, the canyon you cut through is shady, and it is a trifle warm today. And my horse here" — he patted the neck — "seems a bit winded. I could at least get you to the other side of the canyon. Maybe even all the way to Dos Cabezas. There's a saloon there. You can reacquaint yourself with your old nemesis, tequila."

Holden's head shook good-naturedly.

"Well . . . let's just say that I might not make it to Mexico. Dos Cabezas might do me fine. I'll ride along with you, Lieutenant, if you have no objections."

"I always enjoy your company, sir."

"Very good." Foster raised his hand and turned his horse. "Forward, yo-oo."

CHAPTER 3

The wagons creaked, groaned, and the wheels sank in the sand. The new recruits weren't exactly experienced muleskinners, either.

Jed Foster shook his head and found a cigar in the inside pocket of his buckskin jacket. He bit off the end, spit, and shoved the cigar into his mouth, fished a match from another jacket pocket, and struck it on the butt of the Winchester rifle sticking out from the scabbard that faced toward the horse's neck . . . unlike the scabbards on most Army saddles.

"Eight men? That all you got?"

Holden shrugged. "All they sent us."

"The old man was expecting twenty." Foster laughed and slapped his thigh. "So was I."

"You know this man's Army, sir."

"Yeah." The cigar came out, and Foster spit to the side. "All too well I know this man's Army." With bitterness he rarely showed, he pitched the barely smoked cigar into the sand. For a few yards, he said nothing, but finally turned in the saddle and looked at the wagons behind him.

"Two Huns, I take it," Foster said. "Some farm boys. A city slicker. One boy who must've lied about his age. And another who must be older than I am. Plus one swarthy gent who'll desert the first time he gets. Bet he joined up to avoid some law."

The canyon drew nearer.

Foster studied the north wall. Holden looked at the south side. Sergeant Lusk had dropped back about twenty yards behind the last wagon.

When they dipped into the canyon, the air immediately turned cooler.

"Let me ask you something, Mr. Holden," Foster said. "Why do you do it?"

"Do what?"

"Soldier in this man's Army. I know what a first lieutenant makes."

"I don't." Holden laughed and lowered his shoulder to show off the straps. "I'm still a second lieutenant."

"Well, let me assure you, Grat, that you won't get rich on a captain's salary, either."

Holden laughed, but shook his head, and replied in all seriousness, "I don't do this for the money."

"For the glory then? Custer got glory. He also got butchered, got his command killed. And I don't see a whole lot of glory coming to anybody in this god-forsaken hellhole."

"How about for pride?" Holden said.

The captain turned, stared, grinned, and tugged on his goatee. "Pride. Now there's something a man can hang his hat on."

"I'm serious, Captain. Pride in what I do. What we do. What I can do." He hooked his thumb at the wagons. "Those eight new recruits. I'd love the chance to shape them into soldiers. I think I can do it. They're young. But I've been with them for a hundred miles. They're game. And, no disrespect intended, sir, but I don't think that dark-skinned one will run. He's game as a bantam. He'll stick with us because he gave his word."

The white hat got pushed back. Foster leaned back, looked the men and the wagons over, and said, "But what if they're all dead before we reach Dos Cabezas?"

Holden didn't answer . . . but he stared at his senior officer with a bit of uneasiness. Then Foster reached into his saddlebag and pulled out a bottle.

Maybe, Holden told himself, *that explained it.*

Foster bit the cork, pulled it out with his teeth, and took a swig. He took another swig from the bottle and corked it. "How much do you think those rifles and ammunition would bring?" He took another pull from the bottle.

"Sir?"

"How much money could you get?"

"I don't understand, sir."

Foster laughed and held out the bottle toward Holden, who shook his head.

"It's not tequila, Grat. Rye. Not the best I've had, but you can't find the best in southern Arizona."

"You're on leave, sir. I'm on duty."

Foster cackled and shifted the bottle to his left hand. "How much money would they bring, if we were to sell them?"

Holden smiled, but he also brushed his hand casually across the flap of the holster. He had not refastened it. Maybe his nervousness before Captain Foster showed up had some founding to it. Maybe Foster, drunk as he appeared, wasn't the hero the lieutenant had thought.

He made himself answer. "If the colonel is right, Captain, the weapons aren't worth the time and manpower it took to get them from Fort Lowell to here."

"Depends on the buyer, I guess. Ain't that

25

the case!" Foster reined in. "Hold up, Grat. No sense in both of us getting shot off our horses."

Before Holden could say anything, Captain Jed Foster turned in his saddle, and ordered the drivers to stop and wait. Then he spurred the steel dust ahead, slowing only when he reached the edge of the canyon. Cautiously he loped out of the canyon several yards, gun in his right hand, whiskey bottle in his left, reins in his teeth. He spurred the gelding to the north, fell out of view, came back into view trailed by dust and disappeared on the south side only to reappear a few yards ahead.

He stopped, looked up, down, behind him, and at length, using his knees, guided the horse back to the edge of the canyon.

"All clear, come ahead."

Holden breathed easier, but still kept his hand near the holster, and kicked the horse into a walk. As he cleared the canyon, Foster again held out the whiskey bottle.

"No, but thank you, sir."

"Then hold up for a moment, Grat. I want to talk to you. See if you can do me a few favors while I'm gone. No, it's not paying off any of my gambling debts." He winked. "And, no, it's not about filling in on any of my myriad dalliances."

He waved the Germans on. "Keep riding. Don't slow till you've topped the grade. It rained recently, and the sand's soft."

He sent the next wagon on, then called out to Sergeant Lusk. "Sarge. Best ride back down the canyon. Make sure nobody's following us. Look for dust. Then get your arse back here in a hurry."

By then, the third wagon was out of the canyon, creeping along.

He kept holding out the bottle. Jed Foster was persistent. He called Grat Holden stubborn. "Or a teetotaler."

"Wouldn't call me that, sir. But, again, I'm on duty."

"Hold up!" Foster yelled. The recruits — even the Germans — obeyed.

Holden cocked his head. It was an odd place to stop four wagons.

"Come with me to Mexico, Grat. We'll have us a high old time."

That's when Grat Holden reached for his holstered Schofield. But he never got to it, for Jed Foster still held his long-barreled Colt, and swung it with crushing force across the top of Holden's head.

CHAPTER 4

Grat Holden tumbled out of the saddle the moment gunfire erupted up the trail. Jed Foster watched the gallant young fool hit the ground hard as his horse took off at a gallop toward the wagons. Blood ran down Holden's face. He did not stir. Quickly, Foster slipped off his horse and drew his 1873 Winchester from the scabbard.

The Army issued Springfields to its soldiers, but officers could always, at their own expense, outfit themselves with something that shot more than once like a Springfield, and something that was unlikely, after many rounds, to fix things so you had to pry out the empty copper cartridge from the breech with a knife — before the Apaches were riddling you with arrows.

Foster's horse was trained not to run with all the gunfire popping around him. Foster did not concern himself with the eight green recruits on the four freight wagons. He focused on Sergeant Byron Lusk, galloping down the canyon with his Springfield single-shot carbine ready.

Deftly, Foster worked the lever, jacking a .44-40 shell into the chamber. Resting the twenty-four-inch barrel on the seat of his saddle, he drew in a deep breath, and braced the stock against his shoulder. He lined up Sergeant Lusk's back in his sights, released his breath, counted one-two, and squeezed the trigger.

The rifle kicked, the steel dust did not move. Stepping away from the smoke the Winchester belched, Foster saw the sergeant's horse still running. He saw Sergeant Byron Lusk, who'd won some Confederate medal while fighting as a captain with Jeb Stuart's cavalry, lying in the center of the trail. Then Foster shot the horse.

He turned, spit in disgust, and worked another round into the Winchester. The Army preferred carbines for troopers. Foster liked the rifle, especially the Winchester. It held three more rounds than the Winchester carbine. He had fired twice. That left him with thirteen. He knew he should have kept a live round in the chamber. Then he would have started with sixteen .44-40 cartridges.

"Thirteen," he said. "Bad luck." He sent another round into the air and worked the lever again.

Foster glanced at Holden, still unconscious in the dirt. *As hard as I clubbed him,* Foster thought, *Grat will sleep till Independence Day.*

The men Foster had hired remained in the rocks on both sides of the road. Foster couldn't see the lead wagon, but he figured the two Germans were dead. He couldn't see Lieutenant Holden's horse, either, and that troubled him.

The rest of the raw troopers, however, must be game. Smoke belched from inside two of the freight wagons and troopers returned fire in both directions. Foster shook his head. Young Grat was right. Those fellows might have made something of themselves in this man's Army. Just not the one who ran toward Jed Foster.

Tears cut through the gunpowder residue that darkened his pale face. He was the city boy, young, red-headed, freckles on his nose. Blood poured from his left arm, and dribbled down his fingertips. He had dropped his Springfield. Seeing Foster, the kid slid to a stop. He blinked. He said, "Mister . . ."

Foster shot him in the chest.

Moving to his right, around the new corpse, Jed Foster inched his way toward the last wagon. No problem there. He could see the driver, the farm kid, lying on the seat, not moving, the top of his head a bloody mess. Foster went to the back of the wagon and peered inside. The crates were wrapped in canvas, tied down with thick ropes. Foster had to give Grat Holden a nod of respect. The kid knew what he was doing.

He moved to the mules, stamping their feet, snorting, braying, nervous, and wanting to stampede. But the driver had set the brake. The wagon wasn't going anywhere until Jed Foster wanted it to go. He gave the off-mule a wide berth as he moved toward the next wagon.

At least one man left in that one. Foster saw the driver come out of the box and fire at the bandits on the north side of the road. Waiting, hoping those idiots he had hired wouldn't accidentally gun him down, Foster braced the rifle and waited.

The man came up, but as Foster prepared to pull the trigger and put a bullet in that hardcase's spine, another trooper came up from the back of the wagon. Foster had figured he was already dead. This was the one Foster had predicted would desert.

He spotted Foster and knew exactly what to do. He had been aiming at the gunmen

31

on the ridge to the south but swung the rifle at Jed Foster and pulled the trigger.

CHAPTER 5

Foster let out a curse and dived as the bullet burned his blond hair. He rolled over, snapped off a quick shot, and saw the man dive back into the bed of the wagon, and the other rider disappear inside the driver's box to reload.

Foster levered the Winchester, which felt hot in his hands.

His men seemed to be concentrating on this same wagon. He hoped that meant the recruits in the wagons in front lay dead.

Taking cover in the rocks, Foster aimed at the tailgate of the wagon. He could send some bullets through the wood. Make the dark man in the back nervous. Maybe get lucky and hit him. He swore.

And risk ruining one of those Springfields. Or somehow hit the ammunition. The odds of blowing up the wagon by some chance shot were so high, it never could happen. But Foster had too much invested to risk any damage to any rifle.

He would have to get his men to charge. He might lose a few, but that would be no loss. Or better yet, he could work his way up the hill, find a spot and shoot down on the two soldiers. Pick them off. They were sitting ducks.

But not any longer.

Foster blinked and came up swearing as the mules began pulling the wagon off the side of the road and toward the wagon in front. He could just make out the gloved hands that gripped the lines to the mules. The driver — that young kid who couldn't be old enough to enlist — was pulling out. Not retreating. No way any of those boys were cowards. He was showing some brains.

The swarthy man in the back of the wagon popped up, snapped another shot that sent dust and chips of rocks into Foster's eyes, and disappeared as a bullet from one of Foster's men splintered the tailgate.

Furiously working to rub the grime out of his eyes, Foster yelled, "Stop that wagon!" He tripped, fell to his knees, came up, and ran, blinking and rubbing, clutching the Winchester. He tripped over the body of the one soldier who had showed yellow, the one Foster had gunned down back when he thought everything was in hand.

He could see. His vision was blurred, but he could see. The steel dust remained exactly where Foster had left him. The whiskey bottle he didn't remember dropping beside Grat Holden wasn't broken. Foster grabbed the reins, and started to find a stirrup, only to see Holden rolling over, pushing himself up with his hands.

"How — ?" Foster cursed again, kicked his left leg free of the stirrup, and ducked underneath the steel dust's head. Viciously, he brought his boot up, heard the crunch as the heel slammed into Holden's head and sent him into a clump of cactus. He was out cold. Maybe dead. At that point, Jed Foster didn't care one way or the other.

Leaping into the saddle, he spurred the steel dust into a lope.

Past the first wagon, the fleeing Studebaker started picking up speed. Those four mules were either fresh or scared.

"Don't shoot the mules!" Foster yelled as he loped by the other three wagons, a few riddled with bullets, and the soldiers either dead in the wagon seat or lying in bloody pools that were quickly being sucked into the Arizona dirt.

Everything was going to hell.

Then, luck — as frequently came to Foster — prevailed.

The kid couldn't see exactly where he was going, unless he wanted to get his head shot off, so he left that up to the four mules. At the speed they were going, when they started downhill toward Dos Cabezas, the back of the wagon slid, and the wheel landed in the ditch.

Foster held his breath, fearing the wagon would tip over. Once again, his luck held. The wagon drug for ten or twelve feet, then stopped. Stuck for the time being.

His men hurried on foot. Foster reined in his horse. Those two in the wagon had showed they were fighters. They wouldn't give up so easily.

The boy jumped out of the seat, landing on the road. Two bullets ripped into him. He staggered back as one of the bandits — a portly fellow who had been a civilian mule-skinner down at Camp Huachuca — laughed and brought up his Remington. The kid, though, didn't drop his Springfield. Somehow, he braced it against his bleeding side, turned, and touched the trigger. The bullet tore through the portly skinner's throat, and he landed against a paloverde tree. Dead, his head was almost torn off.

Four or five more bullets drilled into the kid, who fell beside the front wheel. The mules started dragging again, practically pulling the wagon out of the ditch.

"Surrender!" Foster yelled.

The green recruit didn't. He came up, put a .45-70 slug into another idiot Foster had hired, and the soldier disappeared behind the wood.

Standing in his stirrups, Foster yelled, "Rush him! Rush him! Before he can reload!"

Some of the men turned and stared at Foster as if he were mad. Foster put a bullet at their feet and jacked another round into the rifle. "I said charge him!"

They ran.

Foster remembered riding with George Custer during the war. Remembered what Custer had once told him. *Men are expendable. Sometimes it takes a lot of dead men to win a battle.*

The gunman came from both sides and the rear. The swarthy man came up again and fired, sending a bullet that went through one man and then dropped the fool immediately behind him. The dark man dropped behind the wood again, but the boys had the bloodlust. They ran to the wagon. Some climbed onto the wheels. Some just jumped up and fired. They fired. They fired. They fired. One even reloaded, stuck his Colt over the tailgate, and emptied the pistol again.

CHAPTER 6

Foster touched the horse with his spurs and rode down the hill.

"Enough. Enough!" He reined in and peered inside the back of the wagon.

"All right," he said, out of breath. Sweating. *Hell, Jed Foster never sweats,* he told himself. He started to sheath the Winchester, but saw his man the dark one had shot. The one with a bullet through his belly and his back.

The man groaned, begged, bled.

"Can you ride?" Foster asked.

The man tried to answer but only managed to spit out blood.

Foster didn't ask again. He brought the rifle up, shot the dying man in the head, then took charge. "Get that body out of the back of this wagon, and get this wagon turned around. All of the wagons must be turned around. Are any of the drivers and guards alive?"

The two in the wagon currently in the lead were dead. No doubt about that.

"I don't think so," one of the men said. "Except the one you hit on the head."

"Want me to finish off that bluecoat you coldcocked?" said a greasy vagabond with a gold-capped tooth.

"I told you that the lieutenant in charge must remain alive. But only him."

"You also told us," said another, "that these boys would turn tail or just curl up and die."

Foster glared. He could shoot that loud-mouth, too, but, well, he needed drivers and guards. "Never mind. What about the bay? The lieutenant's horse? Did you shoot it?"

No one answered. Obviously, they had not killed the bay. Sighing with bitter contempt, Foster nudged his horse down the trail. He saw the tracks of the galloping Army mount, and he knew part of his plan had gone to hell.

"Damn it!"

"But you told us not to kill the —"

"I said not to kill the *mules.* We need the mules to get these wagons to Mexico." He turned the steel dust around. "That horse will run straight to Dos Cabezas. Some drunk will stop him. Someone will see the US brand and get word to Bowie. Or that horse will gallop straight to Bowie. Either way, the Army will be sending a company when even that dumb colonel we have realizes that's Holden's horse. Now get these wagons turned around. It's a long way to Mexico and we don't have as much time to get there as I'd hoped."

The tailgate was opened, and the bloody corpse in the back rolled onto the ground.

Foster rode back to the original first wagon, saw the two dead Germans, shot and killed before they knew what had happened.

He wanted to check on the other soldiers, make sure they were indeed on their way to hell or heaven. Maybe order a few of the boys to walk around and give every one except Grat Holden a *coup de grâce,* a bullet in their brains. But after far too much gunfire and too much gone wrong, he had no time for that. They needed to be moving. Heading south as fast as those mules could go.

His men were hurrying. They feared Jed Foster more than they feared getting caught by the Army. At best, they'd be spending a long time in the prison in Fort Leavenworth, Kansas, if the Army caught them. More than likely, they would be hanged at the fort or over in Tucson. But if Jed Foster turned against them . . .

That was another thing Custer had told him. *Fear makes good motivation.*

Foster rode past Grat Holden, still bleeding, still breathing, and still lying in the cactus. He kept going, past the dead horse he had killed, and came to Sergeant Byron Lusk. He swung out of the saddle, keeping a grip on the reins and Winchester, and kicked the man over. Unseeing eyes stared up at him, and just a small amount of blood appeared on the noncommissioned officer's blue tunic. Foster grinned at his shot. Through the heart. At a gallop. One hundred yards distance, maybe a little more.

He climbed back onto the horse and rode easily until he was out of the canyon. Again, he dismounted, studied the progress his men were making. Satisfied, he reloaded the Winchester before he put it into the scabbard. Then he moved closer to Grat Holden. There was the whiskey bottle, and Foster's luck had held. It had not broken.

Taking the bottle and setting it aside, he knelt and reached into the cactus, put his hand underneath Holden's head, and lifted it toward him.

Holden's eyes shot open as his right fist came up swinging. The blow caught Foster's jaw, and sent him reeling. Holden shook his head and lunged. One hand slipped inside the captain's tunic. The other tried to smash Foster's throat. He missed. His eyes filled with rage. Foster shot out with both hands, catching the lieutenant in the chest. He heard the ripping of his tunic, and Holden went down on his side. He tried to come up, but Foster was in much better condition. His right fist slammed into Holden's temple, and once again, the lieutenant fell silent and still.

"You need to learn when to quit, Holden." Foster tested his jaw.

He grabbed the bottle, but did not bother lifting Holden's head. He pulled out the cork and poured whiskey over the lieutenant's open mouth. Then dropped the bottle beside the unconscious officer.

"I never really liked you, Grat. You're just too . . . decent. Enjoy Leavenworth or, if you're lucky, being a private."

Once again, he mounted the steel dust and loped to the wagons.

"Come on. Mexico and a fortune wait for us!"

CHAPTER 7

His jaw hurt. He couldn't fit a hat over the bandage that covered his head. And Colonel Carlton Smythe told him he could not wear his dress uniform. At least, Grat Holden decided, he was allowed to walk to the funeral. House arrest was restricted. At least for the afternoon.

When the door opened, he stepped outside. Another hot day. Hotter than usual.

Holden brought up the rear, following the procession that moved past the flag flying at half-staff, and on the road that led toward Apache Pass, stopping at the post cemetery. No one spoke to him. No one even looked at him.

The colonel said some words. The chaplain prayed. The honor guard shot their Springfields over the coffin before Sergeant Byron Lusk was laid to rest. He should have rested beside seven other fresh graves, but the recruits killed at the canyon near Dos

Cabezas had been buried at the little village. It was too hot to transport blood-soaked corpses all the way to Bowie.

They had transported one boy, though. To Holden's surprise, he learned one of the soldiers, a kid from an Illinois farm who had a badly wounded right leg and a bullet in his groin, still lived.

That made Holden wonder. Had the bandits and Foster left the kid alive? Or had they just overlooked him? Holden would have to ask Jed Foster that question when he found him, and just before he killed the traitor and butcher.

The funeral ended too quickly. Soldiers filed away, still refusing to look at Holden, or even acknowledge his presence. Holden walked to the hole. He found the shovel. He studied the coffin, frowned, and sent dirt onto the wooden box.

"What do you think you're doing?" Colonel Smythe demanded.

Holden did not look up, just put himself into the job. "Burying my friend."

One of the grave diggers, the ruffian Smythe had let out of the guardhouse to do the job, laughed. That turned the colonel's attention to the post drunk and left Holden alone to his job. A drunk wasn't fit to bury a man like Byron Lusk, formerly an officer

45

in the service of the Confederacy, now a sergeant killed in the line of duty for the United States cavalry.

While he shoveled, another figure stepped to the mound of dirt. He wore chains, too, and the white cotton garb of an Army prisoner, except for his blouse. You could still see where his chevrons had been.

Holden studied the man. Private, formerly a sergeant, Ben "Hard Rock" Masterson. Holden had busted him down to private. He wasn't fit to bury Lusk, either.

"I can do this myself, Masterson," Holden said.

The ex-sergeant threw dirt into the hole.

"You're the one who's not fit, Mister Soon-To-Be-Ex-Lieutenant. You're the one who got drunk, let this good man get killed . . . and a bunch of others. You're the one who's been slanderin' Capt'n Foster's name. You're the disgrace to that uniform."

Holden dug the shovel into the mound savagely, but he would not brawl with a ruffian over a brave man's grave.

"Besides," Masterson said, sending more dirt and pebbles into Sergeant Lusk's grave. "He was my friend."

That's good enough for me, Holden thought. They filled the grave in silence.

■ ■ ■ ■

Back in his Spartan quarters — his roommate had moved out, finding quarters elsewhere, saying he would not stay with a coward and a drunk — Holden withdrew a scrap of paper.

In the desert, he had awakened to the sounds of buzzards and coyotes, drawn the Schofield, and fired into the air. Then he saw the paper he had dropped. Ripped. Wadded up, probably in his hand. He'd picked it up and remembered his scuffle with that traitor, Jed Foster, and knew it must have come out of Foster's jacket during the fight. As the carrion birds left the carnage, he'd seen something else. Four or five armed men riding slowly, leading his horse.

They'd come from Dos Cabezas. Or they might have been Foster's men, coming to finish the job. He'd slid the paper back into his pants pocket, and, still holding the smoking .45, had tried to stand. He had passed out.

Alone, he looked at the paper and tried to make sense of it.

What was there to make sense of? Two words — *Dolores. Muncie.* And the start of a date — *July.* The rest had been torn off.

He heard the footsteps and slipped the paper back into his pocket. Pushing himself off his bed, he felt a sudden spat of dizziness and had to grab a bedpost to steady himself. The door opened.

When the Army thinks you guilty of at least drunkenness if not treason, soldiers forget to knock.

"Colonel wants to see you," the corporal said. There was no *sir* added.

"How's the kid?" Holden asked as soon as the door shut behind him. He stood in Colonel Carlton Smythe's office.

"Kid? You mean Mitchell. So he can swear, as you claim, that he never actually saw you take a drink. Just saw Captain Foster offer you one."

"Because he, and the others killed, were good men."

Smythe fumed. "Trooper Mitchell is dead. Shock, that sawbones says, from the amputation of his leg."

"Damn," Holden whispered.

"Damn?" Smythe sent a glob of mucus into the spittoon. "Damn because you think he could've saved you and your preposterous story? My feeling is damn you, Holden. Nine men killed. You found with whiskey on your breath and a bottle at your side. You're the sole survivor of a massacre . . . and you're responsible for the loss of four wagonloads of Springfield rifles and enough ammunition to start a war!"

"I told you what happened," Holden tried again.

"Yes. You slandered the name of the gallant Captain Foster. He served under the martyred George Custer during the late war, Holden. Do you think anyone will believe your outrageous story?"

CHAPTER 8

The stagecoach slid to a stop on the rugged road leading to Bisbee. The driver cried out in fear. The guard stood in the box and brought the twelve-gauge shotgun to his shoulder, but before he could even thumb back the hammers, six arrows hit him in the chest and four more in the back. He tumbled over the coach, causing the mules to pull hard. The driver felt like letting them run, but that was one hard grade to climb, and he didn't want to wind up looking like a porcupine.

He also didn't want to be tortured to death by Apaches so he dropped into the box, found the shotgun, put it under his chin. The Apaches let him thumb back both hammers. And they laughed as he fingered both triggers.

The white-haired leader with a fat nose, fat face, and red silk headband kicked his pinto into a walk. The horse walked around the dead guard, ignored the smell of blood and death in the booth, and halted by the door. The Indian jerked it open.

"¡Vete!" he yelled in Spanish. "¡Vete! ¡Vete! ¡Vete!" He motioned with his hand, gesturing for the passengers to get out, then he kicked his pinto and went to the wagon's boot.

Motioning to eight Apache warriors, he dismounted and nodded at last to the other two Apaches. They swung from their stolen horses and hurried to him, to open the boot and go through the luggage.

The tallest of the Apaches hurried to the open door, reached in and pulled out the saloon girl who had just been run out of Tombstone.

"Oh, my God," she wailed, and dropped to her knees. "God have mercy. God show pity. God save me."

Four men — a drummer, a gambler, a banker, and a dentist — came out of the coach. They were all white, paler than usual, and the drummer had already wet his britches.

"Ain't you got a gun?" he whispered to the gambler.

"I lost that in Tombstone, too."

"They'll take me into the hills," the woman said, "and ravage me till I'm dead."

"Better than getting staked to an anthill and have honey poured over your face and private parts," said the banker.

One of the warriors, a young brave in his teens, walked up to the dentist. He held out a pillowcase and grunted something in a guttural language none of the passengers could understand. He grunted again, more forcefully, and two of his comrades raised their Winchester repeaters at the dentist.

"By Jove," said the banker at last. He looked at the dentist. "I believe they're robbing us."

The men with the old leader scattered the clothes and items from the luggage in the boot. The old man frowned at the pickings and moved his horse back to the side of the stagecoach. He spoke sharply in Spanish, then Apache.

"That's Crooked Nose himself," whispered the gambler.

"How . . . can . . . you . . . tell?" whined the drummer.

The gambler rolled his eyes.

The warriors ripped the brooch from the saloon girl's dress, threatened to chop off her finger to get the ring before she managed to slide it off, and pulled off her earrings. She yelped in pain, fell to the ground, and buried her head in her hands, sobbing, waiting for the assault that never came.

They took the gambler's vest, and slapped him senseless when they realized he had nothing of value, although the younger one pulled the vest over his bare chest and began strutting around. They scored cash and gold pocket watches from the banker and dentist, and took the banker's diamond stickpin as well, and they emptied the drummer's samples but took his suitcase, which proved better than the pillowcase.

Finally, one of the braves climbed into the driver's box, tossed the mangled corpse of the suicidal driver over the edge, which caused the drummer to faint and the banker to throw up. Next the brave hoisted the Wells Fargo box and dropped it into the dirt.

That seemed to satisfy Crooked Nose, who barked something in Apache, and two of the braves picked up the strongbox and carried it into the wooded hills on the side of the road.

The rest of the Apaches busied themselves. They cut the mules loose from the Concord and herded them into the woods. They took the pillowcase and anything else that struck their fancy — the gambler's hat, the woman's stockings, the shotgun, the driver's wallet and St. Christopher's medallion.

Crooked Nose barked some more orders in the rough language, and kicked his horse into a walk.

A moment later, the passengers were standing alone in the road. They listened for a moment, heard the sounds of the mules and the Indians climbing up the hill, stones rattling, branches breaking. Within a few minutes they could hear nothing but the saloon girl's sobs and banker's gags.

At length, the gambler said in a shaky voice, "They . . . didn't kill . . . us."

"No," said the dentist. "They didn't."

Hearing this, the saloon girl lifted her head. The dentist covered the bloody remains of the driver with one of the coats the Apaches had pulled out of a suitcase.

"Do we walk to Bisbee or do we sit here and wait?" the gambler asked.

"Walk," said the banker, who found a handkerchief and wiped his mouth. "They might be back."

"What happened?" asked the saloon girl.

The dentist laughed. "No one will ever believe it, lady, but we were just held up by Crooked Nose and his Apaches."

CHAPTER 9

The name of the cantina in the town of Rancho Los Cielos, just across the border in Sonora, was called Mariscos, which meant seafood . . . which was a joke. You couldn't get any seafood in the cantina, and even if you could, you wouldn't want to eat it.

When she heard the jingling of traces and the snorting of mules outside, Soledad Tadeo stepped through the open door and waited.

Four wagons. The mules were played out. Four-mule teams pulling two. Another wagon had three. The last wagon had two. The harnesses had been cut. The men, fourteen, by Tadeo's count were bleary-eyed from the hard ride. The mules and the wagons had been burned with the US brand, but none of the men wore the uniforms of the *soldados norteamericanos* except the dashing one with the fringed

55

leather jacket, and he wore only the pants, boots, and spurs of the *Yanquis.*

The first outrider swung off his winded, sweat-lathered brown gelding and rushed to Soledad Tadeo. He grabbed one of her breasts and pushed her against the outer wall of Mariscos.

He found himself against the wall as he grimaced in agony. She had his testicles in her left hand, and she was squeezing like a vise. She had a knife against his throat and had pricked just enough skin to draw blood. Sweat burned the cut, but the man could not feel that because of the agony below his gunbelt.

"Touch me again," Soledad Tadeo whispered, "and I will cut off your manhood and shove it in your mouth." She did not let go.

Most of the men who had ridden in with the gringo now laughed at their colleague's predicament.

She said so that all could hear, "If this *borracho* sees me again, I will kill him. And if any of you dare look me in the eye, I will kill you, too. So when you see me, cast your eyes upon the dirt. The graveyard at the top of the hill is filled with men who I did not like." She moved the knife from his throat, nicked his left earlobe, spit in his face, and gave his balls one final twist. When she turned, the man slid onto the dirt, moaned, puked, and fell on his side.

Only the man in the buckskins was staring at his boots.

She yelled out a war cry in Spanish and brought the knife up as though to throw it. She also drew a nickel-plated double-action Colt and aimed it at the closest man. That did the job. All of the men stared at their dusty boots. To Soledad Tadeo, it appeared that even the mules were looking at the ground, refusing to make eye contact.

She nodded, but lowered neither gun nor knife, and made her way through the men. As she passed each wagon, she looked into the beds. She also noted the depths the wheels had made in the road. It was a rather hard road, but the wagons had made substantial tracks.

When she reached the other cantina in Rancho Los Cielos, she tilted her head back and cried out the name of the revolutionary, *"¡Viva Amonte Negro!"* squeezed the trigger of the pistol, feeling it kick twice, and slipped through the closed door of *La Cantina Que No Tiene Nombre,* The Cantina That Has No Name.

Unlike Mariscos, this place was empty tonight. The owner and bartender, Juan Gomez, stood at the bar. The gringo with

57

the thick gray beard and battered gray hat sat sipping coffee. Soledad Tadeo turned sharply and looked through the window, her back against the wall so the invaders could not see that she was staring at them.

She was, and she knew it, a beautiful woman. Bronzed skin and long to her waist raven-like hair so dark it shined. Her eyes were darker, but they never shined. She wore a tight-fitting muslin dress, a red sash around her slim waist, nothing covering her legs from her knees to where the moccasins slipped over her feet and came up to her ankles. She was twenty-one years old.

"Freighters, miners, or bandits?" the old gringo asked and sipped more coffee.

"Yo no se," she answered then switched to English. "Their mules and one horse say that they are *soldados norteamericanos.*"

The man set the tin mug on the table.

"You sure?"

"Sí," she replied.

Silently, the old man rose from his chair. He checked the Colt holstered on his hip, pushed back his old hat, and let his bowlegs carry him to the other side of the window. His boots — big, tall, heavy — made no sound as he moved across the floor. He looked like a bear. He moved like a bird.

When his back was to the wall, he, too,

spied on the street as Soledad Tadeo did.

She saw what he saw. Four wagons led by mismatched, worn-out mules. Most of the men had gone into Mariscos where they would fill themselves on frijoles, cerveza, and tequila. Six men, however, remained with the wagons. No, she realized, eight. One stood in the corner where he would have a good view of the road that crossed the border. But if he did not stop smoking his cigarette, whoever might be following them would see him first. The other had climbed into the bell tower of the church. She would not have spotted him had the moon not picked that moment to show itself from behind a cloud.

"Eight outside," the old man said. "How many inside?"

She studied the old man again. He was good. Very good. His hair said he was old, but his eyes were that of a much younger man, which might explain why he was something else. He was alive.

"Six."

That told her something else. They were protecting what they hauled in the wagons. "Those are Army wagons. Can't read the brands from here on the mules."

He looked across the window at her.

"You saw what those Studebakers are

hauling." It was not a question, but he was waiting for an answer, and his eyes were as intense as her own.

"Canvas covered them, but they are boxes. Crates."

"What did the men look like?"

"They were pigs." She reconsidered. "Except one." She nodded toward the hitching rail. "The one who rode that horse."

The old man looked outside again. His face changed.

"What did he look like?"

"Tall. Long hair the color of ripened corn. Mustache. Beard on his face, but the mustache will stay after he shaves. He looks young but may be older. Buckskin jacket. Buckskin gloves." She would not let the old man know that she thought him handsome, dashing, so she added, "But he is no Amonte Negro."

"No." The old man looked older now, worn out. Tired. "I reckon he ain't." He fished a coin from his vest pocket and tossed it to her. "Gracias." As he walked past the table, he dropped more change beside his coffee and nodded at José.

She heard him mutter a soft curse as he moved toward the back door.

Then he was gone, leaving Soledad Tadeo

holding a double eagle and feeling . . . rare
for her . . . confused.

CHAPTER 10

Captain Jed Foster leaned against the bar. Without even having to ask, the Mexican bartender with the greasy black mustache poured tequila into a glass he slammed on the plank bar.

Foster gave a weary grin.

"That glass is dirty."

Without looking, the bartender said with a heavy accent, "Not anymore."

That made Foster laugh, and he lifted the glass, holding it up in a toast to the bartender's humor and hard attitude against gringos. Even in a town like Rancho Los Cielos, if anyone actually called it a town, gringos often stopped here, leaving the American law fuming on the other side of the international boundary.

His good mood did not last very long. Almost as soon as the bartender and his petite little helper in a tight-fitting dress had served all of Foster's men, the doors banged open and in walked six Mexican hardcases. Foster saw two others outside, standing in front of the one window to Mariscos. He did not think these men came for seafood, either.

He recognized the one who stopped about fifteen paces in front of him with two others stepping a little behind him and to either side. He wore russet-colored boots, blue denim britches with two percussion revolvers low on both hips. His shirt was red velvet, and bandoliers of ammunition hung in pairs across his chest for the heavy rifle he held in both hands. His kepi, most likely, had been a trophy from the *Rurale* he had killed to get it. His eyes were as black as his teeth.

"Amigo," the bandit said, "you are a man of your word. You brought the rifles and ammunition you promised. You have helped our revolution with your generosity."

Holding the glass of tequila in his left hand, Foster raised it in salute. He grinned again, amused at the thought that anyone would consider this lieutenant's leader, Amonte Negro, a revolutionary. Negro was no George Washington, not even a Benito Juarez, but a cutthroat and killer.

"I told Amonte Negro that the rifles, bayonets, and ammunition would go to the

63

highest bidder," Foster said. "I told him, and you, when and where my auction would take place."

The man's big head nodded. "We decided that you would take our offer . . . tonight." He smiled his dark smile. "Why waste time?"

Foster finished the tequila, and put the glass on the plank.

"I think you've decided that Amonte Negro doesn't need those wagons. You'd like them for yourself."

The man answered with a shrug.

"I like a man who shows enterprise," Foster said.

"We will take the wagons," the bandit said.

"How much will you pay?"

"We might let you live."

Foster's smile widened. "Take the wagons then."

That surprised the cutthroat.

"The mules are all but done in. Probably couldn't carry even an empty wagon back to the border . . . which is what you'd be buying, amigo. Empty wagons." Foster stepped away from the bar. "Do you think we'd be foolish enough to bring the Springfields, bayonets, and ammunition to a miserable town like this?"

The Mexican bandit spun, shouting at the

64

two men he had left outside, *"Buscar en los vagones,"* and suddenly realized his mistake. Swinging back toward Foster, he tried to bring the barrel of his rifle up, but the revolver was already in Foster's right hand, and the last thing the leader saw was the fire and smoke that belched out of Foster's Colt.

Keeping his legs spread wide part, Foster did not move anything but his head and right arm. He always figured that men who moved were those who died. *Stand your ground.* That was something else George Custer had told him during the war. *If a bullet or shell is meant for you, no matter how you duck, dip, dance, or dive, you will still just die. Besides, it's hard to hit a target when you're moving. Be still. Focus. Don't blink. Don't worry. Don't hesitate.*

He bent his wrist to the right, thumbed back the hammer and shot the man who had been standing to the now dead bandit's left . . . shot him in the throat.

Too high, Foster thought as blood spurted and the man left his feet and landed on a table, overturning it, and rolling to the floor, leaving a trail of crimson behind him.

Straightening his wrist, Foster brought the Colt to his left and fired again. That bullet hit the outlaw to the dead leader's right . . .

in the gut. The man spun around, dropping his old pistol, clutching his belly, and dropping to his knees. The dying man tried to lift one of his hands to make the sign of the cross, but Foster put a bullet in the man's back, shattering his spine. He collapsed in a heap, groaned, coughed, shuddered, and lay still.

Foster's gunshots were echoed by his own men as they cut loose on the men who'd come to steal their wagons. Glass shattered from the window, which was broken in two places before they had even ridden into town. The barmaid was on her knees, clutching a bottle of mescal, eyes tightly closed as she grimaced. The bartender, frozen in shock, stood against what passed for a back bar in a hellhole like Rancho Los Cielos.

Foster decided that his men could handle the pathetic, two-bit thieves, so he began shucking the empty casings from his Colt and reloading as he moved back to the bar. He found the bottle the bartender had left, studied his glass, and used the clear liquid to rinse out dirt. He added two fingers of the rotgut, laid the Colt on the table, and sipped.

The men he had hired had done a poor job at the ambush near Dos Cabezas, but they'd learned quickly — most of the Mexican bandits were dead. Some of the boys were busting out into the streets to find and kill any more bandits who had ridden up to Mariscos to steal the wagons.

Foster glanced through the shattered window. He could see the four wagons and knew that he had lied about those wagons being empty. Eventually, they would move the guns, but there had not been any time to do that chore yet.

He saw one badly shot-up bandit crawling on the floor near the bar.

Foster picked up his Colt, aimed, and shot the man in the head. Then returned to his tequila.

When everything had quieted down, he reloaded his Colt again, holstered it, and nodded to the man who called himself Cossey.

"You and the boys take whatever you want off these fellows, not that it'll amount to much, then strap them on to their horses. Fire a couple shots, and the horses, most likely, will take these fools back to Amonte Negro's camp . . . if this was Negro's idea. Then I guess we can ride out of here and put these wagons in a safe place. Help yourself to some tequila for the trip."

He looked at the bartender, still frozen in

terror, and dropped a few greenbacks on the plank. He nodded at the girl on the floor, but with her eyes open, and tossed a half-eagle in her direction.

"Custer's luck," he said with a smile. "Foster's luck." He reached inside his buckskin jacket and pulled out his papers.

That's when he saw the ripped piece of paper. That's when he had a bit of a scare that Foster's luck might be running out.

CHAPTER 11

"Lieutenant Holden?" The voice sounded respectful and came after a soft tapping on the door.

Grat Holden folded the piece of paper he had pulled out of Captain Jed Foster's uniform and slid it into his pants pocket.

"Yes?"

"Begging your pardon, sir, but I've been ordered by Colonel Smythe to escort you to headquarters."

Holden sat up, considered that, and rose from the bed. He never cared much for spending all day lying around in bed anyway. "I'll be right there." He pulled on his tunic, found his hat, and went to the door.

Lieutenant? Knocking on the door? Even a "Begging your pardon, sir?" Something was up. Something had changed.

"Grat Holden," Colonel Smythe said with no hesitation, and nodded at the gray-haired, lean man in Mexican denim trousers, Apache-style moccasins, a calico shirt, tan vest, and gray hat. "This is Sam Florence."

Holden straightened. He had heard a lot of stories about Sam Florence, one of the best scouts in Arizona Territory, a man who had known Cochise, Mangas Coloradas, and even Geronimo, not to mention old Crooked Nose himself. So . . . Florence didn't stand seven-feet tall and he didn't look like Hercules.

Still, Holden bet the old man could handle just about anything thrown his way. "I've heard a lot about you, Mr. Florence."

The man ignored the comment. "This the bub who lost the wagons?"

Holden felt his shoulders slump.

"Yes. Now do you mind telling me what this is all about, Sam?"

"From what I hear," the old man said, "you say that Captain Foster, Captain Jed Foster, winner of the Medal of Honor, rode up to you near Dos Cabezas. Then he whacked you on the head with his pistol just as bandits started firing at the wagons, and the troopers in them."

"That's what I say."

"Which is preposterous," Smythe chimed in.

70

"Shut up, Colonel," Sam Florence said, and Carlton Smythe obeyed with meek resignation.

"You were knocked out?"

"I came to," Holden said. "Twice, I think. I know at least once I got into a bit of a scrap, but Foster hit me again. Then I woke up. That's about it. Passed out. Next time I woke up I was in handcuffs in the back of a wagon returning here."

The old man nodded.

"You'd swear that to my face."

"I'm waiting for a chance to swear it before a court-martial."

"Swear it to me. But know this. Jed Foster saved my life in the war."

Holden stared at the old man, trying to match the fierceness in his eyes. He said in a respectful voice, "As much as you may worship Captain Foster, and as much as I respected him before last week, I swear to you that Jed Foster led the ambush that left all nine men under my command dead. And I believe the only reason I was spared was so I would get the blame. I wish to God that it had been the other way around."

The only sound inside the colonel's office was the ticking of the Regulator clock on the wall . . . until Colonel Carlton Smythe spoke again. "As I said, *preposterous.* Scan-

71

dalous. I shall add slander to the charges for which we will drum you out of this man's Army."

"Shut up, Colonel." The old man's shoulder's sagged, and he moved to the settee in front of Smythe's desk. Wearily, joints in his knees popping, he sat and hung his head. Finally, he removed his hat, laid it on the floor, and ran his fingers through his thick head of hair.

At length, Sam Florence raised his head. "The kid ain't lying, Colonel. I was across the border the other night. Just a little place west of Agua Prieta. Fourteen men rode up in the middle of the night . . . outriders and four wagons. Army wagons."

Smythe protested, "Lieutenant Meade is leading a scouting party, trying to find where the bandits took those wagons."

Florence shot back, "And when your Lieutenant Meade rides back here, he'll tell you that they crossed the border into Mexico."

"You rode that far." Smythe tried to sound respectful and astonished so he wouldn't be told to shut up again.

"Jed Foster was leading them, Colonel."
"You saw him?"
"I saw his horse. The steel dust. A young revolutionary described him to a T."

"But . . ." Now it was Smythe who sank into his chair.

"Have you alerted the Mexican government?"

"Well . . . no . . . not . . ."

Grat Holden decided to join the conversation. "Colonel, have you alerted General Willcox or anyone with the Department of Arizona?"

"I hoped . . . well . . . if we can get . . . You see . . ."

"Did you let anyone in Washington know?" Before Smythe could answer, Holden asked another question. "Or the Springfield Armory?"

CHAPTER 12

Colonel Carlton Smythe hemmed and hawed for a while, made his way to the cabinet against the wall where the American flag, a cavalry guidon, and a portrait of Abraham Lincoln hung, and found the decanter. After filling a snifter and refortifying himself with Napoleon brandy, he managed to say, "There's no sense in passing blame around or wondering who knows what. The bottom line is that we must get those weapons back before they fall into the wrong hands."

"They're already in the wrong hands," Sam Florence said.

"But maybe Captain Foster —" Smythe sighed, shook his head, finished the brandy but did not refill his glass, and walked back to his desk. He kept the glass with him, likely not realizing he had not left it on the cabinet. He set it down on the edge of the desk. "I cannot believe Jed Foster, a Medal of Honor winner . . ." He sighed again and sank into his chair. "Why? Why would he do it?"

"Money."

Florence and the colonel turned to stare at Holden.

After breathing in deeply and exhaling slowly, Holden tried to explain. "We all know Jed. He can be reckless. He loves to gamble. Horses. Cards. A shooting contest. He likes to be showy. He likes to dress to the nines. And he would rather be rich."

Florence nodded. "How many investments has he made that went south and took his pay with them?"

After grunting and groaning, Colonel Smythe shook his head, "I just can't believe Jed Foster would turn outlaw. No, not just turn outlaw but betray his very country."

"Greed changes a man, Colonel," the old scout said.

The lengthy silence that followed was broken by a solid tapping on the door.

"Yes?" Smythe said with irritation, and the door opened.

The sergeant major, a lean man, clean shaven, and well-tanned for a man who spent his days behind a desk, came in, holding a piece of paper in his left hand. "Beggin' the colonel's pardon, sir, but I have a message from the post commander at Camp Huachuca."

Smythe seemed even more irritated. "Can it wait, Sergeant? We're busy here."

"I see that, sir." The sergeant saw the snifter on Smythe's desk. "I don't know, sir. The message is being relayed to all forts and camps in Arizona and New Mexico. And" — he scratched the side of his face with his left hand — "It's sorta . . . well . . . peculiar."

There came that sigh again, and that look on Colonel Smythe's face. "All right, Sergeant. Read it. And skip all the pompom and crap that I don't need to hear."

"Yes, sir." The man found the spectacles in his coat pocket, slipped them on, and held the paper close. "It says a stagecoach from Tombstone was held up near Bisbee late yesterday afternoon."

Carlton Smythe swore. "Bandits holding up a civilian passenger conveyance is a problem for the local civilian peace officers, not the United States Army. What in blazes is Colonel Reid at Camp Huachuca thinking?"

"Sir," the sergeant said, "the bandits that held up the stage were . . . well . . . Apaches."

"You mean Apaches attacked that stagecoach?" Smythe asked.

"No, Colonel. The message here says that they held it up."

"What kind of nonsense is this? Colonel Reid is playing a joke, playing us for fools."

"Sir, this is going to every post in two territories," the sergeant reminded.

Sam Florence didn't buy the story, either. "How drunk were the passengers on that coach?" He wasn't grinning, though.

"I don't know, Mr. Florence." The sergeant major looked at the message. "The driver and the guard were killed. The mules pulling the coach were stolen. Guesses to the number of Indians involved ranged from eight to eighteen. Four passengers — three males and a woman. All robbed."

"Robbed?" Grat Holden had spoken for the first time. "Of what?"

"I can imagine what they took from the woman," Smythe said.

The brandy, that one little snifter, must have gone straight to his head, Holden thought.

But it was only eight-thirty-two in the morning.

"No, sir," the sergeant said. "They didn't molest any of them. And the witnesses, or survivors, or whatever you want to call them, said that the Indians only killed the guard. The driver killed himself."

"What did they take?" Holden asked, sharper this time. He wanted to know the answer.

"Wallets. They don't give a figure of exactly how much money was stolen. Some watches, jewelry, and they also took the strongbox."

"How much did it have in it?" Sam Florence seemed to be following Holden's line of thinking.

"It doesn't say, Mr. Florence. Just that it was money from Tombstone's Laughlin Mining Corporation to the Bank of Bisbee."

"Rogue Apaches?" Smythe questioned, and shook his head. "No, more likely white men, or probably Mexicans being that close to the border, pretending to be Apaches." He snorted and shook his head. "The Boston Tea Party, Bisbee-style. Thank you for the interruption, Sergeant. Tell Colonel Reid —"

"Ask Colonel Reid to let us know how much money was in that strongbox," Holden interrupted his commanding officer. "And ask him if he has heard of any other reports of Apaches robbing civilians."

Smythe looked furious, but held his tongue.

"Very good, Lieutenant," Florence said. "And I don't know about any Apaches holdin' up folks around here, but there was a report about some injuns robbin' a copper mine in Sonora last week, or thereabouts."

"Very good, Sergeant. Please, no more interruptions until I have finished my interview with Mr. Florence and Mr. Holden."

The sergeant major nodded and bit his lower lip. "There's one more thing, sir."

"Be brief, Sergeant."

"Colonel Reid also says that the survivors in the stagecoach said the leader of the Apaches was none other than Crooked Nose hisself."

CHAPTER 13

The front door to the second adobe building on Officer's Row was locked.

"You got a key, Colonel?" Sam Florence asked.

"Of course not. I don't live here."

Florence glanced at Grat Holden, who did not hesitate. He stepped back and kicked hard against the door, which shuddered but did not give. His second kick busted the bolt, and the door slammed open.

"This is highly improper and in all likelihood illegal," Colonel Smythe said.

"So is killing nine soldiers and stealing four wagons of rifles and ammunition," Holden said with contempt as he entered the quarters of Captain Jed Foster.

A map of Arizona Territory, a photograph of George Custer surrounded by several officers, and a portrait of George Washington hung on the wall.

Washington, Holden thought. Should be

Benedict Arnold.

The furnishings, by Arizona and Army standards, seemed quite opulent.

"You know anything about the captain's family?" Sam Florence asked as he squatted beside the trunk at the foot of Foster's four-poster bed.

Smythe stood in front of the door, outside, on the porch. He wasn't about to step into Foster's quarters . . . likely to protect himself from court-martial and dismissal, or even a stay at the penitentiary at Fort Leavenworth, Kansas.

"He never talked about it," Holden answered as he went to the dresser.

From the doorway, Smythe said, "His parents are dead. They were dead when he joined the Michigan regiment at the outbreak of the War to Preserve Our Union. It's in his personnel files. No family. No next of kin listed."

"No inheritance, most likely," Florence said, as he drew his revolver and slammed at the lock on the trunk. "Joined for the money the Army offered."

"Or for the glory," Smythe said. "Or the honor. Or for his loyalty to his —" He stopped then.

Loyalty to his country? Not after stealing new Springfield rifles.

The third blow from the revolver's handle broke open the lock. Florence opened the trunk. Holden looked at the top of the dresser. Whiskey bottles. Wine, even champagne. A calendar propped up by the mirror and various photographs of girls slid into the cherrywood sides of the mirror. Holden began going through the drawers.

"What were your folks like, Holden?" the old scout asked.

Holden stopped tossing socks and unmentionables — women's undergarments, spoils of conquests, he figured — and turned. "My parents?" He studied the scout, who did not look back, kept pulling out tintypes, books, and clothes from the trunk.

"Alive? Dead? Rich? Poor?"

"Both alive," Holden said. His lips tightened. Embarrassed, he finally said, "Not . . . poor. Well . . . my father runs a shipping . . . he owns . . . a shipping line in Boston."

"Rich then," Florence said.

"Very," Holden admitted.

"So you go to West Point instead of some fancy school?"

"I told Father and Mother I wanted to make it on my own."

"Jed know that?" The old scout turned and waited for the answer.

Holden nodded. Then he cursed. "If the

damned fool needed money, why didn't he come to me? I could've asked my parents."

"Pride," Colonel Smythe suggested.

"Nah." The scout went back to the trunk. "The adventure. To see how far he can push his luck. That's Jed Foster."

Cursing, even angrier at Foster, Holden ripped out a drawer, dumping its contents on the floor then dropping the drawer on the shirts. He moved to the next drawer.

"Here we go." Florence rose and sat on the bed. "Bank book." He began thumbing through it. "What you'd expect for a captain with his taste in liquor, horses, and women."

Holden swore again, held up a handful of letters, and ripped the next drawer out. It landed hard on the floor, and the front-facing, carved wood fell off. "Letters demanding payment for" — he read and dropped each letter — "a saddle . . . that Winchester he carries . . . an abor—" He didn't finish.

He turned back to the mirror, looked at the faces of the women in the photographs, and saw Sam Florence tossing the bank book onto the bed. Colonel Smythe's head was bowed.

"Colonel."

Holden heard the scout's drawl.

"I think you'd better get word to the commander of the *Rurales* down in Mexico and the Mexican government."

Smythe entered the home, pulled the door shut as best as he could, and leaned against the rifle case next to the door. "There must be another way. We must — I would rather we get those weapons back."

"How the hell you gonna do that, Colonel? Those rifles are already across the border in Mexico. And I gotta think that an old injun butcher like Crooked Nose ain't robbin' stagecoaches in Bisbee and copper mines across the border for the fun of it. He's gettin' money. Money to pay . . . and he ain't payin' off Jed Foster's saloon debts."

"I cannot — I will not believe that a Medal of Honor winner like Jed Foster would sell four wagonloads of Springfield rifles to Apaches."

"No," Holden said. "You're probably right."

Florence gave him a questioning look. Smythe looked more hopeful.

"Four wagons. Crooked Nose would have to rob a lot of stagecoaches and mines to get enough money to pay for those."

"An auction," Florence said. "Sell them to the highest bidder."

"That can't be," Smythe said.

Which is when Grat Holden reached

inside his pants pocket and pulled out the torn slip of paper. He brought it over to the bed and showed it to Florence. Colonel Smythe walked over, too.

"I guess I somehow ripped this out of Jed's jacket when we were fighting outside the canyon near Dos Cabezas. Tore it, anyway. Haven't been able to make sense of it. Maybe you can help."

Smythe straightened and demanded indignantly, "Why did you not present this to me when you were first placed under house arrest?"

"What?" Holden barked. "A ripped piece of paper with a few words? Show that to you . . . as evidence?"

"Why'd you keep it?" Sam Florence asked.

"Because if I got court-martialed or if the Army dragged things on much longer, I was going to break out and go to Mexico myself."

"Muncie," Florence said. "That's means there's hell to pay for sure."

"What's Muncie? Who's Muncie."

Smythe whispered, "Son of a bitch."

Florence nodded. "Yep. Best description I ever heard for Will Muncie."

CHAPTER 14

The Bonnie Blue flag popped in the hard wind that scoured the land in Sonora. Colonel Will Muncie stepped out of the verandah and admired the blue flag with the single white star in the center. It was a new flag. The first had been taken by Yankees at Shiloh, a black day, a black mark, to be sure. The second had lasted, though stained with powder, blood, and riddled by grapeshot and bullets, till the shame of Appomattox that led other generals, including Muncie's superior, to surrender. That flag now had a place of honor, displayed in a glass case, in his library. The newest one came from France.

So did his uniform.

A gray frock coat, and, yes, he did feel the warmth of the Mexican sun in late June. He was wearing heavy wool, but no one would ever say William Henry Muncie IV sweated. The collars, cuffs, and piping were blue, for he would always be an infantry officer. Foot soldiers, the mainstay of any army. Those were the men who won battles and won wars and won glory for the cause. How many cavalrymen had Muncie ever seen dead? And artillery soldiers? Muncie scoffed at that thought.

Spotless brass buttons were arranged in pairs, eight per row. The blue sash was knotted perfectly above his left hip. The black belt fit perfectly over his sash, secured at his midsection by the two-piece oval belt plate, gold-plated, with an embossed wreath circling the *CS* in the center, and just below the letters the Latin words *Sic Semper Tyrannis.* Thus Ever To Tyrants.

He had borrowed that from Virginia, but the words rang true in Texas twenty years ago, just as they applied to Mexico today.

A saber hung sheathed from his left side. A black leather holster housed his LeMat revolver. His trousers were of a darker gray with twin blue stripes down the sides. The legs of the pants came over his boots made of black Italian leather, which glistened in the sun.

The French and the Italians would sell anything to anyone, even a new Confederate uniform and boots, fifteen years after it all ended . . . for nothing . . . and left Will

Muncie with . . . nothing.

Maybe not quite nothing.

Twenty-seven men still rode with him. When he had first crossed the Rio Grande into Mexico, having refused to take the oath of allegiance to the victorious United States of America, he had better than a hundred and ten men, plus at least sixteen families of the men who had ridden with him across Texas, Louisiana, Tennessee, Mississippi, Kentucky, Arkansas, and Missouri. He had buried more than a handful. A whole lot more had eventually given up and returned in defeat and disgrace back home to Collin County.

As if Collin County had ever been home.

Back in '61, his neighbors, his friends, had voted against secession. Almost two-to-one against leaving the Union. He had arrived in '49 with fifteen slaves and a dream of making his fortune in cotton. He couldn't sell cotton in Collin County. It was too far to get the crops to market. So eventually, he had turned to wheat and corn. Not the glamour one got from cotton, but those crops had made Will Muncie a rich man. At least, by Texas standards.

They burned his home, the Yankees did. Or rather, his Yankee neighbors did, while he was fighting for the rights of Texas and free Texans, while he was burying his boy, killed in battle by the Yanks at Corinth. So when word reached Muncie in southern Texas that those four hard years had been for naught, Muncie took the men who worshipped him and their families to Mexico. To fight for the French, Maximilian's boys.

And when he realized that Maximilian didn't stand a chance at winning, Muncie had joined the other side. Fought for Juarez, who'd paid a little better, and who'd won.

Other unreconstructed Rebels had left the defeated South and settled in Mexico. A few even went farther south, into South America, but most of those had gone home. Even Fighting Jo Shelby of Missouri was back praying to God for his country. For all Will Muncie knew, they were even voting Republican and letting the Negroes vote.

The three officers remaining, Knight, Fountain and Truett, walked to him, stopped, came to attention, and snapped their salutes.

Without returning the salutes, Muncie nodded at the new flag.

"What do you think?"

Mexico had aged him. Sonora wasn't as green as Collin County. The soil wasn't rich. It was a hard, hard, hard place to live. No, one didn't *live* there. People just tried to survive. And he had. Survived . . . endured. He would turn sixty years old soon. The sun had bronzed him. The fighting had left him haggard, gaunt, and he had developed a nagging cough that some feared was consumption, though Muncie had never spit up blood. His nose was crooked, and he still wore the black patch over the left eye the Yankees had taken from him at Yellow Bayou along the Atchafalaya in miserable Louisiana back in '64. Frijoles and enchiladas and Mexican beer had added a paunch to his midsection, but no one ever doubted him, and no one ever disobeyed one of his orders.

"Like old times, Cuhnel," Knight said.

Pleased, Muncie nodded. "I despised the flag our government chose for us. All of them. The battle jack. The so-called national flags. Red, white, and blue. Always red, white, and blue, just like the flag of our enemy. This flag" — he nodded, and his one blue eye gleamed — "blue and white. That's all the colors we need. Blue for the infantry. Blue for our blood. And white. White . . . for the color of our skin." He called out a name. "Sergeant Winters."

One of the last of the men who had joined him from Collin County stepped forward.

He held a rifle, still slippery with grease, in his gloved hands.

"Report."

CHAPTER 15

Nelson Winters had raised horses in Collin County, just six miles from Muncie's farm. He should have served in the cavalry, as well as he rode, but he swore by Will Muncie. And he was a damned fine shot.

He held the gun toward the officers. "Trap-door model. Not much different from Springfield's previous model, the '73. Here's your trap door. What the Yanks call a breechblock. It's on a hinge. Here's your hinge. Here's how you open it. Like this. Slide the cartridge in here. Shut the door. Cock the hammer and you're ready to fire. Shoots a forty-five-seventy. Same as the old model." He held the weapon out for inspection.

Winters went on. "Barrel thirty-two and one-half inches. They done a good job of bluin' the barrel. You got a front sight here with a hood over it, and here, this rear jump sight will go up to twelve hundred yards."

He butted the weapon on the ground, holding it straight next to his body, which went into rigid attention. "As you can see, total length is a little better than four feet." The gun came up perfectly to his shoulder. "You can put a sling on it. Good for carrying on a march. Stock's walnut. Metal is case-hardened." He let Truett hold the weapon.

"Heavy," said the man from Dallas.

"Yes, suh," Winters said. "Nine pounds, thirteen ounces. Shoots a forty-five-caliber cartridge with four hundred and five grains of power, weight seventy grains."

"How does it shoot?" Fountain asked.

"The Yankee tested it, suh, when I met him near the Texas border. Then I tested this one. At two hundred yards, the bullet penetrated a chunk of white pine eleven inches deep. When I moved that target back to a thousand yards, the penetration was eight and one-half inches."

"Not much of a difference," Fountain said.

"I reckon you's right, suh. Pretty accurate, too. Lot better than the old models we have, them from '61."

"But not a repeater," Truett said.

"No, suh. But a good man, and we've got good men, can get off eight to ten shots a minute. It's no muzzleloader, suh, like we had in the war."

"I dislike using a Yankee gun," the colonel said. He smiled then, evil mischief showing in his one eye. "Unless I'm using them on Yankees."

Uneasily, the men laughed with their commander.

"So is it better than the model the Yanks have been using?" Knight asked. "The '73 Springfield?"

"Haven't fired it enough to know for certain," the old horse wrangler said, "but it packs a wallop." He massaged his right shoulder. "Likely left a bruise after only ten shots. But right now, suh, all we have are the old muzzleloaders that we fit with back durin' the war. And what we've managed to steal or buy or borrow since then. These is new rifles. There's gotta be somethin' to be said for that."

"So," Knight asked again, "why did the Yanks replace the old model?"

Winters nodded and brought the rifle up for inspection. "The way the Yank explained it up north, suh, was this. It's not so much the rifle they was replacin', but this." He withdrew the bayonet. "They, bein' the gunsmiths and engineers at that damn Yankee armory in Massachusetts, figured they needed a better design for the cleanin' rod and the bayonet. So they come up with this here beauty."

He withdrew the bayonet and passed it to Captain Knight. "More of a triangle style, you see, than the old bayonets we all used fifteen, twenty years back. The thing that makes this boy dif'rent is the bayonet. The lockin' spring here keeps this hog sticker in place. Got serrated ears on both sides, you see. So if you lift this spring, you can slide this long knife up till it locks here. Plus you can remove the whole contraption and turn this sticker into a cleanin' rod, usin' the threads here at the end to attach the clean- in' devices. A rifle ain't good for nothin', you officers know, iffen it ain't a clean gun."

Will Muncie's good eye brightened again. "Now, that's what I wanted to hear, Winters. There's nothing more glorious in battle than a charge. A charge with bayonets. Smelling the blood, seeing the whites of the enemies' eyes, the fear on their faces. Hearing our hallowed Rebel war cry. Glory. Glory. Glory. How God must love war."

He walked forward and took the bayonet, feeling its edge and grinning, then handing the "hog sticker" back to Sergeant Winters.

"Thank you, Sergeant, for your keen and clear report. How many rifles did the Yank say he had?"

"Two hundred and fifty. The Army sent

'em out here from Springfield to get some testin' done. Plus bayonets for all the rifles, with a few extries and boxes upon boxes of ammunition."

"Can the Yank be trusted?"

"No Yank can be trusted," Winters replied. "You know that better than anyone."

"How much did he charge you for this rifle?"

"Thirty Yankee dollars, but he throwed in the ammunition, such as it was. Just enough to get this baby warmed up a mite. That was what he called a deal. He wants fifty per rifle, and twenty dollars for each thousand rounds."

Muncie stared at Fountain, the mathematician of the ex-Rebels. "Twelve thousand, five hundred dollars, sir. For the rifles. I don't know how much ammunition he has, but I would guess five hundred to a thousand dollars' worth. The Yankee government doesn't like shooting much power and shot. Otherwise, the soldiers would have Winchesters or Spencer rifles."

"We wouldn't need two hundred and fifty rifles," Truett said. "We'd only need say thirty . . . thirty-five to include a few extras as replacements."

"Nonsense, Lieutenant," Muncie said. "When we begin our march, the oppressed

Confederates of Texas will rise up and join us to push the Yankee horde north till they are out of our country. Or dead."

"Yes, suh," Sergeant Winters agreed.

"We don't have that much money, sir," Knight pointed out.

"We didn't have money in the war, either, especially during the last few years. But we learned how to take what we needed. And we need these rifles." Muncie spun back to face Winters. "And where did the Yank say this meeting — this trade, this auction or whatever he wants to call it — will take place?"

CHAPTER 16

Holden had heard enough about Will Muncie, some insane former Confederate with an ax to grind. He asked Sam Florence, "And what do you know about this *Dolores?*"

The old scout hesitated. "It could mean anything, Lieutenant. A woman's name. A place."

"A place," Holden said. A guess, but it seemed pretty logical knowing what he had learned so far.

"If I were guessing, it would be *El Cañon de Los Dolores,*" Florence said. "The Canyon of The Sorrows. Something like that. Apaches, Mexicans, and Yaqui Indians used to do some trading there. It's in Sonora. Can't say I've ever been there."

"Could you find it?" Colonel Smythe joined the conversation.

"Not sure I want to. Nobody — no *white* man — knows where it is. At least, no *hon-*

est white man. It's a place where Apaches used to sell Mexican captives, sometimes white captives, too. We know it's near Rancho Los Cielos, but that's about all there is. There's a bandit who has been holed up outside Rancho Los Cielos for a year or so. Maybe not quite that long. Amonte Negro — he's as mean as Crooked Nose and as crazy as Will Muncie. Foster might try to sell the guns to that crazy Mexican, too."

"I will go," Holden said.

Smythe made a beeline for the cabinet and the brandy. After fortifying himself with another snifter, he shook his head. "You seem to forget, Lieutenant, that Jed Foster is now in Mexico, beyond the reach of the United States Army."

"Well," Sam Florence said, "you can always alert the authorities south of the border."

Smythe refilled his snifter. He gulped this one down. "That I do not wish to do, at this time. No need in worrying the residents of Sonora or all of Mexico."

Holden clenched his fists but said nothing. No need in worrying the residents. The residents who would be butchered by the Apaches if they got their hands on that many new weapons. Or the *Rurales* who might be killed by those Mexican bandits, properly armed, before the bandits rode to Mexico City to kill and plunder. And if Will Muncie got those Springfields? As crazy as Smythe and Florence had described him, Muncie wouldn't rest until the entire South-west ran red with the blood of the in-nocents.

"We don't have much time," Florence said. "The other word on that paper the young lieutenant grabbed says *July.*"

"Which is a few days from now, Sam," Smythe said, "and July has thirty days in it."

Actually, thirty-one, but Grat Holden was not going to contradict the colonel on that picayune detail. But he did say, "It won't be at the end of the month."

"And I suppose you know the exact date of this . . . auction?" Smythe asked.

Grat Holden remembered riding beside Jed Foster, before the ambush. He heard their voices clearly.

"There's nothing like celebrating Independence Day on the Fourth of July in Mexico."

"I don't believe Mexico celebrates our independence, Captain."

"Then I'll celebrate her. By myself if I have to."

"Independence Day," Holden said to Florence and Smythe. "The Fourth."

"Why then?" Florence asked.

"Foster mentioned that day on the trail."

"That means nothing," Smythe said.

"No," Sam Florence said. "The shavetail here might have a point. It would be a good joke. That's the way Jed Foster would see it."

They all realized the truth of that statement.

"I'll still volunteer to go, Colonel," Holden tried again.

"Mr. Holden," Smythe bellowed, "I cannot send a lieutenant, especially one with only five years of experience on the frontier, across the international border. It would lead to scandal, an incident that would embarrass our Army, our generals, the Secretary of War, and our president. That will not happen."

"Then," Sam Florence said, "you'd better let your commander know what has happened here, and you had better let Mexico know what's about to happen down there."

Smythe stared at the brandy, but refrained from getting too intoxicated.

"What," Holden tried again, "if I went into Mexico out of uniform?"

The colonel tilted his head, intrigued.

"Are you serious?" he asked after a long

thought.

"De— Yes, sir. Very serious." He had almost said *dead* serious.

"One man?" Smythe shook his head. "How many renegades still ride with Will Muncie?"

Florence shrugged. "Twenty. Thirty. No telling."

"And with Crooked Nose?"

"No more than with Muncie. Maybe a good deal less. Apaches are notional, temperamental. Muncie and his boys? They're just crazy."

"And what about that bandit you mentioned?" Smythe snapped his fingers trying to think of the name.

"Negro. Amonte Negro." Florence shook his head. "I don't know. He calls himself a revolutionary. A fighter for the peons, the peasants, the people. He could have five. He could have five hundred. It would just depend on the mood of the people down in Sonora."

"I'd still like to go, sir," Holden said.

And if the colonel declined the offer, Holden would resign his commission and go down himself. He had a score to settle with Jed Foster.

"Would you go with him, Sam?" Smythe asked the old scout.

Sam Florence did not answer. Instead, he said, "The boy's got a point, though, Colonel. So do you. You can't send a whole troop of cavalry across the border. Mexico might declare war. Probably not, but that's a crazy country. And that many people would draw the attention of Negro, the Apaches, Muncie and, especially, Jed Foster. He has to think the Army and the US government won't let that many brand-spanking new rifles get into the wrong hands without a fight."

"Two men," Smythe suggested.

Holden tried not to roll his eyes. *Two men.* What chance would two men have over an army?

"Two men wouldn't get much attention, if they knew what they were doing," Holden said.

Seeing that the colonel was nodding his head, Holden decided to rethink his original position. "I'm going, sir," he told Smythe. "I'd like to pick the man who goes with me." Holden was looking at Sam Florence, who did not meet the lieutenant's eyes.

"No," Smythe said. "No. But you will have a man with you." His head bobbed again. "Understand, if you are caught or captured or killed, we will disavow any knowledge of your activities south of the border."

"That's fine with me, sir."

"Then I'll send Private Masterson with you." Smythe liked the idea. "He'll go. Or he'll go to Leavenworth for ten years."

Masterson. Holden, his mouth open, shook his head.

Ben "Hard Rock" Masterson, once a sergeant, now a private about to do hard time in the federal pen in Kansas. Ben Masterson, who hated Grat Holden's guts. Holden would be lucky to get to Mexico alive with "Hard Rock" riding with him.

CHAPTER 17

For yet another time — Jed Foster had lost count of how often he had looked at the paper — he studied the damaged paper. That reminded him of something else Custer had told him. *Keep the written orders to a minimum. Written orders can get an officer in trouble. Even lose a war. Remember what happened at Antietam to Robert E. Lee's Army of Northern Virginia.*

Foster looked at the ripped left-hand corner.

What had he written there?

One thing was obvious — *July.* He saw the *4th* and beyond that *noon.* And beyond that and underlined *payday.* He had been doodling nonsense.

July wouldn't tell that greenhorn Grat Holden anything. Yet the other words might give the boy some hope. *A long shot,* Foster thought, *but wars can be lost or won on long-shot gambles.* He needed to prepare. He had to guess that he had written Confederate officer Will Muncie's name on the paper. Amonte Negro's and the Apache chieftain Crooked Nose's names were written in all capital letters just beyond the tear. After that was mostly ciphering, guessing at how much money the Reb, the Apaches, and the Mexican bandits might be able to bring. Foster had also written the name of the nearest *Rurale* leader and the alcalde of the largest and closest village. He had considered letting them bid on the weapons, too, but had dismissed those. The Apaches and Negro's mercenaries wouldn't come if they understood the *Rurales* or the local magistrate might be coming. Apaches didn't trust Mexicans. Mexicans didn't trust Apaches. Inviting Crooked Nose and Amonte Negro was risky enough. *Rurales?* No. Porfirio Díaz was on his way out as president of Mexico, and Foster had never trusted any Mexican government official.

Another thing Custer had told him. *Don't get too big for your britches. The man who goes after the golden goose instead of just one golden egg usually gets his goose cooked.*

Most likely, Foster was just being overly cautious. He remembered the fight with Grat Holden near Dos Cabezas. That reck-

106

less fool. Should've played possum. Yet he had too much spunk for his own good. Foster remembered feeling Holden's hand reaching inside his jacket. He recalled bringing his upper arm and forearm down against the hand. He didn't recall seeing anything come spilling out of the pocket, landing on the dirt or cactus, but he had been a little preoccupied with the treason he was committing. When he closed his eyes and thought back, he could see Holden's clenched fist. The ripped corner of one stupid little page could have been in that fist. On the other hand, it could have blown down the canyon or toward the "Two Heads" or gotten stuck on a cactus needle two miles from the middle of nowhere.

He told himself to forget it.

Yet he still walked to *La Cantina Que No Tiene Nombre,* The Cantina That Has No Name. The raven-haired beauty sat at a table studying tarot cards.

After a nod at the bartender and holding up two fingers, Jed Foster dragged up a chair and sat opposite the woman known as Soledad Tadeo.

"Reading your future?"

Without looking up, the young woman said, "I play a game, much as you *Yanquis* play your poker or your faro. I do not

107

practice divination." She turned over a card and shook her head. "But you come in and I turn over The Fool."

The bartender came over and put a glass of tequila in front of Foster and a glass of goat's milk in front of the woman.

"I consider myself the king," Foster said. "And you are the queen. Perhaps the king and queen should get together."

"I would rather sleep with a pig."

He laughed, although inwardly he wanted to drive the wench's head into the rough floor. "You misunderstand my intention, *Señorita* Tadeo."

Actually she had not misinterpreted anything. For a girl with tarot cards who didn't practice divination, she had read his mind perfectly.

"I come with a business proposition." Jed Foster waited.

The woman finished her game, or at least a hand, and looked up. Her eyes were pitch black, her face unreadable. She stared, waiting, and did not touch the glass of goat's milk while he drained the tequila.

"I do not work for gringos. I do not work for deserters."

He gave her his best smile, a look that had left many married women and once even a preacher's daughter falling into his arms and allowing him to carry them away before he left them in tears, ruin, and shame.

"But you work for Amonte Negro," he said when he realized his look had no effect.

She nodded at the bartender. "I work for *mi amigo.* Mostly, I work for myself."

"Then I will pay you for your services," Foster said, "and all I ask for you to do is to lead me to Amonte Negro."

"Again?"

He smiled. She had arranged the meeting when he had made his proposition.

His head nodded. "Again. But" — he rose — *"muy pronto."*

"Do you think Amonte desires to see you again after what you did to his men the other night?"

"Those men either betrayed *Señor* Negro or *Señor* Negro tried to betray me. But I am willing to let bygones be bygones if the latter was the case. And I will pay your pal Negro for his time and trouble. And" — he winked — "I will pay you much more than I pay him."

"Get your horse," she said. "I will saddle mine. We shall ride out of Rancho Los Cielos in fifteen minutes."

109

CHAPTER 18

The mule couldn't pull a wagon, but Foster figured it might have enough strength to carry a few things, so he had a couple of the boys fit a packsaddle on it, and loaded the weary old Army animal with a couple boxes. Then he swung into the saddle of his bay and gave the men a wide grin.

"If I'm not back in a day or two, I'll see y'all in hell." He touched the spurs to the gelding and pulled the mule behind him.

On a zebra dun, Soledad Tadeo waited for him across the street.

"What do you think, Madame Tarot?" Foster asked. "Will your amigo like his gift?"

Without looking him in the eye, she eased her horse ahead of his and led the way out of town. "If they are hungry, they will appreciate the mule."

For the life of him, Jed Foster couldn't understand why the Mexicans and the

110

Apaches fought over this patch to hell. Scorpions and rattlesnakes, Gila monsters and cactus. The wind blew hot. The sun baked you. On the rare times you found water, it proved hard to drink. And if you did drink it, the water might kill you quicker than a rattlesnake.

Arizona wasn't any better, but the Army and the white settlers kept fighting the Apaches over the raw desert, too.

Soledad Tadeo slid back in the saddle as her dun picked a careful path down a sandy arroyo. She rode better than a bunch of recruits the Army kept sending to Bowie. And he really liked riding behind her when she kicked her gelding into a trot. Too bad she didn't do that very often. Then again, it was a really hot day, and the mule, considering its load, did not want to trot at all.

The dry wash twisted like a rattlesnake's trail, but it was deep enough and the scrub brush that grew alongside it provided some shelter from the wind. He realized that they were heading into the hills, and before long the sun had disappeared behind the high rocks.

Despite the coolness, he still had to loosen his bandanna to wipe sweat.

As they kept riding, Foster heard the woman's soft curse and a few words she said in Spanish. Understanding the Spanish word for *fools,* Jed Foster smiled. He had to agree. He had heard the men up the arroyo long before the raven-haired beauty in front of him had.

They rounded another twist in the dry wash and there stood Amonte Negro.

Soledad Tadeo turned her gelding to a pool at the western side of the bend and let her horse drink. Jed Foster merely reined in his mount, kicked one leg free of the stirrup, and rested it over the stock of his Winchester.

He grinned and said, "I do remember asking the señorita to tell you to come alone."

Six men flanked Foster. Two were a few paces in front of the man who considered himself a revolutionary. Two more were along the edges of the arroyo, up on the banks, hidden in the junipers. The other two stood behind Foster, who had pretended he had not spotted the imbeciles when they had ridden past them.

Amonte Negro hooked his thumbs in the bandoliers that crisscrossed his chest. He wore a sugarloaf sombrero, fringed leather pants, and a blue jacket that had gone out of style and certainly out of favor about the time Juarez was killing Emperor Maximilian. Negro's sandals were mismatched. He wore no socks.

His teeth were crooked, but at least he had some, and his face bore scars and patches of dark beard. Neither slim nor fat, neither short nor tall, he did not cut a dashing or dull figure. He was just one of the thousand poor men trying to figure out how to get rich or at least a good meal before they died. Mexico was filled with such men. Amonte Negro was just the closest to Rancho Los Cielos.

Foster shook his head. He felt sorry that a beautiful young maiden like Soledad Tadeo had only an illiterate wastrel like Negro to pin upon her hopes for this country.

She translated Foster's comments while the horse slopped up the water.

The man laughed and sang out in Spanish.

"He says you did not come alone either. You brought a starving coyote that you dressed like a mule." The horse raised its head as the girl shrugged. "It is his idea of a joke. You may laugh. Or not."

She didn't laugh. Maybe she was growing tired of Negro.

Foster did not laugh, either.

"Tell Negro I thought he would like a few weapons to test before our gathering to see who shall be lucky enough or rich enough to win the golden prize."

She put little emotion in the words, but Amonte Negro certainly did in his reply. He puffed his chest in and out, paced back and forth, and punctuated exclamations with jabs of his fingers or pumps of the right fist. He kicked sand and pounded the bandoliers where they crossed his heart, finally finished.

"He says he has seen nothing in his life but hardships. He was born during the reign of Maximilian and has gone through men like Juarez and others whose names he cannot remember." She rolled her eyes and told Foster, "de Tejada and Iglesias."

"And now that Porfirio Díaz is finished as president, all Mexico gets is a puppet, for Flores will not give Mexico what it needs and when Díaz is back after the puppet —" She stopped. "To get to the point, he says you should merely give him the weapons. You would be blessed."

"Blessed," Foster said, "isn't rich. Tell him that I am blessed. Blessed with luck."

CHAPTER 19

Negro did not give the girl a chance to relay Foster's response. He was at it again.

When it ended, the girl was rolling a cigarette for herself. Unlit, she stuck it in her mouth and said, "He does not like that there will be Apaches in the canyon where the trade will occur."

Foster laughed. "Tell him that when he kills the Apaches with the Springfields he buys, he can take their scalps and turn them in at the alcalde's for the bounty. That'll help him earn back what he pays for the rifles."

She turned to Spanish, and Foster watched the man's dark face. The Mexican grinned, but there was little mirth in the bandit's face. He spoke a short sentence this time.

"He does not trust you," the girl translated.

Foster hooked his left thumb toward the

two cutthroats standing behind him.

"And I am to trust him?"

She translated again.

He spoke, and she said, "He will look at your gifts."

"They are not gifts," Foster explained. "They are weapons which he may use to test. I expect to be paid for these, too."

He could tell that Negro nor the men whose faces Foster could see, did not like that answer.

Foster bowed and said, *"Con el permiso del galante general Negro, mostraré a todos las armas que he traído para que él y sus hombres prueben."* There was no trace of English in his accent. He spoke as if he were born in Mexico.

Even the woman looked impressed and shocked.

"You speak Spanish."

"And French. Despite all the demerits I chalked up at West Point, before they kicked me out, I did learn a few things."

He swung out of the saddle with ease and walked to the mule to show the bandits who called themselves revolutionaries the Springfields.

"Six rifles," he said after he had laid the new rifles on a blanket in the sand. "Sorry, one of you will not have one. I didn't know you were bringing six men. I thought you and I and the girl maybe would shoot a few targets and I'd send you on your way. Now one of your amigos will be disappointed. He might even kill someone for the Springfield he doesn't get. Don't translate that for your hero."

"I will not," she said.

He asked if anyone knew how to load the weapon. None did. He showed them. He showed them how to aim, how to adjust the rear sight. He told them how far the Springfield could shoot with some accuracy. He showed them how to affix the bayonet and how to use the rod to clean the barrel after firing. He doubted if the bayonets would be used for anything except plucking bread or spearing cantaloupes.

He fired only one round himself, clipping a branch off a juniper at two hundred and fifty yards.

The men were impressed, but he did not reload the Springfield. Instead he presented the smoking beauty of a firearm to his excellency, the cutthroat killer from Sonora.

"Would he like to try this rifle?"

"Ask him yourself," the woman told him in English. "You did not need me."

"Oh, yes, I most certainly did. He would not have met me here alone. But were I to bring a woman, well, no gallant gringo would risk putting a woman in harm's way. He would, of course. He still wants to kill me and get the guns."

She asked Negro, who shook his head and answered.

She did not translate, but he didn't need it. The old fool did not want to waste any bullets. He would take the gift.

Foster raised and wagged a finger as he smiled. "But remember" — he spoke Spanish — "I said that these weapons — the rifles, the bayonets, and the boxes of shells — are not gifts. There is a price for these, too, just as there is a price for the rest that we will sell in a few days. Remember?"

Negro kicked dirt and spit between Foster's boots.

"And what is the sum?"

Foster grinned. "A favor."

She translated. Negro did not understand.

"No money. The weapons and ammunition are yours. But I want you to send some men to the border. The American Army will not let these weapons disappear into your country without trying to get them back. And they will not trust your government to recapture the guns and send them back. The *Rurales* would keep them for themselves. You know that. So I think some troopers, not wearing the uniforms of the American Army, will be headed this way. They will be able to follow our trail at least to Rancho Los Cielos. Before they get there is a nice little canyon that would be the perfect place for an ambush."

CHAPTER 20

Grat Holden considered himself pretty strong, but even he had to grunt and summon up every muscle in his arms, legs, and back to heave the cell door up and over. It landed with a deafening clang on the dirt, and he peered into the black hole.

"All right, Masterson, come on out."

"Who's that?" a creaking, dry voice rose from the hole in the Arizona earth.

"Holden," he answered.

"Holden." That was all for half a minute. "Holden? Oh, yeah. The . . . lieutenant."

"Out, Sarge. Out Trooper Masterson." Standing above the pit, Holden tried to figure out how deep the sweatbox, that place of solitary confinement, went.

A ragged, hoarse cough rose from the shadows, and then Holden made out movement. White . . . no gray clothes that once had been white . . . rose into the light. Masterson looked completely different from how he had looked at Sergeant Byron Lusk's funeral only a day or two earlier. He was thin, pale, gaunt, a ghost in filthy clothes. With him came the stink of the sweatbox.

To Holden's surprise, he realized that the pit — the prison cell — was no more than seven feet deep and maybe seven feet wide. A man could not stand, could barely sit.

In five years, Grat Holden had never known such a cell even existed at Fort Bowie. Ben "Hard Rock" Masterson was no soldier and was bound for Fort Leavenworth's penitentiary, but no man, no prisoner, *no one* deserved to be confined in a place like this, even for an hour.

The former noncommissioned officer bowed his head and shuffled his feet. Solitary, Holden had heard, had broken everybody who had spent time in the sweatbox. Just looking at the pathetic figure almost broke Grat Holden.

"Come on, Masterson," Holden managed to say, with sympathy that he felt.

The soldier shuffled his feet, kept his head bowed, his body hunched and moved to the edge. Without raising his head, he said in a pleading, almost inaudible whisper, "Beggin' the gen'ral's pardon, sir, but could you lend me a hand? I ain't got no strength to climb all the way up."

All the way up. Holden grimaced. Any soldier on the post could have leaped out with hardly any effort at all. Any soldier . . . but this one.

Holden leaned forward and extended his hand. "Here you go, Masterson. Put your hand here."

"Where?" Masterson shielded his eyes, though the sun had already dipped low on the horizon. The gloaming must have felt like staring directly into the sun at high noon.

Holden moved his hand until it brushed against the one-time sergeant's.

"Feel it?"

"Oh, yes, sir. Yes sir." He closed his hand around Holden's.

"Sarge . . . Masterson," Holden said softly. "You'll need to squeeze a bit tighter."

"This good enough, Gen'ral?" Masterson asked.

What Holden wanted to do was to leave Ben Masterson there, storm into Colonel Smythe's office, kick the martinet out of the adobe building, across the parade ground, and all the way to the pit, and then kick him into it. He could see Smythe having a good laugh, joking with the sergeant major and maybe a few officers, perhaps even the post chaplain, that he would like to see Mr. Holden's face when he realized what kind of soldier he had been saddled with to accomplish an impossible mission. But Holden also wanted to help this poor, wretched creature out of the sweatbox.

He would see to Carlton Smythe later.

"A little bit tighter, Ben," Holden said.

Then his right hand felt as if it had been caught between a Percheron's hoof and a blacksmith's iron. A second later, he felt himself flying into the hole, face-first. Masterson released his grip on Holden's now throbbing hand and laughed as the lieutenant fell into the black pit. He landed in the wetness and excrement that Ben "Hard Rock" Masterson has been living in, with nothing to eat but hardtack, and nothing to drink but tepid water.

Holden landed and groaned. He felt revulsion. He felt anger. He felt betrayal. He felt his head jerked up by the hair and slammed into the pungent ground again.

"Like it, Holden?" Masterson shouted, but did not wait for an answer.

CHAPTER 21

The soldier's boot came between Holden's legs, but the court-martialed sergeant's legs weren't as strong as his hand and arms — not after being cooped up in the box for that long. The blow hurt, but did not cripple Grat Holden.

Understanding that his legs were of little use, Masterson bent down to ram Holden's face in the filth and rocky floor again. He glanced up and behind him, surprised to see that Holden had arrived at the guardhouse with no enlisted men. Even the sentry was gone. That caused Masterson to hesitate.

Trap! he thought, and whirled.

It was a mistake. Holden was here alone. This wasn't some way to have a sentry open fire and shoot Masterson down, kill him, save the Army the trouble of feeding and housing him in Leavenworth for the next ten years.

He moved back toward Holden just in time to see that the lieutenant had raised his right foot, brought it back, and then Ben Masterson felt the crushing blow of the boot against his thigh.

The blow drove him back against the top of the hole. He collapsed, his leg throbbing, and his shoulder caught against the side of the hole as he fell back toward the bottom. His arm felt like it had almost been ripped out of the socket.

He lunged to his left, letting Holden's second kick go wide, and watched the lieutenant fall.

Masterson rose, or tried to, while instantly moving toward Holden, but the leg Holden had kicked gave way. He was on his knees just as Holden came up out of the black void and threw a haymaker that sent Masterson back into the darkness.

Holden bent down, intending to find Masterson's throat and strangle the fraud and fiend.

Instead, he found Masterson's left fist and went sliding back into the muck and mess, his back and head slamming against the rocks that lined the end of the cell.

A savage roar helped Holden regain his senses. He saw the catamount-like blur of a man in rags as he leaped for the kill. Holden lifted his legs, bent his knees, and raised his hands. He caught Masterson as he soared. Holden heaved and cursed and watched the determined man fly out into the yard.

Holden pulled himself to his feet, breathing and gagging and determined to join Masterson in clean air, out of the pit no one deserved to be in — not even Jed Foster.

Out of the pit, Holden tripped on the rocks and pebbles, fell to his knees, and saw Masterson rolling over, shaking his head, and trying to push himself up. Holden also saw several blue-coated men rushing across the parade ground. Someone blew a whistle. Someone tapped the drums. Others came running from the stables, from officer's row, from the enlisted men's barracks. Even a few galloped over on horses.

Holden rose. He waved his hands over his head.

"Stay back!" he shouted. "Stay back. This is personal."

The last word came out as a gasp as Masterson drilled a punch in Holden's kidneys.

He landed on his knees, gasping, groaning, stinking, and about to vomit.

Masterson grabbed a handful of hair and tried to twist Holden's neck. Tried to pull off his head. Tried to break the lieutenant's neck. But his hands kept slipping in all the wretchedness that coated Holden's hair.

So Masterson drilled a knee into Holden's spine. Maybe he could break the dog's back.

Holden fell face-first like a tree cut by a logger, face-first, while Masterson lost his balance and fell hard on his buttocks. That almost broke the old sergeant's backbone and tailbone.

He grunted and fell to his right, telling himself to get up, feeling his weakened legs move like they were pedaling one of those newfangled velocipedes. He rolled onto his back, saw Holden pushing himself over and up.

He also saw the men gathering in a circle. Soldiers — officers and enlisted men — and civilian muleskinners and teamsters. Maybe even two or three post laundresses. Nobody knew what to do. No one wanted to take charge.

Then the truth hit Ben Masterson.

Nobody wanted to touch the filthy, reeking, brutalized men.

He made himself stand. He took one step backward, two, three, and thought he might keep backing up till he was against an Arizona walnut tree. Somehow, he stopped. He stepped forward, felt his right knee buckle, and tasted the sand and blood and his own foulness.

Somehow, Masterson pushed himself up.

A woman gasped.

Two saddlers handed money to a corporal of infantry.

He was moving right toward that green pup of a lieutenant. In Masterson's blurred vision, he thought he saw the strangest thing. He thought he saw Grat Holden off the ground and heading right in his direction, bringing a fist back and driving it forward.

The fist caught Masterson right above his nose and between his eyes.

He went down and felt Holden coming with him. Masterson managed to lift his legs and kick out, sending the lieutenant somersaulting into the darkening skies with a crash and a prayer.

The prayer came from another laundress.

Voices came to him.

"That's it."

"The lieutenant's done for."

"A bottle of sutler's beer says Holden gets back up."

"You're on."

"Goodness, the stench is going to cause me to —"

"Hey, did you see that? Major Nelson is throwing up."

"Shouldn't we stop this? Colonel Smythe

will blow his top."

"I ain't putting my bare hands on those two until they've had a month of Sundays in the bathhouse."

"Hey, you owe me, boy, Holden's back on his feet."

"Yeah. Well he won't be for long. That old reprobate Masterson's standing up, too."

Indeed, Masterson realized he was standing, moving toward the weaving, staggering, bleeding, stinking Grat Holden.

"Stop this, men!" the chaplain called. Or maybe it was the archangel. "Stop this brutality!"

Masterson tasted griminess in his mouth, but he had no saliva to spit it out. He certainly didn't want to swallow any dirt. His breathing felt ragged. He was dragging his left leg, but Holden's left arm hung useless at its side, and with a few more blows, Masterson thought he could close up the lieutenant's left eye for good.

One of the laundresses began praying, and quickly turned the prayer into a psalm or song. The chaplain turned away from what he might witness, knelt, and began praying earnestly and silently. The soldiers and civilians and even the post sutler began laying down more bets.

"Five-to-one the sarge is finished."

"If they're both standin' when this is all done, I'll give you even money . . . I'm finished, pal."

"C'mon, Holden, show 'em how we do it in . . . where the hell is the lieutenant from?"

"You can pay me as much as the president of our United States makes in his entire term of office, but there ain't no way I'm a-doin' either one of their's laundry!"

To everyone who had gathered around the sweatbox, the stench got worse.

Former Sergeant, now prisoner, Ben "Hard Rock" Masterson swung wide, hoping to deliver a blow with all his might, something that would keep this bantam rooster down for the count. He saw Holden swinging, too, the one arm that still worked.

Masterson felt his punch land, and he was sure Second Lieutenant Grattan Roosevelt Holden III, middle of the Class of 1875, United States Military Academy, wouldn't know what hit him.

Or course, Ben Masterson didn't know what hit him, either.

They both lay on the ground in a steaming, stinking heap.

CHAPTER 22

Grat Holden poured more whiskey from the bottle into his mouth. There was no need to waste time and effort by putting the rye into a glass first. He swished the burning liquid around in his mouth, leaned his head over the tub, and spit the whiskey — and whatever else remained in his mouth — into the ground soaked by two bottles of rye or whatever the post sutler sold as rye. He brought the bottle up again.

In the bathtub next to him, Ben "Hard Rock" Masterson did the same. Only Masterson's bottle was labeled IRISH WHISKY, though it tasted pretty much the same as Grat Holden's bottle of rye.

It tasted like filth.

When the third bottle Holden had purchased was empty, he tossed it onto the ground and sank again beneath the suds in the water that had been hot when he had first stepped into the tub. It was on the cold side, especially since the sun had set and the temperature had turned cooler, common for this desert country.

His head came up, he sucked in air deeply, exhaled with an exclamation, and began rubbing his fingernails with much vigor against his scalp.

Three bottles were gone. Holden was on his fifth tub.

Sam Florence sighed and rose from the bench, where he had been whittling. He dropped the stick, folded his pocket-knife, and walked back into the bathhouse. A few moments later, he came out with two bottles. The rye he handed to Lieutenant Grat Holden. The Irish he tossed to the next tub, where Masterson let it splash into the water.

Masterson was on his fifth bottle, but only his second tub. The post had only ten tubs for enlisted men. The orderlies were beginning to worry about who would have to clean out the tubs when the convicted sergeant and the second lieutenant, who also had recently been placed under house arrest, were finished with their . . . baths.

Florence waded through the wet ground and found his spot on the bench. He thought about opening up the knife again, trimming another twig into a toothpick, but instead he returned to the building and walked out with a bottle of beer. This he opened. Sitting, he leaned back against the adobe wall and took a healthy swallow.

In the dirty water, Ben Masterson watched and took a chance. He uncorked the bottle of rye in the filthy water — all the suds had vanished or retreated or disintegrated — and brought the Irish whisky to his lips. Instead of rinsing and spitting, he swallowed.

The whisky burned a path into his stomach, but Masterson's fears proved unfounded. He did not die immediately of instant cholera.

Likewise, Lieutenant Grat Holden must have felt relatively clean, because he stood, reached onto the bench next to the tub, grabbed the bucket, which he lifted and dumped over his head. He exclaimed from the frigidity of the watcr, tossed the bucket, which made a damp splash on the ground, and found a towel. After drying himself off at least a little, he took his nakedness out of the tub, grabbed a pair of underdrawers on yet another bench, pulled those on, and sat in a camp chair next to Sam Florence. Holden had not forgotten the bottle of rye.

"Feel better?" Florence asked as he stared at his beer bottle.

"At least I smell better," Holden replied.

"Not sure. This place stinks like a pigpen. Not sure if it's just all the tubs filled with your messiness. Or yourself."

"Yer a couple nitwits," Ben Masterson said as he pulled again from the bottle of Irish. "Try spendin' ten days in the sweatbox."

If I commanded this post —

Grat Holden choked down that silly notion. He was a shavetail lieutenant, last in seniority at the fort, maybe last in this man's entire army. And he wasn't about to apologize to a man like Ben Masterson.

"All right," Masterson said as he climbed out of the tub and sat on the edge. He kept his legs and feet in the dirty water until he studied the water and what was floating on the surface, then hurriedly climbed out, splashed his way to the side of the adobe building, and dried himself off slightly before pulling on a muslin shirt and stepping into a pair of cotton underwear.

He pulled hard on the bottle and sat on a boulder that served as a chair or a clothesline, or a headstone or whatever.

"All right. I'll bite. What's the offer? What keeps me out of Leavenworth, or at least out of the sweatbox?"

CHAPTER 23

Grat Holden disappeared inside the laundry and came out wearing a pair of clean, pressed officer's trousers while dabbing a fresh silk handkerchief against his swollen lips. Eventually, he dipped the tip of the square into the rye and pressed that against his cut, swollen lips. Grimacing, he alternated between bathing his lips, cuts, and bruises with the whiskey-soaked piece of silk and just drinking straight from the bottle.

Masterson drank from the bottle of Irish as if he were guzzling tea.

That's what made Holden pitch the bottle of rye into the filthy water on the ground alongside the tub. He remembered all the times he had seen Captain Foster drinking whiskey or wine or champagne or even beer. One drink became two, which soon turned into twenty. Jed Foster never turned into what folks on the frontier called a mean drunk, but he certainly often kept himself a good distance from sobriety. Holden realized if he were drunk, or even just slightly in his cups, he would not stand a chance against the traitor.

"We're going after Foster and those Springfields he stole," Holden answered Masterson's question.

"I don't believe the capt'n stole nothin'." The whisky was taking effect, and Masterson's wounds were starting to heal. He was becoming his arrogant, obnoxious, Army-hating self.

It was Sam Florence who came to Holden's defense.

"It's true, Hard Rock, for I saw it myself." Florence took a long pull of beer, swallowed, and tossed the empty all the way into the tub that was the farthest away.

"Then good for the capt'n. 'Bout time he learnt that this man's army ain't good for nothin'. He can make his own fortune in" — Masterson snorted — "private enterprise. Yes, sir. Good for the capt'n."

"Good for the captain, maybe," Holden said. "But not so good for the settlers in Arizona. Or New Mexico. Or the citizens of Sonora."

"No skin off my nose, bucko," Masterson said. "I'll be in Leavenworth by the time this country's runnin' red with blood. Ten years of three square meals and a clean bunk." Mockingly, he drew in a deep breath as if he were admiring the aromas from Delmonico's. Exhaling, he said, "Fresh Kansas air and not this rank-smellin' sheee-iiii —"

"You ever spent time in Leavenworth, Masterson?" Holden cut him off.

The prisoner laughed. "I spent time in Colonel Smythe's solitary chambers. You think any horror tale you can give me about Leavenworth is worse than that? It's Kansas, for Pete's sake."

"Two days in the sweatbox here," Holden said. "Ten years in Leavenworth . . . or" — he paused for effect — "an honorable discharge. Free to go your own way. With no provost marshal, no law, nobody trying to put you back in . . . the sweatbox."

"Makes nary a difference to me. I just got a bath. You can go ahead and put me in the hellhole and I'll be good to stay there for another ten days, twenty, thirty. They don't call me Hard Rock for nothin'."

"Where did you earn that handle?" Sam Florence asked, just to say something.

"Texas."

Florence nodded. "I see."

So did Grat Holden.

"Lots of Texans have settled around Douglas," Holden said, remembering something he had read in one of the Tucson newspapers. "Not to mention the town of Nogales, the one on our side of the border. Even find quite a few Texans over Tucson way."

The wind changed direction. It began blowing the stench from the water quickly becoming stagnant in the tubs, toward the three men leaning against the adobe wall to the bathhouse.

Grat Holden began wishing that he had not pitched his bottle of rye into the nasty water that had soaked into the Arizona sod.

Suddenly, Ben Masterson yawned. "How do you buckos want to play this? Me and the shavetail fit ourselves to a draw. All this Texas honor and family honor and ever'thing else don't bother me one way in the least. So if you want me for somethin', you best start speakin' my language."

"What we want," Holden said, "and the only thing Colonel Smythe wants is for you to accompany us across the border . . . out of uniform . . . to fetch back those stolen rifles. And bring back the man who stole them, Captain Jed Foster."

"Plain enough," Masterson said. "Here's my answer. No. You hear that?"

Holden shot a quick glance at Sam Florence, then, without waiting for any signal from the old scout, decided to call Ben Masterson's bet.

"Very good, Sarge . . . Trooper Masterson. I'll escort you back to your . . . cell."

The color seemed to leave Ben Masterson's face.

"Not so fast, Lieutenant Holden." Suddenly, he drew in a deep breath of the foul air, held it, and somehow managed to exhale without gagging or vomiting. "Let's enjoy some of this fresh Arizona Territory air. Always smells so refreshing on a night like this."

Silence.

Then Masterson asked, "What's in it for me?"

"The colonel, as I've previously stated, will grant you an honorable discharge."

"And my sentence?"

"Set aside. Vacated. You'll be free to go wherever you want, with whoever you want, whenever you want."

Masterson considered this. "It won't get me far . . . on the pay . . . of a sergeant . . . busted to trooper . . . and with the money I owe at the post sutler's . . . and the hog ranch . . . and the saloons at the border line . . . not to mention over in Dos Cabezas."

Tired of playing games when time was essential, Holden sang out, "How much do you want, Masterson?"

Masterson froze. He was no good at playing that kind of game. Fifteen dollars would be a fortune to him, but not for a rich man's son like the lieutenant. He said at last, "You can't pay me enough, Lieutenant. Besides, what would prevent you from just murderin' me once I found your boy and you cleared your honor?"

"What would prevent you from murdering me in my sleep fifteen miles outside this post?"

Masterson grinned.

"Make me a proposition, Lieutenant," he said after a while.

That's when Grat Holden realized exactly what he had over Sergeant-now-Trooper, Ben Masterson.

"Here's what I can offer you, Ben. I can give you a chance at getting the man who shot Sergeant Byron Lusk dead out of his saddle."

CHAPTER 24

"Just because you are both out of uniform," Colonel Carlton Smythe reminded, "does not mean you do not salute your commanding officer."

Grat Holden and Ben Masterson gave lazy salutes. The colonel, his right hand preoccupied with the decanter of brandy, did not return the salute. Once he set the glass on the cabinet, he raised his snifter and looked at the two men in disgust.

Their faces and hands were bruised and swollen. They dressed like ruffians. Smythe did not like Army men out of uniform. He did not even care for the standards many of the officers adopted in the desert, but he had allowed that.

Holden wore civilian boots, stovepipe style, a reddish color with thick square toes and long mule-ear pulls that flopped toward his Mexican spurs. Stuck inside the boots were gray-striped trousers. A navy bib-front

141

shirt, flowing red and white polka-dot bandanna, tan vest, and tan hat completed his getup. His revolver remained the thumb-busting Schofield .45, but the lieutenant had replaced his Army-issue belt and holster for a shell belt, and the holster was tied down on his right leg. A pair of deerskin gloves were stuck inside the gunbelt.

Even with his military bearing and posture, Grat Holden would pass for a civilian, Smythe decided. The battered face certainly helped.

Masterson wore nondescript black boots, tan-colored canvas trousers, a boiled shirt of large black and white check, but no vest. He also sported a blue silk bandanna and a wide-brimmed, flat-crowned straw hat. He had a pair of double-action Colt Lightning revolvers — one nickel-plated with an ivory handle and the other blued with walnut grips — stuck butt forward in a red sash. A bandolier holding shells for the revolvers hung over his left shoulder.

He doesn't look military at all, Smythe thought and sipped his brandy. Then again, Ben Masterson had never been military. Never.

"Long arms?" Smythe asked.

"Winchester," Holden answered.

"Springfield," Masterson said.

"That's an Army rifle, Masterson," Smythe reminded him.

"I stole it," Masterson said, and grinned.

He probably planned on stealing it, too, Smythe figured. A man like Masterson would desert as soon as he got close enough to Mexico. He might even kill Holden along the way . . . would make things a whole lot easier to explain to the Springfield Armory, General Willcox, the secretary of war, and the president of the United States if the mission failed. As it most certainly would.

"Horses?" the colonel asked.

"Not Army," Holden answered. "Civilian saddles. No brand on the horses. We got them from a trader in Dos Cabezas. We thought about a pack mule but decided against it. A mule would just slow us down. The horses we got can run." He seemed to know what Smythe was thinking. "I paid for them with my money, sir. Not the Army's."

"Very good," Smythe said as he made his way to his desk, sipping the brandy as he crossed the room.

He did not sit, but set the snifter, now empty, on some reports he had no interest in reading. He pressed his hands against the wooden top and stared at the two men before him.

"You will ride out immediately. You have

143

no orders. Understand that. You are working on your own, at your own risk. If you are caught below the border by Mexicans, you are on your own. There will be no help from this side of the border. You understand that. You must understand that."

"We got it, Colonel, darlin'," Masterson said.

Smythe pressed his lips together. "Here is what I can do for you." He moved to the map that hung on the wall.

"Captain Garrison has this crazy idea that he wants to try. He served in the Signal Corps. The Apaches have been cutting our telegraph wires, as well you know, and then they splice the wires with rubber bands. Makes it hard to find out where the connection has been broken. Garrison thinks he can devise another way for Army patrols to communicate with one another."

He tapped a spot on the map. "I am allowing this experiment. He will be posted at the top of this peak. The plan is to communicate with another few men here" — he tapped another spot more to the north — "and one more here." That was closer to Bisbee. "I have informed Mr. Garrison that Sam Florence might try to send a signal from here." He tapped a rise below the border.

"Colonel," Masterson said, "even with a spyglass, a body ain't gonna be able to see no red signal flags that far —"

"Not signal flags, you damned fool," Smythe said. "Flashes of light. From a mirror. Mr. Garrison has a friend at Fort Whipple in Virginia, where they have been experimenting with this type of telegraphy. They call it a heliograph. With our fine sun in this godforsaken desert, Mr. Garrison believes this territory is the perfect place to communicate by this . . . heliography. He suggests that a heliograph signal can be seen up to thirty miles."

Holden cleared his throat. "What does this have to do with us, Colonel?"

"You will carry a heliograph mirror in your saddlebags. If you are successful, you can climb a hill and signal to the closest point." He tapped the spots on the mountain again.

"You do know Morse code, don't you?" the colonel added sarcastically.

"They still require that at West Point, Colonel," Holden said.

"Then you will send the message 'Happy Independence Day.' "

Holden frowned.

"You have until the sun sets on the Fourth of July to get that message delivered. If I

145

have no word from you or Mr. Garrison or anyone by that time, I will be sending word to Washington and the Springfield Armory that those four wagonloads of rifles were stolen. And that you two are missing, absent without leave."

Smythe returned to his desk and sat down. "Carry on, gentlemen."

Holden headed for the door.

Masterson followed, pausing long enough to say, "Ain't you gonna wish us luck, Colonel, darlin'?"

He slammed the door shut before Carlton Smythe could respond.

CHAPTER 25

They taught you at West Point that, if you were commissioned in the cavalry, a horse could walk four miles an hour, trot six miles an hour, and gallop nine miles an hour. By resting your mount for five minutes each hour, varying your speeds, leading the horse on occasion, and putting it into a gallop to keep the muscles loose, you could make forty miles a day.

Which would have put Grat Holden and Ben Masterson across the Mexican border in a day and a half, maybe two. It wasn't an easy trail south.

Holden decided not to follow the Army's recommendations. They had two Morgan horses, both browns, and they loped them out of Fort Bowie and rode hard in a hard country.

Four hours later, when they first spotted the buzzards circling in the pale sky, they reined in their mounts and let them breathe.

147

Holden drew the Winchester from the scabbard. Masterson checked the cylinders in his double-action .38-caliber revolvers, slipped both back into his sash, and pulled out the heavy Springfield carbine, which he braced against his thigh, the barrel pointed skyward.

They eased their way south into rugged hills.

Holden took the point and nodded at an impression in an arroyo as they climbed in and out of it.

"Moccasin print."

"Yep," Masterson agreed. "But that buck's following a mule and two white men."

He nudged his horse until he drew even with Holden's Morgan, and tilted the barrel at other tracks, faint impressions in the shadowed edge of the chasm.

"God gave you a good set of eyes, Masterson," Holden said.

"Which is why I'm alive."

Twenty minutes later, their horses showed nervousness. They soon knew why.

Holden reined in and brought his Winchester to his shoulder.

"No," Masterson said from behind him. "Don't shoot. Those bucks might still be around."

"Wasn't planning on shooting," Holden

said. "Just getting ready."

He waited a moment, the horse tried to turn around, but he made it stop. With his free hand, he removed his hat and waved it until the buzzards flew away.

Both men choked down bile at the grisly sight before them.

Two prospectors, by the looks of what remained of them. One had been smart enough, or fast enough to have taken his single-shot pistol and put a bullet through his head. The Apaches had then used knives and hatchets and rocks to smatter him into a bloody mess that now fed ants and drew flies by the hundreds.

The other had been captured alive. His partner had been much luckier.

"No time to bury them, Holden," Masterson said.

"I know that."

"Can't do a thing for them."

"I know that, too."

"Then if it's all the same to you, I'd like to move on. This does little for my digestion."

"Can you tell how many there were?"

Cursing, Masterson swung off the Morgan, handed the reins to Holden, and moved around the scene. There was little room in the tight canyon. Holden looked at the rocks above, trying to see where the Apaches had hit them first.

"Can't be certain," Masterson said. "Rocks are hard. Not much tracks here, unlike where we were before. But not many. I'd guess no more than four or five. But one would be all that was needed for these fools."

"And the mule?"

"Never known an Apache to turn down a chance at havin' mule for supper, Lieuten—Holden." They had to remember to forget the ranks, which would give them away when they were in Mexico. Even a lousy soldier like Ben Masterson found that habit, to his surprise, hard to break after far too many years in this man's army.

"All right," Holden said. "Let's ride."

"With pleasure."

Two miles farther along, Holden reined up and nodded at a steep trail that led into the hills. He pointed at a sandy spot at the base of the trail.

"The Apaches didn't take that mule to eat, Masterson."

The former sergeant saw the track and nodded. "Deep. Left the packsaddle on, or whatever those fools had been using."

"Left what was in the packs, too."

"Gold?" Masterson asked.

Holden shrugged. "Some ore, by my guess. Gold? Maybe. Silver? Copper? No telling. And there's a chance that those boys were going hunting for ore, hadn't found it yet, were just carrying in enough supplies, but I don't think the Apaches would have any interest in coffee and hardtack. They would have rifled through that back where we found the bodies of the dead miners . . . then taken just what they needed. They didn't. So my bet is ore. Of some kind."

He kicked the horse into a walk, and told Masterson about Crooked Nose's war party holding up a stagecoach outside of Bisbee, and a report that a Mexican copper mine had been robbed by Apaches, too.

"Down payment," Masterson said, "for a few hundred new-model Springfields."

They rode on.

"Holden."

The lieutenant glanced at his partner in the mission, saw him nodding at the hills ahead and to Holden's left. Holden looked, but kept his horse moving, stepping over the stones and rocks that slowed their progress. Finally, he saw what Ben Masterson had spotted a few moments earlier.

"An Apache, even if he's on his first war party, isn't going to be foolish enough to let the sun reflect off his rifle barrel."

"I agree," Holden said, "but it might not be a rifle barrel."

"Well." Ben Masterson spit. "It sure ain't no damned heliograph."

CHAPTER 26

They climbed out of the narrow confines and saw where the country opened wider. It would be the place to give their horses their heads and make up the time they had lost traveling through the rough arroyo and deep canyon. But that flash of metal kept them at a deliberate pace. They spread out, rifles ready, eyes focused on the hill in the distance.

Too focused, maybe, because a stone rattled, and both men turned to the right, bringing their guns up.

It was no Apache standing behind a pale boulder, but a white man in a blue jacket with a lever action rifle against his shoulder.

Realizing he would never be able to get off a shot first, Grat Holden leaped out of the saddle, seeing three more figures rise out of the rocks. He landed, rolled, and heard a gunshot. Yet the shot did not come from Ben Masterson, nor the man in the rocks, nor close. It was muffled, distant.

His horse took off. Holden came up, saw the man slamming against the rock, his rifle spilling into the dust, unfired. Out of the corner of his eye, Holden also saw Ben Masterson leaping from his horse, slapping its hindquarters with the barrel of his Springfield, and snapping a shot at the other men, who stood there, equally confused.

The man who had been shot staggered away from the rock, leaving a dark spot where the bullet had chiseled into the sandstone after drilling through both of his lungs. Then he toppled out of view.

Holden rose, rifle ready, and squeezed the trigger, levered another cartridge into the chamber, fired. Jacked the lever again and fired. Again. Again. The men scattered, and Holden dropped as another bullet sang over his head.

He rolled, came to his knees, and dived to his left.

Bullets riddled the spot where he had been.

On his back, he watched Ben Masterson reload the trapdoor Springfield, shoot, then stand and run. He was running to a narrow opening between two rocks. The opening was suddenly filled by another man. He was wearing a porkpie hat and red and green checked britches — the ugliest pants Holden had ever seen. The man held a shotgun in both hands and seemed to be grinning . . . until he realized that Ben Masterson had palmed one of the .38s in his sash and opened up. The man did some wild dance, spun, and dropped out of the opening that Masterson quickly filled before the rocks were dented by bullets.

A bullet ripped off one of the pulls of Holden's left boot, leaving a scar across the leather top. Rolling over, Holden saw the figure of a man in Mexican denim britches and a black hat working the lever of his Henry rifle. Then down went the man to his knees, blood spouting from the fist-sized wound a powerful bullet had made when it exited. The man's eyes rolled into the back of his head, and he pitched forward into the sand.

Holden had seen the muzzle flash and the smoke.

It had come from high up in the hills, from where he and Masterson had seen the reflection of the sun. The man up there was no enemy. At least, not yet. He was helping Masterson and Holden.

But who the hell was he?

"Did you see that, Hank?" a man cried out from the rocks.

"Where'd it come from?"

"Up yonder. Somewhere."

"Hell, Buster, Pete and Slim's done fer. Let's get the hell out of here."

"Muy pronto."

Holden came to his knee, rifle at the shoulder. One man stepped out of the rocks, and Holden fired. The bullet caught the man in his left shoulder, spun him around, so that he was on his knees, staring at Holden's Winchester. He tried to bring up his six-shooter, and Holden, having instantly cocked the rifle after firing, touched the trigger and blew the top of the man's head off. Another ran for the pocket of woods on the other side, only to be drilled by a .45-70 slug from Ben Masterson's Springfield rifle.

One more jumped up to the left of Holden, but he was already swinging around. Holden fired. Masterson fired, using his other Colt Lightning, and Holden heard another blast from the hillside and saw the smoke again. All three bullets struck and staggered the man, who dropped to his knees, looked confused, and died confused.

Echoes bounced all around the canyon. A white handkerchief started waving above the rocks, and Holden slowly realized that someone was trying to surrender.

"Stand up!" Holden said, levering another

shell and aiming at the dirty handkerchief.

Two nervous white men, one bald, fat, and sweating, the other short with a mustache and goatee, rose. Their hands remained high over their heads.

Ben Masterson stepped out of his hiding place and brought the Springfield up, but he aimed the Army rifle at the rocks. The man took no chances. Just because somebody had helped them out in this gunfight did not mean he didn't plan on murdering them.

Holden moved toward the men.

"You best do some talking," he said, and jabbed the hot barrel of the Winchester into the bald man's fat belly.

"It was Pete's i-de-er," the bald man said.

"That's right," said the other one. "Pete." He pointed a bent finger at one of the dead bodies.

"We seen 'em buzzards," said the bald one. "Knowed some ol' boys was up huntin' fer gold. Figgered we'd see if they found any."

"They found Apaches," Masterson said, but he kept the rifle aimed at the high hills.

The other brigand's head nodded. "Pete figgered that might be the case, too. Then we'd just kill them bucks and sell their scalps down in Mexico for the bounty."

Part of Grat Holden wanted to just shoot down those two vermin.

"Holden," Masterson said.

Holden waved the barrel of the Winchester, and the two stupid outlaws understood. They dropped to their knees and clasped their hands behind their heads. Masterson was nodding toward the hill.

A man had stepped out of the woods. Too high up, too many shadows to make out anything about him, but he was holding a rifle in his left hand and waving his hat in his right. Then he pulled a horse out of the timber and began walking down a deer trail.

CHAPTER 27

"Keep your eyes on our two amigos here," Ben Masterson said to Holden. "I'll catch up the horses."

Holden nodded. He looked at the two trembling bandits. "You thought we were the prospectors," he said, not a question.

"Sure, sure," the bald one said. "We wouldn't have tried to waylay you good peoples had we knowed you wasn't the ones we was huntin'." He made a feeble attempt at a grin.

"Where did you put your horses?" Masterson asked them, and when they didn't answer soon enough, he pulled one of the Lightning revolvers. "I'm not walking after our horses, boys!"

Both men pointed to a wall formed by a rockslide on the other side. "Beyond yonder," the short one said.

Masterson lowered the .38 and made a hurried march to the makeshift livery.

"Bring a shovel?" Holden asked.

The two bushwhackers glanced at each other. One chewed on his bottom lip.

The other hesitated and tried to smile as he turned back to Holden. "I reckon we forgot."

Masterson loped away from the fallen rocks and debris on a bay. If he ran, Holden knew he would not be able to stop him.

He waved the barrel up and down, signaling the two men to rise. Slowly, sweating more profusely, they did.

"Cover your pals with rocks."

They scrambled to the chore, and Holden shot one glance at Masterson off after the horses, then turned back to study the man riding a pinto pony down the steep ridge. Holden found a place in the shade where he could sit on a rock and keep an eye on the burial party, Ben Masterson, and the stranger who had saved their bacon. He wished he could take a drink of water, but the canteens were on the Morgan horses, and it would be a few minutes before Masterson brought those back.

When the rider had made it halfway down the slope, Grat Holden relaxed. Recognizing the man at last, he turned his attention to the short man and the bald man, watching them drag the bodies off to the side and begin finding rocks to cover the corpses — after they plundered the dead, their colleagues if not friends, of any valuables.

"Don't take any weapons, boys," Holden called out to them. "Knives or guns or anything. I find you holding something, and you'll join your pals."

The bald one smiled, straightened, and lifted his left hand slowly, held out a finger and thumb, and carefully reached behind his back. Even more deliberately, he brought up a Remington derringer into view, holding the hideaway .41 with thumb and forefinger, he dropped it into the makeshift grave. The short one slipped a Bowie knife out of his boot and pitched it into the pile, and then pulled a single-shot Sharps pistol from the small of his back and gently rested it on one of the dead men's chest.

They went back to work.

Masterson was back with the two Morgans before the man on the pinto had reached the bottom of the hill. The former sergeant dropped the reins of the two horses and swung from the saddle of the bay. Rising, after checking on the two outlaws to make sure they kept doing what they were supposed to be doing, Holden went to his horse and found the canteen.

He shoved the Winchester into the scabbard and nodded over the saddle.

"Recognize him?" he asked Masterson.

The former sergeant studied the figure whose pinto leaped the last two feet, kept its balance, and began picking a path toward them.

"Figures," Masterson said, and slid his Springfield into the scabbard.

"Thanks,"

Grat Holden told Sam Florence when the old scout reined in the pinto and reached into his pocket to find a chaw of tobacco.

The old man shrugged.

"What were you doin' up there?" Masterson asked.

Once his jaw started working on softening up the old plug of chewing tobacco, Florence jutted his chin down the trail. "Found those poor folks, took Cochise here" — he patted the pinto's neck — "up a ways to follow the Apaches."

He watched the two men carrying a large boulder to the new graveyard.

"You done well," he said to Holden.

"Would've been a different story had you not taken a hand."

"I doubt it." Florence spit. "They ain't got no sand. Doubt if a one of 'em could shoot straight."

"Thanks just the same," Holden said.

The scout kicked free of the stirrups to stretch his legs.

"What about the Apaches?" Masterson asked.

Florence wiped his lips with his sleeve. "Took the mule. Got their horses. Went south. Don't think they'll be comin' back."

"Was the mule still carrying its pack?" Holden asked.

"And all those poor blokes put in it."

"Gold?"

"No tellin'. Maybe. Maybe just supplies. Apaches might be able to sell the pack to some trader in Sonora, get a few pesos for it. Sell the mule, too. If they don't eat it." Florence snorted. "Bad timin'. For the Apaches, I mean. Had they come along a tad later or waited a spell, they could've gotten me, you two, and them." He nodded as the two bushwhackers, exhausted, knelt and started scooping up sand and gravel and small stones and tossing those over the dead. "Taken our horses and everything else."

"Which might buy them a few new model Springfields," Holden said.

The scout shrugged. "If those that done this are part of Crooked Nose's bunch."

"You don't think they were?" Masterson asked.

Florence shrugged again. "I learned a long time ago not to guess nothin' about any Apache."

CHAPTER 28

The village, the town, the few buildings, and corral that made up Rancho Los Cielos was asleep when the hooves thundered and about four Mexicans yipped and shouted as they drove mules down the one street, raising dust, raising hell.

The leader reined up his blood bay mare and laughed as he directed one of his riders to open the gate to the corral and the others to drive the mules inside. He hooked one leg over the saddle horn and laughed again as Captain Jed Foster stepped out of Mariscos.

"Buenos dias, amigo," the big man said.

He wore a Mexican sombrero of straw with a dented crown that had to be at least eight inches high and a brim about the same width, except where it was twisted and curled up at the front. The hatband, made of twisted horse hair in three contrasting colors, had to be worth six times as much as the awful hat.

A dark brown poncho covered his blue silk shirt, and two ivory-handled Colt revolvers were stuck inside a large russet-colored belt that was buckled over brown and tan striped cotton britches. Leather *botas* were strapped just below his knees, and the plain tan leggings came down to his black cowhide Congress gaiters. He wore well-oiled, well-used gloves, and popped a quirt in his left hand. His right came down to rest on the handle of one of the Colts.

"Good morning to you," Jed Foster said. "You made good time."

"Siempre, mi amigo," the Mexican said. He made a gesture with his hand and bowed slightly. *"Mi nombre es Muerte . . . a su servicio, señor."*

Foster bowed. "It is a pleasure to meet you, Mister . . . Death."

The man laughed. "You are . . . *mi capitán . . . Señor . . .* Foster?"

"At your service."

The man who called himself Death waved at the corral, that was now being closed by one of his riders. The rider, Foster noticed, wore a brace of Colt revolvers butt-forward on his two hips. Another rider carried a Spencer carbine. The last one was reaching for a machete.

"You will see that you have the very best mules a man could buy in Sonora," Death said.

"Or steal." Jed Foster laughed.

"You brought gold, my friend, to pay for these mules."

"That is what we agreed upon, my friend . . . Mister . . . Death."

"My friend. It is your money. It is your troubles. But you are new to our country. You are a *norteamericano.* You . . . well . . . if I may be of your assistance, I should point out that you are buying too many mules, my friend. I count four wagons. Those wagons have heavy loads — *eso es verdad* — but you are not pulling a load of borax across Nevada or California. You have more than three times as many mules as you need for four wagons."

"*Gracias,* amigo," Foster said. "But I am a man who likes to be prepared."

"As do I, amigo," Death said. "Jimenez."

The rider with the machete swung down from his saddle.

At that moment, two of Foster's men — two of the men he thought he might be able to trust — stepped outside. Reese, the lanky Texan, came out of The Cantina That Has No Name, holding a double-barreled Parker shotgun in his arms, with two belted guns on his hip. Foster had hoped the young Mexican girl would come out, too, but she was staying inside.

From around the corner of Mariscos stepped the blond-headed kid, Whittaker. He wore two Colts on his hips. He looked ready. The damned fool even looked eager.

"You have friends, amigo!" Death slapped his thigh.

"It's good to have friends," Foster said.

"But three men, including you, *señor*. And four wagons? That does not quite add up."

"My men had a long journey," Foster said. "The others need to rest. Me . . . and my two compadres . . . that's all I need to finish this little transaction."

"*¿Es eso cierto?*" the Mexican asked.

"It is very true," Foster said.

The Mexican called Death laughed again. He raised his hand to push back his massive sombrero. "*Señor,* when you hired me to bring you many, many, many excellent mules, I was pleased. But when we rode into this fine little town, what pleased me even more was when I looked at the wagons. The wagons, if my mind is not playing tricks on me after such an arduous ride in the heat of the day and in the cold of the desert night, appear to belong to the *Yanqui* Army. And you have left the boxes out for all eyes to see. I read something that says . . . Spring-field . . . Armory?"

"Your vision is perfect. Your English is *el mas excelente.*" Foster touched his lips with his fingertips in a mock kiss.

"My English," Death said. "It is not that excellent. This word . . . *armory.* Does that mean . . . arsenal?"

"It means *death,* Death." Foster lowered his hand closer to the butt of his Colt.

The Mexican who called himself Death laughed and brought his right hand up. He pointed dramatically at Foster. "You" — Death shook his head — "are a man who makes me laugh. *Por Dios,* I wish you could ride with me." He shook his head. "Let us celebrate, my friends. Let us dance. Let us —" His hand slapped his thigh.

But Foster knew that little game. He filled his hand with the Colt in the holster and the Mexican named Death swept his hand from his thigh to one of his ivory-handled Colts in the belt around his belly.

CHAPTER 29

The bullet from Jed Foster's .45-caliber Colt caught the man named Death in his side. It would have drilled him in the belly had not his horse shied away as Death palmed his ivory-handled pistol.

"Por trueno, como esto duele," the man named Death moaned as he toppled out of his saddle and landed in the dust.

Foster had to think a bullet in the side, probably perforating the blowhard's liver indeed must hurt. The man named Death pushed himself up, trying to find the Colt he had dropped, but the horse he had been riding brought a hoof down on the man's shoulder blade. Death groaned. The horse galloped back toward the southern edge of town, kicking Death in his right arm as it galloped away from what was thick with white smoke from pistols shooting black powder.

The kid named Whittaker whipped a Colt

from his holster. Foster kept the barrel trained on the body of the Mexican named Death, who rolled over onto his back and moaned and cried and cursed. Foster watched the blond-headed kid. The boy's speed seemed to blur. Like a lightning flash, you saw it and then you didn't.

The Colt spat out death and flame, and two bullets that sounded like one shot drilled the man with the machete against the corral. The big blade with the long walnut handle dropped to the ground. The man groaned and reached for something behind his back. Two more bullets smashed his head.

Jed Foster wondered if his mind was playing tricks on him. It appeared that one of the bullets from the kid's Colt had drilled through the machete-wielder's left eyeball while the second shot smashed through the orb in his right eye socket.

It was no illusion. Because blood pooled out of the two holes in the man's head, and the big Mexican who carried a machete spun around, tried to keep himself from falling by clutching for the top rails. His muscles refused to cooperate, however, and he was on the ground, rolling over and coming to a stop. Luckily for anyone who did not like the sight of blood or gore, the dead man lay facedown on the street. Face-down . . . meaning . . . what was left of his face.

Reese, the savvy Texas gunman, was showing his prowess, too. The big Remington revolver belted on his right hip shot out and drilled one of the riders in the throat. The man coughed blood out of his mouth as the pistol went somersaulting through the air. He landed in the dust as blood spurted from the ghastly hole in above his Adam's apple. The man's left foot remained caught in his stirrup, and the palomino gelding thundered out of the village of Rancho Los Cielos, dragging its rider through the dust. The body bounced this way and that, hit a stump, a mound of mule droppings, and was pulled through a patch of prickly pear before horse and the rider it was dragging rounded the bend and disappeared as though heading for the border with the United States.

That left one of Death's riders. He had leaped out of the saddle, pulling the Spencer repeating rifle with him. The last of the Mexican mule thieves brought the stock of the .56-caliber carbine to his shoulder, and his finger found the trigger. But that's all he managed to do.

The man named Reese dropped to a knee,

aimed, and sent a bullet into the man's up-per right arm, shattering a bone. The heavy Spencer tumbled out of the man's hands and fell into the dust after a slug from the kid's Colt ripped through the man's left side, just above the gunbelt and holster. It exited the right side and tore a savage hole a bit higher up than the entrance wound. That dropped the bandit to his knees, and Jed Foster put a bullet in the center of the man's head. The killer's eyes rolled into the back of his head, but he still did not fall until all three men fired simultaneously.

The bandit spun around, twisted as doing some crazy dance, and fell into the dust, his body shuddering as life ebbed away and the man discovered what hell was really like.

Inside the corral, the horses were braying, snorting, and dancing nervously around, but as far as Jed Foster could say, no stray bullets had hit any of the animals. He would need those mules, all of those mules, soon. Real soon. From inside Mariscos and The Cantina That Has No Name, the men he had hired slowly emerged. Most held their weapons loosely. Foster kept his eye on the entrance to The Cantina That Has No Name as he walked to the writhing figure of the bandit who called himself Death.

Foster stood over the pathetic little figure

and leveled the Colt so that the barrel was aimed at the man's forehead. Foster's eyes, however, remained on the cantina. Eventually, the pretty girl with the stunning eyes and the black, black hair stepped outside.

That's when Foster smiled and looked down at the dying mule thief.

"Death," he said, "you're dead."

The Colt barked. The slug blew a hole in the man's head, and Death died without another word.

Foster walked away from the dead men. He plunged the empty shells from the cylinder of his Colt and quickly reloaded. He stopped at Reese and smiled.

"You're not bad, my friend. Thanks."

He moved over to the kid. "You're almost as fast as I am, Whittaker. Thanks for taking a hand."

He turned back and barked at the men who had watched from the safety of the two businesses of Rancho Los Cielos. "The rest of you, check those mules. Make sure every last one of them is all right. Then get those dead idiots off the street and out of my sight. Bury them. Bury them deep. And then someone better start breakfast. I'm hungry."

By that point he was standing in front of the black-eyed beauty.

He holstered his Colt and removed his

hat. "Ma'am," he said, affecting a Southern accent, "I sure hope those four men were not friends of yours."

"I have no friends," she told him, and walked back into *La Cantina Que No Tiene Nombre,* The Cantina That Has No Name.

CHAPTER 30

Buzzards circled overhead, waiting for the men to leave. The short man and the bald man staggered over to the three men.

"Finished?" Holden asked as he tightened the cinch on his saddle.

"W-well . . . y-yeah . . . I-I m-mean . . ." the bald one stammered.

"I suppose that'll do." Holden glanced at Masterson, who sat on a rock while he cleaned his revolvers, and then at Sam Florence, who stood in the shade, looking at the ridgetop to make sure the Apaches did not come back.

"All right," Holden said, and pointed to the rockslide. "This is your lucky day. Get your horses, all of them, and ride out. That way."

He pointed down the trail.

The two men looked at each other uneasily.

"That's why you came here, isn't it?"

Holden put his right hand on the butt of the Schofield. "Those two miners you planned to kill, they're back there. You're going to go to them, both of you. You're going to bury them, and you best do a better job than you've done here. Bury them. And take the horses and keep riding north."

"You mean . . ." the bald one said, "you ain't gonna kill us? Or turn us in to the law?"

"Shut up!" snapped the short one.

"If you don't get out of my sight, I might forget that I'm an officer and a gentleman." Holden tugged the big .45 halfway out of the holster. The two men ran, but the short one remembered the bay horse Masterson had used, hurried back, grabbed the reins, and pulled the horse toward the rockslide.

"Hey!" Ben Masterson rose.

The short one stopped and turned with a petrified grimace.

"I'd sell those horses as quick as you can and keep riding," Masterson said. "Out of the territory and as far away as you can get. Montana, maybe. Or Canada. Maybe the North Pole. Because if I see either one of you again, I'm shooting. Shooting to kill."

The man scurried away to join his running, stumbling, sweating comrade.

■ ■ ■ ■

The army men rode easily through the canyon, which caused Grat Holden to bite his lower lip.

He risked talking. "We don't have much time."

"You lope through here, Holden," the old scout said, "and your horse'll either step into a hole or trip over a rock, and if you don't break your neck in the fall, you'll be afoot." Sam Florence turned his head and spit tobacco juice onto a tarantula. "We'll make up time, sonny, when we're in flatter country."

Sighing, Holden nodded. "You're right."

"Usually am," Florence said, and laughed. "Don't believe that, boy."

"What are you doin' here?" Masterson asked.

"Ridin'," Florence answered. "And mindin' my own business."

Masterson's face flushed, but Holden said, "You weren't minding your business when you saved our bacon back there."

"Old habits," Florence said.

Having a conversation with Sam Florence took a lot out of a person.

"Did the colonel send you?" Masterson asked.

Florence chuckled. "Nope."

"Where are you going?" Masterson asked.

The smile left the old scout's bronzed face. "Boy, you got a lot to learn about this deal I call mindin' your own business."

Holden sensed a fight, but Masterson said, "And I guess you were mindin' your own business when you brought word to Colonel Smythe about Foster and those guns bein' in Rancho Los Cielos."

"Happens that that was my business."

"I don't understand," Masterson said.

"That's your business."

A thought hit Holden, and he belted it out before he had time to reconsider. "Maybe we can make this your business, Mr. Florence." He waited until the scout, riding slightly in front of him and Masterson, turned in the saddle and eyed the lieutenant. "You could help us."

"I did that back at the canyon."

"Which wasn't mindin' your own business," Masterson said.

"Like I told you already —"

"Old habits." Holden cut him off. "I know. So maybe another old habit is hard to break."

"Such as?" Florence turned back to look at the trail ahead.

"Helping your country."

Florence laughed. "You mean helping a shavetail lieutenant who doesn't want to face court-martial. Or a real horse's arse of a sergeant who should be spendin' the next ten years in a federal penitentiary."

"I mean," Holden said, "preventing both sides of the border from turning into a slaughterhouse."

The scout's head bobbed. Without turning around he said, "Then maybe I ought to take the advice you give 'em two scoundrels back down the canyon. Go north. See what Montana looks like. Or Canada. And I bet, after fifteen years in Arizona Territory, the North Pole would feel a bit nice. Cool me off some. Always wondered what a seal tastes like. And I ain't never seen none of those Eskimos 'cept a drawin' oncet in *Harper's.*"

"You are a piece of work, old man," Masterson said.

"I'm alive."

"We'd like to stay alive, too," Holden said.

They rode a few more yards in silence while Sam Florence studied the country, the only sound coming from the horse's hooves and the creaking of leather.

At length, he said, "Put it plain, youngster."

He reined in the pinto.

Masterson pulled up his Morgan on the old scout's right. Grat Holden stopped on Florence's left.

"All right," Holden said. "The colonel sent us to get back those Springfield rifles. Just the two of us."

Florence spit again. "You know why he done that, don't you?"

"I can guess," Holden said.

Florence chuckled. "It ain't no guess. He's sendin' you south to get killed, which will save him from findin' hisself before either a Board of Inquiry or a full-blowed court-martial. He can blame you and Foster for the loss of the weapons. Now, he'll still have to answer a few questions like how come he took so long to report the rifles stole, but he'll figure somethin' out. And the Army brass ain't knowed for bein' the smartest thinkers, and with those guns in the hands of Apaches or Mexican bandits or, most likely, that crazy ol' coot who thinks he can bring back the Confederacy, the Army will have plenty of work to do. They'll even need a stupid, worthless martinet of an idiot, Carlton Smythe, colonel, U S of A."

He spit. "I've done talked myself out, boys. You speak if you want."

"All right," Holden said. "Neither of us knows Mexico. You do. Masterson knows

Apaches better than I do. He's been on the frontier longer. You know more than either of us. And you know who we'll be dealing with. You know *El Cañon de Los Delores,* The Canyon of The Sorrows, which is where Foster will be selling the rifles."

Florence stopped him by lifting his head. He corrected, "Where you *think* Foster'll be."

Where he's got to be, Holden thought. *Where he must be . . . for all of our sakes.*

When Holden did not respond, the scout said, "And remember, back in the colonel's office, I said that I'd never been to Los Delores."

Holden came to the point: "You can find it better than we can. Will you help us?"

The silence lasted forever.

Shaking his head, the scout sank a bit into the saddle.

"Can't do it." Sam Florence kicked the pinto into a walk, and he remembered.

CHAPTER 31

"Remember the date, Sergeant. Eleven May, 1864." General J.E.B. Stuart circled his prancing horse in front of Sam Florence on the road out of Richmond. "Today we win the war. Or we die trying."

Florence smiled. "Not you, General." He thought, *But me? Most likely. And most of the rest of us.*

Florence could smell the cologne on J.E.B. Stuart. Barely thirty years old, Stuart was dashing, bearded. His hat with an ostrich plume flopping in the side of it was cocked at a rakish angle, and a red flower was pinned onto the lapel of his coat.

The First Virginia Cavalry would follow Stuart anywhere. They were about to follow him into hell.

He rode away to shout encouragement to other divisions, other soldiers, and instruct his junior officers.

The captain of Florence's troop pulled up

alongside him. "What's that up ahead, Sergeant?"

Florence was checking the caps on his Navy Colt. "Yellow Tavern, sir," he answered.

"Yellow Tavern indeed. I could use a drink right about now, Sergeant. What about you? I'll buy the first round."

The hammer on the Navy came to full cock before Florence gently lowered it. He did not holster it.

"I'm afraid the tavern's closed, Capt'n. Been closed a long while."

"Damn." The captain winked. "War is hell, Sergeant."

"Hell indeed, sir."

The road led past Yellow Tavern to the Yankee lines, but there, Major General Philip Sheridan, commander of the Union cavalry, had come to meet the South.

"You know what the infantry always says about the cavalry, Sergeant?" The captain unsheathed his saber.

"About never seein' a dead horse soldier, sir?" Florence said.

"That's the one, Sergeant. Well" — the captain drew in a deep breath, and let it out with a bit of a cough, or maybe it was an amen to a prayer — "today, Sergeant, I'm afraid there will be a lot of dead horse soldiers. God willing, more in blue than gray."

That would be unlikely, Florence knew. J.E.B. Stuart had maybe two brigades. The Yanks ahead of them had to number three divisions — ten thousand soldiers, maybe as many as twelve thousand — with better than two dozen artillery pieces. Against what was left of the finest light cavalry in the world, General J.E.B. Stuart, the South's most dashing hero, and five thousand men.

Sabers came out. Florence spit out his tobacco.

"Charge!" came the command, and thousands of horses bolted toward the ramshackle little building. Rebel war cries filled the air. The Yankees answered with shots from their fast-shooting Spencer carbines.

It was right around noon.

Along the low ridgeline next to the road, saber met saber. Horses screamed. Carbines and pistols left the woods and road shrouded in a fog that smelled of sulfur and brimstone. Hell, indeed.

A man rode past Florence — who couldn't tell if the man were North or South — screaming, reins dragging as the poor, wretched man gripped his right arm with his left. Blood spurted from where his right forearm had been sliced off with a saber.

He kept riding until, mercifully, bullets riddled his body and ripped him out of the saddle. The horse rode on toward the Union lines.

Charge and countercharge. Fall back and regroup. Charge again. Dead, men in blue, men in gray, and horses of various colors littered the field, the road, the woods, and even the porch of the abandoned inn. Smoke burned Florence's eyes. They were back at the bottom of the hill. Riderless horses thundered one way and then another, confused.

They had been at the slaughter for three hours. It felt like three days.

"Charge, boys, charge! We can push the Yanks back with one more charge!" It was Stuart. His horse reared, and the general waved his hat. He led the way.

Florence spurred his weary horse after him.

The Confederates were winning. Somehow, they were winning the fight, despite the odds, despite the numbers, despite Spencer repeaters against carbines, Colts, and sabers.

The Fifth Michigan came out to meet them. Reins held by his teeth, Florence deflected a saber with his own, and brought back the saber, surprised to find the bluecoat lifting a pistol in his other hand. Florence still held the Navy Colt in his right hand, and he brought it up, ducking as the Yank rushed his shot. The bullet burned the back of Florence's neck and he squeezed the Colt's trigger. The .36-caliber ball slammed into the Yankee's chest. The man fell off his horse, the saber rattled onto the ground, and the bluecoat's horse bolted south toward Richmond.

Florence's horse went down. Spitting out the reins and kicking out of the stirrups, Florence fell into the leaves and grass. He had thrown the saber away from where he was leaping, or falling, not wanting to be speared by the weapon. He came up, still clutching the Navy, and fired again at a charging Yankee who grunted and dropped low in the saddle as the horse carried him into the trees.

Florence looked for a horse. Grabbed at the reins of one, but missed, and hit the ground. He came up, blowing the cylinder of the Colt, hoping to clear it of dust and trash. His hat was gone. He saw a man clutching his arm as it pulsated blood. The man fell onto his back.

Florence shoved the hot Colt into his waistband and ran to the wounded man whose eyes were rolling back in his head.

Quickly, the young sergeant ripped a long silk handkerchief from a pocket of his shell jacket, wrapped it above the soldier's arm, and tied it quickly. Drawing the Colt, he tied the ends of the bandanna around the hot barrel, and twisted and turned and twisted and turned until the bleeding stopped.

That's when he looked down into the eyes of the soldier. The kid had awakened. He was a Yankee. He wore the blue.

"Here." Florence laid the arm across the kid's chest. He put the other hand on the butt of the Colt. "Loosen it every now and then, boy. Let it bleed a little. Then tighten it. That'll hold you, I hope. Till some Yankee or one of our sawbones can patch you up."

Florence stood, searched for a horse, another gun, anything, when a bullet slammed into his back. He fell, rolled over, cursed and groaned, and saw a Yankee slide his horse to a stop. The soldier worked another round into his Spencer and drew a bead on Sam Florence.

"Hold it!"

Another Yank stopped his horse between the Spencer-wielding back shooter and Sam Florence.

"The war's that way, bub," the other one said. "In case you haven't noticed, we're retreating! Get to it!"

The soldier lowered the Spencer, then slammed the barrel against the horse's rear, and bolted away.

The bluebelly officer slid out of the saddle. He found a rag in one of his pockets and placed it against the hole in Florence's back.

"Saw what you did there, Sergeant. You ought to be a Wolverine!"

Then the Yankee was climbing back into the saddle of his horse. He smiled, saluted, and said, "You owe me a life, Reb." He spurred the horse and disappeared.

CHAPTER 32

"Why?" Grat Holden asked as they rode across Arizona.

"My business," Sam Florence said.

The lieutenant and the convicted sergeant cursed, sighed, and shook their heads in exasperation . . . but they kept riding south.

Sam Florence sighed himself.

He remembered lying on the ground with a Yankee's handkerchief plugging up the bullet hole in his back. He remembered seeing J.E.B. Stuart fall from his horse, shot by some Yankee trooper as he was retreating. And he remembered the surgeons and officers coming, and watching them lift the great cavalry leader and take him away. Two riders swung off their horses, and Florence thanked God that they were First Virginia boys. They helped him away. They left the Yankee with the tourniquet. He always wondered what happened to that boy.

In Richmond, J.E.B. Stuart had died the

following day. That's when Sam Florence had known the war was over. Lost.

As he rode between Holden and Masterson he remembered more.

Thirteen years after Yellow Tavern, he took a job as a civilian scout. Off duty, he was in a dark adobe hut better than two thousand miles from that part of Virginia when an officer slammed through the door, walked to the bar, and slapped his hat down.

"The best you have, amigo," the man said. "The best liquor. The best woman. *Muy pronto, muy pronto.*" He slapped a gold coin and turned around, and studied the men and women in this dusty place in the middle of a dusty territory. "The cleanest woman and whatever passes for whiskey will have to do."

When the officer's gaze found Sam Florence, he stopped.

Florence set his empty glass down. The red scarf reminded him of Yellow Tavern. All those Michigan boys wore red, just like their general, George Custer, who was given command of a division after Yellow Tavern. But it was the face, the eyes, and that long hair that held Florence's attention.

The man raised a hand as if he recognized Florence, but wasn't quite sure.

Florence wasn't certain either. "Say somethin'," he told the newcomer.

191

That's when the cavalry trooper smiled.

"You owe me a life, Reb."

Sam Florence straightened. He also whispered a soft curse.

"But for the time being," Jed Foster said, "a bottle of tequila will suffice."

Of course, the Yanks had not given Jed Foster the Medal of Honor for saving a Rebel sergeant's life, but they had given him one for all he had done to help save the day, and win both battle and war at Yellow Tavern back in 1864.

That afternoon in the adobe saloon at Dos Cabezas was the only time either Florence or Foster had brought up Yellow Tavern. Neither one spent much time thinking about the past . . . or at least talking about it. Florence never mentioned that he had served in the Confederate cavalry, although his accent likely dropped a few clues. The only person Jed Foster ever mentioned was George Custer, and that name had not come up too much since Little Bighorn.

Holden, Masterson, and Florence rode out of the canyon at that moment. The scout shook off the memories and stared ahead at the Arizona desert. They had a long way to go yet.

He spit out the tobacco and wiped his lips on his sleeve. "We can put our horses into a gallop. Limber 'em up some."

They rode.

And when they slowed to give their mounts a breather, Florence had made his decision.

"I'll get you boys to Rancho Los Cielos. And I'll introduce you to a person who can get you to *El Cañon de Los Delores.* Whether or not Soledad Tadeo will do that for a couple gringos, I don't know."

CHAPTER 33

Crooked Nose did not like what he was about to do, but some of his braves enjoyed it. It made them feel Apache, and even better, it made them feel Chiricahua Apache. His braves were young, and, if they lived long enough, they might begin to feel as he did. Old.

He drew in a breath, exhaled, and walked toward the Mexican his braves had captured. *It had been,* Crooked Nose thought, *a fine raid.* A burro and three mules — one butchered, and the steaks were perfect. Some money. One woman whom Badger Killer had enjoyed several times before he had sliced her throat. Four Mexicans had been killed, two more captured and tortured which made his braves even stronger. They wanted to kill the middle-aged Mexican who wore a fine pale-eyes suit and glasses that made his eyes look bigger than they actually were. The man carried many books in his black bag, but those books were filled more with what the pale eyes called numbers and not their chicken-scratch marks they used to draw what they were thinking, and what was supposed to be in their hearts.

The books interested Crooked Nose, which is why he had made Badger Killer and the other braves bring the captive along instead of killing him down on the road north to Agua Prieta, or better yet, torturing the man until he begged to be put out of his miserable existence so that Badger Killer and the other braves could take his spirit, his existence, and his bravery . . . if he had any . . . to make them all the stronger.

The man with the glasses had been stripped naked and staked on the rise where Crooked Nose had led his braves and their squaws. The women kept sharpening their knives, waiting for the opportunity to do their best on the Mexican still living. Apache women, Crooked Nose knew, were much better at torture than Apache braves, even Badger Killer, who was quite handy and enjoyed it more than he enjoyed killing bravely in battle.

The Apaches had left the man's glasses over his eyes. This they enjoyed. It made the Mexican look funny.

Where they were camped was the highest point for miles. It was cooler, filled with trees, and the rocks jumped up in several palisades, like many, many fingers pointing to the sky. White man's fingers. Not Apache's. But one did not question the wisdom of Ussen, the Apaches' Life Giver, and well . . . white was one of the four sacred colors. The Mexican's suit was black, which also was a sacred color among Crooked Nose's people. His tie was yellow, yet another sacred color. And his vest was made of the cloth the pale eyes called blue. The fourth of the Apaches' sacred colors. This meant something to Crooked Nose so he had brought the Mexican to their camp.

Badger Killer had protested. He wanted Crooked Nose to hurry up and die. Badger Killer wanted to take over the band and lead them to . . . *ruin,* Crooked Nose figured.

To Badger Killer's thinking, even worse than taking a miserable Mexican who could not see without the help of those pieces of glass he wore over his ugly eyes was the fact that Crooked Nose had cut loose the rawhide thongs that bound the Mexican's hands and feet, had let the Mexican see all that Crooked Nose had taken in raids, and had let him take his writing stick that he called *un lápiz.* Crooked Nose had even drawn his knife and sliced the stick so that the gray lead showed and allowed the Mexican to make his numbers and do what he called *aritmética.*

The Mexican with the glasses over his eyes had counted all the coins, all the papers, everything Crooked Nose's braves had stolen from that House On Wheels north of the border in the land of the bluecoats, things taken from the pale eyes and Mexican miserable beings who dug in the ground for rocks to sell to other miserable beings on both sides of the border between the Mexicans, the bluecoats, and the killers of Mangas Coloradas.

Once he had counted everything and had carved with his lead stick a number at the bottom of the second page, Crooked Nose had brought one of the old rifles used by the bluecoats to the north. It was not the rifle that Bluecoat With Golden Hair Longer Than The Hair On Some Pale-Eyes Squaws was promising to give to Crooked Nose and his war party . . . providing Crooked Nose could offer more pale-eyes money than either the miserable Mexicans or The Pale Eyes In Gray Who Once Fought And Still Hates Our Enemy.

Crooked Nose had tossed the old rifle, what the pale eyes called a Springfield trapdoor carbine, 1873 model, at the eyeglass-donning Mexican's bare, bloodied feet covered with cactus needles and cuts from rocks.

"*¿Cuántos?*"

Beneath the glasses, the Mexican's dark eyes had widened. The fool did not understand how superior the Apaches were to Mexicans. Of course, Apaches had learned the language of the Mexicans. Mexicans were too stupid to learn the tongue of the Apaches.

"How many?" the Mexican had responded in his own tongue. "Do you mean how many . . . Maybe . . . you wish to know how many of these —" he had patted the stock of the rifle the bluecoats north of the border called a Springfield carbine — "you can buy for this." He patted the deerskin bag that held all Crooked Nose's men had taken from pale eyes north of there and the miserable Mexicans all over the Apache country. "Is that what you wish to know?"

Crooked Nose had not answered. He had no use talking to a Mexican more than he needed to, and he had said enough.

The Mexican had realized this. He had scratched his earlobe, the one Badger Killer's youngest wife had not sliced off back on the road to Agua Prieta.

Eventually, the man with the glasses had shrugged his shoulders and shaken his head. *"No mucho,"* he had answered. *"Lo siento."* Then he had shrugged as if apologizing and said, *"Diez, doce, quince a lo sumo. ¿Quién sabe?"*

Ten. Crooked Nose had sighed. No more than fifteen.

He'd stepped away.

Crooked Nose breathed deep. All of that work, all of the raids, all of that time spent not acting as Apache braves but as pale eyes and Mexicans, robbing for plunder, not for glory. All of this time wasted, for Crooked Nose's war parties had not stolen enough money to buy enough new Springfield rifles with their sticking sticks to arm the twenty-four braves who rode with him, and that did not include the six women who, many wise Apaches thought, were much braver, smarter, and better fighters than Badger Killer or his friends.

Badger Killer would be having fun, now . . . at Crooked Nose's expense. If he had enough tizwin, the weak Apache beer, he might even start spouting off his silly talk that he should become leader of Crooked Nose's men, that Crooked Nose should wander off into the Sierra Madres to die or just learn to cook maize with the old

199

Apache women.

Crooked Nose returned and knelt by the Mexican who had told him how many weapons Crooked Nose's money would buy. He stared at the man's big eyes made bigger by the glasses he wore over his eyes, and Crooked Nose reached down and touched the Mexican's shoulder.

"Lo siento," he said in the miserable man's own tongue.

But deep down, Crooked Nose was not sorry. He rose and nodded at the squaws, who began shrieking with joy and ran toward the bound Mexican, naked and sweating and scared out of his mind. They began working their knives on him.

The Mexican screamed, but his screams would be lost among the tall rocks and the endless sky.

No, Crooked Nose did not enjoy that. It did not make him feel brave. But, well, the man would be dead soon. Besides, he was a Mexican. And Crooked Nose hated all Mexicans.

CHAPTER 34

"Well, hell," Sam Florence said as he reined in the pinto horse. He stared at the canyon ahead, shifted the tobacco to the other side of his jaw, and leaned back in the saddle.

Grat Holden nudged his Morgan up alongside Florence and drew the Winchester from the scabbard, planting the stock on his thigh and keeping his right hand in the lever, ready.

The canyon before them was narrow, with high steep sides of craggy boulders and a few trees. The tops on both sides looked barren, but there were plenty of nooks and crevasses just below the ridgeline for Apaches or bandits to wait. Holden studied the bottom, seeing some dead juniper trees and a few places where boulders had toppled over. It was a straight path that began a descent about halfway through. Beyond the canyon the country likely flattened out for a while. A few miles farther lay the village of Rancho Los Cielos.

"Is there another way around?" he whispered.

"Sure. Plenty of ways to get there." Sam Florence spit juice onto a cactus. "East and west of here. Main road, in fact, is over yonder about three miles."

"If I were an Apache," Holden said, "I'd think this would make an ideal spot to set up an ambush."

"I would, too," the old scout said, "and I'm not Apache."

Ben Masterson eased his horse alongside Holden's. The one-time sergeant had his Springfield cradled across his lap, gloved finger in the trigger guard and thumb on the hammer. He said nothing.

"We could take that main road," Holden suggested.

"Sure. We could take the main road or follow a coyote. Could make our own road, too. It's not like you're going to run into any fences or farmers who don't want you crossing their property."

"Then why are we here?" Masterson asked.

Florence leaned forward, and pushed back the brim of his hat. He turned and locked his gaze on Grat Holden.

"What kind of name is Grat?"

It wasn't the question Holden expected. He answered, though. "Short for Grattan. My mother's maiden name."

"You like it?"

"Grat? Or Grattan?"

"Either." Florence turned away and spit again.

"Not particularly. Either one. Grat's easier to handle. My folks didn't give me any say in the matter, though."

"Got a middle name?"

Holden stared at the man, wondering if Florence had lost his reason, or if he was playing some prank. Still, he had been brought up to respect his elders, and Sam Florence had saved his life and Ben Masterson's life, back in that other canyon they had passed through.

"Roosevelt." Holden almost blushed. "I've no idea where that one came from."

Florence laughed. "They stacked the deck against you, sonny." He leaned over so he could have a better view of Ben Masterson. "And you, bub?"

"Benjamin Patrick Masterson. And you know it's not polite in this country to ask a man his name."

"Yeah," Florence said. "But I always want to know the name of the folks I'm gonna die with." He sighed.

"We don't have to die," Holden said softly. "At least . . . not here."

"We don't. Maybe we won't." Florence nodded at the trail ahead. "But you think a mite, Lieutenant. You served under Captain Foster. Put yourself in his place. He just took four wagonloads of Springfield rifles, pig-stickers, and ammunition to Mexico. Stolen from the United States Army. So what's he thinking? And what's he doing? And what's he planning?"

CHAPTER 35

The image of Jed Foster popped into Holden's mind. He saw that bright smile, the cocky gleam in his eyes, the hat cocked at a rakish angle. Daring anyone to try to stop him, knowing his luck always held.

"Well, he knows even Colonel Smythe will send pursuit."

"How many?"

"Not a full force," Holden answered faster, more certain. "Mexico would consider that an invasion, an act of war. Smythe can't risk that. Jed knows it."

Holden nodded. Jed Foster had served under Carlton Smythe long enough to know that his vanity and his fear of failure would prevent the colonel from contacting Mexican authorities and informing them of the stolen rifles — and of Foster's likely plan to sell them to start a bloodbath.

"Six men," the lieutenant said. "No more than ten. No. Six. That would be the most.

Out of uniform."

Florence nodded his head. "Yeah. But Jed Foster would have forgotten just how big a miser the colonel is."

"Instead of six, he gets three," Masterson said.

"Two," Sam Florence corrected. "I'm just along for the ride, boys. It just so happens that this ride takes me . . . us . . . through this here death trap."

Holden breathed in deeply and said without needing Florence's prodding, "So Foster thinks six men. He knows we wouldn't likely take the main road. Too many travelers."

Sam Florence was grinning.

"But" — Holden nodded as he confirmed his theory, at least in his mind — "he has to make sure. He'll leave a couple of his men on the road there to keep watch."

"Just a couple?" Florence asked.

Holden answered quickly. "He doesn't have that many men with him. Not enough to watch everywhere or set up an ambush at every possible location. And he knows that that Rebel general —"

"Colonel," Sam Foster corrected.

"Colonel. Yes. Those unreconstructed Rebs know about the Springfields. So do the Apaches. And the Mexican revolutionaries —"

"Bandits."

"So be it. They'll want to get those weapons cheaper. By stealing them. So he'll have to keep the bulk of his men with the wagons."

"Or hide the wagons," Ben Masterson said.

"Maybe. But hiding four wagons loaded down with all that iron won't be easy. He can't bury them. There's not enough time. His deadline is coming up, and anyone paying his ransom will want to see the merchandise before they hand over the money. Especially General . . . Colonel . . . whatever his name is."

"Muncie," Florence said. "Will Muncie."

"So," Masterson said, "how does our capt'n protect his merchandise? Keep it safe if he can't spare that many men?"

"I don't know," Holden said. He thought for a minute and then stopped. "And that's not our concern for the moment."

"Right-o!" Florence slapped his thigh and smiled. "You might make captain, sonny. Major even. If you live."

"Right now," Holden said, "I'll settle for the living part."

"Then here's a thought," Masterson said. "We leave here and take the main road. Not all of us at once, but one at a time. They'll be expecting two, four, six men together. One man might not arouse suspicion."

Florence nodded. "Not bad." He eyed Holden. "What do you think, Major?"

Holden thought and then asked, "How busy is that road, Mr. Florence?"

The scout shrugged. "It sure ain't Front Street in Tombstone when the miners get paid. Depends on the season and the day. I know the season . . . but not the day. A few travelers."

"They could pick us off one at a time?" Holden asked.

"If they were so inclined."

"Why would they do that?" Masterson asked.

"What if Jed Foster were watching? He'd recognize you and me . . . and Mr. Florence."

"Son," the scout said, "let's drop that Mister part. Mr. Florence makes me feel older than I really am."

Holden didn't pay attention. He kept answering Masterson's question. "And if you did get past those watchdogs, we'd be entering Rancho Los Cielos alone. If Foster's not on the road, he'd be waiting in that town, most likely."

"He'll be wherever the Springfields are," Masterson pointed out.

Holden's head nodded in confirmation. "And those Springfields might be parked on the main street in Rancho Los Cielos. We just don't know. I don't think we can risk riding into town one at a time."

Masterson thought, frowned, and finally nodded. "That's why I am . . . or was . . . a sergeant. Not a shavetail second lieutenant."

"Soon to be major," Florence said with a grin.

"If he lives," Holden added.

Holden let out a heavy sigh, and studied the Winchester he was carrying.

"We could," Masterson said, "take another road or follow that coyote Florence was suggesting."

"We could." Holden nodded and eared back the hammer on the Winchester. "But we're outnumbered. I'd like to reduce the odds a bit." He tilted his jaw toward the canyon's entrance. "I'll ride in. You work your way up that side of the ridge, Masterson. Florence" — he looked at the old scout — "I can't ask you to do a thing. Like you said, you're just riding along with us till we get to town. And I reckon we can find our way from here."

Florence swung out of the saddle, and drew his rifle from the scabbard.

"You can't ask me to do a damned thing, Mr. Grattan Roosevelt Holden, but I can do what I please. And it pleases me to work my way up this side of the canyon."

Holden wet his lips. Masterson was tethering his gelding to the branch of a juniper a few yards back before the canyon began. Florence was leading his pinto to the other side, and after tethering it, he reached into his saddlebag and pulled out an extra box of ammunition.

Masterson started up the rocky edge. "I'd like to be riding my horse into Rancho Los Cielos real soon. I could use a beer about now."

He moved up the slope like a cougar, quiet, intense. Every sense of his was aware of anything and everything.

Sam Florence nodded at Holden. "Give us five minutes. Probably ain't enough, but if some fellows are waiting for us up above, they'll be getting impatient real quick."

He turned to go, but Holden called out, careful not to speak too loudly. "What's your full name?"

The old scout turned and beamed. "Why, sonny, don't you know it ain't polite in this country to ask a man his name? If he wants you to know it, he'll tell you himself."

Then he was gone.

Holden felt himself grin. He waited. Those five minutes passed almost instantly, and he kicked his horse and walked into the darkening, deepening death trap.

CHAPTER 36

The best of his bunch, which wasn't saying much, went into Mariscos out of breath.

Jed Foster was sitting alone at a poker table, dealing blackjack to himself and his imaginary partner. A cup of coffee rested near his revolver, the long barrel pointed at the entrance to the saloon.

"They're comin'," said the man who called himself Russell.

Foster looked at his cards. He had a ten of diamonds and a six of spades. Sixteen. His imaginary opponent had a four of clubs showing. Ignoring the man in the doorway, Foster said aloud, "I'll stay." He reached and turned the card lying facedown over. It was the ten of spades. He dealt another card up. Eight of hearts.

"Busted." Foster grinned. "I win." He turned back to Russell, a tall man in blue jeans, black boots, and a tan shield-front shirt. A battered gray Stetson sat on his head and on his hips were two Navy Colts that had been converted to take brass cartridges in .38 caliber.

"Which way?" Foster asked.

"The road that leads south."

Foster sank back into his chair. He picked up the cup and sipped coffee, blowing on it to cool it off. The bartender had just topped it off a minute before Russell came in with the news.

"South." Foster sipped again. *South.* That wouldn't be any soldiers the imbecile Colonel Carlton Smythe sent and — He stiffened. Had Smythe showed backbone and common sense and alerted the Mexican officials?

"How many?"

"Lot of dust. Fifteen. Sixteen. Somewhere around there. Traveling at a trot. I figure it's the greaser army."

Not enough. The Mexican army or the *Rurales* would have sent twice that many, at the least, had they known what they were dealing with. And Foster just would not accept the notion that Carlton Smythe could ever do the right thing, the logical thing. So if not the Mexicans, then who?

Not Apaches. Russell and the others on sentry duty would never have seen any dust. They wouldn't have seen a damned thing until the Apaches were killing them . . . silently.

Not Amonte Negro and his bandits, either. If that stupid Mexican had planned on trying anything, he would have done it by now, and Foster figured he had paid Negro and his boys off with his gift of the new Springfields and the chore he had asked them to do. That would occupy their time.

He laughed and rose. "Did you see a guidon? A flag? Some banner in the breeze?"

Russell's dirty head nodded. "That's why we figured them to be greasers. The Mex army."

"No." Foster picked up the Colt and holstered it. "It's not the *Rurales* or the army of Mexico. Stay in here, Russell. Cover me from the doorway. Don't shoot unless you hear the whole world end in thunder."

After pulling his hat down low, he started out the door, looked around and smiled at the four wagons still waiting in the street, guarded by one man per wagon. The mules and other livestock stood contentedly in the corral next to the saloon across the street. He turned back to Russell and asked, "How far away?"

"Close by now," Russell answered. "Like I said, they was raising a lot of dust. Trotting pretty hard."

"Good."

Foster left Mariscos and when he was in the center of the street, he looked at the men guarding the wagons. "We'll be having company joining us soon, boys. Don't kill them unless my luck runs out and they kill me . . . which won't happen. So make sure you don't make any mistakes. Do that, and I'll have to kill you."

As his smile widened, Jed Foster hurried through the dust and into *La Cantina Que No Tiene Nombre,* The Cantina That Has No Name.

He whipped his hat off and bowed at the stunning Soledad Tadeo, who sat in a chair, drying her glistening wet hair with a towel. A bowl of soapy water was on the table in front of her. Foster could smell the fragrance of yucca. She was beautiful, but her dark eyes gazed at him with hate.

"Your monthly bath, señorita?" he asked.

She replied with an indelicate and quite offensive phrase.

He laughed again.

"Well, once you've made yourself present-able, I think you might like to watch a conversation I am about to have outside with some of your dear pal Amonte Negro's competitors. They want the rifles as bad, perhaps even worse, than your, ahem, revolutionary. I thought that you could watch as we do some horse-trading. Then you can tell your boyfriend —"

"He is not my boyfriend," she said icily.

"Well. You can tell your heroic fighter for the people what he has to compete against."

By then, he heard the hooves pounding outside. Russell was right. Those boys were not dillydallying at all.

"I can't keep my guests waiting." Foster bowed, blew Soledad Tadeo a kiss, and told the bartender, "I'd keep my head low and my face out of sight, amigo."

Casually, Jed Foster walked back outside.

CHAPTER 37

Colonel Will Muncie lifted his gauntleted left hand and brought his Andalusian stallion, the grayish color of gunmetal, to a halt. The dozen men riding behind him all stopped their horses. Sabers in scabbards rattled, leather creaked, and the horses began blowing or urinating. Muncie used that moment to remove his deerskin gauntlets and begin pounding his chest and thighs, trying to remove the dust from his new French-made Confederate uniform.

The long-haired rapscallion and miserable Yankee stepped out of the doorway of some pathetic watering hole to Muncie's right. The man was a traitor. Worse, he was a cocky traitor. Muncie would have had an officer in his legion flogged for showing that kind of attitude. Drummed him out of the service. Maybe even had him shot by a firing squad. No, that was a death for a soldier, not a traitor. Jed Foster — No,

Muncie would have hanged that type of man. He might hang Jed Foster yet.

He decided to ignore the Yankee soldier and as he beat his clothes, he looked at the four freight wagons in the street. The tailgates were open. He could see the canvas covering boxes. To his amazement, some of the canvas had been rolled up and tied near the front of the wagon. The boxes were there, just sitting there in the back of one of the wagons, beckoning.

Wooden boxes, long, firmly made and stamped on the side.

SPRINGFIELD ARMORY
Springfield, Massachusetts
US RIFLE, CALIBER .45-70-405,
MILITARY

One crate had even been opened, and Muncie saw the emblem — two crossed cannon with a black cannonball at the center and flames shooting above the wide oval that covered parts of the crisscrossed cannon. It was burned into the lid leaning up against other boxes.

SPRINGFIELD ARMORY read the top of the circle. And at the bottom was SINCE 1794.

He wet his lips. He felt envious. He could

taste victory. The breeze picked up and he heard the battle jack flapping in the wind. Like old times. He could smell the battle, hear the muskets, see the banners waving and brave men dying. Will Muncie almost smiled.

Then Jed Foster had to speak.

"You're early, Colonel," the traitor said. "Our deal is not scheduled for a few more days. Not here, either. Remember? On Independence Day."

Muncie stiffened. *July fourth.* He would never celebrate that day again. The day Vicksburg surrendered. The day Gettysburg was lost for good. The day his only son was . . .

Foster finished his sentence. "At The Canyon of The Sorrows."

Sorrows. Muncie's shoulders slumped. He had gone through enough sorrows. But he regained his composure, found his dignity, and unbuttoned the coat just enough to shove his gauntlets inside. He took a quick look at Foster and the men and the nearby buildings. Four men in the wagons, plus the traitor. Likely a few more inside the buildings. But nowhere near enough to survive if Will Muncie ordered a fight.

But that must wait.

He pointed a finger at the open crate.

"Wanted, suh, to make sure I would be biddin' on merchandise in the best order. But seein' how that lid is open, well, a good rainstorm might give me cause to lower my bid on . . . July fourth."

"Reese," Foster said. "Why don't you hop up on the back of that wagon and put the lid back on where it belongs. But be careful. Don't rock the wagon even a hair. Don't want our friend the colonel to have to lower his bid and reduce our profits."

The gunman leaned his rifle, an old Henry, against the rear wheel and started to pull himself into the wagon bed.

"Gentle," Foster reminded him. "And show the colonel one of those babies."

Reese moved slowly and gingerly bent to pull out a Springfield. He held it up, and Will Muncie's eyes beamed.

"Two hundred and forty-nine, Colonel," Jed Foster said. "Just like that one, sir. I'd let you borrow it. But you're all dusty. And you don't want to buy a rifle that has dust on it. Do you?"

Reese took the hint and returned the rifle to the crate. He slid the lid up and onto the top, but did not nail it shut. Slowly . . . agonizingly slow . . . he moved to the side of the wagon and crawled down. Most men would have jumped. He took the Henry and resumed his stance.

Muncie wet his lips.

"What do you think these rifles will go for?"

Foster shrugged. "Well, I think I'll set my minimum purchase at fifty a rifle."

The colonel laughed. "When the factory would charge thirty?"

"You can always place an order in Springfield, Colonel. But that would mean you'd have to do business with a Yankee outfit in a damn Yankee state."

"Do you think anyone in this country can come up with that much money?"

Foster grinned. "Well, sir. I don't know. But let's say that you and Señor Amonte and that old Crooked Nose himself don't have enough money to make it worth my while. Well, then I'll just travel south. There are other outfits who might have enough money. Maybe even the Mexican army. Or since I find myself now to be a man of leisure, I might travel all the way to South America. This country is just full of opportunities."

The colonel leaned forward and put his hand on the flap of the revolver in its holster.

"And what would you think if we decided to take these guns for ourselves? Right now. Just take them from you and leave you and your men dying in the dust."

"It wouldn't be quite honest, Colonel. Not the way a Southern gentleman does business."

"I could crush you like an ant."

Colonel Will Muncie pulled the flap loose.

CHAPTER 38

"Colonel, Colonel, Colonel . . ." Jed Foster chided the ex-Confederate officer as if he were addressing a child, or maybe a boorish old man who had lost a war, a son, and most, if not all, of his faculties. "Do you think you are dealing with a fool?"

"A damned fool!" Colonel Muncie thundered. "Not only that, but a damned Yankee fool! I can take those rifles from you right now."

"And we'd all be in hell, Colonel" — Foster shook his head — "if Lucifer could find enough of us left worth his while." He turned just a little and pointed to the seat of the nearest wagon. "What do you see on the driver's bench, my good ol' Rebel colonel? You aren't wearing eyeglasses, so I reckon you are like most old men in this country. You can't read a newspaper six inches before your very eyes, but you can see the snow on a mountaintop forty miles away. That wagon's maybe twenty yards from you right now, Colonel. So tell me, what do you see?"

"A bottle," Muncie snapped. He roared, "Of gin or something clear. Not Kentucky bourbon, suh."

"I wouldn't know, Colonel. About Kentucky bourbon, I mean. Now, were we talking about Pennsylvania bourbon, well . . ." Foster laughed at the look on Muncie's face. The fool probably thought all bourbon hailed from Kentucky. "Of course, if I recollect correctly, Kentucky wasn't a member of the Confederacy, either."

"But a number of Kentuckians fought on our side."

"And lived or died to regret it."

The colonel's face flushed with anger, and his right hand gripped the handle on the revolver.

"Colonel," Foster called out coldly. "That's not gin in that bottle, sir. You want to die and take me and all your boys and most of this dot on a map . . . and every last one of those new Springfield rifles . . . you go ahead and pull that hog leg."

Muncie's hand seemed to be glued to the revolver's walnut handle, but the pistol remained stuck in the holster.

Soledad Tadeo had stepped into the doorway of *La Cantina Que No Tiene Nombre,* The Cantina That Has No Name. The old skinflint of a bartender, however, must have taken Foster's advice and was hiding, shaking in his sandals on the floor behind a keg of whiskey.

The sight of the beautiful woman excited Jed Foster. He loved to play in front of an audience, especially before a stunning woman like that black-haired, dark-skinned girl. "Look at the other wagons, Colonel," he commanded.

The old man's eyes moved. That pleased Foster, as well.

There was a West Point graduate, class of 1843, a hero of the war down in Mexico, a man who had served with distinction in the United States Army for eighteen years before resigning to go home and fight for the doomed Confederacy. There he was . . . obeying orders from a mere captain, and a blue-bellied captain, at that.

Foster did not glance behind him. He just watched Muncie's eyes as they moved from wagon to wagon . . . specifically from driver's seat to driver's seat on each freight wagon. Even more specifically, from whiskey bottle to whiskey bottle that stood in the center of each seat. He also studied the men behind the old soldier. They were looking at the bottles, too, and he could see a few brows start to knot, a few men glance at the companion mounted on the next horse over.

Confuse and confound your enemy. That was another thing Custer had drilled into Foster's brain. *That's half the battle. Confuse him, and you have a fine chance at killing him. And even if you do not kill him, confounding him will send him retreating with his men in wild panic and his reputation ruined.*

Colonel Muncie's gaze once again landed on Jed Foster. "Your drivers, suh," the colonel said in that slow drawl, "appear to have a preference for gin. I certainly hope they do not imbibe too much of such liquor, for I would sure hate for your wagons to suffer some terrible accident." He said that softly, sarcastically, but that was an act.

Foster knew the bottles had left the man confused and confounded. Muncie wanted to sound confident, but the voice came across as concerned. Uncertain.

The battle, Foster already knew, had been won.

"Colonel Muncie, my good man." He laughed. "You fought down here against the Mexicans before you took up with that losing army of the South." He liked to see Muncie's face redden and those eyes just about pop out of his face. "You served in armies of the North and the South for a good long time. Surely, sir, you must remember that any teamster or any soldier worth his salt would never, not in a hundred years, not in a thousand years, leave a bottle of gin or bourbon — Pennsylvania or Kentucky — corked and sitting in plain view of other teamsters, other soldiers, other vagabonds, and wastrels. Because if he did that, well, all he would find would be an empty bottle waiting for him. Now, sir, isn't that right? From your own personal experience?"

Muncie removed his hand from the revolver. He was at a loss for words.

The Mexican beauty had stepped out farther. She had only glanced at the bottles on the wagons and was focused entirely on Colonel Muncie and Captain Foster.

"What are you saying, suh?" It took Muncie a good long time to work up enough courage to ask the question. His voice came out as strained and, to Foster's delight, helpless.

Jed Foster stepped closer to the horses. "I'm saying, Colonel, that you are a damned fool. That's right. You're a damned fool for treating me like a damned fool. Did you think I'd just leave those rifles out here so you could swoop down like one of Nathan Bedford Forrest's Southern caballeros or some of Mosby's irregulars? Did you think that I would not expect you to try such a cowardly act? What happened to Southern honor, Colonel? Have you spent so many years hiding down here that you have forgotten all that made Southern men, Confederate officers, idolized by all the good folks of the South. *Suh.*" He mocked Muncie's thick accent. "General Robert E. Lee is a-rollin' in his grave at ya. Ya lack honor, Colonel Muncie, ol' boy. But I daresay what y'all lack in fine, Southern, gentlemanly honor ya make up with wagonloads of stupidity."

He palmed his Colt, cocked the hammer, and whirled. But he did not aim the revolver at Colonel Muncie, nor any of his men. He pointed the pistol at the closest wagon.

CHAPTER 39

"Tell me, Colonel Muncie!" Jed Foster bellowed. "Have you ever heard of nitroglycerin?" He kept his back to the former Southern aristocrat who had become a penny-ante thief south of the border. Foster was gambling again, but this hand, he felt, was a winner. He did not even try to keep Colonel Will Muncie in view out of the corner of his eye. He just grinned, and aimed that big .45 at a bottle of gin that was only half full.

He heard the gasps from Muncie's men. Several of their horses stepped back and stamped and snorted, as if they knew what nitroglycerin was capable of doing. Most likely, Muncie's boys were showing their true colors and just wanted to get out of the miserable little village in the middle of nowhere as fast as they could.

"I'll give you a history lesson, Colonel. This instructor I had at West Point — before

I got expelled — was utterly fascinated by this harmless little liquid. An Italian chemist concocted it back around the Mexican War, maybe just before it ended or a year or so after it was over. I'm not that good at dates. But I do remember that colonel at the Point just marveling over how a lot of folks experimenting with nitroglycerin at some factory had blown themselves and most of the factory to bits at some town in Sweden. That was in '64 . . . just before the commandant called me to his office and told me to get the hell out of his academy."

Foster grinned and glanced at the girl. She did not seem afraid of the nitro or, for that matter, anything else. Then again, she was just a stupid, ignorant Mexican girl who likely had never even heard of nitroglycerin.

He kept talking, mostly to give the shapely little wench a lesson.

"Not too long after that, some Germans tried to make it available as explosives. They blew themselves to bits, too. Finally, folks worked very carefully . . . and I do mean very carefully . . . so they could ship a handful of crates of this stuff across the ocean and all the way to California . . . to help build the railroad that connected the western United States and her territories with the eastern United States. When one of those crates blew up the Wells Fargo office in San Francisco and reduced fifteen Californios to little bitty pieces, that got the transportation of nitroglycerin banned in California. And many other places. Dynamite took over. It's a little safer. But doesn't pack the wallop . . . or produce the fear . . . that nitro does. Still, you can make your own nitroglycerin. A lot of mines do that by sweating out dynamite sticks. I'm not sure it's any safer, but — Well, it's highly available in places where railroads are being built and where mines are making lots and lots of money.

"Like the Territory of Arizona. And —" Foster turned around, but kept his arm steady, and the sight of the .45 trained on one bottle on one wagon. "Well, you see, Colonel, I have plenty of access to plenty of mines and enough nitroglycerin to blow those rifles, me and you, and most, if not all, of this town . . . all the way to hell and gone."

He waited.

Colonel Muncie's face glowed with sweat. The men behind him looked deathly white.

Jed Foster grinned and thanked Ascanio Sobrero for all he had done when he had pretty much discovered nitroglycerin back in 1840-something.

"You wouldn't blow yourself up, man," Colonel Muncie said, but his voice could not hide his fear.

"If I don't get paid, Colonel, you don't get guns. Nobody gets nothing. You deal in money. I deal in death. So what's it going to be, Colonel? Money for Springfields? Or the most horrible death you and your boys can imagine?"

The colonel did not answer. So Foster told him, "The Fourth of July, Colonel, at The Canyon of The Sorrows. Around noon. Don't worry, Colonel. I won't have the band strike up 'The Battle Hymn of the Republic' when you ride in to make your bid."

Foster saw that Muncie was not ready to quit. Not yet. The man didn't like the taste of defeat, so Foster came up with another gamble. He was confident he would win this bet, too.

"I'm told, Colonel, that you are a sporting man. That you like to bet on horses and games of billiards and, on certain occasions, other games of chance."

Muncie said coldly, "So?"

"So, Colonel. I hate for you to make that journey all the way here for nothing. I tell you what. I'll give you a chance. Reese."

The gunman near the first wagon grunted.

"Draw your Colt, Reese, and keep it

aimed at the bottle. Just so our guests don't get any fool notions."

Reese did not appear to like the order. He stood closest to the wagon, which meant he would not only be the first to die, but he would likely be chewed up worse than anyone in the town. And if he pulled the trigger that destroyed the gin bottle, he would also be committing suicide.

Still, he pulled the Colt from its holster, and aimed it at the bottle. The cocking of the hammer sounded like bells ringing in the stillness of the day.

CHAPTER 40

Once Reese's .36-caliber Navy Colt was aimed at the gin bottle Jed Foster slowly lowered the hammer on his Colt and drop it into the holster. He winked at the Mexican girl and grinned at Will Muncie.

"Pick one of your boys, Colonel. *Mano a mano.* Man to man. Him against me. We face each other. You call it, Colonel. On three. If he kills me . . . or even just wounds me . . . you can ride out with all the Springfield rifles. But if I win, you ride out and don't give us any more trouble. You can take your boy home and bury him."

"What if you just wound him?" Muncie asked.

Foster laughed. "Colonel? Really? I never leave a man wounded, suh. That ain't my style, ol' boy."

Now the girl had moved to the hitching rail. She leaned against it and studied both Jed Foster and the crazy old Southern officer and gentleman. She was sizing up the grizzled old soldier, wondering what he would do.

Foster knew, of course. Will Muncie's honor . . . and the honor of all Southern soldiers . . . had been challenged.

Muncie twisted in the saddle. He looked at his men. Every hand shot up. Every man was willing to die for Colonel Will Muncie, and that, Jed Foster had to admit, was a surprise. And Jed Foster did not find himself surprised very often.

Then again, maybe it wasn't that surprising. Those old fools weren't willing to put their lives on the line for the stupid colonel. Foster had challenged Southern pride. They weren't volunteering for a duel to the death for Will Muncie. They were fighting for Southern honor. They were fighting for themselves.

"Corporal Bowdre," Muncie called out in a soft voice, sounding weak.

A slight man with buck teeth and a brown mustache slid out of his saddle, and handed the reins to the younger trooper mounted next to him.

"Thank you, Colonel." He sounded pleased and confident.

Foster studied him closely.

He had to be in his middle forties. Too

old to be faster than Foster, who tried to guess why the colonel had selected this man, sentenced the particular gallant gentleman to death. Unmarried. Yes, that had to be the reason. Or a man with no relatives, no brothers or sons or neighbors serving alongside him.

It was as good a reason as any, Foster thought. Not that it mattered.

He wasn't doing it for show, although he felt certain that's what Colonel Will Muncie figured. Likely, Soledad Tadeo figured something similar. But Foster felt out of practice at that kind of thing — a real gunfight. Man to man. Separated by twenty paces or so. He had not done anything like that in years. It got his heart racing. He could taste the sweat. He enjoyed it.

He'd always thought it the ultimate gamble.

Since he would have to face Apaches, the US Army, and possibly more . . . *Rurales* and those damned Mexican bandits . . . he needed all the practice he could get.

If that practice had to be against an over-the-hill former Confederate soldier, well, so be it. Everyone had to die sooner or later. Foster decided he would make this one quick. Besides, Colonel Will Muncie had taken too much of Foster's time already.

Foster wanted to sip some tequila, and maybe get better acquainted with that handsome little filly who was watching him now with intense interest.

And yet, Corporal Bowdre demanded more of Foster's attention.

The old man — old by Foster's reckoning and standards — removed one of his gloves, the one on his right hand, and laid it atop the seat of his saddle. The left glove Bowdre kept on. Probably, Foster surmised, the corporal was right-handed. Fitting a gloved finger into the trigger guard of an 1851 Navy was a hard thing to do. Especially squeezing a gloved finger into the trigger guard in a fight where half a second could decide between living and dying.

Next, Corporal Bowdre unbuttoned his tunic and removed it, folding it gracefully and laying it atop that lone glove. He stepped back, found the sun, and since it would be neither behind the corporal or Foster, removed his hat as well and placed it on the horn of his saddle.

Corporal Bowdre then stepped away from the horses and Colonel Muncie and the command, unfastened the flap over the holster, and bent it so that it would not interfere with his draw. After taking a few steps away, he stopped and pulled on the belt, twisting it so that the holster now lay against Bowdre's right thigh instead of his left, as was military fashion. Finally, he pushed the holster down a little bit, lower on his hip.

He reached for the butt of the Navy. "May I?" he asked respectfully.

Foster bowed. "By all means, Corporal."

"Thank you, suh." Bowdre slowly drew the long-barreled relic from the Civil War out of his holster.

The gun had not even been modernized to take modern cartridges. Foster could see the percussion caps on the cylinder of the old pistol.

Keeping the muzzle of the Colt pointed at the dirt and away from Foster, Corporal Bowdre rotated the cylinder, checking the loads, the caps, and making sure no dust or debris would keep the cylinder from rotating once he cocked the hammer.

He would fan the hammer, Foster decided. That's why he had kept the glove on his left hand.

Corporal Bowdre had been picked by Colonel Muncie for another reason. The man was a quick-draw artist. A real shootist. He might be old, might use a weapon that most gunmen found antiquated, but Bowdre was a real professional.

And that made Jed Foster happy.

This would be a good show. A bet that was not stacked. This would be for real.

CHAPTER 41

Bowdre slowly slipped the old cap-and-ball Navy Colt into the holster and stepped into the street, closer to the cantina where Soledad Tadeo still leaned against the hitching rail. He stopped about six feet to Tadeo's right and dropped his arms to his waist.

"Do you mind?" Foster asked, and tapped the handle of his Colt with his trigger finger.

"No objections at all, my friend," Bowdre said. "I have always been one to observe courtesy among professionals."

"You are truly a professional, my friend." Foster pulled the Schofield from the holster, drew the hammer to half-cock, and rotated the cylinder. He stopped at the empty chamber, and fished a spare .45 cartridge from his pocket, and filled the hole with the brass casing. Finally, he pulled the hammer to full-cock, and then softly lowered it to its resting place.

With his eyes on Bowdre, Foster let the

heavy pistol drop into the holster. He walked away from the wagons of rifles and Colonel Muncie, and moved casually toward The Cantina That Has No Name. Yet his eyes never left Corporal Bowdre.

The man might be a professional gunfighter, but not all professionals were completely trustworthy.

I know, Foster thought to himself, *that I'm not.*

He grinned. He also made sure not to let Muncie or Muncie's other riders out of his sight.

This would truly be a test.

He came to a stop about six feet to Soledad Tadeo's left.

Bowdre raised a finger on his right hand, near the Navy, and pointed at Foster's holster. "You prefer those cannons, I see."

Foster nodded. "A .45 makes sure." He nodded at Bowdre's direction. "Yet I see you like those old Navies."

"They shoot true," Bowdre said. "And the ball stays inside the body of the man who is dead. That .45, it could go through a person and kill a couple innocent bystanders."

Foster chuckled. "Then it is a good thing I'm standing in front of the wagons, Corporal. If I were standing where you are, when I shot you, my .45 slug might've hit one of

241

those bottles of nitroglycerin."

"Wouldn't that be something to see!" Bowdre also laughed slightly. "Don't worry. My .36 ball will stay in your heart."

"I'm not worried," Foster said. "Those wagons are out of range for a kid's toy like a Navy. I mean . . . in this wind."

"There is not much wind, sir," Bowdre said.

Foster laughed again.

The lean Confederate gunfighter turned away from Foster and bowed at Soledad Tadeo. "Ma'am. You'd be wise to return to that saloon. I'm not a wild shot, but when people get hit by bullets, they aren't always so gallant. They shoot wild. I'd hate to see you harmed."

She acted as though she did not hear.

Bowdre shook his head and looked at Foster. "Does she not speak English, Captain?"

"I think she just wants a front-row seat. This kind of show doesn't play very often at Rancho Los Cielos."

"Where were we, Captain?" Bowdre asked.

"Talking about your preference for old Navy Colts."

"Ah, yes. They served Wild Bill Hickok well," Bowdre said. "The Navy .36 was his pistol of choice."

"Indeed." Foster smiled. "Of course, Wild Bill Hickok is dead."

"But not," Bowdre said, "on account of his choice of weapons."

"Indeed, sir, you are right. It was his seating arrangement that led him to cash in his chips."

"How true, Captain Foster. We must all know where we take our seats."

"Yes. Too bad you are seated on the other side. I could use a man like you, Corporal."

"Well," Bowdre said, "such is the way fate deals the cards."

Foster sighed. "I suppose that if I offered you, say, one hundred dollars a day, a bag of gold, and your pick of an 1880 Springfield rifle, you would be repulsed."

"I would be insulted, sir. Once you wear a uniform, you do not disgrace that uniform. Once you give your word, you do not break your word."

"You are truly a Southern gentleman, Corporal Bowdre, and I knew you would be." Foster grinned. "I, of course, am no Southern gentleman. I offer you my sincerest apology."

Bowdre shrugged. "There is no need to apologize, Captain. You were thinking hypothetically. Thinking out loud. And, sir, for your edification, I would have enjoyed serving under your command . . . if you were not a damned bluebelly . . . but . . . well . . . any such union between two men of our backgrounds would have had an unpleasant finish."

Foster nodded. "Yes. Two men like us cannot survive for long. At least, one of us couldn't."

Bowdre laughed. "Sooner or later, we'd have to know, wouldn't we? A couple of fast guns mix like oil and vinegar."

"Or a .36 paper cartridge," Foster said, "in a chamber made for a Colt .45."

Bowdre laughed again, and his laugh was filled with the confidence of a seasoned veteran.

"I'm glad you volunteered, Corporal," Foster said.

"I'm glad Colonel Muncie gave me the opportunity, sir. It has been an honor." Bowdre bowed.

Foster returned the bow. "The honor, Corporal Bowdre, has been all mine."

Each man took a slight step back. Their hands fell just above the handles of their revolvers. They crouched.

Foster's heart raced like a thoroughbred that had just finished the Kentucky Derby. His throat turned dry. He hadn't felt anything like this since before he had met up with Grat Holden just before that ambush near Dos Cabezas. And Grat Holden was nowhere near the man Jed Foster was facing. Grat Holden was a boy. Grat Holden could never kill Jed Foster. But the man in gray named Bowdre?

Such challenges made life worth living.

"Your count, Colonel," Jed Foster said.

"On three," Corporal Bowdre added.

They did not breathe. Nor did they dare blink.

Colonel Will Muncie's voice sounded weak, as though he already knew the outcome. "One . . . two . . . three." Muncie did not even shout the last number.

CHAPTER 42

Foster's right hand shot down for the .45, and the Colt practically leaped into his hand. He saw Bowdre's .36 coming up instantly. Foster dropped to his left and moved closer to the Mexican woman standing by the hitching rail. That, he figured, was one direction a Southerner like Corporal Bowdre would never have anticipated.

Indeed, he had calculated correctly. Corporal Bowdre had aimed in the opposite direction and quickly tried to adjust the .36 Colt's barrel.

All that was happening so fast, no one could say what had exactly happened. They just saw two men slapping leather and clawing their guns. They just heard two gunshots that sounded like one. For all Soledad Tadeo or any of Foster's men or any of Colonel Will Muncie's Rebs could say, no one had even moved. They had just pulled their pistols and fired.

They would be able to say, however, that Corporal Bowdre's body was lifted off the ground and driven back three feet. They would be able to say that Bowdre's .36 slug dug up dust in the street a few feet behind Jed Foster. They would be able to say that the Colt bullet went completely through Bowdre's body and left a fist-sized and gory, bloody hole in the back of his muslin shirt. They would be able to say that Bowdre landed hard, kicking up a mound of dust, bounced up slightly, and rolled onto his side.

His eyes remained open. His mouth was locked in an eternal smile.

Corporal Bowdre was dead. But he had died game.

The woman looked at the dead man, she looked at Jed Foster, and then she stepped away from the hitching rail and moved back to the door, out of the sun. But she did not return inside The Cantina That Has No Name.

"You lose, Colonel," Foster said. "Reese, keep that pistol aimed at one of the nitro bottles . . . in case these Southern gentlemen want to try this bit again." He thumbed back the Colt's hammer, but kept the barrel aimed at the dusty street.

"Colonel. You can leave Bowdre here for

me to bury. Or —"

"He will be buried, suh, in the post cemetery," Muncie said. "He will be buried as a soldier who gave his life for his country."

Two men quickly dismounted. They picked up the corpse of the man who had been incredibly fast with a pistol and carried him to his horse.

They left his smoking Navy .36 in the dirt.

Post cemetery? Foster had to stop from laughing. Deep down, he figured a gunfighter like Bowdre would have preferred to have been buried near the street where he had died. But, well, when you're dead, you don't get a say in such trivial matters.

Foster had to give Colonel Will Muncie credit. The man knew how to make himself look as if he were not turning tail and running away. Muncie straightened, and methodically closed the covering over his revolver in the holster. He found the gauntlets he had stuck in his frock coat, and these he pulled back onto his hands with a show. He straightened his hat, and trained those eyes of a madman directly at Captain Jed Foster.

"Then, suh," Muncie said. "I will see you at that canyon."

"I'll send a man to fetch you, Colonel,"

Foster said, affecting an over-the-top Southern accent. "Since I don't believe you or your boys have had the privilege of visiting that canyon."

The colonel frowned. "I would not say, from the stories that I have heard, that visiting The Canyon of The Sorrows is a privilege, Capt'n."

"You are most correct, Colonel."

"But you happen to know this nefarious place, Capt'n?"

"Well." Foster shrugged his shoulders. "What would you expect from a nefarious scoundrel who wears the blue."

"Indeed."

"I'll see you at The Canyon of The Sorrows, Colonel."

Will Muncie bobbed his head. "Noon. July fourth. I bid you good day, suh."

"Be here on the evening of the third. I will send a guide to take you to the canyon where we shall begin the auction. With luck, you'll ride out of there with plenty of rifles to resume your war."

The colonel saluted.

Jed Foster touched the brim of his hat with the barrel of the Colt and lowered the .45 again, keeping it cocked and aimed at the nearest gin bottle.

"Gentlemen," Muncie called out to his

command. "About face."

The men turned their horses. It wasn't the best Foster had ever seen, but considering just how scared out of their wits those old boys appeared, it ranked pretty good nonetheless.

The flags whipped in the wind. Colonel Muncie yelled out a command, and he led his men out of Rancho Los Cielos.

"Reese," Foster called out softly when the former soldiers of the Confederacy were too far away to hear anything anyone in Rancho Los Cielos said.

"Yes?" the gunman said.

"Mount your horse. Take one of the boys with you. Make sure the man knows how to follow men and not get spotted. Follow Muncie. You ride just far enough out of here to make sure that crazy old coot isn't coming back. Your boy needs to follow him all the way back to his camping spot. He should stay there. Out of sight. With his eyes always open. If Muncie decides on another plan of attack, if he leaves or sends out a rider anywhere before he needs to take off for *El Cañon de Los Dolores,* your man needs to get back to us. That means he's to ride hard and fast and I don't care how much dust he raises."

"You bet, Foster," the man named Reese

said. He appeared happier than a possum on a stump, wanting to get away from the wagons and those bottles of gin as quickly as possible. "Bateman. Get your horse. Make sure you got enough water and jerky to last till the fourth."

When Bateman and Reese were gone, and when the dust from Colonel Muncie's command had faded from view, Jed Foster smiled across the street at the Mexican beauty. He winked at her.

"Did you like the show, Soledad?"

The woman stepped back toward the hitching rail.

Foster moved to the nearest wagon. He reached carefully and took the bottle of gin off the seat, and he grinned at the woman as he held the bottle up as though raising a glass in toast.

"Have you ever tasted nitro, honey?"

She was picking up the Navy .36 that had once belonged to the gunfighter named Bowdre.

Foster suddenly frowned. He saw the dark-skinned woman thumb back the hammer, lift the Colt, and he heard the shot, saw the flame from the muzzle. She missed the bottle.

But Jed Foster was diving into the dirt —

251

while the bottle he had been holding plummeted to the hard, hard ground.

CHAPTER 43

The bottle shattered.

Rancho Los Cielos was not destroyed. The only casualty was a bottle of Old Tom Gin — and Jed Foster's dignity, along with the dignity of many of his men who had dived for cover, begged for forgiveness, or wet their britches.

The bottle struck the ground at an angle, snapping the neck cleanly so quickly that the cork did not even pop out. The jagged edge of the rest of the bottle bounced off the dirt, somersaulted in the air, and smashed to pieces on a rock that rested just inches from a mound of mule droppings. The ground promptly sucked the clear liquid deep into the bowels of the earth.

The liquid was not nitroglycerin. It was gin. Cheap gin at that.

Foster came to his knees, drawing his Colt .45 again, cocking the hammer and drawing a bead on Soledad Tadeo. He did not squeeze the trigger for one very good reason — the Mexican woman had the late Corporal Bowdre's .36-caliber Navy Colt trained on Foster.

For all Jed Foster had joked with the now dead Confederate gunfighter about the accuracy of that particular weapon, he knew any pistol Wild Bill Hickok had used was more than reliable, and although Soledad Tadeo had missed her shot at the bottle Foster had been holding, he didn't think she would miss again.

Foster wet his lips and waited until he had regained the façade of composure. He watched his own men picking themselves off the ground. Some made the sign of the cross. A few tried to crawl a ways to hide the telltale signs of embarrassing urination by coating the front of their trousers with sand.

Eventually, Foster lowered the hammer on his long-barreled revolver and made himself stand.

"You take chances," he told the woman, and made a fine display of sliding the .45 back into the holster. He reached inside a pocket and pulled out the makings of a cigarette.

"No," the woman spoke in English. "I do not."

"You were that sure?" Foster cocked his head and made himself grin. Deep down, though, he wanted to strangle the lousy little wench. He wouldn't be disrespected and embarrassed by some Mexican hussy who hung out in a miserable cantina in the middle of nowhere, raving about and practically worshipping a cut-rate Mexican bandit who pretended to be a patriot of the people and a revolutionary like John Adams, Patrick Henry, and Francis Marion. Foster would have to bide his time, but eventually Soledad Tadeo would rue the day she had ever shamed Jed Foster in front of his men.

She lowered the Navy but did not uncock the pistol, which she kept in her right hand — ready to lift it and pull the trigger quickly and accurately should the need arise.

"All right, señorita, pray tell. What made you call my bluff?"

She did not answer.

"Come on, sweetheart. This is purely for my own education. I want to know how I could fool a man like Colonel Will Muncie and not a charming, wonderful, gorgeous little beauty like yourself." He switched to Spanish. *"Por favor. Concédeme este pequeño deseo."*

She was too far away for Foster to read her eyes, yet she did grant him that wish.

"You left those bottles on the wagons last night."

Foster had to consider this. Had she watched him take the bottles out of the cantina and place them on the hard wooden seats of the wagons? No. No, he wouldn't have made that mistake. He had done that when no one else was looking.

"And you know this," he asked in Spanish, "how?"

She shrugged. "They were not there when I retired to bed. They were there when I awakened to the crow of the rooster."

"A present for the night guards?" he asked in English.

Her head shook.

"Digame," he pleaded. *"La mayoría lo sé."*

She told him in rapid-fire border Spanish . . . almost too fast and too hard for him to comprehend, but his ears remained sharp, and he could make out just enough of what she was saying to realize his mistake. One thing Jed Foster prided himself on was not repeating any mistake.

If bottles of gin, gringo whiskey, or even tequila had been left outside during the night, Soledad Tadeo told Foster, those bottles would have been drained completely empty by the time the rooster crowed to announce the dawn of another day. Soledad

Tadeo had been in Rancho Los Cielos long enough to realize that much about men — Mexican men and *norteamericanos.*

There was, Foster had to concede, a certain amount of truth to that logic. He shook his head and sniggered, correcting himself. There was a hell of a lot more than a certain amount of truth. The little Mexican hussy was dead-on. Lucky for Foster, Colonel Will Muncie didn't know exactly when the bottles had been set on the wagons.

"But," Foster countered, "if my men thought I had placed nitroglycerin on those wagons, that would explain why no one had taken liberties and emptied those bottles."

She shook her head and went on in her Spanish. One would not leave bottles out overnight in such a place as Rancho Los Cielos. Just sitting on a wooden bench? In a place where the wind has been known to blow down trees? Or where an owl might swoop down, or a packrat might climb up to investigate?

"No," she told Foster in Spanish. "You told your mercenaries that those bottles held the potent explosive, but you are not that stupid, even for a *Yanqui.* You are just cocky, like all *norteamericanos.* You think all Mexicans, and especially Mexican women,

257

are stupid. You will pay for your arrogance one day."

Foster laughed, though he told himself that someone would pay for that arrogance, and that someone was Soledad Tadeo. He would enjoy making her pay. And she wouldn't look so beautiful when he was finished with her.

"What," he asked, "if you had been wrong? That I had put nitro in those bottles?"

Chapter 44

"Then," she said in English, "we would all be dead. So be it." She turned to go, saying, *"Los Cielos sería un lugar mejor."* She stopped and added, *"Sin ti y tus asesinos."*

He waved at her and watched her disappear inside the cantina. *Would Los Cielos ever be a better place?* He wondered. He fumed at her remark that it would be better without the presence of himself and his hired men. Did that bandit Amonte Negro do anything for the people there? *Yes,* he told himself, *the uppity witch would pay, and pay dearly.*

For the time being, he had other concerns. "Jesús," he told one of his men. "Get mounted. Just make sure our lovely little lady's pistol shot didn't draw any attention."

The young Mexican asked if he should ride after Muncie.

"No." Foster choked back the insult he wanted to hurl at the idiot. "I think Reese

259

and Bateman will let us know if that's happening. Get to the main road. If anyone's coming or if anyone's holding up and trying to figure out what caused those two shots, gallop back here."

He found another of his men and told him to fetch another bottle from Mariscos. "Put it on the wagon seat to replace the one just shattered.

I don't care what our sassy little witch thinks, Muncie's an idiot and you can fool idiots all the time. Don't drink too much of the gin or tequila or whatever you bring out. Or drink it all and fill it with water. I just want a bottle on all those wagon seats."

Captain Jed Foster walked across the dusty little street to the spot where Corporal Bowdre had fallen and died. The toe of Foster's boot scraped the ground and covered the dark spot of drying blood. Foster thought of the irony, how he could have used a good man, a top gun, like that Rebel gunman, instead of having to rely on the fools he had hired to help him.

On the other hand, if he commanded an army of mercenaries like the late Corporal Bowdre, it would be hard to get rid of them all and be in decent enough shape to make it to the port at Vera Cruz where he could pack up his fortune and sail away. To London, maybe. Or Paris. Or some island in the Mediterranean. Maybe the Sandwich Islands in the Pacific. Or deep down into South America.

Anywhere would suit him.

He twisted the sole of his boot over the blood of Bowdre, spit in the dirt, and crossed the street. A new bottle of gin was resting on the seat of the wagon, and the men under his command were going back to their usual business. He went inside Mariscos and ordered a bowl of green chile stew and a bottle of the best tequila in the town.

He wouldn't get drunk. Getting drunk would be more dangerous than facing a gunman like Corporal Bowdre. He found a seat where he could see the wagons and the door to The Cantina That Has No Name.

The food was filling. The tequila was awful, but most likely, it was the best to be found in Rancho Los Cielos.

He ate. He drank. He watched. Mostly, Captain Jed Foster thought.

So far, he had anticipated everything — except Soledad Tadeo's challenge. The hussy had not only challenged him, she had outthought him, and that was something he could not let happen again. It would not happen again.

He wasn't concerned that much with the Apaches. He brought the Apaches into the game to up the ante, make the Mexicans under Amonte Negro and Will Muncie and his Southern losers think more, raise more money, get a little bit scared at the competition they would have to deal with.

Muncie had played into Foster's hands exactly as expected. And those diehard Southern expatriates had scurried out of that border town with their tails tucked between their legs and their best gunman slung over his saddle with a .45 hole through the center of his body. Muncie would still be a nuisance, but Foster had never met a Reb he could not outfight or outsmart.

And the Mexican bandit that little girl across the street worshipped? Foster had paid off Amonte Negro with some free Springfield rifles. He had gotten the bandit to do some of his fighting for him. And that was what concerned Foster at that very minute. Some of Negro's boys were watching the back door to Rancho Los Cielos. Negro wouldn't do anything until after that little set-to was over. Then he'd flex his muscles and show off his wares . . . and prove to everyone that he was just a stupid Mexican bandit.

But that left the American Army. Foster

expected whoever Colonel Carlton Smythe sent from Fort Bowie to rescue those stolen rifles and bring back Foster's body or at least his head or scalp to have made the first play already.

Had Smythe showed his yellow back? Had he even reported the rifles stolen and alerted the Mexican authorities? No, had that been the case, the Mexican army would be surrounding Rancho Los Cielos. So what was taking the Army so long? The little ambush in the hills above Rancho Los Cielos should have started.

He heard the faint report, and he set the spoon in the bowl in front of him. Foster sucked in a deep breath. He listened again.

The next pop sounded more definite.

Foster glanced at the owner of Mariscos, who pretended to ignore the muffled echoes of a gunshot or two. Foster wiped his mouth and rose, crossed the room, and pushed his way into the streets.

The men were listening too, and looking off to the northeast . . . exactly where Foster expected the Americans to try to sneak into Rancho Los Cielos.

From The Cantina That Has No Name, Soledad Tadeo walked into the street. She also looked in the direction where Amonte Negro's cowards were ambushing whoever

Colonel Smythe sent to do his secret dirty work.

Pop. Yes, that was a rifle. Winchester, maybe. Or a Henry. *Pop. Pop. Pop. Pop.* Yes, that came from a repeating rifle.

Then . . . Ka-boom! Ka-boom! Those had to be from Springfield .45-70 single-shots. Army issue. Foster had heard those guns fire many times, just not from this newer model.

Another series of shots sounded too faint, too soft, to be from any kind of rifle. That had to come from a pistol, and counting how fast those shots had been fired, either more than one pistol or at the least a double-action revolver. Foster had to laugh at that. How could a pistol, even a self-cocker, be effective against the power and might of a Springfield rifle?

The hussy with the dark hair and the brains of a white girl turned around. She understood what was happening in the canyon above her pathetic little village, too.

Her eyes met Foster's.

Realizing he had taken a glass of tequila with him, he raised it in Soledad Tadeo's direction and grinned.

She had not thought of this little development, now, had she?

CHAPTER 45

Second Lieutenant Grat Holden, out of uniform and practically out of this man's Army, eased his horse deeper into the canyon. The Schofield .45 remained holstered on his hip. The Winchester repeater was cradled in his arms. The only sound he should have been able to hear was the metallic ringing of the hooves of his horse on the hard-rocked ground. But Holden thought he could hear everything.

His own heart pounding against his rib cage.

The blood pulsing through his horse's veins.

The wind that blew.

The sweat that dripped down his forehead and his cheeks.

He knew his job. He was the sitting duck, sent into the canyon to draw the fire of the lookouts atop the canyon. He just had to figure out a way to live long enough so Sam

Florence and Ben "Hard Rock" Masterson could do their jobs, which weren't as dangerous as Grat Holden's . . . but were anything but easy.

He kept his head down as though he was looking straight ahead, just a casual traveler with no thought of being bushwhacked. His eyes, on the other hand, studied both sides of the canyon wall. He was looking for anything that would give away the location of the ambushers. Something that might just save his life.

An instant later, he thought he saw a flash but could not be certain. It might have been sunlight reflecting off a rifle barrel, but it could very well have been the sun bouncing off a shiny stone. Even more likely, it could have been Grat Holden's frightened imagination. That meant he had two choices.

He dived out of the saddle and to a large boulder on his right, near the canyon's thick, dark wall.

As soon as he was in the air with his boots cleared of the stirrups, he heard the roar of a heavy-caliber rifle shot. He heard the bullet buzz over his falling body and whine into the rocky wall.

He had guessed right.

Holden hit the ground hard, and rolled over as the second shot shattered a small rock to his left and sent shards from the chunk of granite into his cheek and left arm. It stung like hell, but that didn't hurt nearly as bad as a .45-70 slug tearing through his intestines.

His horse thundered down the canyon.

There was another shot, and he heard the horse scream. Holden just caught a glimpse of the horse as it somersaulted head over tail before coming to a rest in the middle of the canyon's floor. He saw the horse, dead, and he had to fight back the anger. There was nothing he could do about that now.

Leaning against the boulder, he brought the rifle's stock to his shoulder and he aimed where he thought he had seen the reflection of the sun, where he guessed that first shot had been fired. He squeezed the trigger, cocked the lever, and fired again. Three more times he touched the trigger and jacked the lever. He was shooting uphill at a target he could not see, but that did the job he wanted.

Bullets roared past him, slamming into the front, side, and top of the boulder. He sank back down to the dirt, wet his lips, and fished cartridges out of the bandolier that crossed his chest. He fingered them into the Winchester's magazine and jacked a fresh load into the chamber.

If he was guessing right, two rifles were shooting from above and to his left. Two more were firing above him and to his right. Shooters were on both sides of the canyon's top, but that had been expected.

Four men?

That didn't sound right. Four men wouldn't be enough. There had to be at least one more, probably two or three more. Jed Foster was not an idiot, and he would have made sure the ambush worked. For that, Foster would have used more than four men. More than five.

Voices called down into the canyon. Holden couldn't make out the words, but the echoes that bounced across and down the canyon told him that the men above, the men trying to kill him, were Mexican. They were yelling in Spanish.

So . . . he thought . . . *what if the men upstairs were not Foster's boys?*

He fired again to his right, cocked the rifle, swung around, and sent another round to his left. Then he retreated into his hiding place, pulling himself into as tight a ball as he could possibly contort himself. Bullets rang all around him.

"All right, boys," he said softly. "I've done my job. You damned well better do yours." Another bullet smacked the rock across from him and sent shards of lead fragments into his cheek. This time, he tasted blood.

"And you damned well better do it in a hurry."

CHAPTER 46

The roar of the Springfield rifle took Ben Masterson by surprise. It had come a little earlier than the former Army sergeant expected. Sinking behind a juniper, he brought the Colt Lightning up and aimed through the twisted branches of the tree. The blast of the big rifle still rang in his ears. Whoever had started the ball with the first shot was pretty damned close. Masterson had to grin. He was supposed to be up there trying to save Lieutenant Holden's life, but the little pup of an officer had drawn the first shot. And that shot had likely just saved Masterson's hide. Had he not have been warned by the shot, he most likely would have stepped right up to the man . . . who could have blown a hole through the former sergeant's belly big enough to send a Baldwin locomotive through. Another shot rang out from the other side of the canyon.

A horse screamed, and Masterson frowned. Some dirty dog had just killed Lieutenant Holden's horse, and that was the lowest thing a body could do. But that shot had been fired from the far side of the canyon, so it would be up to Sam Florence to kill that bushwhacker.

More shots boomed. Masterson listened intently. So, two men were up there, one just a few feet from him and the other at least a hundred yards up the trail. Probably even farther than that.

He concentrated on shots from the other side. If he could count right, that meant four men. Two for Florence. *And two,* Masterson thought with a grin, *for me.*

Masterson backed away from the juniper and inched his way closer to the drop-off, staying low enough that he'd be hard to spot by some gunman on the other side. He spotted the dead horse then looked back and found where the bullets were hitting a boulder. That had to be where Lieutenant Holden was hiding. If those ambushers were worth a tinker's damn, they would be working their way around to catch him in a crossfire, and rip him to pieces with the heavy slugs. They didn't have to see him to kill him. If they knew how to shoot, they could perforate the shavetail's body with

271

ricochets. More often than not, ricocheting bullets did a more thorough job of producing a corpse than head shots or shots straight to the heart. A ricochet could cut a man to pieces.

Even though his ears rang from the gunfire, Masterson could tell the man he wanted was in the rocks just a few yards ahead of him. He dropped to his stomach and began crawling to a little depression in the ground. Like a rattlesnake sneaking up on some unsuspecting jackrabbit, he moved quickly, but silently.

Once in the hole, he waited. He listened. The Lightning remained in his right hand, but he did not bother cocking the pistol. That wasn't because the .38 he held was a self-cocker. Unlike a single-action Colt, all a self-cocking double-action pistol required was to pull the trigger. That cocked the hammer and released the hammer, while the older single-action Colts had to be cocked manually before they could fire.

Cocking a revolver made noise. Masterson didn't want the Mexican behind the rock to hear anything — until Masterson put a bullet in the man's head or chest.

The man behind the rock sent another .45-70 bullet into the canyon floor. Masterson heard him laugh, heard the metallic sounds of the breech of the Springfield being opened, a spent shell coming out, a fresh cartridge going in, and the breech closing. The hammer was cocked then the man called out across the canyon to one of his compadres.

The killer farther down yelled out something. The man nearest Masterson laughed and shouted back at him. The gun roared. The bullet ricocheted off a rock, and two men on the far side of the canyon answered it with gunshots of their own.

Down the trail toward Rancho Los Cielos, the farther gunman on Masterson's side yelled again. The near Mexican busied himself with reloading his Springfield and did not bother to answer.

Masterson looked at his .38 and frowned. If he used the pistol, chances were it would give away his location to the gunman down the trail. That wouldn't be good for Masterson, and it wouldn't be good for Grat Holden. Most likely, it would also let the killers on the other side of the chasm think somebody might be on the top trying to kill them . . . which wouldn't be good for Sam Florence.

So, Ben "Hard Rock" Masterson told himself, *I'll have to send this old boy to hell the old-fashioned way. I'll just have to kill him with my own hands.*

That thought made him smile.

He had not beaten a man to death with his bare hands in a few years, and that had been an Apache sentry on a patrol he had strangled to death.

Except, it did not work out that way.

The Mexican bandit had decided to move in order to catch Grat Holden from behind. He stepped around the rock and saw Ben Masterson lying in the small little hole just six feet in front of him.

CHAPTER 47

Sam Florence was leaning his Winchester against a rock and drawing the Bowie knife from its sheath when he heard the rapid reports of a double-action revolver across the canyon. He kept one hand on the rifle, and his left hand on the handle of the Bowie, as his keen eyes swept over the canyon to the far side.

He watched the dark-shirted man, a fat man it appeared, stagger back, driven against a dead tree by multiple shots. The man dropped a rifle at his feet, stepped toward the edge of the canyon, and dropped over the side. He fell silently, dead already from the .38 bullets Sergeant Ben Masterson had pumped into the killer's chest. The fall appeared mesmerizing. The corpse flipped silently, head over boots, until it smashed into an overhanging mass of rocks.

The sickening crunch made Florence cringe as the body bounced off and spiraled

— no longer a graceful tumble — in a hideous dash to the ground. It landed in a heap of bloodied rags and smashed bones.

"Miguel!" a voice shouted from the opposite side of the canyon. A Springfield roared. "Miguel!" the man yelled again.

The name floated across the canyon, echoing the name repeatedly as if pleading for a response from the crumpled remains of a cold-blooded assassin that lay unmoving down below.

When the echo died, Florence focused on his task. He couldn't give any more attention to what had just happened across the gap. If the Mexican sharpshooter's aim had been true and Ben Masterson was dead, well, there was nothing Florence could do about that. Nothing Grat Holden could do, either, stuck as he was behind a boulder on the canyon floor. Sam Florence had a job to do on his side of the canyon's top. And that was to kill the two men he knew to be up there. One was just a few feet from him.

Eliminating that man might have been easy. Florence had figured to sneak around the rock and drive the Bowie knife into the man's heart. Or slice the throat, cutting as deep as possible to prevent any cry, any alarm, any noise the second sharpshooter might hear.

Ben Masterson's killing of the man dead on the canyon floor had ruined any element of surprise.

The man had been shot multiple times with a fast-shooting pistol, and then — if that had not been enough of a warning, he had fallen over the edge to be seen by all of the killers.

Even the biggest fool in Mexico and Arizona Territory would likely figure out the man trapped down below was a decoy. At least one man was on the other side of the canyon, and he had just killed one of the ambushers. The pair on Florence's side had to be thinking that, most likely, the Americans had sent a man up there as well.

Florence took his hand off the rifle. It stayed where it was, cocked and ready to fire, but he decided to stick with the Bowie. Its edge was so sharp, he could shave with it. He could have trimmed Abe Lincoln's beard with it.

He moved it up and close. He breathed silently as he listened for any noise. A twig snapping. A rock rolling. A sandal, a moccasin, or a bare foot touching the ground.

The man he had to kill first was on the other side of the rock. But which way would he come? To Florence's left? To Florence's right? Or would he merely back away to find another hiding place where he could keep watching for Florence or wait for Grat Holden to make a mistake and be killed, all the while looking across the canyon and waiting for Ben Masterson to show himself. The bandit had one advantage. He had a Springfield rifle, a gun that could kill Holden down below or Masterson on the far side. At the close range, he could blow Florence in half.

The scout did what he knew might keep him alive.

He turned rigid. He did not move. Men who moved were usually the ones who died. He leaned his back against the boulder, keeping the knife close and ready with the blade pointing up. He breathed silently, slowly, and confidently. He waited. Mostly, he listened.

The assassin two hundred yards away screamed for Pedro. Pedro, who had to be the one on the other side of the rock, did not answer.

At least, Florence thought, *now I know your name.*

When Pedro did not answer the call, the man farther away gave up and shot again down at Grat Holden.

That shot caused the Mexican on the other side of the canyon to chastise him.

"Hold your fire, hombre!" the man yelled in Spanish. "The one below is trapped like a rat."

Hombre and *rata* — the Spanish word for *rat* — bounced several times down and across the canyon.

"Do you see anyone?" the far man on Florence's side yelled.

"Silencio," the killer across the canyon shouted.

The echo rang out hauntingly. *Silencio . . . Silencio . . . Silencio . . . Silencio . . .*

All fell silent.

Nothing to hear except the wind.

Florence felt the sweat all over his body. His armpits were damp. His tongue tasted the salt of sweat on his lips. Luckily, no sweat rolled into his eyes, which darted to his left and right as he waited to hear or to see from which side the killer would make his play.

A moment later, he heard the noise. He smiled, and his eyes stopped moving left and right. They looked up.

Smart, Florence thought. The man had pulled himself to the top of the rock.

Slowly, painstakingly, Sam Florence came up to his feet. On soft feet, he turned around and brought the knife up. He drew in a deep breath, let it out, and listened.

The man on the top of the rock moved like a cougar. Softly. Silently. This one was a real professional.

Florence waited until his senses took over then he leaped and his left hand grabbed the man's arm just above the wrist. Coming back to the ground, he yanked the man forward. The knife the silent killer held toppled to the ground as he let out a shriek and fell.

He landed on his back with a thud. Air whooshed out of his lungs. The man tried to rise, tried to find the Remington .44 in his waistband, but the Bowie drove into his chest all the way to the hilt. He died with his eyes open, locked on Sam Florence.

Chapter 48

"Pedro!" the voice screamed from the other side of the canyon.

The reply was the echo.

Pedro . . . Pedro . . . Pedro . . . Pedro . . .

Ben Masterson emptied the cylinder of .38-caliber casings. He had put six bullets into the chest of the man who had fallen over the side of the canyon. Six bullets in one man. That was wasteful. That was unprofessional.

Masterson had left his 1873 trapdoor Springfield down below in the scabbard on the saddle of his horse. The two double-action revolvers he kept in the sash would do him little good against the man on the far end of the canyon, the one with a Springfield rifle. Yet the man whom Masterson had filled with lead and sent to a long drop to the canyon floor, had left him a little present.

He crawled out of the depression, and his

fingers touched the warm metal of the Springfield rifle the man had dropped. Gripping it and holding it in front of him, Masterson moved like an Apache on the dirt. He rounded the corner, squeezed in behind some rocks, and brought the big rifle up close for his personal inspection.

At first, he thought the bandit had been using the regular Springfield, the one the Army's foot soldiers had been using for roughly seven years or so, but as he examined the rifle, he understood what he was holding.

It wasn't the 1873 Trapdoor. It still smelled brand new, hardly had a scratch. It had to be one of the new models . . . from one of the boxes that Captain Jed Foster had stolen.

Evidently, the old captain and traitor had parceled out a few of his stolen weapons to lay an ambush. That meant the army men were on the right trail.

Masterson wet his lips. *Well,* he thought, *let's see if this needle gun's worth all the fuss that has been made over it.*

He was old enough to remember the first Springfield, the old "needle gun," first produced and delivered to Union troops in the last days of the War of the Rebellion. That one had been designed by Erskine S.

Allin himself, who had become a legend at the Springfield Armory in Massachusetts. "Allin's Alteration," the rifle was called, although Masterson liked *needle gun,* even though the firing pin was longer than plenty of needles Masterson had seen. Muzzleloaders were out of fashion — actually, outdated — so Springfield had commanded Allin to convert those old rifles into breechloaders. That would save a lot of lives, the Army and the factory figured, if soldiers didn't have to stand up to ram a ball, patch, and powder down the barrel.

It was a wonder, of course, that the Army stuck with Springfield after Allin's first try at the breech-loading rifle. The .58-caliber bullet, seated in a copper-cased cartridge and charged with sixty grains of powder, made too much gun. What Allin eventually did, of course, was reduce the caliber to .50, but the weapon still had a big problem. The breech block would often fly open, and that wasn't what a soldier wanted when he was facing a swarm of charging Sioux warriors who could riddle a body with arrows before those old 1865 and 1866 models could be reloaded.

Eventually, the Ordnance Department of the United States Army found something from Allin and Springfield that the boys really liked. It had been called the No. 99, and later the Springfield Model 1873, but to most soldiers, and most people, it was just the Springfield Trapdoor.

Those first weapons issued to the Army's foot soldiers came with a barrel that was thirty-two and five-eights inches long and shot a .45-70 cartridge charged with a four-hundred-and-five-grain bullet. The steel of the new rifles came with a blued finish. Older guns, well, the sunlight reflecting off those bright weapons could blind a man.

By 1874, the Army was outfitting cavalry regiments with Springfield carbines and taking away the old Sharps carbines. Springfield's version of the shorter weapon had a barrel twenty-two inches long, and the cartridge had been reduced to .45-55, decreasing the powder charge of the rifle by fifteen grains.

Masterson remembered the first time he had ever fired a Springfield carbine. The kick of the rifle was so hard, he had lowered his trapdoor and told the captain, "Cap, this here baby's powerful enough to drop two men with one shot — the fella that got shot, and the fella that did the shootin'."

Masterson hefted the rifle, still warm from the shots the bandit — now dead — had been sending down toward Lieutenant

Holden. Rifles had certain advantages over carbines, but not if you happened to be a horse soldier. The barrel on this one seemed to be a tad longer than the 1873 model. So maybe it would have great range. In his mind, the biggest change had to be the bayonet.

He shook his head at the way the Army brass did its thinking. What good was a bayonet to a cavalry trooper? Horse soldiers didn't even like carrying sabers into battle. All those long knives did was get in a trooper's way. And a bayonet? Nobody ordered bayonet charges anymore, especially those who had lived through the foolish charges during the Rebellion. A while back, the boys of the Ordnance Department had asked for bayonets that could be used for digging trenches. That went over about as well as a reduction in pay. So bayonets had been going back to the old style, good for spearing meat over a fire's coals, but not much good for anything else.

But the one Masterson held? It looked more like a cleaning rod than anything else, which might be useful after all.

Otherwise, the Springfield looked about the same as the 1873 trapdoors. It shot a copper cartridge in .45-70 caliber.

Masterson looked around. He saw the

crushed butts of several cigarettes, the dead man's sombrero, and plenty of ejected copper casings from the Springfield. The question he had to answer first was

Is this trapdoor loaded?

CHAPTER 49

Masterson opened the latch and smiled. Just to be sure, he removed the single cartridge, kissed it, and reinserted it, then closed the latch — the trapdoor that earned the rifle its nickname.

If the dead bandit had any extra bullets, however, he had taken those with him to the canyon's floor.

One shot. That's all Masterson had, other than the twelve bullets in his two .38-caliber Colt revolvers. The man at the other end of the canyon was too far away for the pistols to be effective.

He heard shots on the other side of the canyon, and Holden's Winchester returning fire. Bullets whined off rocks. Echoes made it sound like Custer's Last Stand was being fought again. The man with the big rifle on Masterson's side shot, too.

Masterson pulled back the hammer of the Springfield and came to his knees. Leaning against the boulder, he peered around the corner and started to bring the heavy rifle to his shoulder then he stopped.

The Army did one thing pretty well. They issued single-shot rifles to foot soldiers and horse soldiers alike. Some troopers complained that was because the Army was too cheap to buy ammunition. The brass did not want the soldiers shooting more than they had to. But Masterson's shoulder had been bruised from target practice, and every trooper he had worked with had learned to sight in a rifle. You didn't go into a turkey-shooting contest without a little target practice first.

Sights needed adjustments. Some rifles shot high. Others tended to be low. A few were damned near perfect. Some got too hot. Others jammed. Masterson was holding a new rifle that had only been fired a few times, and he had never fired it at all. He had only one shot. He had to make that one shot.

The man Masterson had to kill sent another bullet at Grat Holden. Masterson drew the nickel-plated Lightning and popped three quick rounds at the two-bit assassin hiding in the rocks. He brought the weapon back, emptied the spent cartridges, and replaced them with fresh loads. By that time, the man he had to kill sent a .45-70 slug into the tree to the former sergeant's right.

Masterson looked at the splintered branch. "Is he that bad of a shot?" he asked aloud. "Or is he trying to run a bluff?"

He stuck the .38 around the rock and felt the Lightning buck in his hand twice, then brought it back and waited for the killer to answer with his big needle gun.

The man did not bite.

The gunfire continued on the other side of the canyon. Masterson shoved the hot Colt pistol inside his sash, grabbed the Springfield rifle, and rose to his feet. He glanced over the side of the boulder, saw the muzzle flash as the killer down the trail fired again at Holden, and made his break.

Seeing the man whirl toward him before ducking behind the rocks and shrubs, Masterson counted as he ran, timing how long it would take the killer to open the breech, eject the casing, reload the weapon, close the trapdoor, cock the heavy rifle, and bring it back up to fire. A good trooper could fire ten shots from a Springfield in one minute.

Masterson didn't think the man holding the 1880 model was a good trooper. He counted out fifteen seconds before he dived behind some brush to his right. Sliding to a stop, he kicked a few pebbles and pinecones over the side. A few seconds later he saw the barrel of the killer's rifle appear.

Almost twenty seconds, Masterson thought. *Really slow at reloading.*

Using the dead limbs as shooting sticks to rest the barrel against, he brought the rifle up to his shoulder, adjusted the rear sight for distance, checked the wind, and made that calculation in his head.

The barrel disappeared behind the rock.

Masterson studied the terrain. The only place the killer could shoot from was the side. The top would be too high, and unless he wanted to climb up the treacherous slope, he wouldn't be trying to make a play from the ridge above him.

Masterson waited, expecting the man would turn fast, make a quick shot, then dive back behind cover.

The man appeared, and Masterson squeezed the trigger. The stock slammed against his shoulder. The 1880 model hammered the shooter even worse than the 1873 Trapdoor. To his surprise, he saw the puff of dust a good foot or more from his target's forehead then felt the slug of his assailant's rifle slap the brush over his head.

He swore, tossed the Springfield to the ground, and drew both Lightnings. Then he ran, charging but not screaming, not even opening his mouth. He just ran with the nickel-plated .38 in his right hand, the blued model in his left, fingers in the trigger guards.

Silently he counted . . . seven . . . eight . . . nine . . . spacing the numbers a second or so apart. Ten . . . eleven . . . twelve . . .

The man had not appeared. Not even when Masterson reached twenty.

The giant slab of reddish-white rock was just before him. His mind roared at him to stop, take cover, but he thought of something else. He rounded the corner and saw the big man.

The rifle was in his lap. A skinning knife was in his right hand. He was trying to pry the copper casing out of the breech. The big man swore and came halfway to his feet, dropping the rifle in the dirt and trying to throw the knife at Masterson.

Both revolvers bucked in his hand. The .38 bullets slammed into the center of the two pockets on the Mexican's shirtfront. Masterson pulled the two triggers again and then he ducked, more from instinct, and felt a .45-70 slug whine off the rock just above his head.

One of the killers on the far side had tried to save the life of his partner and take off the back of Masterson's head.

Catching his breath, Masterson looked at the man he had just drilled with four bullets. The man was studying his bloody chest before he toppled over and lay still.

Masterson lowered the two hot Colts, grabbed the smoking Springfield the man had dropped, and pulled it close. The copper cartridge remained stuck in the barrel.

After wiping the sweat off his brow, Masterson shook his head. "Erskine S. Allin," he said in a dry whisper, "I think you've got some more work to do, ol' hoss."

CHAPTER 50

Sam Florence heard four fast pops across the chasm, followed by the blast of a heavy rifle two hundred yards down from where he stood. The first shots would have been from Ben Masterson, and since Florence had not heard any kind of return fire, he could assume the old cavalry sergeant had just sent the second killer on the other side of the canyon straight to hell.

The whine of the heavy rifle bullet convinced Florence that the assassin's shot had missed Masterson. So . . . three of the bushwhackers were dead.

How many men would Jed Foster have put up here to stop the Army from getting their rifles back? Florence studied the man he had just knifed to death then said to himself in a soft whisper, "No. Wasn't Captain Foster who sent them."

The man who lay dead in the dirt and debris wore sandals. His pants were dingy tan cotton, ripped and patched. His shirt was filthy calico, with a blue and gray silk bandanna that had faded from years in the sun. He was short, skinny to the point of nearing starvation, and his fingers were covered in grime, grease, and . . . blood.

He did not even have a shell belt for the cartridges of his stolen Springfield rifle, but a white canvas sack that hung over his shoulder. Florence studied the man's face. An old, practically ancient face on a young, young man. He was not the kind Foster would send to do a man's job. So Foster had hired it out.

"Amonte Negro," Florence whispered out loud. He nodded in understanding and picked up the 1880 Springfield rifle the dead man had dropped.

Foster had hired the Mexican bandit to do that part of the job for him. That meant Jed Foster didn't have many men with him. There was some sense to that, Sam Florence decided. Fewer men you hired meant fewer men you had to pay — or kill. Foster was also used to the Army's way of doing things, with as little manpower as possible. Smaller patrols could cover more ground. The fewer people you had to trust or depend on, the better off you most likely would be.

But . . . if Jed Foster trusted Amonte

Negro to take out American soldiers, Jed Foster was losing some of his own faculties. Amonte Negro had sent a handful of men to do a job that needed ten or twelve.

On the other hand, the old scout told himself, *it just takes one bullet to kill you.* He picked up his Winchester as the bushwhacker's rifle shot roared down the canyon, and the bullet whined loudly off a rock across the gorge.

Belly to the ground, Florence peered down the path, if anyone would call that a path, and began crawling like a snake. Every twenty yards or so, he would stop, study the way ahead, and listen. The only sound came from the moaning of the wind through the crevasses and the trees, most of which were dead on his side of the canyon.

He moved again, keeping his rifle in front of him, his head up, eyes aware and constantly looking. The man, maybe the last one of Amonte Negro's boys, knew Sam Florence was there, and even knew Florence had killed his partner. Likely, he had taken a few potshots across the canyon at Ben Masterson to make Florence think he had forgotten all about him. Seemed that would be something one of Amonte Negro's idiots would consider.

The man jumped out, the Springfield at

his hip, not more than thirty feet from Florence.

Immediately, the scout rolled, realizing that bandit wasn't as stupid or as clumsy as the others. He had moved up a good hundred yards or so from where Florence had last spotted him, and there the killer had remained quiet as a mouse, just biding his time and waiting for the gringo to make a mistake . . . which he had done. He had underestimated his adversary's intelligence.

The Springfield roared like a howitzer, and Sam Florence figured he was dead. But he heard the bullet slap into the dirt two inches from his face, blinding his left eye. The killer swore, tossed the empty rifle at his feet, and palmed for an old Remington revolver stuck inside his waistband. By that time, Florence had the Winchester butted against his shoulder and was raising the barrel. He couldn't see anything out of his left eye, but his right eye was all that he needed.

The Winchester bucked. A splotch of crimson appeared just below the ribs in the center of the Mexican's gray shirt, and he staggered back. The Remington slipped out of his fingers, striking a rock, and discharging a .44-caliber bullet into the dirt. Florence was sitting up and levering another cartridge into his rifle. The Mexican bandit was dying, but he reached behind inside his shirt.

Florence shot him again, driving him to the edge of the cliff. Somehow the man managed to pull a leather thong from underneath the gray shirt. The crucifix slid off the broken thong as he toppled over the side, crying out as he plunged to the rocks and brambles below.

"Hell, mister," Sam Florence said apologetically. "I didn't know that's what you was reachin' for."

Chapter 51

The screaming man crashed into a dead juniper, breaking limbs and smashing his lifeless body on the rocks and cactus.

Grat Holden spit the taste of bitterness and disgust out of his mouth. The echoes of rifle fire and the dying man's screams faded in the canyon. Grat had seen two of the bushwhackers plunge to the bottom, one on each side. He had to figure Sam Florence had killed another up there. Holden looked down the ridge and the high walls to his left. By all logic, Ben Masterson had killed the second bandit on that side of the canyon.

Four dead. Most likely, anyway. So how many were left? Or had there only been four?

The little ambush had turned into a guessing game.

Holden studied both sides of the canyon's floor. Four men. Two on each side of the canyon, but up high. That could do the job, but that's not how he would have staged the affair. You needed at least one man on the canyon floor. But where?

So far, all Holden had done was provide a target for the sharpshooters up on the high ground. He had some cuts on his face from splintered bullets and rocks kicked up by gunfire. He had a dead horse, and that really got his dander up, even though the man who had killed that fine horse was now dead, too.

Holden waited. A minute passed. Then another. He waited five more, but still heard nothing.

He had to work up enough spit in his throat to swallow, and he didn't know for certain if what little saliva he could form would do the job. He raised his left hand to the side of his mouth and called out, "Masterson?"

His voice bounced across the canyon floor.

"Yeah!" Masterson called out.

So the old sergeant was still alive.

Once that echo faded, Holden turned to his right and called up toward the canyon's rim, "Florence?"

Again, the name rang up and down the canyon.

"Yo!" came the response, and that syllable also echoed long and lasting.

Holden did not look toward the voices. He did not even look at the top of the canyon. His eyes were locked on the floor and the myriad hiding spots a bushwhacker might set up for a killing shot.

The canyon measured roughly two hundred yards before it opened into rough terrain and raw desert, and there had to be two hundred thousand good hiding places in those six hundred feet. But which place would be the most effective to lay down a murderous barrage?

Holden stood.

"Florence!" he yelled then listened to his echo and, eventually, the old scout's terse reply.

"Other side of the rocks," Holden called out. "On the floor below Masterson's position." He let those echoes fade. "Empty your Winchester into those."

At the first crack and whine from Sam Florence's repeater, Grat Holden was moving, hugging the wall below the scout. He moved quickly, weaving from rock to tree, boulder to cactus, while lead slammed into rocks and whined and ricocheted, splintering branches, clipping leaves, and ringing like thunder in his ears.

Fifteen shots from the Winchester sounded like five times more. One ricocheting bullet even buzzed over his head, but he had covered half the distance he needed. With luck, the killer . . . if anyone was indeed still left . . . had kept his head down during Florence's cannonade. With even better luck, he was dead or dying, torn apart by .44-40 slugs.

Waiting, catching his breath, studying the terrain ahead, Grat Holden found his patience. Another five minutes passed. He did not even move to wipe the sweat from his forehead. One thing he'd realized was that if he yelled, the echoes would make his location impossible for a bushwhacker to figure out.

There were some times Grat Holden did not care for command. An officer had to make decisions, decisions that could lead to the death of another soldier, or in this case, even a scout. If you couldn't live with that, there was no reason to put on a uniform. It wasn't pretty. It wasn't decent. But, hell, neither was war.

"Florence?" he yelled.

"Yo!"

The echoes faded.

"They must be gone."

Gone bounced across the canyon.

Holden sucked in a breath, exhaled, and said, "See if you can spot dust."

He had no time to feel repulsed or remorse. He was setting the old man up as bait, and would likely get just one chance to save the scout's life. He could have chosen Masterson — hell, he might have even preferred to risk the temperamental sergeant's hide — but a man in the rocks would likely be protected by those rocks if he had to take aim at Ben Masterson. If he wanted a shot at Sam Florence, he would have to show himself. And Holden had a pretty good idea where that man would be. Where he had to be.

He did not look up the hill toward where Sam Florence would be showing himself. He looked at the rocks, and when the rifle barrel rose, Grat Holden let his Winchester do the talking.

CHAPTER 52

The rapid *tat-tat-tat* of a repeating rifle faded away, and Jed Foster poured the rest of the tequila in his dirty glass into the dust. The liquor had lost its flavor, and he knew better than to get drunk that afternoon.

"Hell." He tossed the glass into a water trough that was only half full.

He wanted to curse Amonte Negro for his cowardice, his stupidity, and his frugality. That blackheart had the six new-model Springfield rifles to do an ambush and he had sent maybe five men — perhaps six, but not from the sounds Foster had heard — to do a job that should have taken ten. Maybe the bandit figured if he was getting only six rifles, then those were all the men he should risk.

On the other hand, Foster figured, that meant he had six fewer men he'd have to deal with. No. Not six. He knew Amonte Negro well enough. The captain of the so-called revolutionaries would have kept one of those new Springfields for himself.

"Maybe," Foster said, "it'll blow up in that bastard's face."

He called out, "Whittaker!" and one of his men stepped away from The Cantina That Has No Name.

"Yeah, boss."

"Get the wagons hitched. We're moving out. Now. Pronto. Don't dally. Don't ask questions."

"The gin bottles?" Whittaker asked.

"Take them with you. Drink them at our next camp if you want or pour them out. I don't care. Just get moving."

He whirled and shouted into Mariscos. "All of you. We're pulling out. Now. Pronto. Get moving. We don't have much time."

Whittaker barked orders at the men who had been lounging inside or outside The Cantina That Has No Name and those who had stepped outside listening to the distant reports of a battle a few miles from Rancho Los Cielos.

Seeing the men do their work, Whittaker moved to Jed Foster.

"You think the Mex's ambush party failed, boss?"

"You heard what I heard," Foster said. He was checking the loads in his Colt revolver.

"I heard shots. That's all I heard, boss. And those shots were a good distance from here."

Foster smiled and dropped the Colt into his holster. "Guns have different sounds, Whittaker."

He was a young man, eager and a good gunman. Foster knew that much about him, but that youthfulness had one disadvantage. The kid lacked experience.

"You heard shots. I heard four single-shot rifles. A couple pistols, most likely double-action. And a smattering of repeating rifles. Winchesters. Marlins. Maybe a Henry. But not a Spencer. Not enough power for a Spencer."

The kid was amazed. "You could tell all that, boss?"

"I know a few things about guns, Whittaker." He winked. "I know a lot more about women, though."

The boy laughed.

Foster put his hand on the boy's shoulder. "So we're pulling out. Heading to The Canyon of the Sorrows. I'm going to leave you behind, Whittaker, because I trust you. Because I know you can do the job."

The boy straightened. "I'll do my best, boss."

"That's all I can ask for, Whittaker. Negro's boys failed. I shouldn't have left that job to a bunch of stupid little greasers. I should have sent you. So now I'm sending you."

"Where do I go?"

"You stay right here. Stay here and when they come. Kill them. Then rejoin us where we'll be selling those wagonloads of rifles and ammunition. Can you do that for me, Whittaker?"

"I'll kill a hundred of them for you, boss."

Foster chuckled. "I don't think you'll need that many bullets, son. By my guess, there should only be three or four. And with luck, maybe Amonte's bunch got rid of one or two of those."

"Piece of cake, boss."

"See you in a day or so, lad."

Foster looked around. The men were doing a pretty good job of hitching the wagons with fresh mules. He found another outlaw, the best rider of the bunch, and ordered him to mount his best horse and raise dust . . . and keep raising dust . . . until he had caught up to Reese. "Have him and the others head straight to The Canyon Of The Sorrows. Don't stop. Don't stop for anything."

"What about that crazy gray-coated ol' coot?" the rider asked.

"We're not going to worry about him for the time being. Go!"

They would be moving out in ten minutes. That's all the time he needed. Jed Foster walked into The Cantina That Has No Name, saw the Mexican girl eating a bowl of beans with corn tortillas and walked up to her. She did not look up.

"There will be some men coming into town soon," he said.

She ate.

"I'm just telling you that these men will be gringos. Yankee soldiers. Now if your revolutionary friend Amonte Negro wanted to do something for the Mexican people, he could do a lot by wiping out those old boys. And maybe your hero can do a whole lot better than he did a few minutes ago."

She looked up.

That's what he wanted. He slammed his fist into her face and watched her fall onto the floor. When she pushed herself up, he brought his left foot up and caught her in the ribs. The old man behind the bar sat up, and then sat back down and stared at the dirt on the floor.

Soledad Tadeo rolled onto her back, bleeding from both nostrils, clutching her ribs. Tears filled her eyes, but she showed no fear when Jed Foster knelt beside her.

"Most ladies think of me as a dashing young man, a catch to be sure. You look at me as if I'm dirt. So you remember what just happened here, little lady. And if you ever shoot at a whiskey bottle I'm holding again, you better adjust your aim."

CHAPTER 53

Grat Holden fired the Winchester from his hip while he charged the rocky fortress. Dust and bits of rock flew from the rocks, and the barrel of the Mexican's rifle disappeared. Holden did not turn from the rocks and the man he charged. He did not check on Sam Florence above. He did not look to his left to see if Ben Masterson was taking a hand. He just jacked the lever and pulled the trigger.

He adjusted his aim as he ran. He sent the bullets at an angle into the far wall of the little side cave. White marks began appearing on the blackened rock wall, and Holden could hear the whines as the bullets bounced off the rocks. He even thought he could hear the screams of the man hiding in those rocks.

The Winchester bucked and barked. Holden smelled the gun smoke. Then the man dived out low, hitting the ground and rolling over while Holden slid to a stop and swung the .44-40 at the rolling man.

He was a big Mexican with a black beard, buckskins, and a flowery shirt. Coming to his knees, he brought the big rifle up.

Holden's feet slipped from under him, and he landed on his back as he pulled the trigger. The bullet sang harmlessly into the rocks and trees. The bandit had his Springfield ready. The weapon roared, and Holden felt the fire of the blast as the bullet singed the hair above his left ear.

"Hijo de la puta!" the Mexican roared, and opened the breech to the rifle. Quickly he gave up and flung the rifle at Holden, who blocked the massive Springfield with the Winchester. The big single-shot rifle dropped to the ground. Holden swung the Winchester up as the man clawed for a short-barreled Colt holstered on his right hip.

Working the lever, Holden touched the trigger. He heard the hammer strike and nothing else. He had emptied the magazine. He threw the rifle at the big man while diving to his left and drawing the Schofield from that holster.

The Winchester caught the big man in the belly, sent him staggering into the dirt while his bullet blasted a cactus near Holden into oblivion.

Both men lay in the dirt, arms stretched out in front of them, right hands gripping revolvers.

Holden spit out sand and thumbed back the heavy hammer. The Mexican cursed and cocked his Colt.

A pistol roared, and for an instant, Holden found himself wondering who had shot first. Then it dawned on him that if he had not touched the trigger first, he would not be thinking anything at all.

Slowly, Grat Holden pushed himself up, rolled over, and leaned against the rock behind him. The Mexican lay on his side, an ugly hole in the center of his forehead. He still clutched the short-barreled revolver, the hammer cocked, the finger on the trigger. It had been that close. *Too close.*

Holden was too tired to move, but no one else was shooting at him. That meant there had been only five bushwhackers. If there were others, they had fled. He looked up and saw Sam Florence standing on the edge of the canyon's top to Holden's right. To his left, he spotted Ben Masterson waving his hat.

Holden lifted his gun in return, and the two men began making their way back down the trail that ran across the top of the canyon. He figured it would take them ten minutes, probably twenty, to get down to the floor. Somehow, Holden got himself to a standing position. He covered the few feet that separated him and the dead man, and slowly, carefully, removed the Colt from the man's stiffening hand. After lowering the hammer, he shoved the pistol into his waistband and went to check on the other dead men lying on the canyon floor.

He saw his horse, dead in the rocks, and frowned. That was just like an officer in the cavalry. Officers could order men to their deaths but hated to see a good horse shot down. It wasn't fair. He hadn't ridden the horse long enough to really get to know him very well, but it still sickened him.

Sighing, he walked toward the dead animal, trying to figure out what made the bandits shoot down the horse. It couldn't have been to keep Holden pinned down. The horse was going the other way.

It did not matter, he told himself. The horse was dead and there wasn't a blessed thing he could do about that. Likely, he tried to tell himself, the horses belonging to the men they had killed would be somewhere down the canyon. He'd be able to replace the horse. Yet the closer he got to the dead Morgan, the more he felt like cursing the bandit who had shot down the noble mount.

The killer of horses had not just put Lieutenant Grat Holden afoot, he had substantially reduced the chance of accomplishing this mission. And the odds had not been anywhere close to Holden's favor before that little run-in with Mexican bushwhackers.

CHAPTER 54

The saddlebags lay fifteen yards away from the dead horse. That fatal gunshot had caused the horse to cartwheel several yards, and the bags had pulled loose from the rawhide thongs meant to keep them connected to the rear of the saddle. The horse's momentum had basically catapulted the leather bags into the air, where they had smashed against several rocks and boulders that had fallen to the canyon floor during some avalanche or rockslide or mudslide.

One bag was open, and its contents had spilled out onto the rough rocks and debris.

Slowly, Holden walked away from the horse — there was nothing he could do for it other than get the saddle and bridle off — and dropped to his knees as he picked up a piece of metal.

The words of Colonel Smythe rang in his memories.

"You will carry a heliograph mirror in your

saddlebags. If you are successful, you can climb a hill and signal to the closest point."

"Hell," Holden said as he tossed the piece back to the ground near the shattered glass that once had been a mirror.

"You do know Morse code, don't you?" the colonel had asked back at Fort Bowie.

"They still require that at West Point, Colonel," Holden remembered answering.

"Then," Colonel Smythe had ordered, "you will send the message 'Happy Independence Day.' "

It would be hard to send any message with what was left of the mirror. The shards lay scattered in the rocks and cactus like the smallest of all diamonds.

Holden dragged the bags away and opened the second one.

Instructors at West Point had trained Holden that in the experimental method of "sun-signaling," or as they liked to call it, *heliography,* the larger the reflected bit of sunlight, the farther away it could be seen.

A three-inch square of glass could signal observers as far away as ten or twelve miles. Colonel Smythe had outfitted Holden with a four-inch-square, which should be able to cover up to twenty miles. Given the right weather and terrain — Northern Mexico and Southern Arizona Territory usually provided that weather and that landscape — a heliograph might stretch across the sky another twenty miles, increasing the range to forty.

Grat Holden did not have a shard of glass even an inch square.

Two legs of the tripod were smashed into splinters, while the tangent screw used for adjusting the mirror horizontally was missing, lost in the dirt or rocks. The crossbar was bent and the sighting rod had been broken.

He had been given two mirrors, but neither had survived. The cases were fine. The contents were worthless.

Sam Florence had made his way down from the canyon's top and appeared to be looking for Holden, who raised his hat off his head and began waving it. Florence had been scouting for too many years to miss that, and he raised what appeared to be a heavy rifle in a greeting. Holden realized the scout had rifles in both hands, which he leaned against the side of the canyon wall. The scout turned as Ben Masterson came into view. Masterson was also holding rifles, and these he leaned against the wall near the two Sam Florence had brought down.

The old scout pointed toward Holden, and both Masterson and Florence made their way to where Holden sat.

They saw the wreckage of the field helio-graph, as Holden kicked some dirt over the busted glass.

"Be hard to send that message now," Masterson said.

"Hell." Sam Florence shook his head. "I never had a whole lot of faith in those sun mirrors no-how."

Holden rose. "Yeah. And we have to get those rifles back before we could worry about letting Smythe know we were successful anyhow."

"You did good," said Florence.

Holden just shrugged. "Not bad yourself."

Florence laughed. "I staked you out. You staked me out. That's the way the game's played . . . sometimes."

"I thought I didn't do too badly myself," Ben Masterson said.

Florence chuckled, and Holden let a weary smile form on his face.

"We're alive," Holden said. "That means we all did pretty good."

"Come on," Florence said. "I want to show you something."

"Me, too," Masterson said, and the three men walked back down the canyon.

Sam Florence picked up two of the rifles he

had leaned against the wall, and lifted the one in his right hand toward Holden. Holden was looking at the other two rifles, the ones Ben Masterson had retrieved. They were brothers and sisters to the rifle belonging to the bandit that Holden had shot dead.

"I think," Sam Florence said, "this is what we came after."

Holden took the rifle the old scout was offering him. He hefted it. *Heavy.* He didn't care much for the size and weight, but he was an officer. Officers in the US Cavalry could use their own weapons, and Holden liked the Winchester. Just as he liked the heavy Schofield .45.

"Cartridge casing's stuck in the barrel of this one." The old scout pulled open the trapdoor and showed the jammed shell.

Ben Masterson took the two Springfields he had carried down the slope. Holden nodded at the Mexican he had killed, and the rifle leaning against the juniper branch.

That made five Springfield rifles, and not the 1873 models. They had to be the new weapons for they had scarcely been fired, showed little signs of use, and despite multiple shots by inexperienced riflemen, they smelled of grease and wax.

"Well," Sam Florence said with a mirthless chuckle. "We have five of those valuable rifles back. You reckon that would satisfy Colonel Smythe back at Fort Bowie?"

No one else laughed.

Ben Masterson leaned one rifle against the canyon wall and then opened the breech of the other heavy rifle.

"I don't think," the veteran soldier said, "he'd want any of these rifles. I don't think any man who depends on a rifle to survive would want any one of these. They ain't nothin' but junk. Worthless junk."

CHAPTER 55

Three of the five weapons had jammed. The copper casing remained in two of those, but Sam Florence had managed to pry out the metal from one of the Springfields by using his knife.

"One of the boys I shot down," Masterson said, "was doing that when I got the drop on him."

"Maybe," Florence said, "they don't know how to shoot."

"Maybe," Grat Holden said, "Custer's command at the Little Bighorn did not know how to shoot, either."

All three of them knew that story.

Lieutenant Colonel George Armstrong Custer, four years earlier, had led most of his Seventh Cavalry against the Sioux and Cheyenne in Montana Territory. There, they had charged a massive village. There, Custer had fallen with his brothers and most of his immediate command.

At first, a few know-it-alls had blamed the Army for sending men with single-shot rifles against Indians who had, through murder or gunrunners, fought with repeating rifles such as the Winchester, Henry, and Spencer. But other soldiers, those who had survived the slaughter fighting with Major Reno and Captain Benteen, told a different story.

As the Springfield rifles fired repeatedly, the copper cartridges expanded from the heat of the barrel. Getting a spent casing out of the breech proved almost impossible. Soldiers had to use their knives, or a bayonet, or anything just to reload the weapon.

If, of course, you were to follow the field manual for the Model 1873 rifle, you would merely take the rifle's cleaning rod and ram it down the barrel, pushing out the offending piece of copper. That might work fine for the foot soldiers, but there had been no infantry at Little Bighorn. Cavalry soldiers were given carbines, not rifles, and carbines did not come with cleaning rods.

"Springfield rifles have been jamming on us for years," Holden said. "That's nothing new."

"Don't I know it," Masterson said.

"I guess you do," Holden said, remembering.

Two years earlier, Sergeant Ben Masterson had led five troopers on a scouting party that had been ambushed by eight or ten Chiricahua Apaches. The soldiers and the Indians had engaged in a running fight to a water hole, where the boys fought them off.

"I let the boys do the shootin'," Masterson reminded Holden and Florence. "I was the fix-it man. Somebody would hand me a jammed carbine, and I'd claw or cut it out, reload it, pass it to another soldier about the time I got handed another Trapdoor. That's all I did. Just cut out a cartridge, reloaded a rifle, then got another jammed Springfield. As you know, Lieutenant, we enlisted men don't get our picks of rifles."

Holden nodded.

"You'd think the boys at that factory in Springfield would have come up with a way to fix it," Sam Florence said.

"Oh." Masterson took a swallow from his canteen, sloshed the water around in his mouth, and spit onto a cactus. "The Springfield's a good rifle. It'll kill a man, kill a horse, and maybe even both at five hundred yards. It shoots hard. It kicks hard. And if you hit a man with a .45-70 slug, that man ain't likely to be gettin' up no time soon."

"So the cartridge is the problem," Florence said.

"Copper expands with heat," Holden said. "At some point, the Ordnance Department of this man's Army might come around to discovering that themselves. And maybe they'll find something better suited."

"Like brass," Masterson said.

Holden shrugged.

Masterson pulled one of the rifles close and began rubbing the dust off with his bandanna. "Look. The Trapdoor we've been using has problems, but it's still better than anything else I've shot in the Army. It's not the rifle that causes the jams. That's the cartridge. But this here improvement isn't an improvement at all." He held the rifle up as though for inspection. "This piece of junk has plenty of other problems."

He tapped the rod underneath the barrel. "This comes loose. How many times did those hombres shoot at us? A dozen? Fifteen? Maybe not even as many as ten shots apiece. The spring here is supposed to hold the rod in place, but it isn't working. You tell me that a spring's going to come loose after ten, twelve, fifteen shots. That's not going to work. That's not going to work at all."

"That can be fixed," Holden said.

"Sure. That's why they sent those rifles here. To get tested by real soldiers in the field. I'm just saying that if you give me my druthers, I'm sticking with the 1873 model. Because maybe I can deal with a cleaning rod that falls apart. Maybe I'd just shuck the damned thing and find me a willow switch, some axle grease, and a handkerchief to clean my rifle. But this here" — he touched the front sight and then slid his hand down the barrel to the rear sight — "this is a big problem when your life is on the line."

Florence said, "The rifle doesn't shoot straight."

"Right." Masterson's head bobbed. "I shot. I missed. High and wide. And I don't miss often. Hell, I don't miss at all. So maybe that's just one gun. But the fellow shooting at me, he missed, too."

"Maybe he was a lousy shot," Holden said, but he knew that wasn't the case. He shook his head. "By all rights, I should be dead myself. The man I killed had me dead to rights."

Florence's head bobbed in agreement, too.

"When the gunsmiths at Springfield toyed with the design," Masterson said, "they messed up the . . . oh, hell . . . what's the word I'm lookin' for?"

"Ballistics," Grat Holden said.

"Right. You change a gun, even just add

fractions of an inch to a barrel, and you change how that baby's going to fire. We know we have to sight in, but these guns are well beyond that. These guns are pretty much worthless. That's my field report anyhow. Not that nobody gives a damn what a fightin' cavalry sergeant has to say." He dropped the rifle on the ground. "Besides, these guns are for infantry boys. As long as Springfield doesn't try to saddle us horse soldiers with guns like this —" He spit into the dirt again.

CHAPTER 56

"So maybe," Sam Florence said, "you're suggesting that we let Jed Foster take his rifles and sell them? Ride back to Fort Bowie, let Colonel Smythe know that we've done him a favor. We've gotten back five rifles out of two hundred and fifty, but the two hundred and forty-five left won't pose a problem to anybody but the fools shooting them?"

"I ain't sayin' that at all, Florence," Masterson said, stiffening. "You put two hundred rifles in the hands of Apaches or Mexican bandits —"

"Or an ex-Confederate who wants to start the Civil War again." Grat Holden said.

Masterson nodded. "Blood will be spilt on both sides of the border. The guns might not be worth a damn, but they can still kill. They killed the lieutenant's horse. Came pretty damned close to killing the three of us. We got to get those guns back. No doubt about that. The three of us." He shook his head and chuckled. "Three of us. Against Foster and whoever he lined up. And whoever else wants to buy the weapons from him."

"A Mexican bandit named Amonte Negro," Sam Florence said. "And most likely the Apaches."

"And Colonel Muncie's Confederate renegades," Holden added.

"Against the three of us."

"Two," Sam Florence said. He rose, his knees popping, and pulled his hat down lower on his head. "You keep forgetting that I owe Jed Foster my hide and hair. I told you I'd get you to Rancho Los Cielos and ask someone I know there to get you to The Canyon Of The Sorrows. And that's as far as I'm takin' you two."

That took the wind out of the sails of Grat Holden and Ben Masterson.

They found the horses of the bandits on the far side of the canyon. Five horses. Five dead killers. That's all there had been because surely Mexican bandits would not have left any horses behind.

Holden removed the saddle from one of the dead men's mounts, and replaced it with his own saddle and tack. The five 1880

Springfield rifles he wrapped in one of the dead assassin's saddle blanket and bedroll, and strapped the heavy package behind his saddle.

"If we're gonna lug those rifles across the desert," Ben Masterson said, "we ought to get a pack mule."

"You can leave them in Rancho Los Cielos," Florence said. "That guide I told you about knows all the hiding places this side of the border."

They buried the dead, but not very well, covering the bodies with stones and sand and brush. Animals would have to do some work to dig up those bodies, but not that much work.

After that, Sam Florence led the two soldiers out of uniform down the path toward Rancho Los Cielos.

"Maybe . . . they might have left a couple more boys behind. Just in case." Ben Masterson offered this as they came toward another canyon, although it was really nothing more than a winding, narrow arroyo.

"I don't think so," Sam Florence said. "Not enough hiding places here."

Florence was right. All they saw were a few jackrabbits in the shade and some ravens circling overhead. They climbed out of the arroyo, circled around a handful of junipers, and rode toward what some people called a village.

Sam Florence brought his pinto to a stop, and swung out of the saddle. Holding the reins, he knelt and put his right hand in a wagon track. Even in his saddle, Grat Holden could tell the track was deep. He could also see that there had been more than one wagon. By his count, there had to be four.

"How long ago?" Holden asked.

"Not long," the scout answered, and he looked down the road, away from the village of Rancho Los Cielos. "Not long at all."

"A day?" Masterson asked.

"An hour," the scout replied.

Masterson sat up straight in the saddle. "You mean the captain was here . . . during our little fight with those Mexicans?"

"No. I'm saying these tracks were made an hour or so ago. I'm not saying these tracks were made by four wagons carrying stolen Springfield rifles. Not yet."

"But you know they were," Masterson said.

The old man came up, but kept looking south.

"Why would he wait?" Holden asked. "He hired some men to ambush us. Why wait? Why push his luck?"

"You know the answer as well as I do," the scout said, and he grabbed the horn and pulled himself back into the saddle.

"A gamble?" Holden shook his head at the thought.

"The captain's always gambling," Masterson said, just to offer his thoughts on the subject.

"Colonel Smythe could have sent a whole company here," Holden said.

"He could have. Maybe he should have. Your pal decided to bet that he wouldn't. Then he stuck around to see if he was right."

"He's no pal of mine, Florence," Holden said.

The scout had the reins, but he kept looking down the trail.

"Should we follow him?" Masterson asked.

"No," Florence said.

Masterson countered: "The trail's fresh."

"Our horses ain't," Florence said.

"It doesn't take fresh horses to run down four wagons filled with ammunition and rifles that weigh a ton," Masterson said.

The scout pointed out the hoofprints that showed in the sand next to and sometimes on top of the wagon tracks. "You want to go up against that many riders with guns, go ahead. Me? I'm riding into Rancho Los

Cielos. And if you want to meet the person I said could get you to that trading place, you can ride into town with me. You want to risk getting killed, you ride south and follow the tracks. Who knows? One of those boys might have figured out how to make that 1880 Springfield Trapdoor shoot straight."

CHAPTER 57

"This town's dead," Ben Masterson said as the three men rode down the main street, the only street, in Rancho Los Cielos.

"By this burg's standards, this is a boom." Sam Florence pointed at the dun gelding tethered in front of the place known as Mariscos. No horses were tethered in front of The Cantina that Has No Name, but a few worn-out mules lounged in the shade of some trees near the well and next to a barn and a lean-to.

The mules looked like they had been pulling heavy wagons all the way from, say, Fort Bowie in Arizona Territory.

"Foster got fresh mules," Holden said.

"A lot of them," Florence said, "from the tracks I saw. And from all the dung in that corral, more mules than he needed to pull four Army wagons."

"Maybe he had men riding them," Holden said.

"Maybe. But I don't think so."

"Where's your guide?" Holden asked, but a movement caught his attention. His right hand landed on the butt of his Schofield as a young blond-headed man — not yet out of his teens judging by the complexion of his face — came out of Mariscos.

Holden studied the lean pockmarked kid as he smiled like he was taking an afternoon walk and grinning his greetings at the three strangers. The boy, with his blond hair, pale eyes and fair skin, looked about as out of place in a border village like Rancho Los Cielos as . . . well . . . Grat Holden, Sam Florence, and Ben Masterson.

"Howdy," the boy said in a Texas brogue.

Only Grat Holden watched the kid. Masterson kept his eyes on the place called Mariscos. Sam Florence turned in the saddle and looked everywhere else in town, including the little cantina on the other side of the street.

"I been waitin' on you fellows," the boy said.

"Is that a fact?" Holden noticed the punk wore a Colt low on his hip. The boy's eyes said he was just crazy enough to pull it at any moment.

"It is a fact indeed. You Army boys?"

"Maybe," Holden said. There was no

point in lying to the kid. He had to be one of Jed Foster's hired guns, and if Captain Foster had left him behind alone, then Holden figured there was more to this punk than met the naked eye.

"You know" — the kid stepped into the street and backed away from the three riders, moving to the middle of the dusty little road that was more path than street — "I tried to join the Army down at Fort Davis. That's in the Davis Mountains. Western part of the great state of Texas."

"I've been there," Holden said.

"Texas?" The boy's eyes lighted up. "Or Fort Davis?"

"Both," Holden said.

"Oh." The kid shook his head. "They wouldn't let me in. Join up. I wanted to. Thought it would be fun just to kill and scalp me a mess of Comanches or Apaches or Sioux or Cheyenne or even just a bunch of lazy digger Indians."

"That's a shame," Holden said.

"Shame for me. Shame on the Army. They missed a top soldier when they turned me loose."

"Where's Foster?" Holden had grown tired of this silly game.

"He left," the boy answered matter-of-factly. "But he left me behind to take care of you gents. You are from the fort, ain't you? I mean" — he hooked his thumbs on the gunbelt and slouched a little — "I'd hate to kill you fellas for nothin'."

"I think," Holden said, "you know who we are."

"Well" — the boy grinned — "I'll tell you what. I want to make this fair and give all three of you a chance. So here's the way I'm going to do this. I'll take you all, but one at a time. That way, you got three whole chances to shoot me dead. But I need to warn you, I saw your capt'n, that great Mr. Foster, gun down a top gun just today. Golly. Wow. Land sake's that happened not long ago at all. It was something to see. That Capt'n Foster, he's a right fair hand with a six-shooter. He's almost as good as me."

"Three?" Holden had to try not to roll his eyes. "You're going to challenge us to . . . duels . . . one at a time?"

The boy's eyes gleamed. "That's right."

"How many," Sam Florence asked, "dime novels have you read, youngster?"

Those young eyes turned still, deadly and serious. The kid stepped back and turned a bit so that he faced Sam Florence more directly.

"You're makin' fun of me."

"You're wastin' my time, punk," Florence said.

The kid stiffened. "Well, I'll tell you what, old man. You're a rude sourpuss. That's what you are. So I'm going to give you first crack at me. You got that. You get to try first." The boy laughed. "You get to die first."

"Sam . . ." Holden started.

But the old scout shook his head. He kept his eye on the boy. "You'll give me time to swing down off my pinto?"

"Of course," the boy said. "I saw how Capt'n Foster done it. He was a real pro. A gentleman. He gave that old hoss in the gray uniform a fair chance. And sent him to hell with one shot that blew the biggest hole in the man's middle that I ever did see."

"Thanks, son," Sam Florence said. "You're a chip off the ol' block that was Captain Jed Foster."

Florence casually dismounted, keeping the horse between him and the punk with the crazy eyes and the holster tied down on his right thigh.

But when the old scout stepped around the pinto, he had his revolver in his right hand, and the hammer was cocked, and falling.

The boy with the blond hair screamed,

and his hand bolted down toward his holstered Colt, but long before it even neared the ivory handle, the kid was falling back, a bullet in the center of his chest.

The punk fell onto the street, his eyes staring at the sky, his mouth locked in that eternal scream.

"Good God, Sam," Ben Masterson said. "You didn't give that boy a chance at all."

"Hell, no," Sam Florence said. "I'm too old to be playin' kid's games."

He did not even look at the dead punk as he strode to The Cantina That Has No Name. He stopped in the doorway, looked inside, and bellowed, "Where's Soledad?"

Someone must have answered because Florence turned, whipped off his hat, and slapped it against the hitching rail.

"Damn," he snapped. "She's gone off. To Amonte Negro."

"Who?" Holden asked.

"Soledad Tadeo. The person who can take you two to The Canyon Of The Sorrows."

Ben Masterson was about to swing down from his horse, but he stopped and shot Grat Holden a curious look.

Holden looked away from Masterson and across the narrow street at Florence.

"Sam, did you say . . . *she*?"

CHAPTER 58

Three of Amonte Negro's men stepped out of the shadows as Soledad Tadeo rode the entrance of the box canyon where the revolutionary hid out. Irritated, she pulled her horse to a stop, and let the men look her over, up and down, and get their eyes full.

"I am here," she told them, "to see Negro."

"He is busy," the fat one said.

Beyond the three sentries, Tadeo could hear the laughter, and by her ears Amonte Negro was howling the loudest and the hardest.

"Busy?" Tadeo looked at the fat monkey. "Busy doing what?"

The answer came from within the canyon. A gunshot roared, so loud even from that distance it caused her horse to buck and kick out. She had to pull the reins tight, and the scream that followed, loud enough to pierce her ears, caused the buckskin mare to jump around and kick out twice before she managed to get it back under control.

She lowered her eyes and glared at the fat man. He shrugged.

She was about to say something when the second gunshot roared, followed by another agonizing scream, but she was ready for the horse's reaction, and she kept the mare from bolting. It snorted, shook its head, and stamped one forefoot, but Soledad Tadeo leaned over and rubbed his neck.

"It's all right," she whispered.

The painful shrieks had faded, and she thought she heard whimpering instead.

"I am going," she told the fat man, "to see Amonte Negro."

When the middle-sized one started to swing the carbine off his shoulder, she barked at him, "Do not act like the fool you are, Ricardo."

The man stopped, and Soledad Tadeo rode easily past them and into the camp of Amonte Negro.

She rode the horse into the center of camp, but she did not dismount. Reining up, she watched in disgust as Amonte Negro fumbled to shove a shiny cartridge into a heavy rifle. The man stopped long enough to wipe sweat off his dirty brow and take a slug from a stoneware jug by his feet. Finally, he managed to close the breech to the big gun and staggered to his feet. He weaved toward a man staked spread-eagled in the center of the camp. The man twisted and turned as much as the leather straps and stakes would let him, writing in agony. Both of his knees were nothing but a horrible, bloody mess.

Amonte Negro was too drunk to notice Soledad Tadeo. He staggered, having to use the butt of the big rifle to keep from falling down, and eventually made it to the man who was being tortured.

In Spanish, he called out, "Where do you hide your silver, my friend? Tell poor Amonte Negro this and you will suffer no more."

She could not recognize the man, but he was dressed not like a peasant or peon but a man of some means. The barrel of the heavy rifle came down until it rested in the crook of the man's right arm.

"You no longer can walk, my friend," Amonte Negro said. "Do you no longer wish to write, too? Or be able to raise a glass of wine to your lips? Or enjoy the feel of a woman in your arms?"

The man sobbed. Negro braced the heavy rifle and pulled the trigger.

The man wailed, and mercifully, passed out.

"Here." Negro brought the smoking rifle up and tossed it to one of his men. "You reload this son of a bitch. It is too hard to do."

The young revolutionary walked to the fire and began fumbling with the breech of the new weapon.

Suddenly aware of Soledad Tadeo's presence, Amonte Negro turned. The sight of the girl on the horse caused him to step back, and he almost tripped over the grievously wounded man behind him. Alas, he did not fall. He was so drunk, Soledad Tadeo had her doubts that he would be able to rise.

"Blessed be the saints," Negro said, "it is the loveliest angel of Rancho Los Cielos. Have you traveled all this way to see me?"

"I thought," she said, "you might be able to help me. I thought I might be able to help you."

He grinned. "You can help me —"

"Shut your mouth, pig. Or lose your tongue."

The bandit — for that was what Amonte Negro was, nothing more — tensed. Anger crossed his face, and his eyes lost much of their drunkenness to reveal those thoughts of revenge, for no one should insult a revolutionary.

Revolutionary. Patriot. Soledad Tadeo spit. This man was no Juarez. This man was no savior. This man was a louse.

While the drunk tried to think of something to say or something to do, Tadeo pointed at the man being tortured.

"You make a man suffer so you can fill your pockets with his money!"

Negro shook his massive head. "No, no, no. I do this because we need money" — he pointed at the fool trying to reload the big rifle — "for guns . . . for guns. Guns we need to take Mexico City back for the people. Our people. Guns we need —"

"Guns. Gringo guns stolen by a thief no better than you. We would have followed you with hoes and rakes and spoons. And you would be robbing us. Making us suffer as that poor nobleman."

"He does not suffer, my lovely little dancer." Negro pulled a pistol from his pants, cocked the hammer, turned, and put a bullet into the unconscious man's forehead. He looked back at Soledad Tadeo and grinned. "He suffers no more."

"Your suffering," she told him, "will begin soon."

And she spurred her horse out of the

canyon and rode back to Rancho Los Cielos.

CHAPTER 59

When she saw the pinto tethered to the hitching rail in front of *La Cantina Que No Tiene Nombre,* Soledad Tadeo pulled her horse up short. Her left hand let go of a rein, which she draped over the horse's neck, and brought her hand to her nose and cheek. The bruise smarted. She hated the man who put it there. She hated the man she had once admired even worse. She did not want the old gringo to see her face. Yet he was not in The Cantina That Has No Name. He called out from the shadows behind Mariscos.

Soledad Tadeo turned the horse. She watched as the *Yanqui* named Sam Florence stepped into the street and stopped. She nudged the horse toward the old scout and reined in, keeping a good bit of distance between her and Florence, and keeping one side of her face in the darkness, out of his view.

"Did you miss me?" she asked in Spanish.

"When I thought of you," he replied in English. "Did you miss me?"

She shrugged. "Perhaps. If I thought of you."

He smiled, and his gentle smile made her relax so that she almost forgot about Amonte Negro and a gringo dog named Foster.

"How is your boy?" he asked. "Your patriot? The man you just visited?"

She spit. The bartender in The Cantina That Has No Name one day would learn to keep his mouth closed and his tongue from wagging so much. Or one day she would cut out his tongue and sew his mouth shut.

"Amonte Negro is no patriot," she hissed in Spanish.

"I'm glad you finally see him for what he is, which is —"

"We have never discussed politics, old man," she warned him. "We should not break that treaty now."

He nodded and pointed at the corral, now empty except for dung and tracks.

"You've met the man with the rifles."

She shrugged.

"He's taking them to *El Cañon de Los Dolores.* To sell."

She just stared.

"You know the way. I could find it. But . . ." He sighed and spit. "Well, men sometimes find foolish reasons to prevent them from doing their duty. Something about personal honor."

Soledad frowned. He made no sense. Had he been drinking the swill the patron served in Mariscos? He did not look drunk.

"You know the way there."

"What makes you think that?" she asked.

"You told me. Twice."

She paused to reflect, and then she laughed. That hurt her nose and her bruised cheek.

"I have a big mouth."

"It's a pretty mouth."

She frowned again. It wasn't so pretty if the old scout from the United States came much closer.

"I have come to ask you a favor. A big favor." He gestured inside the open doorway to Mariscos. "Two men are inside. Yes, they are gringos. But they have come here to stop a bloody war. They have come to get the guns that were there" — he gestured at the empty corral — "and take them back across the border."

She had to lean forward and stare, just to make sure the old man was not drunk.

She asked, "Two . . . men? Two?"

He held up two fingers. *"Dos,"* he said, and shrugged. "The *soldados norteamericanos* have strange reasons."

"Two men," she told him, speaking English, "could not take those rifles away from the gringo called Foster."

"I believe you are right," Florence said. "But two men might be able to destroy those weapons. Keep them out of the hands of . . . Amonte Negro . . . maybe the Apaches . . . possibly, probably, even the bandit in gray, the man who left after the troubles between the *norteamericanos.*"

"What you ask, is for me to lead two gringos to their deaths." She spit again. *"El Cañon de Los Dolores."* She turned to English. "The Canyon of The Sorrows shall live up to its name."

His voice turned firmer, stronger. "Understand this, Soledad. All you're to do is get them to the canyon. Then all you do is get the hell away from there. What happens will be none of your concern."

"Why do you not go with these gringos?"

"I owe Jed Foster," he said.

"That much?" she asked.

The old man did not answer.

"If I do this," she said after a long moment to think. "If I take those fool gringos to *El Cañon de Los Dolores,* and if they manage to destroy the weapons Jed Foster has brought to my country . . . this will hurt the gringo pig?"

Sam Florence cocked his head and those keen eyes locked on Soledad. She turned her head to make sure the scout could not see the features on that side of her face.

"It'll hurt him," he said. "Badly."

She swung out of the saddle. "I will speak to the two gringos," she said, but she pointed at the scout. "But I will speak to them . . . alone."

CHAPTER 60

The woman had a wicked bruise across one cheekbone, her lips were swollen, and there were traces of blood in both nostrils. That said, Grat Holden could not think of a woman more beautiful than the one who marched into Mariscos like she owned the place, barked at the bartender in rapid-fire Spanish until he was high-tailing it through the front door.

She stared long and hard at Holden, studied Ben Masterson just as thoroughly, and then walked behind the bar, where she found a bottle of tequila and a clean glass. These she set on the bar. She poured a drink, smelled it, tasted it, then downed it without a cough. After refilling the glass, she looked up at the two men.

"My name," she said in English, "is Soledad Tadeo."

"Grat Holden, ma'am." The handsome one tipped his hat.

"Ben Masterson," said the other, who raised his glass as though toasting her.

"Why are you here?" she asked.

They looked at each other briefly, the two gringos, and then the one named Holden, the younger of the two, the best looking, cleared his throat and said,

"Sam Florence says you could get us to a place known as The Canyon of The Sorrows. We would like you to take us there."

"There is nothing to be found in *El Cañon de Los Dolores* except death. Do you wish to die?"

"Not particularly." Ben Masterson laughed.

He drank too much, Tadeo decided. Maybe not as much as that fool and blowhard named Amonte Negro, and maybe not even as much as the gringo called Jed Foster, but she decided that she would not like this man. She did not like the way he looked. She did not like the way he spoke. She did not like Ben Masterson at all.

"I will ask you again," she said, keeping her eyes on the young man named Holden. "Why are you here?"

Holden watched her for a moment as though searching for an answer. He must have found one because he said, "A traitor to the uniform he once wore stole two hundred and fifty rifles from the United States Army. He brought them here. We've seen the tracks. We know he wants to take them to this canyon, this canyon of sorrows, and there he plans to put the stolen rifles up for sale. We believe that a bandit named Amonte Negro will make a play for those guns. We know this. Some of his men tried to kill us today."

She stopped him by raising her right hand. "They are dead?"

He nodded. "Five of them."

"Bueno." She leaned back in her chair.

"We also think what we call in our country an unreconstructed Rebel, an enemy to our country during the war we fought to preserve our union, will try to buy the rifles from the man who stole them."

"Why?" she asked. "Why would that concern me?"

"Maybe it won't," Holden said. "His war is with men who wear the uniform I do, and that Sergeant Masterson here once did, and maybe will again. But we do believe that this Colonel Will Muncie has been robbing your people, too."

"If he takes the guns," she said, "he might leave my country. And torment yours. Should that concern me?"

"I don't know, ma'am," Holden said, "but

one thing I do know. The Apache warrior named Crooked Nose will try to buy these rifles. If the bandit Negro gets the rifles, that's bad for your people. Very bad from what I've heard about the cutthroat."

"And," she whispered, "from what I have seen."

"If Muncie, the old Confederate, gets the rifles," Holden continued, "that would be bad, very bad, for my people. But if the Apaches get their hands on two hundred and fifty Springfield rifles, that will mean much bloodshed. For your people. For my people. For you. For me. For the entire Southwest." He sat back in his chair and kept his eyes on her.

She studied him. "So I will ask you one more time, and this time you will tell me the truth and you will not think of me as a fool. What has brought you here? Why do you come to me? Why do you come to my village? Why are you in my country?"

A long silence filled the room. She felt the man searching her eyes again, but she did not blink, she just looked at him. Eventually, he shot a glance at his companion, the man named Ben Masterson, who shrugged in confusion. Holden looked at her again, and finally he leaned forward.

"Jed Foster took those rifles from a wagon

train that I commanded. He killed men who rode with me. He killed a friend of mine. I want to kill the son of a bitch. I aim to kill the son of a bitch. The son of a bitch was once a friend of mine. What's more, the man is a traitor. He's evil. I was ordered here. That's the truth. My commander told me that I had to get those guns back, and that's what I aim to do. If I can't get them back, I will make sure that Negro, that Crooked Nose's Apaches, and that Muncie's crazy followers don't get them, either. And no matter what happens, I will see Jed Foster dead. So the Army, my Army, sent me here. But I was coming here anyway, somehow, some way. And I came here to kill Jed Foster."

He leaned back. and poured himself a glass from the bottle next to the bigger gringo soldier.

"Do you hate this gringo with the rifles as much as your friend does?" she asked the one called Masterson.

The big man shrugged. "No. I can't say I do. I don't like him. But I don't like no-body."

"So why did you come?"

"It wasn't for revenge." He raised his glass. "I had the option. I could come down here to most likely get killed. Or I could go to prison and rot. I'd rather fight." He drank his tequila.

She rose. "Sleep well tonight. I will meet you outside in the street at daybreak. I will take you to *El Cañon de Los Dolores*. And there I will leave you. There you will find new sorrows. There everyone finds sorrows. There, most find death."

CHAPTER 61

In the Apache camp, Badger Killer was drunk. And Crooked Nose, the leader of his ever-dwindling party of Apaches, knew that nothing good ever happened to his people when Badger Killer was drunk.

"With the weapons the pale eyes promise us, we will return to the mountains north," the young warrior bellowed to the other warriors too young to remember what Cochise and even before Cochise, old Mangas Coloradas, were like. They knew only of men like Geronimo and, now, Badger Killer. "We will drive the pale eyes out of our country. Then we will be free to sweep down here and kill Mexicans whenever we are in the mood to kill Mexicans or whenever we need a slave to make our life easier."

Crooked Nose stepped out of his wickiup. It wasn't like he could sleep with all that shouting going on anyway.

Badger Killer was pleased that Crooked

Nose had stepped into the night. He beamed and hooked his thumb at the Chiricahua Apache leader.

"Crooked Nose," Badger Killer said, "does not want to take the weapons from the pale eyes."

The eyes of the young warriors turned from the tall, raven-haired Badger Killer to old, gray-haired Crooked Nose.

"We are few," Crooked Nose said. "The pale eyes are many."

"Once, a few Chiricahua warriors were all that was needed," the young man boasted.

"Once," Crooked Nose said, nodding sadly. "In those years, we needed only a few warriors . . . because the pale eyes were few. Now there are many."

"You speak like a squaw."

"The Bluecoat With Golden Hair Longer Than The Hair On Some Pale-Eyes Squaws," Crooked Nose said, "is selling the long guns. We have not enough pale eyes money to buy what he sells. The Pale Eyes In Gray Who Once Fought And Still Hates Our Enemy will likely buy those weapons."

Badger Killer shook his head and spit into the fire. "So that is your answer? We let those pale eyes who wear gray take long guns we could use?"

"The Mexicans might take the guns. But I

believe the Mexicans have less money for long guns than we do."

The young brave leaned his head back and laughed. He pointed at Crooked Nose and shook his head again. "This is what the great Crooked Nose thinks. He thinks since we have no gold to make the pale eyes happy that we should just run deeper into these hills where we hide from the men who seek our scalps, from the Mexican soldiers who want to have us join our long-dead warriors. I remember when we took what we wanted. I say we take what we want again. I —" He stopped.

Crooked Nose was nodding.

"I say we take the long guns, too."

The eyes of the young warriors left Badger Killer and focused on the old man in front of the domed wickiup.

"If the Pale Eyes In Gray Who Once Fought And Still Hates Our Enemy leave The Canyon of The Sorrows with the long guns, we will take the long guns from them. They are old, too. They lost their war with the pale eyes who wear the blue coats and carry the long knives. They raid farmers and villages for their money and their food. They are no longer fighters. Taking long guns from them will be easy." He spoke softly but firmly, and the young men seemed to listen to him.

"And," Crooked Nose said, "if the Mexicans leave The Canyon of The Sorrows with the long guns, that will be much easier for us. We have never had a problem taking anything from the Mexicans."

Badger Killer had to walk to the squaw who held the jug of tizwin. He jerked it from her grasp and took several greedy swallows before tossing the jug to the nearest warrior. Most likely, Crooked Nose figured, the young warrior needed his followers to get drunk. It was hard to get drunk on tizwin. At least, it was hard for men like Crooked Nose to get drunk. These young warriors, well, they seemed to be able to get drunk on corn before it had fermented into a sticky, weak type of Indian liquor.

"Why don't we take it from the pale eyes?" Badger Killer roared.

Crooked Nose shook his head. "You are not that young, Badger Killer. You remember when we lived in the mountains north of here. You were just a boy, but you remember our leaders. You remember our country. You remember the times before we were few, before we had to hide in these hills."

"Yes." Badger Killer banged his chest with his fist. "I remember that. I remember everything. I remember when we were men and when our chiefs were men."

Crooked Nose smiled. "And do you remember who drove us out of that country? Do you remember that? The pale eyes drove us out. With weapons like the one they promise to sell to whoever has more gold. The pale eyes are like sand. You scoop out a handful of sand in the desert, and sand fills the hole. We kill pale eyes and we kill pale eyes, and more pale eyes come to replace what we have killed. No. We leave those pale eyes alone. We kill the Mexicans. We kill the pale eyes who wear gray. Then we learn a better way to fight the pale eyes."

"You want to fight the weakest dog," Badger Killer said. "I want to fight the meanest dog. That is the way of an Apache. We will take the guns from the pale eyes. We will not take them gold and have them laugh in our face. We will take what we want. For we are still, and we will always be, Apaches. Who rides with Badger Killer? Who stays with the women and Crooked Nose?"

It was bound to come to this, Crooked Nose thought as he watched eight of his young men stand and follow Badger Killer to the pony herd. Two young men who remained behind, but they were very young, and the four old men who had known Crooked Nose before his nose was so bent, watched the nine men ride away.

Maybe they would come back. Perhaps they would even return victorious, with rifles and bullets and tales of glory. Maybe Badger Killer would return and demand that Crooked Nose leave the camp, that he was too old, and Badger Killer was taking over because he had proved he was worthy by gaining the biggest victory for his people since Cochise had made the pale eyes suffer.

Maybe. Who was to tell? For the moment, though, Badger Killer was gone. The night would turn quiet again. And Crooked Nose could sleep undisturbed.

CHAPTER 62

"I do not do this for my health," Soledad Tadeo told Grat Holden.

The shavetail lieutenant felt mesmerized by the Mexican girl's beauty and her audacity. He kept staring at her, and could not take his eyes off the bruise on her cheek and nose. She kept touching it. Holden found a handkerchief in his pocket, dipped an end in the glass of tequila in front of him and gently brought it to her face.

She watched him, eyes burning but not blinking, and did not move as he touched the cut with the alcohol. Soledad Tadeo grimaced slightly but let him slide the wet rag across the cut Jed Foster had given her.

"Who did this?" Holden asked.

"It does not matter," she said.

He brought the rag down her nose and over her lip, wiping away the darkened, dried stains of blood that had spilled from her nostrils. She stopped him, took the rag out of his hand, and dabbed the bruises and the scratches herself. Then she wadded up the piece of cotton and tossed it in front of the *norteamericano.*

She couldn't do that bit of doctoring the way the young gringo had. When she touched the cuts, the tequila felt like fire. When the man named Holden did it, it felt soothing, almost cool. She did not like anyone doing anything better than she did. She did not like this *Yanqui,* even if he was pleasing to the eye, even if he had a gentle touch, even if he was everything that Amonte Negro could never be.

"I said," she told him, "that I do not do this —"

"For your health." Holden nodded. "Yes. I know. We will pay you."

"How much?"

"Name your price," he told her.

"One hundred pesos."

He smiled and drank his tequila. "This is a mighty poor country."

"A hundred pesos," she said, "and I take you to The Canyon of The Sorrows. That is all I do. I show you the canyon. I leave you to find your own sorrowful end. I do not fight. I do not die. It is not that I am afraid to do either. It's just that I pick who I fight and I will pick where I will die. Do you understand?"

"Completely."

"Then I will take my hundred pesos now."

He had to stand to reach inside his trousers. He was fairly tall. The hand disappeared into a pocket and came out with a leather pouch. Sitting down again, he pulled on the drawstring, turned the pouch over, and dumped out a few gold coins. Not pesos. *Yanqui* double eagles. They rolled on the table and eventually toppled and lay still.

"That should cover your troubles."

"I cannot make change."

"I did not ask you to."

She glared at him. "All you get is a trip to The Canyon of The Sorrows."

"Understood."

He frustrated her. She couldn't figure him out. She raked the coins into her lap, picked them up, and dropped them in the leather bag she carried over her shoulder. He refilled a glass with tequila, but not his glass. Not her glass, either. He filled the glass of the big man with the two revolvers in his sash, the man called Masterson.

"How long have you known Sam Florence?" Holden asked her.

She adjusted the leather bag, pushed it behind her back, and looked at the gringo named Holden.

"Who?"

"Sam Florence. The old man. The scout. The fellow who brought us here."

"Oh. Is that his name?"

"Yes. Well, it's what he calls himself."

"He never told me his name."

"How long has he been coming here?"

She shrugged. She had to think. "I cannot remember when he was not here," she said after minutes of long, deep thoughts.

When she was a child, when her mother still lived, the gringo had come on what must have been an infrequent basis. Not always there. Rarely there, but she had these distant memories of seeing him, maybe from afar. And after her mother had died, when she had just turned fifteen, when the bad things happened, he came more often. At least it seemed that way. Rarely had he talked to her, though, but his presence always made her feel more confident, and more safe.

"Not always, of course, but he always returns."

What she could not figure out was why he would come. Nobody came to Rancho Los Cielos unless they were running from something, unless they had to hide from the *policía* or *soldados norteamericanos.* Certainly, no one came for the food, the whiskey, and the old man — whose name she had just learned was Sam Florence — did not come for female companionship.

"Well, he's not going with us," the man named Masterson said.

"Bueno," she said. Good for Sam Florence. She did not want to think of him dead.

CHAPTER 63

She rose and crossed the floor at Mariscos, stopping at the shattered glass that had been destroyed in one of the many outbursts of violence. From there, she had a good view of The Cantina That Has No Name. The gringo named Sam Florence would be there. That's where he went. That's where he drank. Sometimes, he would go to the cemetery on the hill that overlooked the town. Sometimes he would go to the corral and groom the horses, just to do something to kill the time. Usually, he took his supper and sipped his whiskey. Then, at some point, he would leave.

Most gringos — most men — tried to bed her, but not the old man. When they talked, they talked of trivial things. They joked. He was a comfortable man, comfortable with himself, comfortable with his surroundings — wherever they were — but not one comfortable talking too much.

She had been talking to him for at least six years, probably longer, and she could not remember anything he had ever told her. Then again, he had never told her his name. Come to think of it, she did not remember ever telling him her name. But he knew it. She must have told him at some point. Still, it did not matter.

She knew that he worked for the *soldados* who wore the blue. She knew he came into Mexico even when soldiers could not, chasing Apaches or trying to find out where they were hiding and when they might be planning an attack on the northern side of the border. Maybe seeing if any of the bandits or men like Amonte Negro planned to try some sort of raid in a town like Douglas or Tucson or Lordsburg . . . places she had heard of, but had never seen, and, truthfully, had no interest in visiting.

The man named Sam Florence sat somewhere inside that dirty little adobe hut across the street. It was the same dirty little adobe hut where Soledad Tadeo spent most of her time, where she cooked and sometimes cleaned and where the owner of the place let her sleep.

She had not been to the place where her mother had lived, where she, Soledad Tadeo, had lived for years. Until . . . that day.

He would be sitting across the street now, drinking, but not getting drunk. Or not drinking at all. Many times, he had arrived in Rancho Los Cielos to drink coffee, to abstain from liquor at all. She had never seen him drunk. He knew that a man in control was a man who could control. On a night like that one, he would not be drinking. He would be sitting, thinking.

Once, she had asked him, "What do you do when you just sit there, old man?"

"I remember," he had said.

"What is worth remembering?" she had asked.

"Not a hell of a lot," he had told her. "But when you find something worth remembering, it feels good to remember. When you find someone worth remembering, that feels even better. Mostly."

That made absolutely no sense to her.

So he would not be drinking tequila. Not tonight. The man who called himself Sam Florence would be eating, but just enough so he would not be hungry.

It was foolish, silly, and childish to stand there and look outside and across the dark street to wonder about an old gringo she did not really know. Soledad Tadeo returned to the table where the gringo named Grat Holden looked at old maps he had rolled out in front of him, and where the bigger man named Masterson stared at her and smiled and drank.

"Sam Florence says that he doesn't know the way to The Canyon of The Sorrows," Masterson said. He refilled his glass of tequila and poured one for Soledad Tadeo. "Is that true?"

She slid the glass away from him.

"I do not know, but if the *Yanqui* says he does not know, then I would not doubt his word."

"It just strikes me odd," Masterson said, "that a scout who has been in this part of the country for so long wouldn't know a place like that. I've been hearing about The Canyon of The Sorrows since the Army sent me to Arizona. And I've been in Arizona for a damned long time."

"Then why do you not go there yourself?" she said.

Grat Holden chuckled, although he did not look up from the map that interested him so much. Even Masterson grinned.

"Well," Masterson swished the tequila around in his glass, probably to wash away more dust, "for one thing, it is in Mexico. The Army didn't let us cross the border very often. But I don't think I've met anyone who has ever been there. Well, I've never met anyone who went there and lived to tell about it."

She found the tequila and killed it in one shot.

"But you've been there," Masterson said. "And you're still alive."

The man named Holden stopped studying the map. That had been a waste of time, Tadeo knew, for he likely was trying to find out where The Canyon of The Sorrows was located. *El Cañon de Los Dolores* could not be found on any map. It might be on a good map, probably was, but not by that name. Most likely, the mapmakers and the passersby and wayfarers had called it something else.

A place like that held only sorrow for those who had gone there, but not to pass through.

"Yes," she told the two gringos. "I have been to *El Cañon de Los Dolores.* But I cannot say that I am still alive."

CHAPTER 64

The Confederate battle jack flapped in the desert wind as Colonel Will Muncie refreshed his cup of coffee at the camp they had made between Rancho Los Cielos and his plantation on what was not much of a river. The coffee was not New Orleans chicory, but it did the job. He heard the men griping, but he did not rebuke them.

It was good for soldiers of the Confederacy to complain. They had turned back, having lost a good man, a fast gun, a man with backbone loyal to the South, to Robert E. Lee's sacred memory, and loyal to Colonel Will Muncie. They had seen him shot dead by a bluebelly with a smirk on his face and a damned Yankee accent. They had turned tail and fled. Retreated. Oh, in orderly fashion, but they had gone to that miserable little flyspeck of a town to win a battle, the first battle in what would surely become a noble endeavor and a glorious cause to all white Southern men. They had slunk away with their heads low, their necks burning in humiliation, and their tails tucked between their legs like a whipped hound dog.

It sickened Will Muncie.

Damn, how he missed good coffee. That part of the country was supposed to produce fine coffee, but he had yet to taste any since fleeing the great South. Well, maybe it was the water that tasted lousy and not the beans and grounds.

Captain Knight came to the fire and snapped a sharp salute. "Sir . . ." he began.

Muncie returned a half-hearted salute. Knight had always been full of brass and vinegar, a salty man who knew no fear. If President Jefferson Davis or any of the big generals had listened to Colonel Muncie, Captain Knight would be General Knight. The boy had practically won the Battle of Chancellorsville by himself.

"Go on, Capt'n," Muncie said. He knew what would come.

Captain Knight was braver than Spartacus, but he also had the brains of a slave like Spartacus, or like all those uppity little creatures who now thought they were as good, and as free, as a man like Will Muncie. He spit coffee into the fire. What he needed was fine Kentucky bourbon. Pennsylvania bourbon? To hell with that. Yankees in Pittsburg or Harrisonburg or Philadelphia or Carlisle likely stole bourbon from Louisville and branded it their own. And Kentucky, by God, was a Southern state. He remembered all those "orphans" who had fought alongside the states that had the gumption to tell Lincoln and the Yankee congress to kiss their arse.

He stopped those thoughts and tried to listen to whatever nonsense Captain Knight was saying.

"What's more," the bantam rooster said, "we lost Bowdre, suh. Bowdre was as fine a man as we have in our service, Colonel. And he was shot down like a poor dumb cur dog in the street. Murdered. That man Foster gave him no chance. And then we left those wagons we came to take. Just left them, Colonel. Beggin' the colonel's pardon, suh, but that just don't set well with the boys, Colonel. No, suh. It don't set well at all."

Muncie brought the tin cup to his eye level. He studied the cup and the steam rising above the lip. And he sighed. Captain Knight was passionate. He was also boring as hell.

"Suh?" the captain said.

Muncie brought his eyes up and locked them on the gallant former solicitor from

Shreveport, Louisiana.

"Yes, Capt'n?"

"Colonel, I was just saying that it doesn't sit well, suh, in a man's belly, to turn tail and run. We haven't run in a long time, suh."

Muncie's head shook. "Since 1865 or something like that, Capt'n, wouldn't you say? Fifteen years ago."

"Suh . . . I am just —"

"Capt'n," Muncie said, his voice remaining calm, "I do not recall you with us at Pittsburgh Landing." That was the name the Southern troops called Shiloh, the 1862 fight on the banks of the Tennessee River that spring in Tennessee. What had started out as a rout of Ulysses S. Grant's Yankee devils and what had turned into a heart-breaking Southern loss. General Johnston himself, that gallant gentleman, had died in the first day of fighting. The bloody losses on both sides had shocked the Yankees and the Southern Confederacy.

"No, suh," Captain Knight said.

"Right." Muncie sipped his coffee. "You were still practicin' the law in Shreveport. Helpin' rich steamboat owners get richer."

"Well . . ."

"I was at Pittsburg Landing, Capt'n. Shiloh, as some call it. By any name, it was a glorious slaughter."

"Yes, sir."

"You learn somethin' by studyin' war, Capt'n. You should try it sometime."

The colonel sighed. His patience had its limits.

"Here's what I learned on that awful day in Tennessee, Capt'n. On that first day, we had pushed the Yanks practically into the cold waters of the Tennessee River. We all thought they were licked, no matter how many brave comrades had fallen in battle. It was a slaughter, Capt'n. A brutal slaughter. But we were winnin' the day. We had won the day. Victory was ours. The blue bellies were almost in a full rout."

He sighed again.

"The next day, Capt'n, the Yanks came back hard." Muncie's head shook. "They whupped us good, Capt'n. Whupped the tar out of us."

He poured the dregs of the coffee into the fire, which sizzled and smoked.

"Once you see a man's back, you figure he's whupped, Capt'n. That's why I let Capt'n Foster see my back. He thinks we are whupped, suh. That's why I sacrificed the gallant Corporal Bowdre. Capt'n Foster, dumb Yankee that he is, will not fret over us after today. That will be his defeat, much as it was our defeat in 1862 at Pittsburg Land-in'." Muncie called out a name. "Lieutenant Fountain!"

CHAPTER 65

The bookkeeper of the Southern expatriates slipped from behind the horses tethered beyond the fire, made a beeline for Colonel Muncie and Captain Knight, and snapped a sharp salute. Lieutenant Fountain appeared out of uniform, having shunned his gray shell jacket for a black poncho, and the darkest denim britches Captain Knight had ever seen. Even the lieutenant's face had been covered with greasy tar, making him look like a damned slave.

"Report, Lieutenant Fountain," Colonel Muncie said without returning the lieutenant's salute.

"Two, sir."

"Two." Muncie considered this. "You are sure."

"Countin', Colonel, suh, is my specialty."

"Indeed." Muncie grinned and turned to the stunned Captain Knight. "Mr. Knight, you seem to be out of sorts. Tell me, Capt'n, if you sent your enemy runnin' back to their mamas, what would you do? Think, man. This is war. We don't have time to debate. We must act with a certain amount of spontaneity."

"I would . . . suh . . . ummm . . . I would . . ."

"Lieutenant?" Muncie looked at the black-faced, thin bean-counter.

"Make sure he was indeed retiring to where he said he was goin', Colonel."

"How many would you send, Lieutenant?"

"One should be able to do the job, suh."

Colonel cocked his eyes. "But," he said with a sardonic grin, "you counted two, Lieutenant."

"It takes two Yanks, Colonel, to do the job of one good Southern soldier."

"Indeed." Muncie grinned at the perplexed Captain Knight.

"Bookkeeper," Muncie told the lieutenant, "do a little subtraction for us, if you would not mind, my good man."

"My pleasure, Colonel." The man in black started back toward the desert. He stopped, and grinned, and nodded his blackened face at Captain Knight. "Would the capt'n care to join me, suh?"

"Indeed, Lieutenant, he would. At least, he should. Follow the lieutenant, Capt'n.

Learn a little bit about war. It's different from what you read in all those law books you pored over back in Shreveport."

"Stay here," the dark-faced lieutenant told Captain Knight.

The captain did not like being ordered about by a mere second lieutenant whose main duties were to keep the books for the colonel's regiment, but he lacked the guts to say anything about it.

The man in black clothes with dark grease covering the white of his skin pointed at a dark shadow maybe a hundred yards down an arroyo.

"Whisper," Fountain said. "Do you see it?"

"See . . . what?" Captain Knight asked.

"The cigarette."

Knight stared. He did not see a damned thing but night as dark as midnight. He stared and looked hard everywhere near where Lieutenant Fountain's finger aimed. He saw nothing but black. Sighing, he gave up. His shoulders slouched.

"Yankees like their smokes," Fountain whispered so low it took every effort Captain Knight could summon to hear. "That's why us Southern boys like a good chaw. Which is dangerous itself." His finger shot out like a magnet. "There. See that?" He sighed. "Of course you didn't. You got to keep your eyes open, Pops. Now, you just stay here and watch. I'll do some cipherin'."

The man who was a master at mathematics dropped to his stomach and slithered like a Western diamondback rattlesnake across the desert floor. Captain Knight could only stare, and he soon was staring at darkness, unable to see the bookkeeper, unable to see the man who was supposed to be smoking a cigarette somewhere in the night.

He bit his lower lip. He held his breath. He listened but heard nothing but coyotes yapping in the distance.

Two hundred yards away, Lieutenant Fountain came up slowly, smiling, and inched his way to a man called Bateman who had just stepped onto the remnants of a smoke with the toe of his square-toed boots. Bateman was thinking that he should be back in Rancho Los Cielos drinking whiskey and trying to get the clothes off that girl with those wonderful eyes and that luxurious hair.

It was a nice thought for a man to have.

It proved to be his last thought.

Fountain came up swiftly, brought his forearm tightly across Bateman's throat, so tight the man could not scream or even gasp. Bateman shot his arms up to the big arm, but then the D-guard Bowie knife cut through his back, cut deep between his ribs, and plunged into the back of his heart.

For good measure, Fountain twisted the knife as much as he could, for the ribs were strong and he was a little tired. He heard the quiet sigh that told him the Yankee was dead, and gently laid the corpse on the ground.

Fountain wiped the blood on the dead man's trousers. Then he went to find the second man.

Ten minutes later, Captain Knight heard horses snorting. A moment later, he saw two horses walking straight toward him. After he blinked, he realized that a Negro was leading those two horses. Finally, just before he was about to wet his britches, he realized that the Negro leading the horses wasn't a man of color at all. It was the bookkeeper, Lieutenant Fountain.

The junior officer stopped to tether the two horses to the branch of a dead clump of brush. Fountain grinned at the captain and nodded. Knight, without questioning the man who knew math, followed his junior officer to Colonel Muncie.

"Those two Yankees," Fountain reported,

"have made the balance zero."

"Well done, Mr. Fountain."

The two officers waited, but Captain Knight lacked the patience. "So what do we do now, sir?"

"We sleep. And tomorrow morning, we will start out for The Canyon of The Sorrows."

"But —" Knight wet his lips. "Well, sir, we don't know where that trading spot is. The Yankee is supposed to send for us."

"Exactly," Colonel Muncie said. "But he has to get there first. And that means he has to leave a trail."

"If there's a trail, no one has found it. You have to have a guide."

Muncie grinned. "Guides can be bought."

CHAPTER 66

The two gringos stared at Soledad Tadeo, waiting for her to explain how she knew about The Canyon of The Sorrows. She let them stare. They did not need to know. She did not want to remember. But she did. She always remembered.

She had just brought in a pail of milk to her mother's adobe cabin about two miles from Rancho Los Cielos. Her mother was singing and cooking supper. She had such a beautiful voice. The cabin smelled fine. No, it smelled wonderful.

Her mother was cooking inside because it was January, and the weather had turned cold. The wind howled outside, and Soledad felt warm and comfortable in her home.

"How," her mother asked while frying the potatoes, "does it feel to be fifteen years old?"

It was Soledad Tadeo's birthday. She was very happy. Her mother was frying potatoes to go with the beans and pork, but she would also be making sopaipillas for a birthday treat. Nothing was better than her mother's sopaipillas after coating them with sugar and filling the insides with honey . . . if the honey was not stuck in the jar because of the cold. If it was, Soledad would have to stick her finger inside the jar, sop up what she could, and then lick her fingers and hands to her heart's content.

"This will be my best day ever," she said.

Soledad Tadeo had asked her mother for a pony. She knew she would not get a pony, even a lame one, because they were poor. Everyone was poor in Rancho Los Cielos. She would not be upset when there was no pony, when there were only sopaipillas and supper and something her mother had sewn or beaded together. That would be enough. But, still, wasn't it wonderful to be able to dream? She would dream of a pony. One day, she would have a real horse.

So, she would not get a pony today, but she was fifteen. And when a girl turned fifteen years old, there would usually be a *fiesta de quince años . . . the quinceañera,* a celebration to mark a girl's passage into womanhood. That would be tomorrow, in Rancho Los Cielos, to give thanks to God and to introduce this new woman to the village. That would be better than any pony.

Someone slammed on the door, and she turned around. *Perhaps,* she thought, it was a pony. Or maybe her mother had invited other children to come. Perhaps, the quinceañera would begin this night and not in Rancho Los Cielos in the morning.

Grinning, she raced to the door. She had not barred it when she came inside because her hands had been struggling with the pail of milk, nor had she removed the latchstring. She pulled open the door quickly, just as her mother was saying softly but sternly, "Soledad, no."

The door opened, and she saw the Apache. She saw all of the Apaches.

Before she could scream, one swung a club that caught her on the side of her head, knocking her to the floor. She heard her mother scream, and then the Indians were rushing inside. The one who had hit her leaped on her, tossing his club away. *He* was young, not much older than her, with long black hair, a red headband, and a calico shirt.

Turning her head toward her mother, Soledad tried to say something. Her mother had grabbed a butcher's knife, and she threw it as the six other Indians rushed inside. They did not close the door. The knife must have missed, and then the Apaches had knocked her mother down, behind the stove. They knocked the table over. Soledad could no longer see her mother. She could, however, hear her mother's screams.

Rough hands grabbed Soledad's long hair and pulled her forward. The young Apache buck glared at her. Another Apache, much older and blind in one eye, knelt beside her and the young warrior on top of her.

The old man reached for the crucifix Soledad wore over her blouse, but the young man spat and barked something in the rough language of that tribe. The old man muttered something, but protested no more, and rose to join the others behind the table.

The young warrior leaned closer to Soledad Tadeo. He said in a harsh, hoarse whisper, *"Eres para mi y solo para mi."*

He had spoken in Spanish. You are for me and only for me.

His breath smelled of foulness. His eyes came close to her, and she felt his hands grabbing her blouse. The cloth ripped. Soledad closed her eyes. She tried to fight him, to push him off, but the young man laughed. She felt his greasy skin against her cheek, and his rough tongue on her throat. She pleaded with the Holy Mother to spare her and her mother, or at least spare her mother. She turned her head, but the man grabbed her head and forced it back. One hand went lower. She opened her eyes and saw his ear. She bit it. She bit hard, like a Gila monster, and the man screamed. He pulled away from her, but her teeth would not let go. A hunk of his ear ripped, and the warrior fell as blood sprayed her face.

The man rolled over and clasped his mangled ear. She sat up, spit out the lobe that tasted rotten in her mouth, and glared at him with hatred. She wiped her mouth as she rose. She would kill him. But the old man with one eye had returned, and he grabbed her by her long hair and jerked her to the floor.

Another warrior came from behind the table. He was completely naked from the waist down. He pointed at the bleeding young buck on the ground and laughed. He said something, but he spoke Apache. The old man with one eye laughed, too.

The boy did not laugh. He jumped up and drew the long knife from the sheath. Had Soledad Tadeo seen that knife, it would already be in the man's belly. The young buck rushed toward her, but the one-eyed Apache stopped him. He was old, but his grip was strong and uncompromising as he held the man's wrist and kept the blade of the knife from cutting anything.

The old man spoke to the one with the bad

ear. The young man barked back. The old man grunted louder and nodded at Soledad. Then he released the young man, who raised his knife and sent the blade thudding into the table.

He said something and stepped to Soledad Tadeo, who prayed that she be killed now.

The old man sat down. He picked up the pail of milk and drank from it, the whiteness rolling down his copper skin and onto his buckskin shirt. The man watched as the young man with the ruined ear lowered himself on Soledad Tadeo.

CHAPTER 67

She knew her mother was dead. The Apaches had murdered her after — Soledad Tadeo closed her eyes. They had strapped her over her mother's mule, tying her hands to her feet underneath the mule's belly. They stuck a rag in her mouth, and another rag was tied across her mouth so tightly that the corners of her lips bled. She was completely naked. The wind was bitterly cold.

The Apaches took their time, covering their trail and moving in the night. When dawn broke, they cut loose the cords and pushed her to the ground. She stared at the unmoving faces. The man with one eye pointed to the brush, and Soledad realized that he meant for her to urinate or defecate. They gave her no tissue. The man raised his fist and barked, so she went behind the bushes. She cried. Then she told herself that she would never cry again. She was a woman. She did not have to use the bathroom, but she tried to scrub away the blood with sand.

The Apaches yelled something so she stood and returned to the mule. She looked at the Indians, and she saw the young one, the one who had — She shuddered, reviled, and wanted to throw up. She wanted to kill herself. But she found satisfaction in the young buck's face. He had lowered his red silk headband and used it to wrap around his mangled ear.

They pushed her back onto the mule's back, and tightened the rawhide cord again to her feet and hands. They mounted their horses, and pulled the mule along.

Eventually, they stopped and cut her down but let her ride the mule. They gave her a frock to wear. They even offered her water from a canteen. Her buttocks and her back had been chaffed by the sun and the cold wind. Riding the mule bareback was almost as grueling as being carted on one like a sack of flour. She ached, and she desperately wanted to sleep, to close her eyes and dream and . . . maybe . . . wake up from this terrible nightmare.

She did not close her eyes, however. She observed. She made herself remember the twists in the trail, the turns, the rocks, and the watering holes. Soledad Tadeo knew where they were taking her. She had heard other youngsters and a few men talk about that place.

Soon she would be at *El Cañon de Los Dolores.*

Sometimes, the priest and the nun would try to scare the children they taught. If you are not a good boy and girl then one night the Apaches may come for you. They will take you to The Canyon of The Sorrows. So you must remember to pray and to go to confession and to live the best life you can and remember your parents and your siblings in your prayers.

She had heard those stories so many times that she had begun to think of that canyon as a myth or some kind of fairy tale.

They rode into the canyon, and she heard the singing, saw the men dancing, saw carts and wagons and plenty of horses. Two of the Apaches grabbed the rope to the mule upon which Soledad Tadeo rode and they loped it to a corral at the end of the canyon. A Mexican in the uniform of a *Rurale* opened the gate, but the corral was not for the mule. The man in the *Rurale* uniform jerked her off the mule's back *and shoved* her through the gate. She stumbled to her knees and tried to catch her breath. The gate closed behind her and the Mexican spoke in a mix of Spanish and Apache, but she could not make out any of the words. She heard the mule being led away.

Later, she heard the gunshot. The Apaches killed the mule and roasted it for supper. It had been an old mule anyway.

When she looked up, she saw other women, most of them Mexican but a few who had to be *norteamericanos.* One was blond. Two were redheads. Several were even younger than Soledad Tadeo. All had the same look on their faces that she knew was chiseled on her face as well. Their eyes revealed their hopelessness. *Two,* she thought, *had already lost their minds.*

Soledad Tadeo sat down. She tried not to look at the women. She looked at the canyon. She burned it into her memory.

CHAPTER 68

On the third day at The Canyon of The Sorrows, the raiders came. They brought whiskey and casks of wine, trade goods, rifles that were not worth much money and powder that was wet but maybe would dry out and fire a musket.

After much drinking and much gambling and plenty of eating and three fistfights, the man wearing the uniform of a *Rurale* opened the gate to the corral. He jerked one of the redheads up by her hair and dragged her four feet before he let her rise and walk in front of him. He shoved her out of the gate, and six men — four were Mexican and two dressed like and were as pale as most *norteamericanos* so Soledad figured they were gringos — closed in around her.

One lifted her dirty red hair. Another opened her mouth and stared at her teeth as though he were guessing the age of a horse. One clasped his hands over the woman's breasts, and another clapped his hands and ran to do the same. The woman was too dead to notice or to care.

The *Rurale* shoved both men away and called out in Spanish, "We will start the bidding at fifty pesos."

Apparently, the men came in pairs, for only two Mexicans and one gringo offered money for the redhead. The Mexican in the blue silk shirt and the leather knee britches called *sotas* won the redhead. He snapped his fingers, paid the man in the uniform of the *Rurale,* and his partner grabbed the redhead and pulled her to a covered wagon.

She had been sold for eighty-five pesos.

The gringos outbid the Mexicans for the blonde. They also got Soledad Tadeo, laughing when one of the Apaches pointed to the young buck's mangled ear and then tapped his teeth and made a biting motion at her. They paid two hundred pesos for Soledad Tadeo. She might have gone a little higher, but the Mexicans seemed a bit afraid of a girl who might bite the ear of a customer. The blonde cost them four hundred. They also bought a girl younger than Soledad Tadeo and a boy who they thought would be a good servant for a while and then a worker *in* one of the mines.

As she was led to the covered wagon, Soledad Tadeo saw the young Apache with the ruined ear looking at her. She stared back, unblinking and the warrior had to turn away. She would remember him, and she made herself a promise. This rich gringo planned to sell her into prostitution, but no one was going to touch her that way until she was ready — and she would never be ready and never be in love. And if anyone ever struck her again, she would kill the hijo de la puta.

Inside the wagon, Soledad Tadeo found a seat near a rip in the canvas. She sat, and when the wagon pulled out, she raised her left hand and stuck a finger in the tear. She pulled the canvas down and watched. She noticed everything — the junipers and the cactus. She figured out which way they were traveling. Hours later, when the wagon stopped, she removed her hand from the rip and waited.

The gringo with the derby hat and the checkered coat opened the flap in the back. He looked at his purchases and cleared his throat. "We'll be going through what amounts to a town in this lousy country. I can stick Harry in here with a gun, but I don't want to do that. Greasers are stupid, but they might wonder why I'm pulling a saddled horse behind this wagon. I could tell them it's mine, but they might not buy it. People get kind of edgy after an Apache raid. So you'll stay in here and you won't make one peep. Because if any of you try to warn the greasers, well, those greasers will be dead. And we'll be taking you back to The Canyon of The Sorrows. We'll be giving you back to those Apache bucks. Savvy?" He repeated the threat in Spanish and closed the flap.

No one said a word as the wagon and the outrider, the man who had served as the rich gringo's partner, crept to Rancho Los Cielos. They rode through the small village without stopping. The village meant nothing to Soledad Tadeo. She was dead already. The village was dead. Her mother was with God. When they crossed the border, they turned west.

They camped that night, letting the women drink water but giving them nothing to eat. To the boy, they did toss a piece of bacon one of them had dropped in the dirt. The boy picked it up, looked at it, and tossed it back to the gringos. The man in the checkered coat and derby hat rose from the fire, walked to the boy, and laid a gash on the side of his head with the barrel of a revolver.

None of the others made any attempt to help the boy.

CHAPTER 69

The next morning, they were back in the wagon and traveling west. Soledad Tadeo again put her finger in the rip and watched the desert pass.

Around noon, the wagon and the outrider stopped. She craned her neck and watched. She wet her lips. One man was riding down a hill. He carried a stick across his lap as he nudged a pinto horse toward the man driving the wagon and the man on the horse. When he was lost to her, she slowly rose and moved to the front of the wagon. The man in the derby hat and the checkered coat had kept the flap closed, and there was no tear in that part of the canvas, but she sat on the bags of trinkets and beans and cloth, wet her lips, and raised her finger to the flap. She pulled it back just enough so that she could lower her head and see.

The man on the pinto horse had stopped in front of the wagon. "Howdy.

The rich gringo's partner had nudged his horse up a few yards past the wagon. She could not see that gringo, but she could see the driver of the wagon. He had wrapped the leather reins around the brake of the wagon and was stretching. Not that his muscles were stiff at all, but he was stretching to put his right hand on the butt of a revolver stuck in the small of his back.

"Man," the rich gringo said, "it's a long way and hard on an old man's back traveling from Lordsburg."

"Lordsburg," the newcomer said.

No, she realized. It was not a stick at all, for once he stopped the black and white mustang, he raised the stick up and braced the bottom against his thigh. It was not a stick. It was a rifle.

He was lean and thin and leathery. His hair was gray and long. He seemed oddly familiar but she could not see very well through the small opening.

"That's right. We're on our way to Prescott."

"Is that a fact?"

The rich gringo's hand tightened on the revolver. His thumb slowly began pulling the hammer to full cock.

"You callin' my pard a liar, friend?" the gringo on the horse said.

"Nope. I'm just saying that I've never heard

398

of someone coming from Lordsburg and going to Prescott heading to Rancho Los Cielos first. It's out of the way."

"You've been following us?" The rich gringo started to pull the revolver out of his pants, but still pretended to be stretching his back and his arms and his shoulders.

"I scout for the Army," the old man said. "Apaches raided a couple homesteads. Took some women captive." He spit off to his right. "They also raided south of the border. Killed some good folks. Took some more captives. Women, mostly. Even young girls."

"That's horrible." The revolver was out of the rich gringo's pants. "What will they do to those poor innocent creatures."

"The Apaches?" The man sighed. "They'll do whatever they please. Then they'll sell them to white traders."

"Traders?" the one on the horse asked. "White men."

"I wouldn't call them white," the scout said.

The man stopped with the pistol.

"What would white traders want with kidnapped girls?" The one on the horse was trying to distract the man on the pinto from the rich gringo with the checkered coat, the derby, and the pistol in his right hand.

"Take them to Prescott. For one of the brothels that caters to the lowest form of man there is." The man on the pinto was finished. He did not wait. He did not ask for the two gringos to surrender. He raised the rifle with one hand and shot the man in the derby hat.

Soledad Tadeo did not see the gray-haired man shoot the other gringo, the one on the horse. The gunshot had surprised her so much she had tumbled backward, and then the man in the derby hat and the checkered coat was falling through the canvas, pushing it open and landing next to her and the boy who had not accepted the bacon.

The rich gringo was dead. The bullet from the rifle had taken him in the center of the chest. There was little blood on his buttoned coat. His eyes remained open and would never blink again.

She heard the other shot as she pried the pistol from the dead man's hand. The man on the pinto might not be able to kill the one on the horse, so she would help. She climbed through the canvas onto the seat, leaped over the side, and saw the gringo's horse galloping back toward Rancho Los Cielos. There was no rider. She stumbled to her knees and saw the man who had killed the rich gringo and that he had also killed the rich gringo's partner.

The stranger dropped the rifle and ran to Soledad Tadeo. He looked as though he wanted to pull her into his arms, but he stopped. His eyes looked funny, like he was about to cry. He reached and gently took the pistol from her hand. "Are you all right?" he managed to ask in slow border Spanish.

She did not answer.

He helped her up. "How many are in the wagon?" he asked.

She did not answer again. She knew this man. He was a gringo. Maybe he had been in her house. That made her remember her mother and she turned *around*.

"It's over," he told her. But he was shaking as he stood and walked back to the man he had shot off his horse. She saw him stop over the man, saw him bring up the pistol that had once belonged to the rich gringo who was now dead in the back of the wagon.

Soledad Tadeo saw the gray-haired scout extend the pistol and pull the trigger. The bullet turned the man's head to one side. The stranger who had just killed the two white men kept pulling the trigger until the revolver was empty, and, yet, even then he kept cocking the hammer and squeezing the trigger, cocking the hammer and squeezing the trigger.

CHAPTER 70

Soledad Tadeo had not thought of that ugly episode for years. Yet the memory of the man who had saved her life, the one who had stopped her and the others from being taken by those miserable gringo slavers to Prescott made her picture his face, and she knew he was the same scout who had been visiting her for all those years. He was the man named Sam Florence. This Sam Florence had never asked her about The Canyon of The Sorrows, but he had told the soldier named Holden and his hard-drinking friend called Masterson that she knew the way to that canyon.

How could that be? How did this Sam Florence know?

It did not matter. That was years ago. Her mother was still dead. And few Apaches had returned to The Canyon of The Sorrows to sell captured women to men like the one who had worn a checkered coat and a derby hat.

She looked at the *soldados* named Holden and Masterson who did not wear the uniform of the bluecoats to the north. She told them, "It is enough that I know the way. It is enough that I will take you there. We should go now."

"Thank you," Holden said.

"I will get my horse," she told them as she headed out the door. "We will ride in twenty minutes."

Rancho Los Cielos had never been much of a village, but the Apache raid when she had turned fifteen years old had driven off others. The priest and the nun left their church and school and moved to a larger town where *Rurales* were stationed and guarded against Apache raids. Others decided to move to safer places or to escape the terrible memories that January night had left to haunt their dreams. With fewer people living in the village, businesses closed until practically all that was left was Mariscos and The Cantina That Has No Name — and even those would have been gone had not bandits from both sides of the border made the place a resting spot, a place to drink tequila and maybe have something to eat before riding away.

Those were all that came to Rancho Los

Cielos these days. No one could remember when the last time *Rurales* had come through to make sure all was well. The only decent person to stop was the scout, the old man whose name was Sam Florence. Soledad Tadeo turned and looked back at Grat Holden.

Maybe this *Yanqui* was a good man, too. Not that it mattered.

She found her saddle in the lean-to behind the corral and groomed the horse before throwing the blanket over the back and the saddle on top of the blanket. Once she had the saddle cinched in place, she took the reins and led the horse out. She closed the gate behind her and walked to Mariscos. The two gringos were about to mount their horses.

Soledad Tadeo glanced at The Cantina That Has No Name. The owner and bartender was crossing the street, muttering something, not paying attention. Most likely he was going to the privy that stood on the other side of Mariscos. That was what had become of a town like Rancho Los Cielos. Two businesses. One corral. One outhouse.

The man who owned and who worked at The Cantina That Has No Name was Juan Gomez. He did not see the man who killed him.

The arrow came out of nowhere and struck Gomez in his chest. He dropped to the dirt with no time to gasp or cry out. He simply died and lay in the street, spread-eagled, as the Apaches rushed around both sides of Mariscos.

Soledad Tadeo felt the reins whip out of her right hand, leaving the mark of leather that burned her palm. She heard her horse snort, turn, and bolt down the trail that led to the border. She did not look back. She dropped to the ground.

"Imbecile," she called herself. Her horse was galloping away, and she was lying in horse apples and dirt. She had left her revolver and her rifle in the cantina. A woman her age, with her experience, should have known better. Rancho Los Cielos was not Nogales. It was not Agua Prieta. She deserved to die like Juan Gomez.

All of the Apaches swung their horses to the corral. She covered her head with both hands and felt one horse leap over her. She breathed in dust, rolled to her side, and kept rolling. The Apaches pulled their horses to hard stops, with two of the animals coming to their knees, and one tossing its rider over its head.

No more than ten, she thought, coming to her feet.

The Apaches yelled and almost immediately turned their mounts around. The one who had been thrown, had risen quickly, grabbed the hackamore, and was trying to swing into his Indian saddle when a gunshot rang out — the first. He was slammed off the horse, crashed into the top rail of the corral, flipped over it, and landed in the water bucket.

Soledad Tadeo was running. Apaches must have been coming to Rancho Los Cielos for horses. There were not enough women in the town to make that kind of raid profitable anymore.

On the other side of the street, she saw the man who had saved her when she was fifteen — Sam Florence — swinging the barrel of his smoking Winchester and firing again. She did not know if his shot proved true, but she understood that he had fired the bullet that had killed one of the Apaches. She turned toward The Cantina That Has No Name, to hide behind the scout named Sam Florence.

CHAPTER 71

"Get those horses inside, Masterson!" Holden roared. "Inside. Get them off the damned street!" He saw the dead Mexican in the street, the arrow still quivering.

The Apaches had come out of thin air. Their horses raised dust as they swarmed into the street, milling, regrouping, and took off toward the corral.

The revolver leaped into Holden's hand and he shouted again at Masterson. If those bucks ran off with their horses, Holden knew any slim chance he had of getting those Springfield rifles back would be gone. His heart leaped as the beautiful woman who was to serve as their guide dropped to the ground.

To his surprise, the Apaches did not stop, and none tried to lean over and scoop her into his arms, to carry her away . . . perhaps to The Canyon of The Sorrows. They stopped in front of the corral, yelling, pointing. He couldn't understand anything, but from their gestures most of them appeared to be angry. They had come for horses in the corral, only to find no more than one or two inside.

Holden looked across the street to see Sam Florence working the Winchester from the doorway to The Cantina That Has No Name. He saw the woman running, weaving, and the Indians charging again. Grat Holden cocked the heavy .45 and charged.

The Schofield boomed twice as he ran toward the girl, who seemed to change direction and run to him. One Apache, a vicious-looking devil, leaned over in his saddle. He wanted to grab Soledad Tadeo for himself, but Holden dived. His right shoulder took her in the hips and he kept flying, carrying her underneath the Apache's grasping hand and out of the path of two other horses as they charged past.

They hit the dirt hard. Holden's jaw slammed shut so hard he thought for sure he had broken or chipped every tooth in his mouth. She grunted. He rolled over, and tried to find the Schofield he had dropped. Dust blinded him. He heard two more shots, and an echo that sounded more like a cannon. He had heard that roar before, back when he had played sitting duck in the canyon that led from the American border to Rancho Los Cielos. It was an 1880 model Springfield, and that meant Ben Masterson was covering them from Mariscos.

As long, Holden thought, *as that rifle doesn't jam!*

A bullet tugged at his hat, which somehow had not fallen during the commotion. He heard the roar of the Schofield and through the dust, saw the woman on her knees and firing the big .45 at the backs of the Apaches as they galloped down the street. The gun was so big, so powerful, she had to use both hands to hold it, and she definitely had trouble bringing back the hammer to full cock. But she fired that heavy pistol. And she kept firing.

He went to her as the hammer snapped hard on an empty chamber.

"Here."

She whirled, her eyes blazing with hatred, but softening slightly when she realized that he was no Apache. He took the gun from her hands, helped her to her feet, and they ran.

He saw the Apaches at the edge of the road before it turned to head deeper into Mexico. Their horses were hard to control, and they seemed to be arguing with each other again. One pointed at the corral, and

Holden guessed that they were pointing at the dead brave they had left behind.

Apaches, like most Indians, did not like to leave their dead behind. In that regard, they showed the same attitude as officers and enlisted men in the US Cavalry.

Holden and Soledad reached Mariscos and quickly stepped inside.

"Where the hell did they come from?" Masterson asked. He tossed one of his Colt Lightning revolvers to the woman.

Holden leaned against the adobe wall and began reloading the big Schofield.

He didn't answer Masterson's question. He asked another one. "Where in hell is the bartender?"

Masterson shrugged. "My guess is he's halfway to Vera Cruz by now." He moved to the window.

"They're coming again!" He pulled back the hammer of the Springfield rifle, bracing the heavy barrel against the frame of the busted window.

"Eight," Holden said as he filled the last chamber with a .45-caliber cartridge and cocked the Schofield. "By my count."

"All it takes," Masterson said, "is one." The Springfield roared.

An arrow thudded in the wooden post next to Holden as he fired. Another shot tore into the adobe. Some of the Indians were shooting rifles, others were using bows and arrows. Two of them did not stop. They raced past Mariscos and The Cantina That Has No Name and stopped at the corral.

Holden hoped they were collecting the dead man and the horse. That might mean they had tired of the fight and were withdrawing. He ducked, fired, and watched the Indians spin their horses and kick the sides. They galloped past, and the two who had collected the body of their fallen comrade, turned and rode behind Mariscos.

One Apache remained. He snapped a single-action Colt, sending three shots toward Holden and Masterson and three others at Sam Florence on the other side of the street. He looked to be a younger man, maybe Holden's age. The Apache shoved the empty Colt into his breechcloth and raised his fist in triumph, turned, kicked his horse, and galloped away, ducking under the shots fired by Sam Florence and Ben Masterson.

He had a belligerent face, long hair, and a mangled ear. It looked like someone had bitten or torn off the lobe.

As they rode out of Rancho Los Cielos, Soledad Tadeo screamed. She ran into the street and fired Masterson's double-action

.38 at the last Indian. She kept firing, too, even after she had emptied the six-shooter.

CHAPTER 72

Colonel Carlton Smythe sat in his desk staring at the papers the sergeant major had brought before him to sign. Outside his office, the soldiers at Fort Bowie were scattering to the various duties they had been assigned for the day.

Eventually, reluctantly, he dipped the pen into the inkwell and signed one paper, blew on it, and set it aside to dry. He signed the next paper, did the same, and finished his task quickly. He glanced across the room until his eyes landed on the decanter of brandy. Smythe looked at the clock and checked the time against his pocket watch. It was, he feared, still a bit too early in the day to enjoy a cordial or two. The bugler had just sounded out that mess was over, so Smythe leaned back in his chair and twiddled his thumbs.

He wasn't certain how long he had been doing that when he realized that the sergeant major was tapping on the door. Smythe had become an astute observer, learning which way the many men under his command knocked on his door. The sergeant major, of course, knocked the most so guessing his *rat-tat-tat-tat* was not difficult. Not even worth the challenge.

"Come in, Sergeant," he called out and stood.

The sergeant came in, saluted, and waited for the salute to be returned, which Smythe did half-heartedly. "Corporal Stevens is outside, Colonel."

Smythe blinked. He could use that brandy right about now. "Corporal . . . Stevens?"

"Yes, sir. Dispatch rider. You sent him out to stay with Captain Garrison."

Smythe nodded, but that name was as foreign to him as Corporal Stevens. He waited, but the sergeant major offered no more particulars. Smythe swallowed and said, "Captain . . . Garrison?"

"The heliograph, Colonel," the noncommissioned officer said. "The one stationed at Dismal Mesa down along the border. Monkeying around with those sun-signalers . . . and keeping an eye out for Lieutenant Holden and Sergeant Masterson."

Smythe breathed in deeply and felt his heart begin to race. "Of course, Sergeant.

Of course, Well, don't just stand there, Sergeant, send the corporal in."

Within moments, the corporal had replaced the sergeant and the door had been closed. Smythe beamed, saluted the corporal who was covered with dust and looked as though he had not bathed or shaved in months, though he had only been gone for days. He was a thin man, short, with bowed legs and a bronzed face. He weighed next to nothing. But everyone the rank of sergeant or higher swore that he was the best galloper in the man's Army.

"Corporal," Smythe said, having already forgotten the trooper's name, "you look like you've ridden far. I bet some brandy would cut the dust. Let me pour you a glass."

"Don't mind if I do, sir," the corporal said.

That made Smythe beam with joy. The way his luck had been going, this corporal would be a teetotaler.

He filled one snifter, then poured more into a wineglass. "Sorry, Corporal," Smythe said as he handed the small cordial to the young rider, "but they have misplaced many of my cordials. I'll have to use the wineglass myself."

Corporal Stevens did not notice the discrepancy. He downed his drink in a second, wet his lips, and set the empty glass on the edge of the counter.

Smythe carried his large wineglass to the desk, sipping along the way, and settled into his chair. "Let's hear your report, Corporal." he said, and took another drink.

"Well, Colonel. They made it into Mexico. I don't know how they got there — which way they went, I mean — but I picked up their dust on the other side of Dismal Mesa. They rode into Rancho Los Cielos, using the trail through the canyon instead of the main road. I heard shooting. A lot of shooting. But I obeyed your orders since they were in Mexico by that time and not in the United States. At night, I figured I was off duty, so I got shun of my Army duds, and crossed the border. I reckon whoever had taken shots at them got the worse end of the deal. I saw the lieutenant and the sergeant in that little bitty ol' town. So they got that far."

"You got no further reports?" Smythe asked.

"Per your orders, I rode hell-bent-for-leather back here to Bowie. Captain Garrison is keeping an eye on the border for their return."

"Very good, Corporal. That is all. Tell the sutler that I said it is all right if you have a beer."

"Thank you, most kindly, Colonel." The trooper snapped a salute, spun on his heel, and exited through the door. Smythe followed him, gave the little man enough time to make it outside, and then opened the door and stepped into the antechamber.

The sergeant major rose and saluted, but Smythe was tired of those formalities. "Sergeant, get Lieutenant Paine. Have him assemble a patrol of ten men, issue rifles and forty rounds of ammunition. Enough food to get us to Dismal Mesa and the border. We will ride out in two hours. That is all, Sergeant. Tell Mr. Paine that I will ride with him."

The sergeant major's eyes almost popped out of their sockets.

"Tell Mr. Paine that I will command." Smythe spun, went back to his office, slammed the door shut, and found the wineglass of brandy he had left behind.

He laughed softly and drank. He would be ready in case Holden and the sergeant made it out of Mexico with those rifles. Then he would ride down upon the men, shoot them as traitors, and have the rifles back in his hands. The Springfield Armory would likely send him a healthy bonus. The general and his staff in Arizona would offer him medals and promotions. That was one scenario.

And the other? If Holden's little expedition failed, which, most likely, it would, then Smythe could report that he had chased the coward that had stolen the Springfield rifles to the border, and there, reluctantly he had been forced to stop.

He wouldn't get any medals from the general or a reward from Massachusetts or his name in many newspapers for that . . . but he would save his arse and avoid any Court of Inquiry or, God forbid, a court-martial.

CHAPTER 73

Holden and Masterson raced into the street after the hotheaded Mexican woman. Across the street, Sam Florence practically fell out of The Cantina That Has No Name, cursing, and stumbling, and coming up with the Winchester ready for any Apaches who dared charge again.

None did.

All that was left of the Indians was their dust.

The scout lowered the rifle and roared at Soledad Tadeo. "What the hell was that — ?" He stopped, caught his breath, and lowered his tone and his gaze. "Are you all right?"

The woman glared at him, then turned her anger to Sergeant Masterson. She pitched the smoking Colt .38 toward him, snapping, "Here, take your pistol." She turned around, cursed and said, "I must go catch up my horse." She started walking away.

Sam Florence said, "You'll never catch him by walking. Hold on! Damn it, Soledad, I said stop! *Now!*"

She did.

The scout turned around and moved into The Cantina That Has No Name. Moments later, he led his pinto horse out, stepped into the saddle, and the mustang exploded into a gallop. The woman stopped, drew a breath, and moved to the dead bartender on the street.

Sergeant Masterson was already kneeling by him, checking for a pulse that everyone knew would not be found. He kept his eye on the dust.

Holden knelt beside the dead Mexican just as Masterson let the hand fall back onto the ground.

"Any idea what that was about?" the lieutenant asked in a whisper.

The Indians were gone. He guessed they would not return as there was no reason for them to come back. What would less than a handful of scalps — if those Apaches actually took scalps; most did not — and so few horses do to boost the Indians' glory? Holden wiped his sweaty hands on his trousers.

"You mean the girl and my Colt? Means she don't like Apaches, be my guess. Or do you mean —"

"The raid, damn it. What was that raid about? Surely they didn't send in nine raiders to kill him." Holden pointed at Juan Gomez.

"My mother raised me better than to go around guessing what motivates a red injun," Masterson said.

"They rode to the corral," Holden said. He nodded at the dead man in the street. "This poor fellow just happened to be crossing the street at the wrong time."

Masterson turned to look at the corral and shrugged as he rose. "I don't think that corral ever holds many horses, at least, none worth stealing. And damned few worth eating if you're an Apache."

"I think they were after the wagons," Holden said.

"You mean — ?"

"Foster's wagons." Holden nodded. "They wanted to take the guns from Foster."

"But Foster ain't here."

"He was."

"Crooked Nose is a lot smarter than that, Holden," Masterson said.

"That wasn't Crooked Nose leading that bunch. You saw them. Young. Even the leader isn't any older than I am."

Rising, the sergeant turned and handed his Springfield to the Mexican girl. "You take this, sweetie. Holden and me will carry in your boss."

She took the rifle without a word and crossed the street toward The Cantina That Has No Name. Masterson pulled out the arrow from the dead bartender's chest and pitched the bloody instrument to the ground. Then he took the arms of Juan Gomez, Grat Holden took the legs, and they took him into the tiny saloon where they laid him on a table. Inside, Soledad Tadeo returned the rifle to Masterson and went to find a blanket to cover the dead man.

She was out with the blanket, which she draped over the poor man's body without a word.

"We cannot stay to bury him," Holden said. He had taken his hat off. "I'm sorry."

"There is no need to be sorry," she said and she nodded through the door. "Pico will see to Juan. As soon as the gringo is back with my horse, we must go." She walked out the door.

Holden reloaded his Schofield. Masterson reloaded his Lightning, and picked up the Springfield rifle the girl had left in the cantina.

"It didn't jam," Holden said, nodding at the big weapon in Masterson's hands.

"Didn't shoot it that much." Masterson laughed. "And didn't hit anything I aimed at, either."

Sam Florence rode up ten minutes later. He handed the Mexican beauty the reins to her horse, remaining in his seat until he saw the girl's face. Swinging down off his pinto, he ducked under the horse's head and stopped in front of Soledad Tadeo. His fingers touched the bruise on her cheek.

She pushed the hand away. "It is nothing," she said in Spanish.

His face revealed a harsh anger, but he said nothing in response.

He looked at Holden and nodded at the road that led out of town and into Mexico.

"All right. I'll say it again. I told you I'd get you here. That I'd introduce you to someone who can take you to the trading place. My job's done. You agree?"

Silently, Grat Holden nodded.

"Well, I ain't agreeing. Not anymore. I'm going with you boys, and with you, Soledad. I'm going to kill me one miserable son of a bitch. Back in the war, Foster told me I owed him a life. He didn't specify that it had to be *his* life. His life ain't worth spit.

I'm gonna kill him."

"No," Soledad Tadeo said. "That is something I will do."

"If I don't kill him first," Holden said.

CHAPTER 74

The mules carried the load of weapons through the arroyo, climbing into higher country, and then into the canyon. The sun was bright, but the canyon felt unnervingly cold. The wind moaned like ghosts. Foster laughed as he saw the men he rode with shivering in their saddles. Not cold. Scared.

It was The Canyon of The Sorrows, and they were sorry they were there.

They had lost one man, but only temporarily. A Mexican named Emanuel whose horse had come up lame. Foster had debated killing the man and his horse, but such moves could lead to a lowering of morale. He let the man stay with his horse. Foster wasn't sure about the wisdom of such a plan, but . . . well, it would be fun to put his life in the hands of a worthless greaser. It would test his luck.

He dismounted and wrapped the reins around an old corral where the prisoners had been kept. It wasn't exactly the federal pen at Leavenworth, nor was it Yuma. Anybody could have climbed out or under the fence, but they would have had nowhere to go. Not with Apaches and white slavers surrounding them, and not with a bitterly harsh desert to cross if they could get out of the wretched, terrifying place.

"Foster," said one of the hired killers.

"Yeah."

"This is it?"

"Yeah."

"Man alive, Foster, this is a box canyon. There ain't no way out. We're going to sell these guns here?"

Foster grinned. "No." He laughed and slapped his thigh. "You think I'm going to sell two hundred and fifty Springfield rifles to a bunch of dumb Apaches who likely won't have fifty pesos between them? Or that fool who thinks he's a big man and will be able to command an entire country when he couldn't command two ten-year-olds?" He shook his head and laughed again. "And don't get me started about the great and grand Colonel Will Muncie and his bunch."

"I don't get it," the hired gun said. "I don't get anything you've done since we pulled out of Rancho Los Cielos."

"Well, boys" — Foster opened his saddle-

bag and pulled out a bottle of rye whiskey
— "let me explain it to you. While you
unload those boxes."

Meeting at The Canyon of The Sorrows,
Jed Foster had to think, was brilliant. Knowing that the three groups who wanted to bid
on the Springfields could not be trusted,
that the Apaches, the Mexicans, and the
Johnny Rebs would try to steal the weapons
— and kill Foster and his men — he had
taken a few precautions.

When they had pulled out of Rancho Los
Cielos with the wagons and more mules
than needed, Foster had stopped his command on the hard-packed ground south of
town. He had transferred the rifles to several
mules, and those mules had brought the
rifles all the way to The Canyon of The Sorrows. The wagons had left the hard road
with his drivers ordered to take the wagons
all the way to another canyon in a rough
area known as Madre Blanco — about
twenty-five miles south and east. Of course,
before those wagons had pulled out, Foster
had had his men load the beds with rocks.
Enough to make whoever followed the
tracks think they were following more than
two hundred Springfield rifles and boxes of
ammunition and bayonets.

That still left them with fourteen more mules, so Foster had ordered two of his men to take those mules, whose packsaddles had been loaded with satchels containing more rocks, down to the Rio Fuerta. From there, they would double their way back around Feo Canyon, Ugly Canyon, recross the border north of Rancho Los Cielos and wait in Bisbee for word from Foster and his men.

"Chances are," Foster explained to the six men left with him, "that someone will follow the wagons. Some others will follow the mules." He tapped the hard ground. "No one can follow us here. Few men can read the signs on rocky ground this hard."

"Apaches can," one of his men said.

Foster nodded. "But Apaches already know where this canyon is. I'm not worried about Crooked Nose's bunch." He chuckled. "Hell, I'm not worried about Amonte Negro or Colonel Will Muncie, either."

"So what's our play?" the red-bearded man from Indiana asked.

"We've reduced the odds," Foster said. "Some are following Wilson's bunch in the wagons. Others are trailing Morgan and those mules all the way to Bisbee if needed. What's left will have to wait. We'll send our escort to guide them here. Where we'll be waiting."

The mean one with a hook for his left hand shook his head. "And the Apaches?"

Foster shrugged. "They'll be here. They won't need a guide."

The one with the red beard shook his head and spit a river of tobacco juice onto a sun-bleached bone. "So we're trapped. In a box canyon. With Apaches, with renegade Southern trash, and Mexican bandits blocking us in."

"Not entirely." Foster had that part figured out, too.

Once all of the participants — Crooked Nose's Indians, Muncie's gray coats, and Negro's ruffians — had arrived at The Canyon of The Sorrows, a rifle case would be opened, and the Springfields — empty — would be passed around. All of the bidders would be asked to show their money. Then the bidding would begin.

"Any one of those groups will just start shooting," the man with the hook said. "There won't be anyone safe in this canyon."

"Which is why you won't be in this canyon." Foster pointed at the high walls.

The men still with Foster would be on both sides of the canyon top, armed with Springfield Model 1880 rifles to shoot down upon the Apaches, the Mexicans, and the Rebels.

"We'll blow the entrance up," Foster said. "Everyone will be trapped here. From your perch above, and with all that ammunition you have, you'll be able to take your good sweet time killing every last one of those boys."

The one from Indiana took off his hat and scratched his bald head. "How do we blow up the canyon? How do we stop them from riding out? We're just a handful of men."

Foster grinned. These men weren't as stupid as Will Muncie or Amonte Negro.

Foster moved to a U-shaped cairn of rocks that had likely once been used as a roasting pit for the slavers and the Apaches. Carefully, he brushed off the ashes and dirt that was covering a blanket. He removed the blanket, then five more blankets until he had reached a small box, which he unlocked with a key he produced from his trousers pocket, and then carefully, almost painstakingly, he opened. He reached into the box and pulled out a small bottle that seemed to be steaming from inside the glass.

He whispered, "We had gin in the bottles on the wagon seats back in Rancho Los Cielos. But this . . . this is the real stuff. This" — he grinned — "is nitroglycerin."

Every man jack of them took a step or two back.

Foster wanted to laugh, but didn't want to blow himself to pieces. He knelt again, taking his good, sweet time, and gently returned the small bottle into a well-padded place. He softly closed the lid, but did not lock it, and with a nurse's touch, he covered the box with three of the several blankets.

"This will bring down the walls," he said. "Then we kill them all. After which, we come down and take the gold they brought or whatever they brought to buy these Springfields."

"And then?" the one with the hook asked.

"Then?" Foster laughed before he explained to these fools. "Then we go south, and we do the same damned thing to *Rurales,* to Yaqui Indians, and to the Mexican army."

His men glanced at each other. Likely, they thought they had a madman for a leader. They just did not know how lucky Jed Foster was.

The one from Indiana, however, brought up a very intelligent question. "One thing, Captain, that you'll have to explain. What's to bring all those Apaches, the Johnny Rebs, and the Mexicans in here? So we leave the boxes down here? Empty boxes. Those men aren't going to come in here and just wait. They'll expect us to be here. To make the trade. To start the auction."

"Very good," Foster said. "Yes. They'll expect at least one man here. And they'll find one man here. The leader. I'll be here."

"Hell, Captain," said the one with the hook. "Bullets flying, nitro blowing this canyon to hell and gone. How do you expect to get out of this death trap alive?"

"That," Jed Foster said, "you just leave to Lucky Jed Foster."

CHAPTER 75

Crooked Nose had saddled his favorite war pony, a deep-chested sorrel with a star on her forehead, and began painting the mare for war. He kept his back to Badger Killer when he returned from his little raid.

He could feel Badger Killer's rage, but Crooked Nose kept with his mare, not looking around, not even concerned, and finally Badger Killer roared out Crooked Nose's name.

The old man turned and saw the horse that was being led away by sobbing women. A fine Apache warrior was strapped to that horse. There would be mourning in camp tonight. Also, eight warriors had ridden out with Badger Killer, but only five had returned — and one of those was dead. Crooked Nose frowned before he looked up at Badger Killer, who remained mounted on his weathered dun horse.

He saw surprise make the young brave

with the mangled ear lean back in his saddle. It had been a long time since Badger Killer had seen Crooked Nose's face painted for war.

"What — ?" Badger Killer began but could not finish.

"Four men and I are riding north," Crooked Nose said. "To fight the pale eyes."

"We have already fought the pale eyes," Badger Killer said, so excited that his horse began to jump around. "We have brought honor to our people."

Crooked Nose looked at the riders, the young men who had followed the Indian with the ugly ear and the bad attitude. Most of the men watched the body of the young brave being taken from the horse. They did not look like a war party returning from victory. They looked scared . . . and so young.

"Three I do not see," Crooked Nose said.

"Blind Skunk, Deer Hoof, and Ten Feathers ride after the long guns, which have left the place where the Mexicans and the Americanos drink. But they are not on their way to The Canyon of The Sorrows. The pale eyes have no intention of selling the guns to you or anyone. Pale eyes can never be trusted."

Crooked Nose considered that and shrugged. He had lost interest in taking the pale eyes' guns anyway. He had another idea.

"You run away," Badger Killer said mockingly, but his voice could not betray his uneasiness.

"I run to fight men who, maybe, know how to fight. There is no glory, there is no honor in dealing with men who try to sell us guns. You, Badger Killer, are the man I should thank for this wisdom, for it was you who showed me how wrong, how foolish I was. We do not steal gold from the black robes. We do not torture Mexicans to tell us how many long guns we can buy with Mexican and blue-coat gold we had stolen. We were becoming men like the Mexican bandits who hide in canyons and steal from anyone they can. Now, my brothers and I will ride to glory. We will return victorious. Or we will not return at all."

The young man turned his head, studying Crooked Nose. He tried to figure out what the catch was, the scheme, the trick, the lie.

"I would like very much, Badger Killer, if you and your warriors joined us when we take our fight to the bluecoats or whoever we meet in the land of the pale-face soldiers." That was a lie. He didn't want Badger Killer anywhere near him, but more men would be better. Even Badger Killer.

"You are running away," Badger Killer repeated, which made Crooked Nose smile.

He had extended the invitation, and Badger Killer had rejected it. *Good.* That made Crooked Nose happy.

Badger Killer pointed. "Go ahead. Run with" — he looked at the old men who had agreed to ride with Crooked Nose — "your grandfathers. My warriors and I will ride after the wagons. We will take the long-shooting long guns from the bluecoats. You take your old men, Crooked Nose, and you run away. When you come back, if you are man enough to come back, you will find a place for you in my camp. This I promise you. I will not turn my back on you, Crooked Nose, even though you are weak, even though you are a coward, even though you are a squaw. You ride away. When you return, I will let you clean my long-gun that I will have taken from my enemy's dead hand. The pale eyes will find nothing but death. And I, Badger Killer, will find glory. And honor."

Crooked Nose was already in the saddle of his sorrel by the time Badger Killer finished his speech. The old man did not look again at the brash, bold fool. Crooked Nose looked at his friends, nodded at them, and rode out of camp. His friends followed him. They sang a song as they rode out of the camp and turned north. The song they sang was one of honor.

In the camp that Badger Killer was now commanding, there was much singing, too. But it was a song of mourning . . . for the brave young warrior who had followed Badger Killer . . . to death.

CHAPTER 76

Colonel Will Muncie had led his command back to Rancho Los Cielos, only to find the wagons gone, and the town abandoned except for one of the saloonkeepers — and he was packing his liquor and his tables into a wagon. He said the town was dead, that Juan Gomez was dead — whoever Juan Gomez was — and that he was going to find his brother and his mother in Zacatecas. He wished he had never left Zacatecas. The land there was pink from the beautiful quarry. The land in Rancho Los Cielos was red from the blood.

Outside of town, Lieutenant Fountain found the tracks, a mix of shod and unshod ponies, which meant Apaches — riding their horses and horses they had stolen. They also followed the wagon tracks till it reached the hard-packed earth.

Fountain and two other fine Confederates knelt close to the ground, studying the sign.

The corporal who had lost his arm at Nashville rode off a ways. Fountain walked in another direction, but Will Muncie could see the tracks the lieutenant was following. Those tracks were plain as daylight.

Eventually, Lieutenant Fountain turned around and walked back to his horse, which was being held by a private named Reginald. Fountain swung into the saddle, nodded at old Reginald, and eased his horse to Muncie. By that time, the corporal was loping back. The hooves left the sand, clang loudly on the hard rocks, and the rider reined to a stop just to Fountain's left.

"Report, bookkeeper," Muncie said.

"Wagons head off that way, sir, southeast, but there are mules going yonder, likely toward the Fire River."

Muncie pointed at the wagon tracks. "Those run deep, Lieutenant. Just as deep as they ran when they left that flyspeck of a village."

The bookkeeper nodded. "Your eyes are as sharp as they were at Chancellorsville, Colonel."

"So the wagons still have the Springfields."

"Maybe." Fountain turned to the corporal.

"Mules," the man said and spit tobacco juice onto the hard earth. "Somewhere between ten and eighteen. Not in any particular hurry, but carryin' a lot of weight. You're right, Lieutenant. They're headin' southeast."

"How much weight?" Muncie asked the soldier.

"Enough to be Springfield rifles and boxes of ammunition, Colonel."

"Or rocks," Lieutenant Fountain said.

Will Muncie sank slightly in his saddle. "That damned Yankee wants us to guess. Follow the wagons. Follow the mules. I underestimated that traitor. But he has underestimated me. What would you say, Lieutenant?"

Fountain shrugged. "Mules would make more sense, Colonel. Easier to maneuver through rough country than wagons. And from what I've heard, The Canyon of The Sorrows is a tough place to get through."

"But those are just stories. We've never been to that canyon. For all we know, it's nothin' more than a little dry wash in the desert. Corporal?"

The corporal shrugged. "Wagons are headin' southeast. In that direction, you're not likely to find much in the way of hiding spots or canyons."

"So . . ." Captain Knight, who had remained silent, spoke up, "we have to make a guess. Follow the wagons. Or follow the mules."

"Or," the bookkeeper said, "just wait in Rancho Los Cielos till the yank sends his guide to take us to that trading place."

"There's another option."

The men looked at their leader.

"How many mules did you say you found, Corporal?"

The man shifted uncomfortably in his saddle. "Not altogether certain, suh. More than a dozen. Not more than twenty. It's hard to read tracks in that sand, what with the wind and all."

"How many mules were in the corral?" Muncie asked.

"A lot," the corporal said.

"And none are left."

Lieutenant Fountain said, "Yes, sir, but no one's left in that town, if you'd call it a town, except for some saloonkeeper who has lost his mind."

Captain Knight suggested, "Those mules could have belonged to . . . I don't know. The man who ran that cantina. Or the girl, the pretty Mexican girl."

"Or the Yankee." Muncie nudged his horse and circled the men who stood watching, wondering. And curious. The hooves clanged loudly on the ground, and the colonel laughed when he pulled his horse to a stop. "Corporal, "do you see any tracks?" He pointed behind him.

"No, suh."

"Exactly. So, let me offer a suggestion. If you were a Yankee, and you did not trust me, a Southern gentleman and man of honor, to wait like some black slave to get told to come to some place and follow your beck and call" — he spit with bitterness — "would you go to your secret canyon that only you and slavers and red heathen injuns know . . . and leave tracks that a blind man could follow?" His voice raised with anger, and he removed his hat. "Or would you take a trail that would be downright hard to follow unless you had a good coon hound or an Apache buck in yer employ?"

The men glanced at one another.

Lieutenant Fountain cleared his throat.

"The question, Colonel," he said, "is can we risk that? Do we gamble and bring everyone with us and just follow this hard ground? Or do we send some of our men after the mules, and others after the wagons?"

"Dividing our troops, right?" Muncie let out a light chuckle. "It did not work out well for that yank named Custer a few years back up Montana-way."

"No, sir," the corporal answered.

"Which is something I meant to ask you, Colonel," Captain Knight said. "When you were talking about Shiloh, the overconfidence, and how the bluecoats pushed us . . . you and General Johnston's army back after the first day. Well . . . the only reason Grant's butcherin' yanks were able to do that was because they got —"

"Reinforcements," Muncie finished, and he pointed toward the northeast.

CHAPTER 77

Amonte Negro reined the black horse to a sliding stop. His sombrero almost flew off his head, but he managed to catch it and slap it against his thigh as the stallion recovered, rose, and blew hard from the long run. The men swung out all around him, and they stared, their hands on their guns at the gringos in gray coats who looked on nervously.

"Coronel," Negro said, donning the big hat at the old American who had not been able to beat the *Yanquis* with all that money, all those slaves, all those guns. And the fool still wanted to go back to his country and lose another war.

That would be a good thing, Amonte Negro thought. *At least the fool gringo and his army would be out of Mexico.*

"It is good to see you, *Coronel.*"

"And," the old gringo said, "it is good to see you, Dictator."

Amonte Negro laughed. He wondered what this word, *dictator,* meant.

"I thought we were to meet at Rancho Los Cielos. My men are thirsty. I am thirsty. Let us ride to that town. Maybe that Soledad can fill my glass with tequila and maybe I can fill her —"

"You won't find anyone left in that . . . ahem . . . town to serve you, *Señor* Negro. It has been abandoned."

"Dios mío, eso es una noticia que rompe el corazón."

Negro had not expected such terrible news. And he was quite thirsty from all the riding across the desert.

"But we are glad you have arrived, suh. We are about to pay our friend, Mr. Foster, a visit."

Negro leaned forward. His thirst could wait. "You know the way to The Canyon of The Sorrows?"

"I think we can come close, yes." The colonel pointed at wagon tracks in the sand. "But in case I am mistaken, we need to send some scouts after those wagons."

"Those wagons carry the guns?"

"They carry something. My gut tells me they carry rocks."

"¿Piedras? ¿Rocas?"

The old gringo in gray shrugged. He then

445

explained that mules, also loaded down with much weight, were going in another direction. That meant the guns the gray coats and Amonte Negro needed could be heading in the wagons or with the mules . . . or, as the old gringo believed, on the hard rock into the high country.

It was just too confusing and gave Amonte Negro a headache when he had not had any mescal since breakfast. "So, what is it that you think we should do?" he asked the colonel.

"You pick your fastest galloper. Send him after the wagons. Send four riders with him. If your galloper discovers that the wagons indeed carry the rifles we seek, that the Yankee traitor Foster is welshing on our deal, then he gallops back to catch us. If he sees for certain that this is a decoy . . . a . . . a . . . a . . . ?" He looked at his interpreter for help.

"Señuelo."

"Do you understand?"

"Señuelo. Sí."

"If that is the case, you kill the drivers, cut the mules loose, and return to us." The old man pointed at the trail that led toward the Rio Fuerta.

"I will send my fastest galloper after the mules that left in that direction. And four men. They will have the same orders. If they find the Springfields we need, the galloper returns to fetch us while the others follow Foster's yanks. If they find this is also a . . ." He tried, but could not pronounce the Spanish word for *lure.* "If that is the case, those men are killed and my men return to us. If the mules do indeed carry our weapons, we will catch up to them with our entire force. That is what I propose, *General.*" He pronounced that right.

It made Amonte Negro grin.

"Do you have any objections?"

His horse wanted to run again, and Negro had to bring it under control, while he tried to read the gray coat's face. It was hard, especially without mescal or tequila or even beer, but Amonte Negro was no fool. No gringo could be trusted, no matter if he wore blue or gray or the clothes of some peon.

"We will do as you ask, *Coronel,* but with one change." Amonte Negro grinned. He was so smart. Benito Juárez, have mercy on his soul, could have used a man with Amonte Negro's brains. "My men will ride after the mules. Your men can go after the wagons. Does that please you, *Coronel?*"

The colonel chuckled and nodded. "Your intellect is inspiring, *General.*" He turned, and barked out five names. Five riders pulled their horses out. They did not have to wait for further instructions. One bolted after the wagon tracks. The others followed at a trot.

The gray-coated gringo was looking at Amonte Negro, who had to pick five men to follow those mule tracks. That was also hard for a man like Amonte Negro. Which of his men were smart enough to do the job? Which of his men could he trust? Hell, he would have to go himself, but that was all right. Maybe the mules were hauling tequila.

CHAPTER 78

The iron hooves of the horses made little noise on the hard, hard rock. Sam Florence had seen to that. He had ripped off the sleeves of a coat, cut them into padding with his Bowie knife, and wrapped it over the feet of the mounts. Then he had secured them with rawhide thongs.

There was noise, but not much, and all the riders had a light touch on the reins. They rode deeper into the hills and felt themselves climbing higher, off the desert floor and into a dark, foreboding place.

Every mile or two, Florence would rein in his horse, dismount, and check the padded shoes he had made for the hooves. He tightened those when needed, adjusted them, or even found more cloth to help diminish the noise.

They rode. All three men kept their rifles across the pommels of the horse. The girl carried one of the Springfield rifles in her right hand, the barrel pointed down. It had to be an uncomfortable way to carry such a weapon, but none of the men made any suggestion to the wildcat known as Soledad Tadeo.

"Are you all right?" Grat Holden had just reined in his horse and looked at Soledad.

She had stopped her horse in the middle of a turn on the trail they followed. She shivered in the saddle and kept her eyes closed tightly. He doubted she had even heard him.

He turned in the saddle and held up his right hand, signaling Ben Masterson and Sam Florence to stop then turned back toward the Mexican girl. He started to reach out, to touch her arm, making her aware of his presence, but he stopped. Something about this woman told him that he should not touch her, especially when her eyes were closed.

He repeated his question louder and using her name.

Her eyes opened and she turned, giving him a savage look at first, but eventually relaxing and drawing in a deep breath, which she held briefly, and then exhaled. "I am fine."

Holden considered her for a moment. He

said softly and sincerely, "You don't have to do this, ma'am. We can ride on ahead, try to find that . . . place."

"You would never find it," she said.

He started to nudge her horse ahead, but stopped almost immediately.

She looked up at him with softer eyes. "But I thank you for your kindness," she said, in the quietest voice, with the softest eyes he had yet heard or seen her use. "And this," she added, the softness gone, "is something I do have to do." She rode ahead.

Once she was about twenty yards ahead, Grat Holden eased his horse around and walked him back toward Masterson and Florence.

"We shouldn't have brought some petticoat with us," Masterson said.

"Shut up," Florence said.

Holden turned his horse around again, and the three men followed the girl at a distance, not too far so that she might get out of sight, but not too close, either.

He let his horse fall alongside the old scout's pinto. "How long have you known her?"

The scout kept his eyes ahead, debating on how to answer. Finally, he let out a soft chuckle and said, "I don't rightly think anybody knows her."

"That's the truth," Masterson mumbled.

"I think you've known her a long time, Sam," Holden said.

"What's it to you?"

Holden shook his head. "Does she know you're her father?" He saw the old man's features harden.

But the scout did not blink and did not look at Grat Holden. Sam Florence kept his head straight ahead. A few yards later, his shoulders slouched. The old man kept staring ahead at the girl riding thirty yards ahead, but he answered Holden's question. "I suppose she's wondering about it, making up her own mind. She's always been good about making up her own mind."

Ben Masterson let out a soft curse.

"Why don't you tell her?"

Florence shrugged. "Gave up that claim when I left her ma." He smiled regretfully. "Ana was something. Soledad's mother. Man, could she cook."

"Why didn't you stay? Or marry the woman?"

"She wouldn't have me. That's the long and short of it. Oh, it was all right for me to visit. Nothing wrong with that. I was welcome to come by and say hello and maybe share a cup of coffee, or if I was lucky, one of her sopaipillas or enchiladas. As long as I didn't stay."

"What happened to her mother?" Masterson asked.

"Murdered," Florence said. "Apaches."

"Crooked Nose?" Masterson asked. "Geronimo?"

"Nah. Some kids and a couple old men. They'd raided a few ranches east of Nogales on the American side. Took a few captive women. Came into Mexico and took some more. I guess Ana was too feisty for that bunch. So they killed her. And took — His head nodded ahead.

"My God," Holden said in a terrified whisper. "To The Canyon of The Sorrows."

"Yeah." Florence's eyes turned into slits. "I didn't learn this till later. I was scouting, but you know the Army and you know the government . . . on both sides of the border. The raiders got across the border, so our Army boys had to stop. Turn back. Send some telegraphs to the *Rurales.* But I stayed around — never occurred to me to ride to Rancho Los Cielos — and when I saw a wagon crossing the border and bound toward Tombstone, I paid myself a little visit."

"Aye," Masterson said. "I remember that fracas. Would've been six years back, last winter. The two men — white men they were — were shot dead. You brought the girls and, if my memory's correct, a young lad, back to Fort Bowie."

"She was one of them," Florence said. "That's how I knew she'd been to The Canyon of The Sorrows."

"So why did you make her do this? Lead us back?" Holden felt the blood rush to his head.

"I didn't. I said you could ask her. She decided to come back. And I'm glad. A doctor over in Tucson once told me that you had to face your nightmares at some point. And then they'd stop tormenting you. So she does this, I figure, maybe that helps her, frees her mind. Either way, we get to find The Canyon of The Sorrows. And we destroy the son of a bitch so that nobody ever has to go through what she did, what who knows how many women before and since, have gone through."

Holden slumped in the saddle. He wanted to throw up.

Beside him, Sam Florence quickly reined in his pinto, and turned back. Holden and Masterson stopped. So did the girl, some yards ahead.

"Hell," Florence said.

They heard the echoes of hooves, many hooves, thundering across the stones.

"Whoever that is," Masterson said, "they're coming mighty fast."

CHAPTER 79

Jed Foster wet his lips, wiped his face, and dried his sweaty hands on his pants before picking up the small container of nitroglycerin. He smiled at the young outlaw, Joe Coberly, who had volunteered to stay behind and help him prepare for their . . . well . . . visitors.

Slowly, he moved to the rocky corner where the canyon widened into the boxed part and stopped at the hole Coberly had dug just under the rocks that had been tumbling down for years. Rain, wind, and erosion had caused the rocks to fall since the beginning of time, Foster figured. In a little while, progress would bring more rocks down — burying those and with luck, a bunch of fools, too.

"Is it the Fourth of July, Capt'n?" Coberly asked.

Foster had knelt and was bending over to put the glass bottle on bandannas and old socks that Coberly had made for the nitro's bed. He stopped, not moving his body, just raising his eyes. *You want to talk about nothing while I'm holding four ounces of death?*

Coberly said, "Sorry," in his softest whisper.

Foster put the bottle on the bedding, let out a short breath, wiped his hands again, and covered the glass with one of Coberly's socks. Gently, he stood, removed his hat, and waved it. On the top of the canyon, the sharpshooting Mexican named Ennio lifted his rifle, one of the new model 1880s Foster had given him. He had also fitted a long brass telescopic sight on that particular weapon.

"Can . . . you . . . see . . . it?" Foster yelled, spacing his words, and hearing the echo.

"Sí," Ennio called down, and his word bounced across The Canyon of The Sorrows.

Foster offered a little salute at the Mexican and walked briskly away from the hole that contained the most powerful explosive found in the world. Joe Coberly had no trouble keeping up with Foster as they crossed the floor of the canyon.

The young killer hooked his thumb toward the last of the nitro and then tilted his head up toward Ennio and his Springfield rifle.

"Even with that fancy lookin' glass, Capt'n, that's still one tough shot for anybody to make. Shootin' downhill. At that distance. With who all knows what hell will be breakin' loose once we've started the ball."

"Well" — Foster stopped in the center of the canyon — "that's one of the good things about working with nitroglycerin, kid. You just have to get close to touch that stuff off. Sometimes, not even that close."

The boxes were there, just in front of the old corral. He could see the black stenciling clearly from where he stood. Even an old man like Will Muncie would be able to read that. And even an illiterate greaser like Amonte Negro or some heathen Apache buck like Crooked Nose could figure out what those boxes held.

SPRINGFIELD ARMORY
Springfield, Massachusetts
US RIFLE, CALIBER .45-70-405,
MILITARY

Foster grinned. He thought, *Or what those crates are supposed to hold.*

One box was open, the waxy paper had been wadded up and moved to help cushion the other small containers of nitro. One long box just underneath the rough, weathered bottom post of the corral caught Foster's eye and caused him to grin again. Most of the boxes were empty of everything but dust.

The one behind the others, though, held some wax paper, some cloth, a bandanna . . . and another four-ounce bottle of liquid hell.

He moved beyond the corral, climbed over some rocks, ducked in a depression, and hurriedly made his way to the edge of the wall. He leaned and reached up, his fingers finding the slot.

"I can't believe you found that," Coberly said.

"You have to know something about ancient Indians. Apaches weren't the first to use this canyon. Pueblo Indians were here hundreds of years earlier. They were smart, smart old Indians. They knew if they were attacked, they'd have to climb out. It was either that . . . or die."

"So that'll be our options when the fight starts?"

Foster smiled. "You didn't have to stay here, Joe. Tomorrow, you'll be up there. With the others. I'll be down here. I'll have to climb out."

"I wouldn't want to do that."

"Well, I like to press my luck. This should be fun."

"So . . . tomorrow's the . . ."

"Fourth of July. That must really get old man Muncie's goat. His boy, his oldest son, was shot on the Fourth of July." Foster laughed. "Shot for cowardice. He loses his son, he loses Vicksburg and loses Gettysburg — and most likely the entire war — on one lousy day. And now he has to grovel . . . to Yankees on the day he hates the most."

Coberly shook his head. "You've thought this whole thing through."

"That I have."

"Well, here's something I can't figure out, sir. You sent two boys with the mules carrying nothin' but rocks one way. And you sent those four wagons with only the drivers out another. So that they'd most likely be followed."

"That'll thin somebody out. Not sure who. Mexicans, Rebs, or injuns, but it'll reduce the number we have to kill. Not that killing them will be hard. Not with all the nitro we have."

"Yeah. But ain't you thought about what'll happen to those decoys, the ones in the wagon and the ones with the mules?"

Foster felt so giddy he laughed out loud. He wrapped his right arm over the young outlaw's neck and pulled him close.

"Of course, I have, Joe." He released the killer and stepped away from the only way out of the canyon, the long climb out of the canyon. "They die!"

CHAPTER 80

Amonte Negro was tired from riding so hard. Maybe he should have gone after the wagons. Mules were not stallions, but they did move faster than wagons, although these mules — or the men who were driving the animals — were not moving that fast. But they seemed to not know where they wanted to go.

First, they had been going southeast, and once they reached the Rio Fuerta, which was dry that time of year, they had moved in its sand to Cañon Feo, and that place lived up to its name. It was ugly. Very ugly. And the sand was so thick, it made traveling hard, even on fine animals such as those Amonte Negro and his men had stolen.

Cañon Feo, of course, ran north. The mules might be bound for the United States. If they crossed the border, that would force Amonte Negro to make a decision. Could he ride into Arizona and take the mules and the rifles they carried — if they carried those Springfields — and make it back across the border where he would be safe? The gringos, they did not like Mexicans coming into their country to take anything, even if what they came to take rightfully belonged to Amonte Negro and his people. By the saints, even Arizona Territory should still belong to Amonte Negro and his people. When he was in charge in Mexico City, Amonte Negro would make the United States give Arizona back to Mexico. California, too. And New Mexico.

Just when the burly Mexican was beginning to think that maybe he should have stayed with *el coronel* in his gray coat, he heard a mule braying just ahead. The galloper was loping back, so Negro raised his hand to stop the three men who rode with him.

The galloper slowed his horse, looked behind him, and reined to a stop.

"Dos hombres. Catorce mulas."

Two men with fourteen mules. That should be easy for five men to take care of. Negro asked if the mules carried any rifles. The galloper said that they carried something, in leather bags. Maybe they were rifles, if rifles could be taken apart and made shorter . . . which, Amonte Negro knew, could be done. Not all guns, but the *Yanqui* gun makers, they knew how to do such things.

"The two men are drinking," the galloper told his boss. "They have stopped to rest under the shade at the water hole." He grinned. "They are not drinking water."

Amonte Negro laughed. "Mescal? Tequila?"

"I do not know."

Negro drew his pistol. "We should find out." He cocked the gun and raised it over his head. *"Asalto,"* he commanded, and the five men raced out of the end of Ugly Canyon and toward the lone tree that provided the one place of shade over the water hole.

"Do not kill the mules!" Negro yelled, and he aimed his pistol and fired.

One of the men dropped the bottle and ran for the nearest mule. He and his partner had been riding mules and leading mules. There were no horses that Amonte Negro could see, but that was fine. Mules brought much money to the people of Mexico. And twelve of the mules were equipped with packsaddles. The saddles maybe carried guns. Maybe gold. Maybe tequila.

The second man ran through the water hole, which was shallow and did not slow him down. He came out and ran into the desert, but two of Negro's riders circled around him and forced him to stop. The man raised his hand and pleaded in Spanish — for he was a Mexican like Amonte Negro and his revolutionaries. He had a wife, a sick mother, and seven little children in Pozos Liberales just one hundred kilometers to the south. They shot him anyway.

The man who had dropped the bottle stopped running at the sound of the gunshots that cut down his partner. He turned, drew a revolver from his pants pocket, and shot Diego Matías out of the saddle. He tried to shoot Alejandro, too, but his gun misfired and he tossed the gun to the dirt, raised his hands, and said that he surrendered. But Alejandro, who was Diego's brother, was in no mood, and he brought down his machete that split the man's head open. Alejandro Matías kept hacking the dead man while the galloper leaped off his horse and began removing the watch and the crucifix and the pouch of money from Diego's pockets.

The men were dead. Tired or lazy, the mules had barely lifted their heads during the shooting. Most of them kept drinking as Negro splashed through the shallow water and ran to the first mule. He pulled open the leather bag and reached inside. Pulling out a rock, he exclaimed with much gusto, "Gold!"

But when he looked at the rock more closely, he realized that it was not gold. Not even quartz. Not silver. Not copper. Just granite. He threw it angrily into the water, checked four other leather bags, and found more rocks.

He yelled at his men to get mounted, that they could forget the mules, that they had to get back and see if they could find the gringo in the gray coat.

Alejandro Matías quit using his machete on the remains of the man who had killed his brother, and walked back to his horse. He was climbing in the saddle when a shot rang out. His horse bolted, and Alejandro Matías fell on top of the mutilated body of the man who had killed his brother.

"Rurales!" shouted the galloper plundering Diego Matías's body. Then he fell dead as another bullet sounded.

Amonte Negro whirled. *Rurales* were riding in from all directions. The last of Negro's men tried to fight, but he was shot dead quickly.

The revolutionary sighed and showed the *Rurales* that he was a peaceful man. He removed his pistol and let it fall in the water.

He called out to the *Rurales* that he was glad to see them, that he had been kidnapped, that he was the most peaceful farmer ever to stay in Rancho Los Cielos. He said he was so glad to see them that he would share some tequila with them. He reached the shade and the bottle, and lifted it to them. *Maybe,* he thought, *these fine young Mexican peacekeepers would let him at least taste the tequila* — until he saw the rifles aimed at him.

"*¡Fuego!*" the leader of the *Rurales* commanded.

CHAPTER 81

Badger Killer found the wagons. It was easy. And Blind Skunk knew of the perfect place to ambush the pale eyes who drove the wagons with little enthusiasm. The eight Apaches circled around the wagons, giving the pale eyes a wide berth, and came to the place where the two arroyos met. Deer Hoof and Ten Feathers and the two young Apaches whose names were not worth remembering would stay on the eastern side. Badger Killer would take Hawk's Claw on the western side. Plenty Drunk would move back behind the wagons in case some of the pale eyes tried to run back to Rancho Los Cielos.

It would be fun. It would be glorious. Badger Killer could not wait to show old Crooked Nose the rifles he had captured — captured and not paid a silver coin to the bluecoats or anyone. They had been bought the Apache way, with blood of their enemies.

He breathed heavily as the wagons approached. The drivers looked practically asleep. *This would be so easy.*

Badger Killer grinned and brought the rifle closer to him. He was about to leap, unable to contain himself, and start shooting, when Hawk's Claw grabbed his shoulder and pulled.

Turning quickly, angrily, Badger Killer saw the young Apache jutting his jaw out toward the south. Badger Killer looked in that direction and frowned bitterly. Dust. A lot of dust. Riders were coming and they were coming fast.

He leaned back down as Plenty Drunk made the sound of a raven to let the others know of the approaching men. *It did not matter,* Badger Killer told himself. *Let the new men join the wagons.*

The more pale eyes Badger Killer and his warriors could kill, the more they could laugh in the face of old Crooked Nose — if that fool ever dared show his face in Apache country again.

The driver of the last wagon saw the riders first. He did not look happy to see them for he rose in his seat, spit out the tobacco he had been chewing, and screamed a warning to the men ahead of him. He pulled hard on the brake, leaped into the back, and grabbed a repeating rifle from the seat. The other two drivers stopped, too. The man in the lead wagon turned, saw the dust, and by that time he could see the five riders, but he did not set the brake to stop his wagon. He stood, lashed out with the whip, and his wagon thundered to the intersection with the second arroyo.

"Lott! You dirty, yellow-tailed coward!" one of the men shouted, but the man named Lott did not care. He was not only a dirty, yellow-tailed coward, he was a fool and a bad driver of wagons. He took the turn into the arroyo too sharply. The wagon rolled onto its side, throwing the pale face named Lott into the dust. He hit his head on a rock and did not move, most likely dead, but the mules pulling the wagon ran in their traces down the second arroyo and on toward the land of the bluecoats.

The men attacking wore gray coats. Badger Killer realized they were very, very brave, and fine warriors — for pale eyes.

The driver of the last wagon was the first to die, shot twice in the chest by the men on horseback. The driver in the next wagon, ducked inside the box of his wagon and fired. One of the horses screamed and somersaulted, sending its rider crashing into the tailgate of the last wagon. The man landed hard on the ground, his head tilted at an angle that told Badger Killer that he was no longer a threat to anyone.

Two riders rode on either side of that same wagon, and the man shooting panicked. He tried to leap off the wagon and hide, but he was shot dead by the man in gray who rode right past that wagon and was shot by the driver of the next wagon up the line. The man dropped his rifle, but reached for his belly gun, only to be shot again by the last of the wagon drivers.

The soldier clutched his stomach, groaned a weak, "Mama," and pitched off his horse before he could see Sergeant Winters on the other side blow the top of the last driver's head off.

"Browne!" Winters reined his horse to a stop and leaped into the wagon. "Browne!"

The soldier lay in the dust as his horse trotted to the next canyon. Browne, Badger Killer knew, could not answer.

"Carter!" the sergeant yelled, turning to the next rider. "Check the —" He stopped, stared, and cursed.

"Damn! This wagon ain't got nothin' in it but rocks!"

Badger Killer frowned. He saw the overturned wagon and the rocks lying all around the wrecked wood. All the wagons were the same. They carried not long-shooting rifles preferred by the bluecoats. They carried rocks. Huge rocks.

His bloodlust up, Badger Killer rose, aimed his rifle, and shot the man named Carter through the head.

The Apaches rushed the two men who still lived. One shot Deer Hoof as he leaped over the side, but Hawk's Claw shot the Confederate in the back. Deer Hoof rose long enough to shoot the Confederate in the belly before joining his ancestors.

The last gray coat shot Ten Feathers in the throat then ran down the arroyo, but he ran straight into Plenty Drunk's knife, which the Apache twisted and pulled out, and then plunged again into the gray coat's chest.

And it was over. The Apaches had mules if they wanted them, and the horses of the gray coats, and the guns the gray coats and other pale eyes had used. And they had rocks. Plenty of rocks. Rocks and rocks and rocks and none of the new blue coat rifles.

They had followed the wagons to nowhere. The rifles must still be at The Canyon of The Sorrows.

"Ride with me!" Badger Killer yelled. "We will avenge our brothers and get the long guns from the pale eyes at The Canyon of

The Sorrows."

But Plenty Drunk and Hawk's Claw did not speak to Badger Killer. Plenty Drunk stood over Ten Feathers, trying to stop the hole in his throat from bleeding. Hawk's Claw was singing a song over Deer Hoof's body.

Badger Killer yelled at his brothers again, but they would not look at him. He spit, found his horse, and took one of the dead gray coat's handguns. "You will be sorry when I ride into camp with more long guns than you have ever seen!"

As he rode away, he tried to close his ears . . . because what he heard, or what he imagined he heard, was the mocking laughter from Crooked Nose.

CHAPTER 82

"What the hell do we do?" Ben Masterson shouted. Grat Holden's horse turned, stamped its hooves, and wanted to run, either toward those horses thundering down the canyon or to the end of The Canyon of The Sorrows.

It was the third of July. Holden was certain of that. The meeting was tomorrow. Who in hell could be galloping down the canyon now? Jed Foster? Surely, Foster was already waiting.

Sam Florence swung off his horse. "We got to hide!" he snapped.

Holden looked around. There were rocks, plenty of rocks, and even a handful of junipers.

He dismounted. He was an officer in the United States Cavalry. "What about the horses?" he yelled.

"Let them go!" Florence was running toward Soledad Tadeo, who had swung off her horse but was holding tightly to the reins. The horse pulled her to her knees, but she refused to let go. Florence's pinto, meanwhile, was rearing up, snorting, then circling around. It bolted toward the sound of the approaching fury, turned around, started deeper into the canyon, and stopped again, running this way, then the other way, unable to make up its mind.

Which, Grat Holden realized, was what he was doing.

"Off the horses!" he shouted. "Into the rocks! It's our only chance."

"What about the horses, Lieutenant?" Masterson yelled.

"They'll do . . . whatever they damned well please."

"They'll give us away, sir!"

"If we don't get out of sight, we'll all be dead!" Holden ran to help Soledad Tadeo, reaching her before Sam Florence could. He pulled her away, watching the reins slip from her hands. He jerked her to her feet. "There!" he yelled and shoved her toward the rocks.

Her horse bolted down the canyon.

Masterson swore, and spurred his Morgan. He caught the reins of Holden's mount and screamed, waving his Springfield over his head.

"Masterson!" Holden yelled after he shoved the Mexican girl into the rocks. "Masterson!"

The soldier was pulling Holden's horse and moving his into a gallop. Somehow he managed to turn Sam Florence's pinto, and he rode into the bowels of The Canyon of The Sorrows.

"Masterson!" Holden yelled again.

"Just name a medal after me, Lieutenant Holden!"

Masterson yelled. "Sir! And raise a toast to County Cork!"

He rode hard, leaning low in the saddle.

The pinto of Sam Florence was running ahead, driven by fear and Masterson on his Morgan, pulling Holden's horse behind him. Soledad Tadeo's horse snorted, bucked, and took off after the pinto. Masterson rounded the corner and was gone.

"Masterson!" Holden called out one last time and started to run after him, but Sam Florence roughly shoved him back and into the rocks.

"Get down, Lieutenant!" the old scout said as he faded into the shadows and knelt.

Fifteen seconds later, an army in gray and mismatched Mexican outfits exploded into view. Grat Holden held his breath until the army of killers were out of sight.

Slowly, he rose and stared down the canyon. He wanted to cry. He wanted to throw up. Mostly, he wanted to salute Sergeant Ben Masterson.

Drunk. Belligerent. Disobedient. The worst soldier at Fort Bowie. And the bravest damned Irish son of a bitch Grat Holden had ever had the pleasure of commanding.

CHAPTER 83

Jed Foster leaned one of the Springfields in the corner of the narrow chimneylike crevasse that shot straight up to the top of the canyon. Even with handholds and footholds spaced up it would be a hard climb, but it would be a great test. It would challenge his ability and endurance. It would put his luck to the ultimate trial.

When he stepped away from the wall, he saw Joe Coberly still staring at him with that hangdog, confused look of a green kid. The boy had yet to get over the shock of Foster's announcement that the men sent as decoys with the wagons and mules would likely be killed.

"Joe, Joe, Joe," Foster said, smiling. "Don't believe everything I say, son. The men with the wagons and mules, why, there's a mighty fine chance that they'll just be wandering aimlessly in the desert — like Moses did for those forty years. You heard me tell the boys where to meet us. Don't fret. Tomorrow you're going to be a rich man." *If you live, which is unlikely.*

"But the Apaches, the Mexicans, or the Rebs are sure to follow those trails."

"Just till they figure out it's bait. Come on, kid. Tomorrow's the Fourth of July. Let's get back to the top and make sure everything's looking good."

They moved away from the towering, foreboding rock wall, toward the boxes and the corral. Their horses had been tethered on an old whipping post, far away from any of the explosives.

Foster stopped and checked above. On the rim of the canyon, his men were making their final preparations, putting together shooting sticks on which they could rest the barrels of the Springfields in a sturdy "V" and fire down with enthusiasm and accuracy at the men they would pick off. Apaches. Rebels. Greasers. It would be such fun to watch, especially since Foster would be down in the middle of it, risking his life, putting everything at stake.

If one did not take chances, what was the point in living?

He pulled up short, and his right hand reached instinctively for the butt of his Colt revolver. Joe Coberly stopped, turned, and then looked back to the mouth of the canyon. The kid heard the noise, too.

Horses. Their hooves on the hard rocks rang out loudly, sending eerie echoes bouncing off the towering walls of granite and around the canyon the myriad spaces against which noise could bounce. Foster had often heard that the women and children who'd screamed there could be heard forever.

As if pleading for reassurance, the kid Coberly turned, caught his breath, and seemed to ask, "Maybe it's Emanuel."

Maybe. The Mexican whose horse turned lame once they entered the start of the canyon. Foster corrected that thought. The Mexican who *said* his horse was lame.

Foster drew the Colt and thumbed back the hammer. "That is more than just one horse." He turned and waved the Colt over his head . . . back and forth, back and forth, back and forth.

The fools on the rim could not hear the clanging of hooves on hard rock. He thought about firing a shot, but that would just warn whoever was galloping toward him.

"Ennio!" Foster yelled up at the best of his marksmen.

His answer was the echo.

Ennio . . . Ennio . . . Ennio . . . Ennio . . .

Ennio . . .

Soon some of the men working on the top heard, and they looked down.

God, Foster thought, *how small those men up there looked.* How small must he and Joe Coberly look from those towering over his head. He pointed the barrel of his gun at the cave.

Then he heard Joe Coberly stammer, "M-m-m-my g-g-good-n-n-ness."

A pinto horse, more white than black and a little mustang at that, rounded the corner, its eyes wide with fear. The horse was saddled. There was no rider. It galloped toward Coberly and Foster, saw them, veered, and made a dash toward the corral posts.

Foster swore, turned, and ran at an angle, hoping to intersect the horse, to turn that wild thing back before he ruined everything. Before he caused one of the bottles of nitroglycerin to explode. The kid, Coberly, remained stuck in his boots on the hard floor, paralyzed by fear.

The saddle had a scabbard, Foster realized as he ran in blind panic and fury. The scabbard was empty.

He waved his gun, he cursed, he waved his other hand, and the small pinto mustang turned before it slammed into the fence posts or stepped on one of the crates marked *Springfield Armory.* The horse ran along the wall, realizing that the only way out was the way in which it had entered.

Another horse exploded through the narrow opening. It was a mare, and it was just as frightened — and equally as riderless — as the small pinto.

Foster slid to a stop. He realized quickly that he had seen both of those horses. He just could not place them at the moment.

A few yards away, Joe Coberly was waving his hands over his head, shouting, cursing, and trying to get those two horses under control. Or at least out of there and away from the highly volatile explosives laying all over the canyon.

CHAPTER 84

His chest burned as his lungs heaved and heaved and screamed for air. His heart raced like those frightened horses that started out of the canyon, back down the narrow, long, terrifying trail, but stopped, whirled, wheeled, and whinnied before they bolted around again.

Foster swore and ran toward the beasts, trying to keep them away from the empty Springfield boxes. He realized that another horse — no, more than one — came down the trail and into the trading post in The Canyon of The Sorrows.

A rifle shot fired, and he heard the bullet whine off a rock. He turned, bellowing and waving his pistol again. He shouted toward his men who lined the canyon's rim. "Not yet! Not yet! For God's sake don't shoot. Don't shoot!"

A moment later, a horse — a fine Morgan, judging from the quick glimpse Foster could manage — entered the boxed portion of the canyon. Another horse was being pulled alongside. Two horses. One rider. A big man who waved a big rifle over his head.

Joe Coberly palmed his pistol — the kid had blinding speed — and Foster shouted at the boy, but his order came too late. The bullet roared out of the kid's .44 barrel and hit the horse the rider had been pulling.

"Don't shoot, damn it! Don't —" Foster broke off, realizing that wasn't the worst of it.

A cacophony of horses sounded like an entire army galloping down the canyon, but that could not be. It just could not be. It was July 3, 1880. Independence Day — the Fourth of July — was not until tomorrow. He had not even sent his guides to lead the Apaches, the greasers, and the Rebs to this place.

The rider on the Morgan leaped from the saddle and rolled over several times. He dropped the heavy rifle, which clanged against the rocks. Foster held his breath. The man was tumbling right toward the Springfield Armory box that housed not .45-70 new-issue rifles, but four ounces of nitro.

And the fool kid snapped another shot at the rolling man.

"Coberly!" Foster bellowed as the man rolled to a stop.

As the big man rose and jerked a Colt revolver from his sash, Foster recognized him. It was that worthless, recalcitrant sergeant from Fort Bowie — the king of the guard house, everyone called him, because he spent more time serving some sentence than he did in the field.

Sergeant Ben Masterson, B Troop, the Fighting Mick.

A bullet rang down from above, followed by another, and both shots bounced off several rocks, whining like women passengers in a stagecoach heading down a steep grade in the White Mountains.

"No!"

The Lightning bucked in Sergeant Masterson's hand. He saw the barrel spitting flame and smoke. He saw Joe Coberly spin around and drop to his knee, his side turning dark with blood, but the gun still in the kid's hand.

Sergeant Masterson emptied that revolver, dropped the piece, and reached for the other .38 in his sash. The kid fired again. Men up top poured lead down at Sergeant Masterson, but the bullets whined all around the fighting Irishman. Then, to Foster's surprise, several more riders poured out of the bottleneck. He recognized the gray uniforms, but he also saw Mexican denim and white cotton, and slowly the reality of all that was happening came to him.

Bullets whined from the canyon. Horses screamed, fell, rolled over, died. Men were ripped out of their saddles. One of the gray-coated Rebs pulled out a shotgun and sent two barrels of buckshot into Joe Coberly's chest. He flew five yards in the air and crashed in a bloody heap, rolled over, pushed himself up, and dropped dead on the rocky ground. Foster recognized one of the riders circling around, trying to find a way back through the bottleneck and out of the crazy place, the aptly named Canyon of The Sorrows.

That man was the Mexican Emanuel, who'd said his horse had gone lame. He was the traitor Jed Foster had debated killing. That good nature, that kind heart, would be the death of Jed Foster yet. He should have killed the bastard. Foster understood . . . Emanuel was a Judas. He had sold out Foster and the Springfield rifles to —

Foster turned his pistol at Emanuel and squeezed the trigger in what he thought would be his last act on this earth. The hammer landed on an empty chamber. The Colt was worthless. Yet one of the sharpshooters on the ridge finally got off a decent shot, or maybe it was lucky. Foster would take either.

Emanuel cried out and dropped from the saddle. He bounded off the rock and lay still, blood pooling beneath his body.

That was one double-crossing Judas that Jed Foster would not have to kill.

Colonel Will Muncie eased his horse toward Foster, and slowly, confidently, and even gracefully drew the jeweled, engraved, and etched saber from the metal sheath.

Foster looked around. The gray coats were closing in around him. The men on the high rocks above had stopped shooting. Somehow, to his amazement and eternal relief, not one bullet had detonated the nitroglycerin. He was still alive, although the colonel of the unreconstructed Rebs had raised his saber as he reined his horse in just feet from Jed Foster.

CHAPTER 85

Foster dropped the smoking but empty Colt .45 at his feet. He waited until he thought his voice might show a modicum of steadiness and he grinned at the crazy old colonel who towered above him with that raised saber and that crazed look on his face.

"If you are ready to surrender, Colonel, I will gladly discuss terms with you, sir."

The colonel did not smile. The saber did not lower.

"Your wit, Captain, will be the death of you."

Foster wet his lips. "You have surprised me, Colonel. I believe our date was for tomorrow."

"I never do a damned thing on the Fourth of July, Captain. It's against my religion."

Foster nodded. "I see you joined up with Negro's bunch. Where is the great Amonte Negro, Mexico's next Diaz and Juarez?"

"I have not the foggiest idea. Dead. If we

and the world should be so lucky."

Foster wet his lips again.

"Well, I guess you'll want to hear that the Apaches have sided with me. So that makes us even."

"Don't mock me, suh," Muncie said. "The Apaches would join up with you about the same time I would. When hell was freezing over."

"Then" — Foster forced a smile — "you're saying the Apaches aren't with you, either, Colonel?"

"I'd trust a damned Yankee before I'd trust a red heathen savage, suh."

"I'm honored, Colonel."

The colonel glared. Foster was pushing his luck. He knew that. But, well, Jed Foster was always pushing his luck.

"We'll be taking our rifles now, Capt'n," the colonel said. "I would ask for your permission, you damned Yankee son of a bitch, but I do not think I need it."

Foster shrugged.

He caught his breath when one of the Rebs — a wiry man the colonel had just addressed as Lieutenant Fountain — swung out of his horse and raced toward one of the Springfield crates.

"Wait!" Foster screamed, cringed, and almost ducked in fear as the man flung off the top of the box. The wooden lid bounced on the rocks. The box did not disintegrate and wipe out Sergeant Ben Masterson, who stood with his hands raised next to the wooden crate, nor send the Rebel officer named Fountain to glory — in about a million pieces.

Foster's heart beat again. He picked himself off the floor while Fountain turned around and shouted, "There's no guns in this box, Colonel. Just —" He looked down. "I don't know. A little bottle wrapped up like it was a newborn babe."

"Check the other boxes, men!" Colonel Muncie ordered.

"No!" Foster screamed. "Listen to me. The rifles are —"

He sucked in a deep breath as another lid was flung off.

"This one's empty, too, Colonel," a man wearing the stars of a captain said.

"For God's sake, Colonel, stop it. Stop it. I'll get you your damned guns, but just stop it. Stop it before you kill us all!"

To his surprise, the colonel lowered his saber.

"Where," he asked, his voice turning husky, "are those damned rifles, you fiend?"

Foster was still alive. His luck, somehow, was holding. He had to figure out how he could get out of there before the skies began raining rocks and boulders and the nitro began sending death and destruction everywhere.

His eyes stopped on Sergeant Ben Masterson.

What the hell was that hard-fighting, never-stop-drinking noncom doing here? He frowned and whispered, "Grat Holden."

"What's that, Billy Yank?" Colonel Muncie said.

Foster raised his hand and pointed at Masterson. "That man. That's the man. He's the one. Colonel, as God as my witness, that man has betrayed us all. That man stole the rifles . . . from you . . . from me . . . kill him. Kill that cur dog now!"

At least he had Colonel Muncie, even the lieutenant named Fountain, and most of the men in gray and the Mexicans who had joined with the Rebs staring at Ben Masterson. Foster inched a bit away from Muncie.

"He's double-crossed the both of us," Foster said again as he looked at the bottleneck. *Would Grat Holden be out there?* He remembered the horses. The Irish hardcase had been riding one, pulling another. But there were two other horses. That meant four. And suddenly he remembered where he had seen those mounts.

The mare had been in the corral at Rancho Los Cielos. Foster almost chuckled when he remembered the lush little wench. She had been riding that one. That little mare belonged to that hotheaded Mexican, Soledad Tadeo. And the pinto? He could see its rider tagging along with Sergeant Masterson more than Tadeo. Sam Florence, the old scout from Fort Bowie. The last horse he did not recognize but his gut told him that one had been ridden by Lieutenant Grat Holden.

His luck, Foster feared, was turning. But he had managed his way from a few bad hands, some silly bets at poker and blackjack tables and faro layouts or roulette wheels. He still had a chance . . . if he could get to that chimney without getting blown to bits.

"Get," Foster said, "that mick away from that rifle box, Colonel. Don't touch that box. And stay the hell away from that —" He cringed. "God have mercy, don't you understand what I'm telling you? If you keep that up, you'll kill us all. There won't be a bloody thing left here but our memories."

Foster felt his resolve break. He saw the Rebels, their rifles lowered as they had dismounted and were moving in on Sergeant Ben Masterson. He saw Colonel Will

Muncie turn to study that Irish fighting man.

Foster saw a path that led to the chimney. He cried out and ran, ran like one of Custer's boys at Little Bighorn when the fighting got totally out of hand. He cried out and leaped over the body of Joe Coberly.

And he saw Ben Masterson out of the corner of his eye, drawing his remaining Colt .38 from the sash. Ben Masterson had figured it all out, too. He jerked the weapon but did not aim it at the men coming to kill him. He aimed at the Springfield Armory box.

The .38 bucked in his hand.

The roar had to be a million times louder than the report of any pistol.

Chapter 86

Jed Foster ran. He did not pray. He did not think about luck. Death, smoke, flames, rocks, dirt, and the parts of men and horses rained all around him.

He saw Colonel Will Muncie stand up, leaning on his saber, his gray coat smoldering. The old man looked lost. His eyes seemed to focus on Foster. The next moment, Will Muncie had disappeared. It looked like half the side of The Canyon of The Sorrows had fallen on top of the diehard Confederate.

Foster veered course. A rock whistled by him. More explosions almost rocked him off his feet.

Vaguely, he understood what had happened. Sergeant Ben Masterson had sacrificed himself, detonating one small bottle of nitroglycerin. The explosion and devastating destruction triggered the other bottles to erupt. He had been warned how volatile that stuff was. He just had never imagined it could be that catastrophic.

Foster staggered into a Mexican bandit whose arm had been ripped off. He leaped over one of his own men who had fallen from the top of the canyon. A rock sailed over his head. A twisted, smoking, ruined Springfield 1880 almost tripped him as it slammed into the earth. The nitro must have sent that wrecked weapon sailing like a boomerang.

He remembered one other thing George Custer had told him. *Know your limits. Know your branch of service. If you're in the infantry, follow infantry tactics. If you're a horse soldier, don't try to be an artillery commander. And vice versa.*

Well, Foster was a cavalry officer who had experimented with nitroglycerin. He wasn't an explosives expert, a munitions guy, an artillery commander. He should have stuck with horses and hit-slash-run. *Run.*

Just run, Foster told himself.

If you die, you die.

Just don't stop running.

He moved through dust so thick it blinded him and mingled with so much smoke, it choked him. His eyes burned.

Suddenly, he was out of the smoke and dust and he could see the escape route the ancient Indians had made. If he could just reach that little half-chimney, he might have a chance.

If . . . his luck . . . could hold out . . . for one more . . . hand . . .

CHAPTER 87

Grat Holden, Sam Florence, and Soledad Tadeo were moving cautiously toward the bottleneck's opening. They could hear the muffled shouts of voices, the prancing of ponies, and even an occasional shot.

They guessed that the trade was being made a day early. They couldn't figure anything out for sure, but —

Suddenly, the noise was deafening. The blast of heat and fire that roared out of the hole knocked them onto their backs. Flames singed their faces and hands. Their ears rang. Rocks pounded on them, and the avalanche that followed left them choking dust, coughing, almost suffocating.

Holden did not know how he had done it. He didn't even remember doing it, but among the smoke, and heat, and rocks, he realized he was shoving Soledad Tadeo ahead of him, and dragging the screaming Sam Florence behind him. His clothes were smoking from heat and flames. His eyelids had been burned off. His face felt as though he had been staked out in the Arizona desert for fifteen days.

When he could breathe again, when he saw more than smoke and just the dark, frightening trail that led to The Canyon of The Sorrows, he stopped, and turned to face the man he had just released.

Sam Florence rolled over in agony and clutched his leg. "Damned rock. Damned rock. That lousy rock."

"Is it busted?" Holden heard himself ask.

"Hell, yeah, it's busted." Florence lowered his head and spit out blood and curses.

Then Soledad Tadeo knelt by him and slapped his face. *"Padre, cállate. Muéstrame que eres un hombre."*

The old scout studied her. "Shut up?" he asked, and chuckled. "Show you that I'm a man? Is that how you treat your daddy?" He dropped his head to the ground and writhed in agony.

"Take care of him, Soledad." Holden rose and hurried into the smoke and dust and raining debris. A few minutes later, he was back and kneeling by the scout with the broken leg and his lovely Spanish daughter. "There might be a way through that rubble, but I can't chance it. I'm going back up top."

"Without a horse," the scout said through clenched teeth. "It'll take you a week to get around this maze and up top."

"No," Soledad Tadeo said. "If you can climb, there is a way. There." She pointed. "I saw it six years ago. When I was here. An Apache was taking it when we rode out of this Canyon of The Sorrows." She shrugged. "He might have fallen to his death. I cannot say."

Holden leaned over and kissed her luscious lips. "I won't fall," he said softly. He winked. "To my death."

This must be, Grat Holden thought, *what Santa Claus felt climbing up and down all those lousy chimneys.* His legs were bent, his arms were cramped, and he kept inching his way, bracing his back against the smooth granite, keeping his feet against the wall in front of him, and reaching, gripping, pulling himself up toward the rim of The Canyon of The Sorrows.

He refused to look down.

The entire canyon, and maybe the whole Mother Earth, seemed to shake as another detonation rocked the world. Sometimes the entire ridge shook so violently, and boulders crashed below or dirt and pebbles peppered him like hail, that he thought he would just fall the hundred or two hundred or however far it was he had made it off the floor.

Somehow, he remained moving, climbing, inching his way to the top.

Then he was there. He lifted a throbbing, burning arm, grabbed hold of the trunk of a juniper on the top, and pulled his upper body over the canyon's rim. He lay there with his chest heaving until he caught his breath. He pulled with all his might and felt his legs scraping on the rocks. His right sock ripped and granite scraped his big toe. He had lost his boot. He didn't remember when.

But he was up on the top, rolling over, and sucking in precious air. Around him he felt and heard nothing but chaos. Below him lay . . . hell.

Hooves thundered past, the clanging of metal hooves on the hard rock pounding his ears like a corps of drummers. He rolled onto his stomach, pushed himself up on hands and knees and somehow, maybe a thousand years later, he was standing, leaning against the juniper, and watching the last of the men Jed Foster had hired flee. Galloping hell-bent-for-leather across the ridge.

Holden turned and stared. The riders, so panicked by the massive detonations — caused by nitroglycerin, he guessed — had left the Springfield rifles. Some lay in piles on blankets. Others had been dropped near shooting sticks. One had a long brass telescopic sight affixed to it, and its owner lay dead. When Holden reached him, he saw no bullet hole. To have been shot by someone on the canyon floor would have been remarkable, practically impossible. Based on the blueness of the man's lips and the look of pain on his face, Holden figured the poor son of a bitch had died of a heart attack.

That was completely understandable. Holden looked at the carnage below.

Rocks and boulders and half the side of the canyon covered the ground. Buried beneath the rubble was Sergeant Ben Masterson. The crazed Colonel Will Muncie. And who knew how many others. Most likely, Jed Foster was down there, too.

If Holden was lucky, Soledad Tadeo and Sam Florence were down on the other side of the bottleneck. With God's grace and about eighteen thousand favors called in from the Man Upstairs, Grat Holden might be able to get them home. Maybe. With a lot of prayers and good luck.

He understood that he was horseless. In the middle of the desert in Mexico. He was out of uniform. He was pretty much alone. And there were hundreds of Springfield Model 1880 rifles lying before him. Holden walked to one and picked it up. Sighing, he tossed it over the side.

Colonel Smythe would blow a gasket when he heard Holden's report.

The lieutenant picked up another rifle, and pitched it into the carnage and destruction below.

Holden had no idea how long he had been dropping rifles over the side, nor how many. Sometimes he did it by handfuls. Sometimes he dragged the blankets and pushed the entire load over the rim. Sometimes he dropped them over the edge one at a time. He pushed boxes of ammunition, and heard them crash on the rocks below. When his arms burned from pain, he would lay on his back and push them with his feet, one boot still on, the other holding a threadbare sock full of splinters and pebbles and cactus spines.

At some point — he had no idea when — he had removed his other boot and thrown it over the edge, along with both socks.

He picked up a rifle, dropped it. He

moved as though he were in a trance. Another rifle crashed below. He grabbed another and another, using both hands, and holding the new-model rifles over the edge. He stopped. He listened. He used the rifles he was about to throw into the ruination as crutches to push himself to his feet and hobbled toward the sound. It came from below.

Grat Holden slowly eased onto his knees and inched his way to the rim. Carefully, he peered down into what amounted to a partial chimney. He blinked. He tried to focus. He wondered if he were dreaming.

The figure below him, maybe forty feet from the top, stopped climbing. The head looked up. The face brightened and smiled.

"Hello, Grattan," Captain Jed Foster said. "I don't suppose you'd like to help me up these last few feet?"

CHAPTER 88

The dust had diminished, and the rockslides seemed to come less frequently. Soledad Tadeo bathed the forehead of her father, Sam Florence, with a rag. She looked up at the ladder, the chimney, the hellish way north that required fingers, feet, and determination.

She no longer saw Grat Holden.

Her father slept.

Another boulder toppled from somewhere inside The Canyon of The Sorrows.

No one would ever enter the canyon again, at least they would never be able to go into the opening, the horrible place that had caused so much pain for so many people. *It was,* she told herself, *over.* She felt glad that she had returned, even though she had not caused the place to collapse. That had been the will of God.

She closed her eyes and prayed for the soul of her mother. She opened her eyes and prayed for the life of her father.

Then she heard the hoofbeats.

The horse coming from down the twisting, turning, cavernous trail to hell had been loping. The rider eased the mount to a walk. The *clop-clop-clop* was not as loud as she had heard earlier, and fear grasped her heart. She understood.

The horse coming toward them was not the horse of a gringo or a Mexican. It was unshod. It was, most likely, the horse of an Apache.

She found her father's pistol and eared back the hammer. She bit her lip and waited.

The horse slowed to a stop and she saw the rider as he swung out of the Indian saddle and moved through the dust and the scattered debris. He looked confused. He might have even been worried. He held a Henry rifle in his hands. He wore a red headband over his head. And when he turned and stared ahead and up at the mountain of boulders that blocked the entrance into that horrible place, she saw the mangled ear.

Soledad rose with the pistol of her father in her right hand.

"Hey!" she yelled.

The Apache whirled and fired. She felt

the bullet singe her hair. She smiled as the Apache worked the lever. And then she shot the son of a bitch in his chest.

Maybe she would not get to kill the *Yanqui* named Jed Foster, the man who had caused so much trouble. But she would kill the Apache, the warrior with the bad ear that was made bad six years ago when she was fifteen.

She shot him again. That was for her mother.

She shot him again. That was for all the mothers and daughters he had brought to this place.

She shot him again. That was for *her.*

CHAPTER 89

Second Lieutenant Grat Holden blinked, but the apparition still remained on the slick, rocky ledge. It moved a bit forward, using handholds and footholds. Foster stopped, tried to shake the blood back into his fingertips, and looked again up.

"What happened to Masterson?" Holden heard himself ask.

The captain laughed. "He started the ball."

Holden sighed. He looked at the rubble below him, trying to guess as to where the remains of Sergeant Ben Masterson might be.

"Grat," Jed Foster called up to him. "Help me out of this, pal. We can work this out, my friend. Make ourselves a fortune. What do you say, buddy? Let's see how Jed Foster's luck can play with Grat Holden's persistence."

Holden looked down at the pathetic little

figure climbing up the escape route Indians had used a thousand years ago. Then he looked at the Springfield 1880 rifles that he held in his hands.

He looked down again at Captain Jed Foster and showed him the rifles.

"Captain Foster, I think these are yours."

Holden let the heavy rifles fall. He heard Jed Foster scream as the rifles slammed into his shoulder and his leg, knocking him away from the canyon's dark, slick wall. He dropped instantly as the Springfield rifles fell with him, all the way down. The scream continued as the captain and the rifles fell to the rocks and carnage below.

It was a long fall. Eventually, the screaming stopped, and Grat Holden sat on the edge of the canyon.

He sat there, exhausted, staring at the smoke-filled floor. He searched for survivors, but he saw none, just rocks and debris. He looked again for Ben Masterson and sighed when he knew that hardcase of a soldier was really dead.

Eventually, Holden pulled himself away from the edge and stood. He needed to get back to Soledad Tadeo and her father, Sam Florence. They were in Mexico, but he saw several horses milling around, mounts belonging to some of Foster's men. He even saw Foster's steel dust. Those horses would have to carry them back to Arizona, back to Fort Bowie.

Holden would not be able to send a heliograph signal to the soldiers experimenting with the sun-signals. He wondered how hard Colonel Carlton Smythe would throw the damned book at him once he learned those new-model Springfield rifles were destroyed and that he, Second Lieutenant Grat Holden, was responsible. He looked over the canyon, what was left of The Canyon of The Sorrows, and the view amazed him. It didn't make him feel any better or any less tired. But it was . . . breathtaking.

Dust and smoke rose. *It would,* he thought, *make for a beautiful sunset.*

CHAPTER 90

Sam Florence opened his eyes to see the ceiling of what he recognized as the post hospital at Fort Bowie in the southern part of Arizona Territory.

"Hell," he whispered, "I ain't dead."

He looked at the sheet covering the lower part of his body and he ripped the covers off.

"Hell," he said, with more emotion, "I'm still whole."

A soft giggle reached him, and he turned his head to see Soledad Tadeo, his daughter, sitting in a chair next to his bunk.

Florence smiled. "Hello, daughter."

"Buenas tardes, Padre." Tears welled in her eyes.

The door opened, and Lieutenant Grat Holden walked inside, pulled up a chair, and found a seat next to Florence's bed.

"I reckon," the scout said, "that you can tell me how the hell I . . . and you and her . . . got out of that canyon."

"Later," Holden told him. "Over about a keg of beer at that gin mill in Dos Cabezas."

"Foster?" Florence asked.

Holden shook his head.

"Muncie?"

The head shook again.

"Amonte Negro?"

The head shook once more. "*Rurales* took care of Negro. We got their report when we made it back to Fort Bowie. You don't remember anything about that, do you?"

"No. Must've been out of my head."

"We all were. A little."

"Well, hell, we done all right," Florence said.

"Well . . ." Holden's voice softened. "There's Ben Masterson."

"Yeah. War's hell."

The girl brought a ladle of water toward Florence, who drank its contents down greedily. He looked back at Holden and said, "And what's Colonel Smythe saying about all this?"

"Nothing. He's dead."

"What?" Florence tried sitting up, but pain knocked him back onto his pillows.

"He led a command down south to join those sun-signalers," Holden explained. "No one knows exactly what happened, but

511

he led his command into an ambush. Apaches jumped across the border. They say it was Crooked Nose himself. Anyway, the colonel caught about six arrows in his back. Two of his men were killed."

"The hell you say!" Florence asked for a beer.

Soledad Tadeo told him to be quiet.

The old scout laughed. "Crooked Nose ain't a bad sort. Tough as nails, but he ranks up there with Cochise in my book. Some of his boys, well, they're as rotten as Jed Foster. But that's the way with all people, I guess. You get good. You get bad."

"The Apaches are less one bad man," Soledad Tadeo said then said nothing else.

Florence's head shook. "The colonel dead. Killed in the field. Reckon they'll give him a damned medal."

"Worse. The Tucson papers have demanded they name a fort after Smythe. But don't worry. I hear there was another fort named Smith — but spelled the normal way — and it got burned down after Red Cloud's War up in Montana Territory, so the Army isn't likely to do that. Anyway, we're here, you're getting stronger, and . . . they are talking about giving a medal to Ben Masterson. They're just trying to figure out how to word it."

Florence nodded. He drank another ladle of water.

At that point, the sergeant major entered the hospital and saluted Second Lieutenant Grat Holden.

"Beggin the lieutenant's pardon, sir, but I have a telegram from the Springfield Armory. They're asking about all those rifles they sent here."

Grat Holden knotted his brow. "Why ask me, Sergeant?"

"Well, sir, the major and all the captains — every last officer, to be exact — are out in the field, sir, trying to catch that red devil Crooked Nose, make him pay for killing the colonel. I know you don't like it, sir, but, well, you're in command . . . till the troops get back or the general sends us a new colonel. And there is no way the armory is going to listen to anything a sergeant major has to say. Especially since I don't have a clue and — Well . . . sir, you're the commander of this post."

"I see." Grat Holden pulled a flask out of his pocket and handed it to Sam Florence.

"This might offer a quicker cure than water."

The old scout took the bottle. Soledad Tadeo pulled out the cork.

"Sir," the sergeant major said, "what do I

tell that fellow at the Springfield Armory?"

Lieutenant Grat Holden smiled as he took the flask Sam Florence held out to him.

"Sergeant," he said as he paused the flask just below his lips. "Tell them . . . nothing."

EPILOGUE

Toward the end of 1880, the US Army Ordnance Department reported to representatives of the Springfield Armory in Springfield, Massachusetts, that testing of the new Model 1880 .45-70 rifles in the field had garnered unanimously negative reports. The retaining device for the cleaning rod had proved knotty, soldiers had reported from posts out West, and worse, the sighting was terribly off. Therefore, the one thousand models issued to troops on the frontier were being returned to be put in storage. The Army, however, recommended that further improvements be made, reminding Springfield representatives of the Army's long relationship with the Massachusetts gun makers.

Springfield produced new models in 1882, 1884, 1886, and 1888 before the US Army finally adopted the Springfield Model 1892–99, a bolt-action rifle chambered in .30-40

Krag caliber, as the new standard for the US Army.

Years after the 1880 field-testing run, a bookkeeper in the armory's headquarters wrote the US Ordnance Department that of the one thousand Model 1880 rifles sent for testing, only seven hundred and fifty had been returned. The bookkeeper asked for an explanation or payment for the missing weapons.

The US Ordnance Department never responded to the armory clerk's query.

ABOUT THE AUTHORS

William W. Johnstone has written nearly three hundred novels of western adventure, military action, chilling suspense, and survival. His bestselling books include *The Family Jensen; The Mountain Man; Flintlock; MacCallister; Savage Texas; Luke Jensen, Bounty Hunter;* and the thrillers *Black Friday, The Doomsday Bunker,* and *Trigger Warning.*

J. A. Johnstone learned to write from the master himself, Uncle William W. Johnstone, with whom J. A. has co-written numerous bestselling series including The Mountain Man; Those Jensen Boys; and Preacher, The First Mountain Man.

The employees of Thorndike Press hope you have enjoyed this Large Print book. All our Thorndike, Wheeler, and Kennebec Large Print titles are designed for easy reading, and all our books are made to last. Other Thorndike Press Large Print books are available at your library, through selected bookstores, or directly from us.

For information about titles, please call:
  (800) 223-1244

or visit our website at:
  gale.com/thorndike

To share your comments, please write:
  Publisher
  Thorndike Press
  10 Water St., Suite 310
  Waterville, ME 04901